The Rainey Season

R. E. BRADSHAW

Titles from R. E. Bradshaw Books

Rainey Bell Thriller Series:
The Rainey Season (2013)
Rainey's Christmas Miracle (2011) (Short Story-ebook only)
Rainey Nights (2011) 24th Lambda Literary Awards Finalist
Rainey Days (2010)

The Adventures of Decky and Charlie Series:
Out on the Panhandle (2012)
Out on the Sound (2010)

Molly: House on Fire (2012)
25th Lambda Literary Awards Finalist

Before It Stains (2011)

Waking Up Gray (2011)

Sweet Carolina Girls (2010)

The Girl Back Home (2010)

The Rainey Season

A Rainey Bell Thriller

R. E. BRADSHAW

Published by
R. E. BRADSHAW BOOKS

USA

•R.E.B.BOOKS•

The Rainey Season
By R. E. Bradshaw

© **2013 by R. E. Bradshaw. All Rights Reserved.**
R. E. Bradshaw Books/April. 2013
ISBN-13: 978-0-9883520-5-6

Website: http://www.rebradshawbooks.com
Facebook: https://www.facebook.com/rebradshawbooks
Twitter @rebradshawbooks
Blog: http://rebradshawbooks.blogspot.com
For information contact rebradshawbooks@gmail.com

Acknowledgments

In no particular order:

To the readers that keep asking for more, thank you.

Donna W., thank you for being a real sweetheart and for your service to our country.

Wen, thanks for the grammar lessons.

Hooah, Dutch. Thanks for your service and answering my questions.

Judge Kate, you rock!

Curtie, thanks for the handholding, talking me off the ledge, and reminding me to just write.

Michelle, the three a.m. conversations are lifesavers.

D. Jackson Leigh, my friend, you are a generous soul and a true southern lady. Thank you so very much. I owe you big time.

Toni, thanks for the smiles. Go Duke!

Beta Readers, thank you for your time and helpful suggestions.

Lynne, my sister soul, I got your back. Thanks for having mine.

Jon, you know why. Kendra, you too.

Deb—Always.

About the book…

This is the third in the award winning Rainey Bell Thriller series, following Lambda Literary Award Finalist *Rainey Nights*. Each book is stand-alone. It does help to read them in order, but it is not necessary. In *The Rainey Season,* former FBI behavioral analyst Rainey Bell has settled into her life as a wife and mother with Katie Myers and the triplets. Consulting and private investigative work occupy the time not taken up with the one-year-olds crawling around her ankles. As always, her eye is on the security of her family, because Rainey knows evil is out there and that it is probably watching her. Rainey may be paranoid, but she's generally right. If it feels wrong, it usually is.

REB

"Sadism: The wish to inflict pain on others is not the essence of sadism. One central impulse: to have complete mastery over another person, to make her a helpless object of our will, to become the absolute ruler over her, to become her God, to do with her as one pleases. To humiliate her, to enslave her, are means to this end, and the most radical aim is to make her suffer, since there is no greater power over another person than that of inflicting pain on her, to force her to undergo suffering without her being able to defend herself. The pleasure in the complete domination over another person is the very essence of the sadistic drive."

~ James Mitchell "Mike" DeBardeleben, convicted serial sadist.

"For such offenders, sex and suffering are one and the same. This perversion, or paraphilia, is surprisingly unusual, even among sexual criminals. But those who harbor it are the most dangerous of all aberrant offenders. They are the great white sharks of deviant crime, marked by their wildly complex fantasy worlds, unequaled criminal cunning, paranoia, insatiable sexual hunger, and enormous capacity for destruction."

~ Roy Hazelwood, Former FBI Behavioral Analyst

CHAPTER ONE

When she was a child and afraid of the dark, her father dedicated himself to alleviating that fear. He was an avid spelunker and took her along on his less dangerous cave crawls. Even with perpetual night awaiting her, she happily followed him into the bowels of the earth. Helmet headlamps and handheld flashlights offered the security she needed to get through the absence of light underground.

On one trip, when she was ten years old, her father stopped in an area of the cave that was just tall enough for him to stand. He turned to face her, gripping her shoulders with his strong hands.

"Bladen, I'm going to teach you something, something you should know. It will help you with your fear of the dark."

Bladen's entire body tightened in panic. "You're not going to turn off the lights are you?"

Her father smiled. "Only for a moment and I promise to turn them right back on, but I need you to understand that you can still see in the dark. You have to trust me."

Bladen did trust him. He had never given her reason not to. Still, she could only nod her head, too scared to respond verbally.

"Okay, just close your eyes."

Bladen did as she was told. Even with her eyelids squeezed tightly together, she knew the instant the headlamps were extinguished.

She heard her father's soothing voice saying, "Breathe slow and deep. Calm yourself. I'm right here and the light is a button push away from being back on. Are you okay?"

Bladen could only nod.

"I feel you moving, so I'm assuming you're nodding your head," he said with a chuckle.

Keeping her eyes shut, as if not verifying the lights were out would keep the fear away, Bladen whispered, "I'm okay."

"Now, I need you to remember the light, Bladen. Even here, in the darkest of places, you always have light. Imagine looking out of your bedroom window on a sunny day. Do you see the sunlight?"

Bladen was amazed, because she did see it. Sunshine poured through her window, the honey-colored beams warming her face.

"I see it."

"Good girl, that's outstanding. Remember, no matter how dark it gets, you can always see the light. Just imagine it there."

"I will, Daddy."

"Now open your eyes, honey."

Bladen opened her eyes, gripping her father's arm tightly. The rush of fear returned with the nothingness of the dark.

Her father continued to talk to her. "You can imagine with your eyes open too. Listen to my voice, how it changes when I move my head. Let your mind's eye draw the picture. Let it show you where you are, Bladen. Trust your instincts. Your mind remembers the light."

She trusted him more than her instincts, and following his instructions was able to imagine the cavern reforming in front of her. With only darkness staring back at her, Bladen could feel what she should see, and her mind remembered.

"It's that way," she said, pushing her father in the direction she imagined was the way out.

Her father's laughter echoed through the cave, when the flashlight in his hand proved her correct.

2

"You're going to be all right, Bladen," he said, patting her on the shoulder. "Sometimes when the lights go out, you have to remember what it looked like when they were on. It's not really pitch-blackness, if you can imagine the light. Never give up. No darkness lasts forever."

Bladen learned a valuable lesson that day. Whenever things were going rough, she would close her eyes and see the light. "No darkness lasts forever," she would remind herself.

Bladen fell back on that memory, her current situation forcing her eyes shut, searching for light, any light. There, in the corner of her mind, was her smiling father, sunlight bouncing off his now white hair. She wanted to stay safe under his watchful eyes, but the primal warnings of her limbic system screamed at her to concentrate on survival. She had two choices. Escape inside her mind, or deal with the reality of her circumstance. Her eyes flew open.

"Stay focused, Bladen. Stay engaged." Her words bounced back from the black void. She concentrated on the reverberation for a moment, energizing her brain, giving it something to do. She listened to the darkness, hearing only the sound of rapid shaky breathing, her own.

She took a deep calming breath and released it slowly, a desperate attempt to control the panic.

"Okay, Bladen. Where are you?"

She repeated her name, sparking her mind to remember she was still there—that she still had a chance. If she lost hope, it was over.

Her father's voice surfaced from a memory, urging her into action. "Just because you can't see, doesn't mean you can't figure out where you are. What do you smell, Bladen? What can you feel? What do you hear?"

"All right. What do I smell? I smell fresh paint and wood, maybe leather when I turn around and face the other way. Oil or gas maybe, and bleach too."

She remembered hearing her dad comment, "These freaks love their bleach. You smell bleach at a suspect's house, you know this guy is up to no good."

She talked her way through her senses. It helped keep her calm. She was sure her father had never meant her to use the skills he taught her to survive a situation like this, but then again, it might have been exactly what he had in mind.

"My head hurts and I think I was drugged. It's warm in here, but the floor is cool." She focused on the darkness in front of her, aiming a short "ha" into the abyss, listening to the sound hit a wall and return with little echo. "Small room, solid walls. The ceiling seems to be about eight feet tall," she said. "No ambient sounds. I think I'm underground, but not a basement. It's too quiet. Could be soundproof, though."

Peering up, she was unable to see where the handcuffs binding her wrist were chained above her head. She was stretched out, pulled up so the balls of her feet were the only things keeping her from dangling helplessly. She felt the smooth concrete with her toes.

"The floor is slanted slightly. I think I may be in the center of the room."

She pulled against the restraints, allowing her toes to explore more of the surface beneath her. She followed the slant down for a few inches, before discovering a round metal grate embedded in the floor. She scampered away from the drain as fast as her toes could carry her, stifling the scream trying to escape her throat. Her body began to tremble uncontrollably, as it had when she first awoke and found she was hanging naked from her wrists in this inky black space. Bladen had seen enough horror movies to know what that drain probably meant. She was sure it was where her abductor was going to wash her blood away when he was done with her.

She chastised herself for letting the fear overwhelm her. "Get a hold of yourself, Bladen. Remember what that profiler said. 'Stay focused. Stay engaged. Do not give up.'"

There had been a series of unsolved rapes in the Raleigh-Durham-Chapel Hill area known as the Triangle and surrounding counties during the past few years. In addition to the rapes, an article Bladen read last Friday noted women began vanishing three years ago. The first cases were prostitutes, but in the last eighteen months, coeds, young professionals, and housewives had joined the list. It did not escape Bladen's attention that the public outcry increased with the elevation of the victims' social standing. The new media attention sparked a proactive community response. Women's safety symposiums were popping up all over the Triangle. At the urging of her father, Bladen attended one held at her small college, where she would graduate in May. While sitting in the audience Monday night, she never imagined that milestone would be in question by Tuesday evening. Surviving to Wednesday seemed even less likely.

Former FBI agent and behavioral analyst Rainey Bell, the last speaker on the panel and the most impressive, spelled it out plainly.

"There is no right or wrong way to escape from a rapist once the attack has begun. No one knows how he or she will react under that much stress, until it's been experienced. Fear can paralyze even the strongest of us. If you don't freeze, fighting like hell can make the situation worse, depending on the type of attacker you are dealing with," Bell said. "Knowledge is power, and knowledge is what we've tried to give you tonight. Beyond all the precautionary measures discussed, the various types of rapists and how best to respond to them, I have only one piece of advice. If you are attacked, stay focused, stay engaged. Listen to your instincts. The will to live is embedded in your DNA. Find your strength in that and do what you must to survive."

The tall, chestnut-haired Bell paused and stepped from behind the podium. Her tone softened as her piercing green eyes swept the audience. "No amount of training or education can make you immune to sexual assault." She lifted her shirt from her waist, revealing a white scar leading up from her navel, disappearing at the base of her sports bra. "I was a trained, armed FBI agent actively in pursuit of a serial murderer, when I was abducted by the man I sought. It can happen to anyone."

She pulled her shirt down and walked closer to the edge of the stage. "Look down the row you are sitting on. Go on—look at the women seated next to you. Statistics advise that at least one woman on each of these rows will be raped. The underreporting of sexual assaults suggests there will be more."

Bell took the time to let that sink in. "Be vigilant, but if you are attacked, please remember these words. Although the odds were very much against it, I am one of only two people to have survived being abducted by my assailant."

The pretty blond panelist from the women's shelter stood up. "I am the other," she said.

Rainey Bell reassured the room. "There is always hope. Do not give up."

Bladen already followed most of the precautions the panel suggested. Her father had drilled them into her head.

"Park in heavily traveled areas, no dark places, not next to any vans," he'd make her repeat. "Be aware of your surroundings. Listen to your instincts. If it feels wrong, it usually is."

She always remembered and followed his instructions. Yet, here she was, chained in a small room without having seen the man that abducted her.

Her last memory was of preparing to leave for an evening class, running late, and rushing her parents off the phone, promising to call back after class to talk about her graduation trip. She awoke alone in the dark, chained to the ceiling of a madman's lair.

After the initial shock and horror, Bladen fought to gain control as each wave of terror seized her. For every moment of calm she could muster, there were many more where the reality of her circumstances sent her into convulsions of quaking panic.

She closed her eyes, searching again for the memory of light, and repeated what had become her mantra, "Stay focused. Stay engaged."

"Former Special Agent Rainey Bell is quite enchanting, isn't she?" A deep voice said out of the silence.

Bladen gasped. Her eyes flew open. He was there. He had been there the entire time, watching her. She jerked away from the sound of movement, the handcuffs biting into her already bloody wrists.

Finding her voice, she screamed into the inky blackness, "Stay away from me!"

Her frantic kicks were futile. Still she swung on the chains, striking out until she had no breath remaining, her desperate trapped-animal screams fading to whimpers. Exhausted from the struggle, she hung limply from her wrists and began to lose hope.

She felt the breeze on her neck as he passed behind her, whispering, "Wasn't that magnificent when she showed her scar?"

Bladen jerked forward with another burst of primal survival instinct, but escape was impossible.

His breath licked at her face. "I bet she screamed when he dug that scalpel into her chest, don't you?"

Energy spent and no way to break free, Bladen closed her eyes against the breath-stealing panic, willing her mind to engage. Who was this guy? She didn't need his name. She only wanted to know what kind of sick freak he was. Her brain supplied the desired information, as it began to play a memory of an earlier portion of Rainey Bell's presentation on the types of rapists.

"Should you become the target of an Anger Excitation offender—the most criminally sophisticated of the rapists we've discussed—escape or resistance is generally out of the question. You must be clever in your defiance. You will have to match wits with him, but above all, you must attempt to avoid his rage. Injuries will increase in severity with his intensified anger. This sadist's goal is to achieve gratification from the fear and torture of the victim. These abductions can range from hours to days, and in rare cases—weeks, months, or even years. Surviving the torture for a time is a good thing, believe it or not. The longer it takes him to tire of you, the more opportunities you have to take advantage of his mistakes and get away. These offenders are lethal. The end result is almost always murder. You must do what you can to escape. Do not give in. Do not give up."

If Bladen had any doubt about what kind of offender held her captive, the crack of a whip behind her took care of that. As he worked himself into lather, her captor used it to punctuate his sentences. Bladen shrank from the sound, losing hope with each thunderclap of leather.

"That guy was a hack." Crack! "He had Rainey Bell in his grasp twice and he ends up with a hole where his chest used to be, courtesy of that little bitch Katie Meyers. Did you see her at the conference, the blond pretty one? She's the other cunt he let escape. Did you know she and Agent Bell are raising triplets and claim to be married? I have my parental rights dictated by some feminist bitch in a black robe, and those dykes are lickin' pussy with three kids under the same roof. That's fucked up. That judge is on my list, too." Crack!

Bladen needed to slow the escalation of his temper and distance herself from the object of his rage, Rainey Bell. The words gushed from her in a trembling whisper, "I don't know Agent Bell. I only saw her at the symposium. I didn't know the blonde was with her. I'm not even a feminist."

He was too invested in his rant to hear her. His monologue grew louder and more agitated, the whip cracks more frequent as he circled her.

"They flaunt those kids like poster children for the lesbian movement. It makes me sick." Crack! "And Agent Sexy is supposed to be some great profiler. She let that guy abduct her. How good can she be?" Crack! "Then she's supposed to be protecting little Miss Meyers, but instead, she almost got them both killed because she didn't see him coming, again." Crack! "She let Dalton Chambers nearly kill her from death row. Behavioral analyst, my ass." Crack! "She couldn't profile my dog." Crack! "I'm right under her nose and she doesn't even see me, even questions my existence."

Caa-rack! The whip wrapped around Bladen's calves, trapping her legs together. She howled as the sonic boom rendering tail snapped to a stinging stop. She jerked and kicked in an attempt to shake it loose, but it was futile. He snatched the whip, pulling her feet out from under her, and snapped restraints around her ankles, before clipping them to an unseen fulcrum in the floor. His moves were precise and efficient. Bladen knew she was not his first victim nor would she be his last, unless she somehow made it out of here alive. Agent Bell had been correct. Escape was highly unlikely, but it was Bladen's only hope.

She started babbling rapidly, her tears tangling in her words. "My name is Bladen Asher. I have to be at the elementary school in the morning. I'm a student teacher this semester. It's my first day to lead the class. I have to show up. And my parents—my parents, they are going to be worried if I don't call."

He moved around her, so close she could smell him.

Bladen switched to a desperate plea for reason. "I haven't seen you. You can let me go. I don't know anything about you, except you don't like that Rainey Bell person."

The whip fell away from her legs. She felt his hand run up her side, like a lover tenderly caressing his mate. She shivered against his touch, her breathing fast and shallow—terror-stricken.

"Shh," he whispered next to her ear. "I know all about you, Bladen Claire Asher. I know where you live, the classes you take, where you work, what you eat, what time you go to bed, and that Patrick and Ginny Asher love you very much. You had just finished speaking with them, when we began our little game."

Just when she thought she could not be more horrified, Bladen realized the depths of her captor's iniquity. He had stalked her, planned her kidnapping, and now he held her prisoner in what she imagined was an underground bunker. She knew she should not let him see her fear, but knowing and doing were two distinctly different things when faced with a whip-wielding maniac.

"How—how do you know all that?"

He grabbed a handful of her thick brown hair, yanked her head back, and growled, "Because you're mine."

The lights flashed on, blinding her at first. Bladen blinked the room into focus, as he turned her so she could take it all in. Multiple medieval looking torture devices surrounded her in a small concrete-block room. Her eyes darted from the apparatuses, designed to elicit pain and degradation, to the man who would use them on her. Glowing yellow eyes glared at her from behind a black-leather mask.

Bladen gasped as he released his grip on her hair and raised the whip in the air. Her voice mere trembling whispers, she asked, "What are you going to do to me?"

Sadistic laughter skipped through his answer. "Whatever the hell I want."

CAA-RRRACK!

#

In another part of the Triangle, Rainey Bell was having a little long overdue Mommy-and-me time with Mommy, when her cellphone began to ring just after ten o'clock.

"Don't answer that," Katie said sharply, sweeping Rainey's phone off the table.

Rainey chuckled at Katie's desperation. "I can't answer it, now. I think you threw it in the hamper."

Katie kissed Rainey's neck. "They'll call back," she whispered.

Triplets and a demanding schedule meant they rarely had the time or the energy for sex. The kids turned one year old on Christmas Day, just fifteen days ago. Rainey had only one problem with her children. Rain or shine, no matter how long a night it had been, the Bell-Meyers triplets rose at dawn. Rainey thought she had seen the sunrise over the lake every morning for the past twelve months. She no longer set an alarm. It wasn't necessary. No one could sleep through those three crying during the first months, and now, no one dared sleep if any one of them were awake.

The house was a labyrinth of baby locks and little fences. Rainey never imagined that crawling babies could cover so much ground. Anything breakable was now at least three feet from the floor, but still not safe. The triplets were on the cusp of gaining more independence and had begun taking their first hesitant steps alone. None too successfully, but they were pulling up and buzzing around while holding onto the furniture. Six tiny feet running through the house was just around the corner, something Rainey looked forward to with mixed emotions. She and Katie could barely keep up with them as it was and collapsed into bed exhausted at the end of every evening—but not tonight.

Katie began the stalking the moment Rainey arrived to help with the nightly feeding and bathing. She was a woman on a mission to get laid, and Rainey was happy to indulge her. There was a lot of winking and ass grabbing in between the assembly line of baths, diapers, shoving feet into pajamas, and the removal of some of the strained peas from Rainey's thick hair. Weather, the only girl and leader of the triplet army, thought it quite amusing to throw food and was quickly teaching her brothers, Timothy and Mack, this skill. Once the triplets were tucked into their cribs, Rainey slipped next door to the master suite with the intention of removing the rest of the kids' dinner from her hair. When Katie caught up with her, the plan for a shower and Rainey's clothing were done away with rather quickly—strained peas be damned.

The phone stopped ringing at some point. Rainey wasn't sure when, since Katie was providing ample distraction. She was kissing her way down Rainey's body, her blond head about to disappear under the covers, when the hamper erupted with an alarm fit for a radiation leak at a nuclear power plant. Startled into sitting position, Rainey nearly bucked Katie off the bed.

"What the hell?" Katie exclaimed, wrestling with the cocoon of covers encasing her.

Rainey scrambled from the bed. "That's the emergency app. Something's wrong."

"It sure as hell better be," Katie said in frustration.

Rainey dug into the hamper, retrieving her phone. That alarm meant someone was in trouble, someone she cared about. Rainey loaded the emergency notification application on the phones of everyone in her tight circle of friends and family. Sliding her finger across her phone's screen silenced the alarm and revealed a satellite image, with the standard distress message from Junior, and a blinking red dot pinpointing his location.

Rainey squinted at the dot, enlarged the map to verify her suspicion, and then whispered, "Oh, Jesus. Junior is at Maybelline's."

Katie hopped out of bed. "Is that bad?"

"It probably isn't good. I can't believe he went without Mackie or me." Rainey hit the callback link on the phone, while looking for the clothes Katie had so recently removed from her body and thrown about the room.

11

When Junior answered, he did not wait for salutations. "Rainey, you have to come. Now."

Rainey was not pleased. "Why did you try to pick up Maybelline on your own? You know better, Junior."

Junior defended himself. "Mackie is with me. He told me to call you. I did, but you didn't answer. So, I sent the emergency signal."

"Where is he? Let me talk to him," Rainey said.

She put the phone on speaker, set it down on the bedside table, and continued to dress. A nude Katie brought Rainey a clean shirt, after having retrieved the baby food-covered one from the hallway. Rainey smiled with the memory of how it got there. Her smile disappeared immediately with Junior's next words.

"She shot him, Rainey."

Katie's gasp accompanied Rainey's hurried questions. "Was he wearing his vest? Is he all right?"

"She shot him in the vest on his left side, lower part of his ribcage. I didn't see any blood, but he went down. He was having trouble breathing."

"What hospital are they taking him to?"

Junior hesitated, before answering, "We got a problem, Rainey. He's still in the house with Maybelline. He made us leave him there."

"You left him in there, alone? What the hell, Junior?"

Rainey began buttoning her shirt frantically, while Junior explained. "I got a tip from Bobo that Maybelline had come back home. He said he didn't see anybody else at the house. But Rainey, there was a mess of kids in there when we went through the door. Maybelline pulled a gun, started waving it around and ranting about wanting to talk to you. We couldn't use the Taser on her. She was holding a baby. Mackie tried to talk her down, but the gun went off. He was only a few feet from her. It was a .44. I don't think she really meant to shoot him, but she went wild after that. Mackie told us to get out."

Even with a level-three ballistics vest to stop the bullet from penetrating his chest wall, Maybelline could have caused some serious damage. The kind of damage a sledgehammer could do to a ribcage, like broken ribs, a punctured lung, internal bleeding.

He was more than Rainey's partner. Mackie was her guardian angel and filled the shoes of his old friend, her father, when he was killed almost four years ago. Mackie loved Rainey fiercely and she him. She could not lose him.

She steeled herself and tried to ask calmly, but felt the tremble in her voice. "So he's talking? Have you called 911?"

"Yeah, he's talking, but with the trouble he's having breathing, he can't say much. The cops are already here. The negotiator and the ambulance should be here any minute, but I'm afraid they're going to wait around 'til it's too late."

Rainey wanted the door kicked in and Mackie taken to a hospital. Any number of things could be killing him by the second. They needed to get him out of there. She was at least twenty minutes away from Maybelline's house, and that would be at record speed with traffic. Rainey took a deep breath and let the emotion subside, switching gears from concerned family member to the FBI agent she once was.

"Let them do their jobs, Junior. It's out of our hands now. I'm on my way."

#

Rainey's Dodge Charger SRT8 was the physical embodiment of her personality—dark and fully loaded. Its specifications said it would do zero to sixty in four-point-five seconds. With the added body armor and ballistic glass piling on weight, her tricked-out custom ride achieved that speed a little more than five seconds after she cleared the guard shack of her gated community. She pressed down hard on the accelerator, the digital readout of her speed passing sixty and climbing rapidly, as she raced north toward Durham. If a cop tried to pull her over, he would have to follow her to Maybelline's house. Mackie would walk through fire to get to Rainey if she needed him. The least she could do was spend the night in jail for evading the police when he needed her.

She checked in at the office and saw Mackie nearly every day, but did not keep up with the daily activities of the bond business. When Katie became pregnant with the triplets, Rainey took a step back from chasing fugitives. She now spent most of her time working from home as a private investigator and a consultant with local law enforcement, defense attorneys, and prosecutors. Rainey was happy to be using the skills her years with the FBI Behavioral Analysis Unit afforded her, and Katie was ecstatic she was no longer kicking open fugitives' doors. She was even speaking to her mother again. Rainey's personal and professional lives were in the best condition of her forty-two years.

Mackie and Ernie had been with the bond business, bequeathed to Rainey by her father, since its inception. Miles Cecil McKinney, Mackie, was Billy Bell's best friend and Vietnam buddy, as well as current forty-nine percent owner of Bell's Bail. Ernestine Womble, the sixty-nine-year-old office manager and the backbone of the business for thirty-seven years, practically raised Rainey. It was at Ernie's not so subtle urging that they moved from the isolated Jordan Lake location to the more populated area of Franklin Street in Chapel Hill. Since the move, the number of bonds they wrote swelled. Rainey wasn't sure if it was the economy or the move, but the bail bond business was hopping.

In the middle of her personal happiness and the expansion in business, Rainey was having difficulty shaking the thought it could not last forever. The truth of her life was that the other shoe always fell. Rainey hoped she was merely being paranoid, affected by the daily threat of Ernie's imminent retirement. She had decided it was Ernie's way of preparing her for the time when it would be a reality. She did not know how she would cope without Ernie behind the front desk. There would be no replacing her. They broke the mold after Ernestine Womble took her first breath. There would never be another like her.

Rainey was also worried about Mackie. He was sixty-one years old and slowing down, not to mention he was overweight and his knees were giving out. Junior, Mackie's nephew, and a few other runners did most of the fugitive recoveries without the six-foot-six, more than three-hundred-pound bear of a man ever leaving the office. She could not imagine why Mackie would have gone after Maybelline without telling her, and worse, not verifying who was in the house. It wasn't like him to be caught unaware.

Flying down the two-lane blacktop as fast as she dared, Rainey was consumed with guilt for not being there for Mackie. He had been sick with a virus back around Christmas, missing the triplets' birthday party because of it. He was having a difficult time getting back up to speed, but Rainey had not noticed it affecting his decision-making. Mackie did not make mistakes like walking in on a desperate bail jumper in a house full of kids. It just did not make sense.

The phone ringing through the sound system stopped her analysis of Mackie's behavior. She glanced at the touchscreen display in the center of the dashboard for the caller ID. She pressed the answer button on the steering wheel, activating the hands-free communication system.

"Rainey Bell."

She recognized the smooth good ol' boy drawl of the Durham County Sheriff's Office negotiator, as soon as he started to speak.

"Sorry to drag you out at this time a night, Rainey," he said, in his slow, deliberate delivery. "Captain Wiley Trainer, here. I'm told you are aware of the situation."

People who mistook Wiley's accent and measured manner of speaking as a sign he might be a bit slow were mistaken. He was as wily as his name implied. His ability to remain calm, while those around him experienced adrenaline overload, made him an exceptional negotiator.

"Yes, I'm on my way," Rainey answered, falling behind traffic on the two-lane state road. "Dammit!"

"What's that?" Wiley asked.

"Traffic. I'm getting bogged down by traffic." Rainey turned the emergency flashers on, honked the horn, and roared past two cars, before pulling back into the right lane. At times like this, she missed the blue lights and siren she once had at her disposal.

"From the sound of that engine, you can get here quick. Let me have somebody meet you up on I-40 and bring you in," Wiley suggested.

"That would be excellent," Rainey said, flooring the six-point-four liter Hemi V8 engine around another car. There was a sharp curve to the left coming up, and then a mostly straight shot to the on-ramp of the interstate. "Tell them I'll be at the on-ramp from state highway seven-five-one in about five minutes, driving a black Charger. Tell 'em to turn on their radar. I'm the hot one coming at them," she shouted over the engine roar, as she paddle-shifted down and banked into the curve.

Rainey heard Wiley's muffled arrangements for her escort. She powered the Charger through the apex of the curve and rocketed out the other end, happy to see no other brake lights ahead.

After a moment, Wiley's voice was back in the speakers. "You keep it between the lines, Rainey. I need you here."

"What does Maybelline want, Wiley?"

"She wants to talk to you. I told her you were coming. Talked to Mackie, too. He's hurt, but breathin'. I got her to give up most of the kids and one of her adult daughters, but she still has the baby, a toddler, and the other daughter in there with her. Angeline, I believe it is. She stayed behind. Said she wasn't leavin' her sister's baby in the line of fire, and her two-year-old would not leave without her. So that's where we stand."

"Where's the baby's mother? Maybe she could talk Maybelline into giving herself up."

Rainey could almost hear Wiley rubbing his chin, a habit when he was thinking. The pause he left between her suggestion and his reply told her it wasn't going to be good.

"Well, Rainey, I believe that's the sticking point. Maybelline's youngest daughter, the baby's mother, is missing. Been gone almost four months now. She disappeared from over near State College last September where she was taking some night classes."

"She's one of those missing girls?" Rainey asked, knowing, in this case, missing probably meant dead.

"Not exactly. She had a rap sheet, some minor juvenile stuff, and a pick up for prostitution when she was eighteen, but it was dropped. When cases were being flagged for the task force, Jacqueline's file—that's her name—was dismissed as not fitting

16

the criteria. I guess they missed that part about her being a student at the college. Maybelline is mad as hell that her daughter was not on the list of possible victims that got published last Friday."

"Whose bright idea was that, anyway?" Rainey asked, but didn't wait for an answer. "Publishing a list of 'possible serial killer' victims, without having found a single body or crime scene, was poor judgment on somebody's part. The only things we know for sure are women are missing, and the victim profile shifted from prostitutes and street people to affluent women back in the fall of 2011. Nobody suggested missing women outside that criteria not be flagged. At least those words never came out of my mouth. I can't speak for the task force. I'm just a consultant."

"I told her that," Wiley drawled, "but that didn't make Maybelline feel any better."

"So, is that what she wants—someone to look into her daughter's disappearance?"

Wiley chuckled. "No, not someone. You. She wants you to investigate, and she wants to look you in the eye and hear you say you will."

"Do you think she'd shoot Mackie or harm those kids if you let the SWAT boys go in there?"

Wiley's voice deepened. Rainey could almost see him lowering his eyes on her. "You know damn well that woman is desperate. You knew that when you bailed her out, which doesn't seem like the best course of action to have taken, lookin' back."

"She's always come in before," Rainey answered, only half-heartedly believing her own defense.

Maybelline Upshaw was an old client, one of the first for Billy Bell's Bail and Bait. Since moving from Jordan Lake, Rainey and Mackie dropped "Bait" from the name, but kept many of the same clients.

Billy bonded out a juvenile Maybelline the first time she was locked up for stealing food from a grocery store. She was a pot-dealing grandmother now, having been in and out of jail and sometimes prison her whole life. Rainey had a soft spot for the old woman, who in reality was a mere ten years older. That was why she bonded her out this time, knowing Maybelline might not comply with the order to appear.

Rainey ignored her instincts and Mackie's warning when she got the call to go to the courthouse from one of Maybelline's daughters. Momma was in trouble again. She also dismissed the warning bells when she discovered the charges against the old girl. Maybelline had too many strikes against her and was facing a lengthy sentence. She distinctly remembered Maybelline vowing never to go back to prison after her last stretch and had hoped it was a declaration that she was giving up her criminal lifestyle. The other implication was the fugitive status Maybelline was willing to acquire in order to spend not another day behind bars. Rainey recalled thinking about that at the bail hearing, but posted the one hundred thousand dollar surety bond anyway.

It probably had something to do with what Maybelline said, standing before the judge. "How else am I gonna feed my grandkids? Ain't nobody hirin' an ex-con. The only bi'ness makin' money is dealin' dope. And I ain't messin' with no hard stuff. Folks is depressed. I'm savin' the gov'ment from payin' these doctors to pump 'em full of pills. 'Stead of worryin' 'bout me liftin' people's spirits with a little weed, y'all ought to fix the economy."

It was funny then, but now Rainey faced the added guilt of placing Mackie in his current position. Had she heeded his warning, he would not be a wounded hostage, and she would not be rushing to his side, praying she could bring them all out safely.

She added to her last statement, "I know it's my fault, Wiley. Now, help me fix this."

"Well, all right then. You bring it on to the house. We got some work to do."

Rainey could see the blue emergency lights flashing on the overpass as she approached. "Keep her calm and tell her I'm coming." She paused, and then added, "You tell Maybelline I said this, and I mean you tell her as soon as you hang up with me. Tell her Billy Bell always did right by her and his daughter will, too, but she can't let anything happen to Mackie. If it does, I'll shoot her myself."

18

CHAPTER TWO

A laptop glowed out of the darkness. Voices came out of small speakers on the desk in the corner, the sound a garbled reverberation against her eardrums. Opening her swollen eyes, Bladen peered through the tiny slits she was barely able to create. No longer hanging from her wrists, for which she was grateful, her head and hands now protruded from the holes of a medieval pillory. He constructed the device by hand, he told her, lovingly sanding the hinged, thick wooden planks that now securely locked her in place. He left her standing there, naked, and unable to move, but at least he was gone.

Not long ago, he forced her into a shower stall to wash her blood and his body fluids from her skin. He snatched the stiff brush from her hands, when he deemed she wasn't scrubbing hard enough. He was in the process of rubbing her skin raw and repeating to her what a "dirty bitch" she was, when he suddenly stopped, handcuffed her to a metal bar attached to the tiled wall, and exited the room. He left her there long past the hot water turning icy cold. Bladen didn't care. She stood fast under the freezing spray, shivering, but determined to wash the last few hours away.

The shower was in a small bathroom adjacent to the maniac's chamber of homemade and "collectible" horrors. He was quite versed in the art of torture. He enjoyed telling Bladen the history of each device, its origin and uses, while he demonstrated how it worked on her. He was particularly fond of one ancient horror.

"Now, I'm going to show you the pièce de résistance of my collection," he had said, his yellow contact lenses seeming to glow behind the black leather mask.

She could see only his eyes and mouth, but it was enough to distinguish his ghoulish expression of delight. He was squatting on the floor in front of her while she was tied face down to the ladder rack that he was especially proud of. He had meticulously reconstructed it from medieval drawings, he explained.

"You're the first one to get to use this museum quality reproduction of mine. Sadly, my last guest departed before it was completed. I'll always remember you were the first," he said, as if they had just shared a ride in his new car. He wiped tears away from one of Bladen's cheeks. "Sorry about the whip, but you have to learn. Have you learned, Bladen?"

Bladen had learned. She learned to respond quickly and with the right answer. "Yes, sir," trembled from her lips.

"And what have you learned?"

Bladen looked him in the eyes, because that's what he had instructed her to do. She took a shaky breath and repeated verbatim what he taught her, careful not to make a mistake. Mistakes caused pain.

"I will do what you say, when you say it. I will take my punishment and learn to like it. You are the master."

"Good girl," he said, smiling. Then he held up a pear-shaped metal object with an ornamental key protruding from one end. The pear part appeared to be pewter inlaid with brass vines and flowers. "This is it. Isn't she beautiful?" He paused for Bladen's answer and when it did not come quickly enough, he reminded her of the rules with a backhand across her face. "I asked you a question."

Bladen watched the saliva and blood drip from her mouth and puddle with her fallen tears on the floor beneath her, as she answered, "Yes, it's beautiful."

"This is a reproduction. Most of the real ones are in museums or rich men's private collections, but this one is very accurately rendered. Do you want to know what she does?"

Bladen needed no reminder this time. She said, "Yes, please tell me."

"Good, a girl who likes to learn. This, Bladen, is called the Pear of Anguish. No one knows its exact origins. The first mention of the Pear dates to 1639, from a French publication entitled *General Inventory of the History of Thieves*. Credit for the Pear's invention was assigned to a robber who lived during the reign of Henry IV, ruler of France from 1589 to 1610. There were many styles and sizes, all designed to do the same thing."

He began to turn the ornamental key, which caused the four metal leaves forming the pear shape to open slowly. His excitement grew as the leaves expanded and he continued to describe the Pear's uses.

"See, if you were a heretic, blasphemer, or liar, you'd have this inserted in your mouth. As the screw turns, the Pear expands, breaking teeth, ripping the insides of your mouth. It's a bloody mess. If you were a faggot, this gets pushed up your ass. If it's opened wide enough, you'll think twice about sticking a dick up there again—that is, if you live through it."

He began to close the Pear, now grinning at Bladen, whose wide eyes betrayed that she knew what was coming, but he told her anyway. He delighted in her fear, and what he said next terrified her even more than she already was.

"And for witches and bitches, this was inserted in their cunts."

Bladen knew she must not resist. Things were so much worse when she did, but fear overtook her. She began to fight the restraints, screaming at the top of her lungs, even though she knew no one could hear her. If her previous shrieks of torment had not roused help, then no one was coming to her rescue. Still she cried and begged, "Please, God, no."

He stood up, his sadistic laughter following him, as he said, "Don't worry, Bladen. I'm not going to use this on your pussy. I have better things for that." The whip came down hard across her already brutalized buttocks, as he rolled the ends of the rack closer together, forcing her rear into the air. "Spread your ass."

21

Bladen screamed and writhed to no avail. The whip came down again, with his command, "I said spread those sweet ass cheeks. Now, bitch!"

Later, standing under the cold water, she was trying to forget what happened next, and all that happened before in the short time she had been his captive. Bladen tried to focus on survival, but part of her did not really want to live through this nightmare. She was looking around the small bathroom for a way to end her suffering, before he had a chance to hurt her again, when he came back to retrieve her.

"Seems our girl Rainey is on the move. She's got a hostage situation. It's on the news. I need to put you away for a bit, but I'll be back."

As he spoke, he locked her, cold and soaked to the bone, in his prized pillory. His tone was tender, while his subject matter was not.

"I'd put a shirt on you, but they tend to stick to the lash wounds. Hurts a hell of a lot more when you open them up removing the shirt. You'll dry soon and I'll leave the heat on. It'll help keep you from going into shock."

He cupped his hand under Bladen's chin, lifting her eyes to his. She saw the sadistic smirk. He wasn't concerned about causing her pain. He rejoiced in it. This nice guy act was just part of the psychological trauma he was inflicting with the physical torture.

"You get some rest now. When I come back, we're going to work with my Shrew's Fiddle design. It has a few kinks I need to work out. I'm sure you'll do nicely for a fitting dummy."

The pillory faced away from the lone exit door. Bladen had been able to identify it in the brief moments she wasn't focused on living through the experience. She could not see what lay beyond the door when it was opened. He turned off the lights, just as he closed and locked her escape route behind him. When she heard the deadbolt slide into place, Bladen realized she no longer carried the slightest dread of the dark. It was not the imaginary evil in the darkness of her childhood that she should fear, but the malevolent fantasies of real men played out under the glare of a bare light bulb.

"Stay focused. Stay engaged," Bladen mumbled.

In his haste to leave, her captor left the laptop open, proof to Bladen that he was capable of mistakes, especially if Rainey Bell was involved. She filed that away for future reference. She could only see the glow of the screen, but she could hear the voices clearer now. It was some kind of news broadcast, and it was Bladen's only company. On one hand, it reminded her that the world continued to turn and no one knew she was missing yet, but it offered a distraction from the hell she was in. Whatever worked, whatever would keep the memories of the agony and torment away, that's what she needed to do. There was a reason her mind was trying to bury those moments, and Bladen was going to let it. She concentrated on the sound of the reporter's voice and let it take her to the happenings on a little side street in Durham.

#

Rainey followed the Highway Patrol escort, as the cruiser turned off Holloway Street into the Albright neighborhood, near downtown Durham. It would not have been hard to find Maybelline's house, even if Rainey hadn't known the way. News media vans and SUVs lined the approaching narrow side streets. Over-anxious reporters stood in the beams of glaring white lights, glancing over their shoulders at Maybelline's house a block away, and then turning back to the cameras with concerned, alarmed expressions to alert the public of "danger." In Rainey's experience, most of what the media did not know in a situation such as this, they simply guessed and hoped to be the one outlet to get it right. The Connecticut school shooting coverage was a prime example of imagination and speculation run wild.

Rainey hoped Katie wasn't watching from home, but knew she was. She would be on high alert until Rainey returned. It would then be several hours before she calmed down, but Katie was becoming better at accepting what Rainey did for a living was sometimes dangerous. Nevertheless, it took careful management of the details on Rainey's part to keep the peace. There were still things Katie did not need to know. Katie agreed to those conditions, with the stipulation that she would be informed if they were in immediate peril. Of some of the day-to-day danger Rainey faced, Katie was willing to remain blissfully unaware, but when the serial killers and stalkers came out of the woodwork, the details mattered. Rainey agreed and the concessions on both their parts seemed to be working.

Thoughts of Katie disappeared, as a reporter recognized Rainey's car and ran toward it. The bright white light of the closely-following camera blinded her momentarily. She could hear the shouted questions begin before an officer directing traffic waved her through the barricade. Blue and red emergency lights flashed and reflected back from windows filled with the inquisitive faces of neighbors peeking out through the blinds or openly gawking. Rainey parked behind some city patrol units, near Mackie's Escalade and Junior's Expedition. When she exited the Charger, ballistics vest in hand, the reporter continued to shout questions from behind the barrier.

"Rainey Bell, you've been called to the scene because you bonded out this dangerous criminal and now your partner has been shot. Is that true?"

She turned to face the reporter, smiling a silent, "No comment," which Katie always told her looked more like a smirked 'Kiss my ass', before going in search of Wiley Trainer.

A uniformed officer beckoned, "Come with me."

Rainey thought she knew him, but she met so many cops. This one's name and how they were acquainted escaped her. The name of the next cop that spoke to her—Detective Rex King—was emblazoned in her mind forever. How could she forget the man who swore he'd see her rot in prison for conspiracy in the murder of Dalton Chambers? A Grand Jury investigation produced no bill of indictment, but doubt still lingered among some in law enforcement. Rainey might very well know something about the attack and subsequent death of the serial killer who tried to arrange her demise from death row, but she would go to her grave with it. Bullying and speculation by an overzealous homicide detective would not sway her from that stance. Only two people knew the truth of her involvement in the case, Rainey and her friend, sometimes employer and personal lawyer, Molly Kincaid. Well, one other person knew the whole truth, but Rainey suspected that person would rather remain silent or suffer the consequences.

"Are you armed, Bell?" Detective King's nasally, obnoxious, superior tone arrived before he emerged from the crowd of law enforcement personnel gathered in front of Maybelline's house.

Rainey always thought the detective's parents had high expectations for a son they named King twice. If they were hoping for a physical specimen of manhood, they most certainly were disappointed. Rex was a scrawny, pale man, with constant sinus drainage from allergies, and poor eyesight. Rainey was surprised he could pass the firearms qualification test. If his parents were shooting for a little man with an ego the size of China, then they definitely hit the mark. Rainey had been forced to work with him after being hired to consult with the missing women's task force, of which Rex was a member. She considered him a good detective, just a lousy human being. To say they could barely tolerate each other's presence would be an understatement. Their mutual animosity was not lost on those forced to work with them.

King continued to approach Rainey, hand out, demanding her weapon. "I'm sure the answer to my question is that you are, so hand it over. We don't need you involved in any more questionable shootings."

Rainey bit her lip, in order not to tell ol' Rex to "fuck off." She was working on cleaning up her language at Katie's insistence. Still, Rainey was sure one of triplets' first words would be "shit." She placed the ballistics vest on the back of a nearby patrol car, removed the Glock 19 from her hip holster, ejected the ammunition clip, and cleared the chamber, before handing the weapon over with no fuss. She had more important things to do than piss on trees with a wannabe alpha male and his little-man complex.

"I'll be wanting this back," she said, holding onto the grip of the pistol a little longer than necessary, forcing Rex to tug it from her hand.

He slipped the Glock and the clip in his coat pocket, sneering at Rainey. "Saw your boy, Bobo, down the block a ways. I used to think it was stupid of you to continue that relationship, but I see now that keeping an eye on him is easier when he's still on the payroll. Maybe I ought to chat with him. See if he's ready to clear his conscience."

Rainey smirked back at the man that was at least three inches shorter than her height of five-feet-ten-inches. "Well, if you find him, tell him I want to see him, too. He gave us bad intel on this job. That's why we're in this mess."

"Sure, blame your screw-up on the lackey," Rex began, and would have continued had Wiley Trainer not interrupted.

"Rex, I need you to go to that house down there with the red car in the driveway. You'll find the rest of the Upshaw family there. I need statements from everyone that was in the house when the shot was fired."

Wiley Trainer had been around a long time, was well respected, and outranked Detective King by a bunch.

"Yes, Captain," Rex answered, leaving immediately to do Wiley's bidding.

When she was sure Rex was out of earshot, Rainey turned to Wiley. "Thank you. I'm not sure how much more of King Squared I could take tonight."

Wiley's lips hinted a sly smile. "Took those statements myself, before we let them go in the neighbor's house to keep the kids warm." He paused to rub his chin. "Never hurts to get the story twice though, does it?"

Rainey returned his impish grin. "No, it sure doesn't. I think that was very wise of you."

Wiley then turned his attention to the problem at hand. "I see you have your vest. You go ahead and put that on while I fill you in."

Rainey pulled off the black leather jacket protecting her from the cold night air, feeling the chill immediately. Wiley held out his hand to take it from her.

"Take good care of this," she said, handing the coat over. "Katie gave it to me for Christmas. She'll be mad if I lose it."

Wiley examined the coat. "Nice. I'll put it in my car. Wouldn't want that pretty little wife of yours to be upset with you."

Wiley was one of the few cops that spoke openly to Rainey about her wife and kids. He was definitely one of her favorite people in the Durham County Sheriff's Office. Of course, Katie had sufficiently charmed Wiley when he spoke at the battered women's shelter run by her foundation. Rainey's wife charmed everyone she met. She had charmed Rainey right into marrying her in the New York City Clerk's Office and raising three kids.

With thoughts of the triplets and Katie in her head, Rainey pulled the Velcro straps on her vest extra tight, while following Wiley to his car. He was the same age as Mackie and had been a young deputy when Billy Bell started writing bonds back in the seventies. He called those days the wild times and shared stories with Rainey about her father. She trusted him. His white hair foretold of his impending retirement, a day she hated to see come. Her world was changing on a daily basis, with old friends moving on to the golden years of their lives. As much as Rainey disliked changes, she had to face the fact that life was a long series of adapting to them.

Wiley talked as they walked. "When you go in the front door, she'll be on your right. We got a heat signature camera on the house. She hasn't moved. Still sitting in a chair in the front corner, holding a baby. Her daughter is on the couch. You'll be behind her when you enter. The toddler is moving about, so I can't tell you where she'll be at any given moment. She appears to be having a good time, which is good. Means everyone is calm in there."

"Where is Mackie?" Rainey asked.

"He's on the floor by those two big windows there, head pointed toward us." Wiley pointed at the house with his free hand, while he tossed Rainey's coat in the front seat of his car and continued to the command vehicle parked directly in front of Maybelline's house. "I'd prefer not sending you in there, but I've known Maybelline a long time too. I don't think she'll hurt you, Rainey. She's upset about shooting Mackie. She just wants someone, specifically you, to tell her that Jacquie's disappearance will be investigated."

Junior rushed forward, flanked by three other young muscular men. He was nearly as tall as his uncle, but with the body of a trained athlete. Rainey barely knew the other three men wearing the Bell's Bail logo on the collars of their black mock turtlenecks. She really had stepped far away from the business. It seemed Junior and Mackie had come prepared with plenty of bodies to take Maybelline down. Rainey nodded at her employees, who were still pumped with adrenaline and wide-eyed.

"Evening, gentlemen," Rainey greeted them.

"Rainey, I'm so sorry," Junior said.

Rainey could see the worry in his eyes, for both her and Mackie. She reassured him. "It's going to be fine, Junior. It's not your fault."

"Junior, Mackie's wife is on the phone." A woman with a distinct military bearing handed a cell phone to him. She turned to Rainey. "Sorry to get you out of bed, boss."

"No problem, Gunny. Couldn't be helped," Rainey replied to retired Marine Gunnery Sergeant Naomi Pierce, the newest member of her staff.

Since Rainey was no longer actively picking up skips, they needed another woman for the female fugitive recoveries. Gunny, as she instructed everyone to call her, had twenty-four years in the Marines, before a roadside bomb upended the transport she was in, causing a head injury. The resulting migraines ended her active duty status, so when she came looking for a job last spring, Rainey hired her to work security part-time at the women's shelter. Liking what she saw, and in need of a female runner, Rainey asked Gunny to become licensed for the bond business and hired her full-time.

Runners were what the rest of the world called bounty hunters, a term frowned upon and illegal in the state of North Carolina. A runner had to be licensed and employed by a single bondsman. No freelance fugitive recovery was allowed. Gunny took the test and was in her sixth month of the mandatory year of supervised recovery, with Rainey or Mackie required to oversee her activities. Gunny also began helping Ernie in the office, learning the business from the old pro. The hard-bodied, forty-five-year-old Gunny was five-feet-seven inches of lean muscle. She had a salt and pepper Marine haircut and the "Oorah" attitude to go with it.

Gunny focused her eyes on Rainey. "You watch your six in there."

Wiley motioned toward a technician from the SWAT team. "Rainey, I want you to wear a microphone and an earbud, so I can hear and talk to you."

Rainey held up one finger. "Wait just a second." She stepped over to Junior, who was trying to calm Mackie's wife, Thelma. She motioned for the phone. "Let me talk to her."

Rainey heard crying as soon as she had the receiver to her ear. She kept her voice calm. "Thelma, it's Rainey. Call your sister and meet us at Memorial Hospital. I'm going in to get him now. It's going to be all right."

"You bring him out of there, Rainey Bell. Don't you let anything happen to my Mackie."

"We'll be out of there in no time. You just get to the hospital."

Thelma sniffled, adding, "You be safe, too, Rainey."

"Always, Thelma, always."

#

Equipped with microphone, earbud, and bathed in the bright lights set up by the SWAT team, Rainey strolled up the crumbling concrete walkway toward Maybelline's front door. Two officers in full assault gear and carrying MP5 submachine guns flanked her on either side. Other tactical team members moved in her peripheral vision, assuming positions for a forced entry Rainey hoped would not be necessary.

Her escorts fanned out on both sides of the door as she shouted, "Maybelline, it's Rainey. I'm coming in."

Rainey placed her hand on the doorknob and whispered to the SWAT guys, "Wish me luck."

The one on her right smiled up at her from his crouched position, tapping his headset with one finger. "We have your back. Just say the word."

Rainey turned the handle and pushed the door open. A toddler, sporting two frizzy pigtails captured with large pink plastic barrettes, emerged from the room on the right. She eyed Rainey up and down and then went screaming back out of sight, causing a stirring in the adjacent room.

"It's just me, Maybelline. Nobody else is with me and I am not armed. I'm coming in."

Rainey took two steps forward and then turned to behold Maybelline Upshaw, as she unfolded her considerable body from the chair in the far corner. Maybelline was the largest woman with whom Rainey had ever occupied the same space. She was six-feet-three-inches of thick muscle encased in blanket of fat, and weighed more than three hundred pounds, all of it topped with a mound of frizzy red hair. No one messed with Maybelline, who had grown up on the streets an unwanted, mixed-race child. Had a kind-hearted soul like Katie stumbled on the young troubled girl, things might have turned out differently for Maybelline.

She was smart enough to get herself and her growing family off the street. Toughened by life and cruel men, she built a small empire, raised three daughters, sent two sons to the penitentiary, and ended more than one confrontation with her opponent in the hospital. Even the gangs in her neighborhood left Miss Maybelline alone. She and her two sons moved large quantities of medical grade marijuana from the Pacific Northwest into the hands of upscale dealers, who paid dearly to keep those hands squeaky clean. The gangs were not interested in her clientele, but the law was. That was the very reason Maybelline's sons were in prison, with their mother to follow shortly. Rainey had to give the ol' girl credit. That clientele list was a hell of a bargaining chip and Maybelline had yet to roll over on the khaki pants-wearing, button-down-collared, uptown crowd she provided with the finest weed.

She also had a laugh that could fill an entire room and a sense of humor Rainey enjoyed the few times they were together. Maybelline showed Rainey her soft side on occasion, usually when talking about making life better for her grandkids. This was not going to be one of those instances. Tonight, Maybelline stared back at Rainey, eyes wild. The mountain of a woman pulled the baby she was holding tighter against her chest. The little girl, so small in comparison to the meaty arms that held her, smiled up at her grandmother, masking the danger with innocent gurgles and squeals.

30

"About time"—cough—"you got here," a voice rumbled from the floor, followed by a fit of hacking, obviously painful coughs.

Rainey took a step toward Mackie, but stopped when Maybelline aimed an extremely large handgun at her face.

"Stop right there," Maybelline said.

Angeline, the daughter who was comforting the terrified, sniveling toddler, stood up from the couch, placing herself in Maybelline's line of fire. "Momma, you're not shooting anybody else. Rainey came to help you. Now, put down that gun."

Rainey could see how much pain Mackie was in and how he was struggling to take a complete breath. She could also see that Maybelline was tired and had no intention of shooting her. She was a woman in pain, a mother's pain, and she only wanted to know what happened to her child. Maybelline wanted someone else to care. She had carried that burden alone long enough. Rainey knew what she had to do and seized the moment of Angeline's distraction to start toward Mackie again, this time announcing her intentions.

"Shoot me if you want, Maybelline, but I won't be able to find out what happened to Jacqueline if you do. I'm going to take care of Mackie first, and then you and I are going to work the rest of this out. Just know if you do decide to fire that gun again, those SWAT guys outside your door are going to be in here pretty quick. You're cornered, Maybelline. Let me help you make a graceful exit. Okay?"

By the time she finished speaking, Rainey was on her knees at Mackie's side. She looked up at Maybelline, who lowered her weapon and returned to her seat in the corner.

Rainey pulled Mackie's jacket back to look at his chest. His vest had a hole in it where the bullet entered, and the ceramic plate was caved in. He probably had broken ribs, if not worse.

"How you doin', big guy?" She asked, while taking his pulse. It was rapid, his skin cool and clammy. She needed to get him out of there fast.

He answered, through ragged breaths, "Broke—ribs."

"I don't suppose you can walk. It's going to take some big guys to put you on a gurney."

Mackie attempted to sit up. "I—crawled out—of the—jungle—with your—daddy—"

Rainey put her hands on his shoulders and gently pushed him back to the floor. "I know, I know. Stop talking. You're going on a stretcher, no argument."

Maybelline sat up on the edge of her chair, baby on one knee, pistol on the other. "You are one crazy white girl. Come in here without a gun, just gonna take charge."

Rainey smiled at the colossal woman, large enough to snap her like a twig. "And you, my friend, are one crazy dope-dealing grandma, but I got to hand it to you—you wanted attention, you got it. Jacqueline Upshaw is now the most famous missing person in the Triangle."

Maybelline smiled back. "Go on, get him out of here, then you and me gonna talk."

Rainey stood up. "Okay, we'll do that. May I have permission to ask those two SWAT guys outside the door to come help put Mackie on a stretcher? I'll ask them to leave their weapons out there."

Angeline switched from helping to hindering. "Momma, don't let them come in here. It could be a trick."

This request worried Maybelline, causing Rainey to intervene quickly. "Look, why don't you and I go back there and sit at the kitchen table? Let Mackie and Angeline leave with the children."

Angeline continued to warn her mother. "What's going to stop them from coming in here and shooting you, if we all leave?"

Maybelline smiled at her daughter and held out the baby for her to take. "That's al'right, Angeline. Go on. Take Jacquie's baby and little Tara and go on outside. I got me a FBI agent for a hostage now. Ain't nobody gonna come in here guns a-blazin'."

Rainey nodded her head. "She's right, all except I'm not an agent anymore, but I'm still worth a good couple of hours of hostage negotiation before they finally figure out who they'll blame if they get me killed."

Wiley's voice came through the earbud. "Tell her you'll send paramedics."

Rainey chuckled. "You better send big ones."

"What?" Angeline asked.

Rainey pointed at her ear. "They are talking to me from outside. They can hear us too. They want to know if paramedics would be more acceptable than the SWAT guys? Really, no one wants this to go any further. Let's get you all outside and let me talk to your mother. I promise no harm will come to her."

Maybelline moved toward the kitchen, dangling the gun at her side. Rainey took that as a sign her suggested course of action had been approved.

She spoke clearly so everyone, including Wiley, could hear and understand. "Stand down. Send in only the paramedics. A woman, a baby, and a toddler are exiting the house. I'm going to stay here with Maybelline for a bit. I'll let you know when we're coming out. Did you get all that, Wiley?"

"Yeah, I got it. Sending in the paramedics now. I'm sending four, if that's okay?"

Rainey looked down at Mackie and then toward the kitchen, watching as Maybelline placed the gun on the table and sat down, defeated, and at the same time victorious.

"Send them on in," she said into the lapel microphone under the edge of her vest. She leaned down and patted Mackie's shoulder. "They're coming to get you now. Don't give them too much shit, all right?" She reached to squeeze his hand. "I love you, you know. Named a kid after you. So, you hang in there. I'll be at the hospital as soon as I can."

He tried to smile, but it looked more like a grimace. "Tell Thelma—"

"She's already on her way to the hospital," Rainey said, answering what she thought was his request.

Mackie shook his head a little from side to side, and with difficulty said, "Bring pajamas—no hospital—gown."

Rainey chuckled. "Okay, no gown. You hear that, Wiley? Tell Junior he better have some PJs for the big man or there will be hell to pay."

She heard Wiley laugh in her ear. "Will do, Rainey. Send Angeline and the kids out."

Rainey motioned to Angeline to move on out the door. She hesitated, looking toward the kitchen at her mother.

33

Rainey said softly, "Go on now. Get those kids out of here. I'll take care of your mother."

"You know, she's not a bad woman, Rainey. She just had a hard life. Jacquie was her hope. She cleaned up after she got pregnant with Halle." Angeline indicated the baby in her arms. "Jacquie was smart, going to college, going to break the cycle of poverty she said. She didn't walk off and leave her baby. Momma just wants somebody to look for her."

Rainey knew better than to promise results, but she could make one pledge. "I will use every resource at my disposal to find out what happened to your sister. I will be honest with you and your mother. If she's been gone this long, the chances of Jacquie being alive are very slim."

A tear fell down Angeline's cheek. She kissed the baby on the forehead, before saying, "We knew that when she didn't come home. If Jacquie was alive, she would have come back for Halle. She was a good momma."

Rainey looked down at the child, knowing that she would spend her very last breath attempting to get back to her own. She reached out to twine one of the baby's fine curls around the end of her finger.

"I'll find out what happened, Angeline."

She let the curl drop and started toward the kitchen as Angeline and the children exited. The paramedics entered the door and went to work on Mackie.

As Rainey stepped into the kitchen, she said into the microphone, "Wiley, leave the recorder going. I want this interview on tape."

"Interview?" A voice other than Wiley's said. "She's got a gun. How is this an interview?"

Wiley interrupted. "Quiet the chatter. We're rolling, Rainey. Anything else?"

"Can you get me Jacquie's missing person file and her record? I don't need it right now, but I'd like to have it soon." She paused a second and then asked, "And Wiley, could you tell Junior to call Katie and let her know everything is okay?"

"Is everything okay?" Wiley hesitated to be as optimistic as Rainey.

"Yes, everything is going to be just fine," Rainey answered, as she pulled out a chair across from Maybelline and sat down.

Without asking and with great confidence that her assessment was correct, Rainey picked up the pistol from the table, took out the clip, and cleared the chamber. A single bullet bounced off the tabletop onto the floor and rolled away, as Rainey spoke to Maybelline.

"We're not going to be needing this weapon, so I'm just going to put it over here." Rainey slid the pistol away from both of them, but put the clip in the back pocket of her jeans. She was confident, not stupid. She refocused on Maybelline. "When we're done talking, you and I are walking out of here with no further problems, right?"

Maybelline leaned her elbows on the table and looked Rainey in the eye. "Your daddy done right by me. You say you're going to do right by me, too. I'll take you at your word. I'll come on when we're done."

Wiley understood the exchange and replied, "Okay, weapon secured. The two SWAT guys by the front door, you stay put. The rest of you stand down. This is no longer a hostage situation."

Rainey smiled at Maybelline. "Now, tell me about Jacquie."

CHAPTER THREE

When Rainey stepped out of the house with Maybelline handcuffed and walking beside her, they were bathed in the glare of the camera lights. The cordoned-off area had been reduced, allowing the reporters to get closer to the scene. Cameras flashed and questions were being shouted, but Rainey paid no attention. That is, until one voice rang out above all the others.

"Rainey! Rainey Bell! Is Jacquie Upshaw one of the victims of the serial killer terrorizing the Triangle? Was her mother justified in seeking attention for her disappearance?"

Cookie Kutter. Somehow, she had managed to survive her fall from grace, after being arrested for driving under the influence and leaving the scene of an accident, which occurred in the parking lot of a well-known lesbian bar. She had hounded Rainey and Katie for three years. Katie had even slugged her once, on camera, which made the news and was captured on countless digital recorders around the Triangle. Rainey had her own copy of the video, which she secretly played for a laugh now and then, but always when Katie was not around.

During a live press conference, Rainey created her own popular Cookie Kutter sound bite. She accused Cookie of being a little too interested in her personal life, hinting the reporter might be covering for her own attraction to women. Rainey had called that one correctly. Cookie suffered a very public outing and arrest not long afterward. Still, she had risen from the ashes, wrangling a reporting job with a local cable and web news organization, covering the crime beat in the greater Triangle area. They even gave her an hour-long crime show. Her brand of journalism played to the public's taste for high drama and was regrettably quite popular.

Rainey suspected Cookie was heavily involved in The Triangle Lesbians blog, the one that called her "Agent Sexy," and followed her family everywhere. The blog posted pictures of the triplets, which crossed the line as far as Rainey was concerned. Molly had been trying to shut the page down legally for a while. The successful defense attorney was also a target, dubbed the "Triangle Tryster" by the author of the blog, referencing her former penchant for one-night stands. Her trysting ways mended, the blog continued to recount her every public appearance. Molly, however, had no legal standing to shut down the page. All of the photos of her were taken in public settings, but Rainey's situation was quite different.

As a former FBI agent, Rainey had ample reasons not to want her image on the Internet, and she stated so before a judge. Her old teammate in the Behavioral Analysis Unit, Danny McNally, testified on her behalf as well. The release of personal information and pictures of her comings and goings put Rainey's life, and those of the people she cared about, in much more danger than the average citizen. Some of the photos of Rainey and her family were taken with long-range lenses and showed them in the yard of their highly secured home. The judge agreed the photos crossed the "expectation of privacy" line, ordering the website to cease publishing those types of images and personal information about Rainey and her family.

The shell corporation set up to mask the identity of the website owners did shut down the page. Only to have it reappear, republished by a different entity, and with the focus now squarely on Rainey and her family. Rainey had her good friend Melatiah Brooks, a computer analyst assigned to her old FBI unit, hunting the origin of the site. So far, Brooks had no luck tracking down the source, as the page jumped from server to server around the world. Whoever was behind the blog had extensive computer experience and an unhealthy interest in all things Rainey Bell, which made her very nervous. She glared at Cookie Kutter, somehow knowing she was involved.

"Rainey, will you make a statement? Are you actively involved in the hunt for a serial killer and rapist in the Triangle?"

Rainey handed Maybelline off, telling her, "These officers will take care of you now. I'll be in touch with you soon." She turned to the uniformed men. "Don't manhandle her. She'll cooperate." She looked up at the woman with whom she just spent the last half-hour, holding her hand while she cried over her lost child. "Isn't that right, Maybelline?"

"All the fight done gone out of me. I'll be good." Maybelline suddenly put her head down on Rainey's shoulder and whispered, "Bless you, Rainey. Your daddy raised a good girl."

Rainey patted the huge woman's back. "I'll find out what happened to Jacquie, I promise."

The officers escorted Maybelline to a waiting police cruiser, while Rainey turned her attention to Cookie. She could hear Molly and Katie in her head, begging her to walk away, but the temptation to approach Cookie was overwhelming. Other reporters were shouting questions, but Rainey concentrated on one voice, Cookie's.

"Rainey, how do feel about bonding out the woman who may have killed your partner, Miles McKinney?"

That was it. Mackie wasn't dead or dying. Wiley had come over the earbud to tell Rainey so, while she was still talking to Maybelline. He had broken ribs and some bleeding between the chest wall and his lung, but he was in stable condition. The vest had done its job. Cookie's wording was exactly what Rainey hated about the media. Suggesting a thing was true with a carefully worded question, a "may have" here and an "allegedly" there, was sensationalism at its core. Cookie and her ilk had turned the noble mission of the fourth estate into a melodramatic reality show.

Rainey quickly crossed the ten feet that separated them, moving right up to Cookie's microphone, and forcing a smile. "Since members of Mr. McKinney's family may be watching, you insensitive tart, I'm happy to report he is in stable condition and resting comfortably."

Cookie was an old pro at taking insults. She moved on to her next question without batting an eye. "As a consultant with the multi-county task force formed to investigate the disappearances of nine women in the Triangle area, are you ready to tell the public there is a serial killer among us, raping and killing at will?"

The other reporters had begun to gather around Rainey and Cookie, shoving microphones between them to catch the exchange. Rainey decided this was not the time or place to settle her old scores with Cookie. She stepped back, so that all of the cameras had a good angle and made a short statement.

"I am merely a consultant and cannot speak for the various law enforcement agencies involved. Since a statement has already been made about the sexual assaults, I am willing to comment on that. There is a serial rapist in the Triangle area. He is focusing on college-age and young professional women. He is entering their homes when he knows they will be alone. Precautions should be taken. Double check window and door locks, and report any strange activity around your home, no matter how trivial it may seem. This rapist is watching his victims prior to the assaults. If you find a window screen loose, notice a stranger watching your house, or feel like you are being followed, get to a safe place and call 911. I encourage all young women to listen to your instincts and stay vigilant. If it feels wrong, it usually is."

"What about the serial killer the task force is investigating?" Cookie shouted. "Are he and the rapist the same person?"

She elbowed another reporter out of the way, in order to move her CKCB logo encased microphone closer to Rainey. The logo was for the Cookie Kutter Crime Beat show. She closed the show each day with, "CKCB. See a crime, come see me." Rainey saw a crime every time Cookie opened her mouth.

"Before a serial killer is declared present, there must be evidence, Ms. Kutter. The task force is investigating missing women. I will only say the rape cases do not appear to be related to these disappearances."

Another reporter asked, "Are you going to release a profile of the serial rapist, Agent Bell?"

"I am no longer an agent, guys. We've been through this," Rainey answered, dodging the question.

If Cookie could not entice Rainey into saying there was a serial killer on the loose, she certainly was not going to let her get away with evading the profile inquiry. "You didn't answer the question. Can you give us a profile? The public has a right to know what to watch out for."

Oddly enough, Rainey partially agreed with Cookie. Rainey thought portions of the profile she compiled should have been made public, but as a hired consultant, how the various departments handled the investigation was not her call. The unknown subject, or UNSUB, in this case probably lived near Raleigh, and had committed multiple rapes in all twelve counties within a forty-five mile radius of the capital city. The assaults were spaced out every forty-five to ninety days and were never in the same county back to back. The resulting confusion of jurisdictional lines complicated the investigation, something Rainey thought was intentional. After various departments engaged her to interview several of the rape survivors, Rainey found there were similarities in victim selection, parallel precipitating events, and evidence that the rapes were the work of a single, very deviant, dedicated criminal. Some of the information Rainey gave the investigators might help prevent another rape, but there was no guarantee, and that was why one other element of the profile kept it from being released.

Rainey had summarized for the command officers in the rape investigation, "When you catch this UNSUB, he will be somehow connected to law enforcement, a cop most likely. If not an active duty officer, he will have been at one time. He may also have military training or work in the security field. His behavior during the crime, demonstrating knowledge of current investigative and forensic procedure, makes it probable that he is presently working in law enforcement." The final sentence was what sent most of the departments into a tizzy. "He is more than likely involved in the investigation of these crimes in some form or fashion."

That part of the profile could not be made public knowledge. The unknown rapist did not use a police ruse to gain access to the victims, so concealing Rainey's suspicions did not put more women in danger. Admitting the rapist was probably a cop could scare women into refusing to seek help or not reporting the assaults. The powers that be only released the complete profile to a few select investigators and kept everyone else in the dark. If he was among them, the department heads surmised, it would be unwise to let the rapist know they were looking for a police officer. Rainey agreed with that assessment, but still thought most of the profile should have been released, instead of the whole thing being quashed.

As she pointed out to the reporters in front of her now, "I just offer the profile. What the investigators do with it is entirely up to them."

Wiley Trainer came to Rainey's rescue. "I'm sorry folks, but we need Rainey to fill out some paperwork."

He grabbed her arm and steered her away from the reporters still shouting questions at her back. She was almost home free, when Cookie's voice rang out above all the others.

"Hey, Agent Sexy. How about one more smile for the cameras?"

Rainey pulled away from Wiley and took three long strides, bringing her nose-to-nose with Cookie. "If I find out you are behind the stalking of my family, you're going to need a new microphone. I don't think that one will work after you pull it out of your ass."

#

Rainey already had enough excitement for one night, and she still needed to go to the hospital to check on Mackie. Wiley had pulled her away from Cookie before things could become more heated. He escorted her to his car, where she sat in the backseat and wrote out her statement. She slipped out of the vest, glad to be released from its compression of her diaphragm, and found her coat on the seat beside her. She could smell a man's cologne on the leather, where he had lifted it to move it from the front seat. It was not offensive, but she marveled at how quickly she noticed the manly scent. It was not something she smelled on her clothing often anymore.

She slipped on the jacket and dug in the pockets, coming up with her phone and a small piece of paper. Rainey was about to toss the paper in a fast food bag on the floorboard, thinking it was just some pocket trash she picked up somewhere, when she saw ink on one of the folds. She unfolded the small rectangle to discover a handwritten message, definitely intended for her.

"Profiling the rapist as a cop—not too original," was printed in blue ink.

So much for the profile remaining eyes-only for a few people. The thin blue line had leaks. Rainey glanced around, knowing he would be watching to see her find his note. There were cops everywhere and the rapist was one of them.

She muttered to herself, "Maybe not original, but I'm right."

There would be no fingerprints on the note. He was too smart for that, but Rainey would turn it over to the rape investigators tomorrow, and suggest they look at any video to see who was in Wiley's car. She did not remember him locking it when he tossed her coat in the seat. Of course, if they caught the note writer, he would say the profile offended him, and he was just taking up for his brothers in blue. Rainey knew that was not the reason he left the note. It was the adrenaline rush from doing it. As with the rapes and his involvement in the investigation, this guy lived for the thrill of getting away with it.

Rainey zipped the note up in a never used little pocket and then called Katie.

"Honey, I'm all right," she said, immediately upon Katie's answering.

"I saw you come out of the house on TV. I gathered Mackie is okay from your exchange with Cookie. Really Rainey, 'insensitive tart', that's the best you had?"

"You won't let me say bitch anymore, so that's all I could think of."

"I suppose the microphone up the ass comment was you forgetting that you're working on your language skills," Katie said, suppressing a giggle. "I'm just glad it's cable so they didn't bleep it out."

"You know she drives me crazy," Rainey said, laughing too.

"I love you. I know you're going to the hospital next. Give Mackie a big kiss for me and tell Thelma if she needs anything, just call."

Rainey smiled into the phone. "I will. I love you, too. Go to bed. I'll be late. One of us has to be able to deal with our sunrise-worshipping children."

"I'll let you sleep in. I have to take them with me to the shelter in the morning anyway."

Rainey was amazed at how Katie could handle the triplets. She could feed, dress, and have them buckled in their car seats in no time, whereas Rainey would have still been trying to get Weather's balled up toes in her little shoes.

"Get me up. I'll help you," Rainey said, because no matter how inept she felt at being a parent, she hated missing a moment with her children.

"Okay, honey. Be safe."

Rainey gave her standard answer, "Always."

After hanging up with Katie, she left Wiley's car with her vest dangling from one hand. She was ready to leave, but needed to locate Rex to retrieve her weapon. Rainey was looking for him, when she spotted Bobo on the sidewalk across the street. He was talking to a man, who was writing notes on a pad.

"Damn. That's all I need. Bobo talking to reporters."

She looked around for Junior, thinking he had probably followed Mackie to the hospital. The SUVs were no longer parked down the block. Rainey had no choice but to deal with Bobo alone. She had a few things she wanted to say to him anyway. Now was as good a time as any. She was almost across the street, when Gunny appeared at her elbow.

"Hey, boss. Junior told me to stay here in case you needed anything. He drove Mackie's vehicle and the other guys followed in Junior's. I'm going to need a ride."

"Okay, I'll be leaving in a minute, but I need to find Detective King. He has my weapon. And I need to talk to this numbskull over here." Rainey nodded her head in Bobo's direction.

Gunny chuckled. "I'm surprised he's still here after Junior threatened to kick his ass. Guess he saw him leave."

That made Rainey smile. Junior was cleaning up his mess. Still, she did not like the idea of Bobo giving a statement to the press. Although he held up during the Dalton Chambers investigation, Rainey presumed it was more out of self-preservation than noble intent.

She turned to Gunny. "Could you find Captain Trainer? He's the negotiator I was talking to earlier, the older guy with white hair."

"Yeah, I know who you're talking about," Gunny said, looking over her shoulder at the dispersing crowd.

"See if he can retrieve my weapon from King," Rainey directed, already moving toward Bobo, before turning back to Gunny. "Hey, can you put this in my trunk for me?" She dug around in her coat pocket for her keys. She handed them and the vest to Gunny. "Thanks, and make sure you lock it back. There's stuff in that car we don't want loose in this neighborhood."

"No problem," Gunny answered, leaving on her mission.

Rainey approached Bobo, who saw her and started to panic. The reporter turned to see what was causing Bobo's eyes to bug out of his head. That was when Rainey recognized him. She could not remember his name, but she usually did not forget the faces of people she had held at gunpoint.

"Well, if it isn't former FBI Special Agent Rainey Bell," he said, smiling broadly. "I've been trying to talk to you since you nearly shot me, and here you are, walking right up to me."

"I recognize the shirt. I remember you were wearing a blue oxford, when you sprang up behind my car while a serial killer was stalking me. Not your finest moment, as I recall." She looked down at his khaki pants. "Guess you had to have those cleaned."

The smile left his face, and he appeared to be searching her hands for a weapon. Bobo thought he saw a way out of facing Rainey's wrath and took a step back, but she had her eye on him.

"Not so fast, Bobo. Stand right there. We need to have a chat."

Bobo froze. He knew better than to run. Rainey would eventually find him. He decided to remain and take his tongue-lashing. When Rainey was sure Bobo would stay put, she refocused on the man wearing the blue oxford shirt under his wool pea coat.

"I'm sorry, I know you are a writer, but I can't remember your name."

"Martin Douglas Cross. I go by Marty."

"Oh yes, I remember now. You were writing a book and wanted a comment."

"Yes, I was writing a book about the Y-Man murders, but I'm on to something new now."

"So, why do you still want to talk to me?" Rainey asked, anticipating that she would not like the answer.

"My new book is about you," Marty said, beaming. "I'm talking to Bobo about his involvement in the Chauncey Barber fugitive recovery, and what he may know about Mr. Barber's motivation for stabbing Dalton Chambers. Maybe you could clear up a few things for me, Ms. Bell."

Bobo started stuttering. "Ra-Ra-Rainey, I told him I didn't know nothin' about that Chambers thing, just like I told them cops and that D.A."

"Oh God," Rainey thought, *"I have to get this guy out of here."* She spoke to Bobo calmly, deciding this might not be the best time to tell him he was fired. "As long as you tell the truth, Bobo, you have nothing to worry about."

Marty had done his homework on Dalton's case. "The truth is Chauncey Barber's nephew—the boy that shot you, former Agent Bell—is in his second year of attendance at an exclusive military school, on a scholarship funded by your wife's foundation. You were instrumental in having the charges reduced and quite magnificently stepped in to change his life. That was nice of you, but it does give Chauncey a motive for taking out the serial killer who threatened you and your family."

Rainey had heard it all before. Her answer was the same as it had always been. "You'll have to ask Chauncey about his motive. If I remember correctly, he told the investigators Dalton pissed him off." She chuckled a bit nervously, to her chagrin, before adding, "Having spent so much time with that psychopathic pretty-boy, I can certainly understand how that might have happened. Dalton Chambers was a real ass. Hey, you can use that for your quote."

"Come on, Rainey. Dalton's murder isn't the only time you've been associated with the death of a prisoner. There was that question about whether you killed Jared Howard, after he was already down on the ground. And you probably let Katie take the fall for shooting the Y-Man. No one had the heart to charge her, even if he was already dying when she pulled the trigger."

Katie's had been a righteous kill and Rainey was not going to argue that with this jackass. She dismissed his comment about the Howard shooting. She was cleared of that charge and the real killer was discovered, but the 'prisoner in custody' comment got her attention. Despite her better judgment, Rainey took the bait.

"To what other prisoner in custody are you referring?"

"Michael Paul Perry. You remember him, don't you?" Marty said, with a smirk of satisfaction.

Rainey knew the color drained from her face. She was caught unprepared and let her genuine reaction surface. Too late, she reapplied the mask of no concern. Marty saw it. It seemed to give him the nerve to goad her just a bit more.

"You must remember the eighteen-year-old-boy found hanging in his cell, shortly after speaking to you."

She offered the standard answer, memorized from years in the bureau. "I can't comment on that."

Marty was smug now. Rainey probably should not have made the pants cleaning remark. He dug at her some more.

"That's okay, plenty of people did want to talk about the sad case of young Mr. Perry. I also found some guards at Central prison willing to state they heard you threaten to kill Dalton Chambers, before the state would have a chance to accomplish that deed. But I think the best quote in my book will come from your old friend at the BAU, Danny McNally."

Rainey was tired, stressed, and not thinking clearly. Katie and the kids had softened her. The thick skin she wore against intrusions like this had worn thin. She should have walked away, but she said instead, "Danny would never talk to you."

Gunny stepped up just in time to hear Marty go for the kill shot.

"He may not talk to me, but shall I quote Agent McNally's Grand Jury testimony? 'You asked me if I thought Rainey Bell was capable of following through with her threat to kill Dalton Chambers. My answer is yes, under the right circumstances I think she would have.' See Rainey, even your old partner thinks you did it."

Bobo picked the most inopportune time to defend himself again. "I swear, I told him I don't know nothin'. Your other friends might dis' you, but not ol' Bobo. I got your back, Rainey."

Rainey, still staggered by Marty's revelation, could only manage a terse, "Shut up, Bobo," aimed in his direction.

Gunny chimed in. "Shit, under the right circumstances, I'd follow through on a few of the threats I've made to kill people. I guess it would depend on how motivated I was."

Damn, none of these so-called allies of hers were helping in the least. Rainey needed to move Marty along, but first she had a question.

"How does a crime novelist get his hands on sealed Grand Jury testimony?"

Marty's smile stretched from ear to ear. "Not everybody is a fan of the great Rainey Bell. Some people would like to see you get what's coming to you."

Before Rainey could say anything else, Gunny stepped up to Marty. "Mister, I don't know who you are, but my name is Gunnery Sergeant Naomi Pierce, retired U. S. Marine Corps. Oorah! Now, I'm kindly asking you to move it along. We've all had a long night. I'm sure you understand."

Marty hesitated. "This is a public street. You can't make me leave."

Gunny grinned. "Did you miss that part about me being a Marine? That 'Oorah' means I can kick your ass, and very publicly on this public street, if that's what you're into."

Rainey chuckled. "I've sparred with her, Marty. I'd just leave, if I were you."

Marty was the pale one now. His smug smile replaced by a grimace of fear. "You can't be serious. There are cops everywhere."

Gunny looked up at Rainey. "Did you hear him threaten me? I'm beginning to fear for my safety."

Rainey nodded in agreement. "Yep, you may have to resort to physical violence in order to separate yourself from the threat."

"Wow, you really are nuts," Marty said, backing away.

"You said it yourself," Rainey called after him, "I'm capable of anything, under the right circumstances."

Martin Douglas Cross walked away, but Rainey was sure she would see him again. She looked over at Bobo, who was still standing where she told him to stay. Reaching into her jacket pocket, Rainey pulled out her wallet. She called Bobo to her.

"I was going to fire you tonight, ban all my runners from ever taking another tip from you. We pay you well for good information and you led my guys into a shit-storm tonight."

"I'm sorry, Rainey. They came in the back way. The neighbor said Maybelline had called the girls over there, after she got home. I didn't know. I'm sorry, man."

Rainey pulled a hundred dollars out of her wallet. She handed it to Bobo, saying, "Don't talk to that guy anymore. He'll get you in trouble. Take this and go home. Junior will find you later, after he calms down."

"Thank you, Rainey." Bobo bowed and started backing away, smiling, calling to her, "I got your back, Rainey Bell. You know that." He laughed and ran toward the corner.

Rainey looked down at Gunny. "You know, this evening started out so well."

Gunny laughed. "When did it go bad, about the time that baby food got stuck in your hair?"

Rainey's hand shot to her head. She could feel the dried peas still clinging to her thick chestnut curls. "Damn, I was going to wash this out when Katie distracted me and then Junior called."

"I don't think it will take away too much from your interview with that Kutter woman. They'll probably remember you threatening to stick that microphone up her ass and not the green

48

slime in your hair," Gunny said, barely able to contain her amusement.

Rainey started laughing. "Well, it'll give Cookie something to talk about. She'll be asking viewers about the 'strange substance' in Rainey Bell's hair."

Gunny giggled, which was a strange sound coming from the hard-nosed sergeant. "Maybe I'll call in and say I think you're an alien."

"She'd probably run with that," Rainey said, and then remembered her Glock. "Did you find my weapon?"

"Captain Trainer said Detective King went to the hospital to get a statement from Mackie. He didn't look to happy about it either."

"Come on then," Rainey said, starting toward the car. "We better get to the hospital, before Mackie ends up in cuffs. He can't tolerate Rex anymore than I can."

"This night just keeps going. Is it always like this when you're involved?" Gunny asked, trying to conceal a grin. "Most of the time, we just scoop the fugitive up and go. With you, it's news reporters, dick detectives, and asshole writers."

Rainey sighed. "Welcome to Rainey's world, where there is a storm around every corner."

Gunny slapped her on the back. "Oorah."

Rainey chuckled. "Oorah, Gunny."

#

The emergency room doors had just swished shut behind them, when Rainey spotted Rex King coming straight for her. He started in on her before she could take a step further. Evidently, his conversation with Mackie did not go very well. Rex was flushed and looking for a fight.

"You people don't think the law applies to you."

Rainey was not in the mood for more of his accusations. "Just give me my weapon and give it a rest for one night, Rex."

That only made him angrier, emboldening him to cross the line with Rainey. "The only thing that would make this night worse, after dealing with you two, is if your son-of-a-bitch father were still around."

Rainey felt Gunny's hand on her elbow, just as she was about to launch into Rex King once and for all. Gunny positioned herself between Rainey and Rex, and to Rainey's surprise, was not the least bit confrontational. Her transformation from tough as nails to polite peacemaker startled Rainey out of wanting to throttle King Squared into King Cubed.

"Detective King, I don't believe we've had the pleasure. Marine Gunnery Sergeant Naomi Pierce, retired," she said, extending her hand in greeting. "I don't think anyone will be served well by cursing the dead, do you? Now, why don't you and I go collect Rainey's weapon, while she sees to her friend, and if you want to talk later, I'm sure she has plenty to say to you."

Gunny so shocked Rex, he lost the ability to speak, and before he knew what was happening, she had escorted him out the emergency room doors. Rainey was still standing there with her mouth open, when Junior slid to a stop next to her. He looked frightened, spoke breathlessly, and began dragging Rainey down the hall with him.

"Rainey, Mackie's heart stopped. Come quick."

Rainey felt her face go ashen. She started running beside Junior, toward the doors that barred the public from the exam rooms. A nurse saw them coming, recognized Junior, and hit a button behind the desk. They passed through the doors without breaking stride.

"I thought he was stable. What happened?"

Junior choked back tears with his answer. "I don't know."

When they rounded the corner, Rainey saw Thelma leaning against the wall, in tears. That's when she heard the high-pitched whine of a defibrillator charging and the shout of, "Again!" coming from the trauma room. The flat-line alarm on the heart monitor droned in the background, eeeeeeeeee— Rainey passed Thelma and pushed her way into the trauma room, where her guardian angel lay dying.

"Zzzzchuunk!" The defibrillator sounded, as the doctor sent an electrical pulse into Mackie's body, causing it to convulse, but the flat-line returned immediately on the heart monitor screen.

"No pulse," a nurse said, as he prepared another shot of adrenaline and another resumed chest compressions.

Rainey wanted there to be no doubt about the man on the table. "Don't give up on him," she said from the doorway. "He walked out of a jungle with five bullets in him, carrying my father. Don't you give up on him."

A nurse turned toward her, to force her back out of the room. Rainey stepped back, but not before shouting, "Don't you give up, Mackie! You fight, goddammit!"

"Again," the doctor shouted. "Push the next epi."

"Charging," another voice said.

The defibrillator whine built to a crescendo for the next shock it was to deliver, when someone shouted, "Wait! He has a pulse."

Rainey slid down the hallway wall to her knees and thanked God for another blessing in her life. When she finished, she had one more person to address. She whispered, "I promise to keep him safe, Dad. Thanks for knowing I needed him with me more than you do."

She felt hands on her shoulders. A familiar voice whispered close to her ear, "Come on, let them do their work."

Rainey looked up to see Ernie smiling down at her.

"You all know it'll take more than a shot through a ballistics vest to stop that big man in there, don't you? I've known him longer than any of you, and I know damn well he isn't going to die today. So, let's all go get some coffee and they'll come get us when we can see him."

A nurse came out of Mackie's room, just as Ernie finished. "She's right. His heart is beating normally again and we have him closely monitored. Y'all go on down to the waiting area. The doctor will come out to talk to you."

"Thank you, we'll do that," Ernie said, acting as spokesperson for the group.

Rainey was happy to have someone else take charge for the moment. Ernie was never one to wallow in misery and she wouldn't allow those around her to do so either. She held out her hand to help Rainey from the floor.

"I'm glad you're here, Ernie," Rainey said, standing up.

"Well, somebody had to come down here and straighten you all out. Nothing worse than a bunch of negative energy around sick people. A little positive attitude goes a long way." She paused and tilted her head, a puzzled look crossing her face as she gazed at Rainey. "You know, when I saw you on TV, I was trying to figure out what that was in your hair."

Rainey's hand went to the green slime embedded in her curls. "Weather likes to throw strained peas and anything else she can get her hands on."

Ernie looped her arm through Rainey's, as they started down the hall, following Thelma and Junior. "Well, I know she doesn't have your DNA, but that child is the spittin' image of your personality, and to that I say—you are in for a hell of a ride to adulthood."

It crossed Rainey's mind that maybe this was it, the other shoe dropping. If so, it was working out okay. Mackie might be down, but she felt sure he would pull through this. If he was going to die, she reasoned with herself, a few minutes ago would have been the time. She hung onto that hope, telling herself maybe this would inspire Mackie to get into better shape, start watching what he ate, and live to be one hundred. By then, maybe Rainey would be ready to let him go.

Deciding not to share her thoughts with Ernie, Rainey smiled down at the small gray-bunned woman on her arm, replying to the prediction of future parental woes with Weather, "Let's just see if we can stop her from throwing food first. We'll worry about the storms to come, after she's out of diapers."

"Oh, throwing food will be the least of your worries with that one." Ernie said with a chuckle. "There will be rainy weather in your future, you can count on that."

Rainey laughed. "Clever word play there. Probably should have given that weather theme a bit more thought when we named her."

Rainey's attention was unexpectedly drawn back to the trauma room, where Mackie's heart was now beating again. The sudden sense of approaching doom returned in a rush. Immediately, her father's voice was inside her head, whispering,

"Watch your back, Rainey. There's trouble." She stopped walking and stared back at the door of the room.

Ernie stopped with her. She knew Rainey well enough to recognize when something wasn't right. She also knew to respect Rainey's intuition. "What is it, Rainey?"

"Dad," she whispered. "He's trying to tell me something."

Rainey did not feel strange admitting to Ernie that she heard her father's voice at times, and with good reason.

Ernie squeezed Rainey's arm. "I've heard him lately, too. There's trouble."

Rainey knew Ernie talked to her dead father, often hearing her carry on whole conversations with him in the office. They were very close friends, more like brother and sister than employee and employer. Rainey was not sure to what extent her father's spirit participated in Ernie's conversations with him, but Ernie did credit Billy with finding lost objects on occasion. This was new. Ernie had never passed along a warning from the beyond before. Rainey attributed the messages from her father to her own mind associating him with her instinctual knowledge. Because Billy Bell spent so much time telling his daughter to listen to her inner voice, she was not at all surprised it sounded like him. But for her and Ernie to receive the same message, now that was freaky weird.

"Why didn't you say something?" Rainey asked.

Junior turned back to look for Rainey. She saw him and motioned him to go ahead.

Ernie was usually very direct, but she was a little hesitant to speak. She finally said, "Well, you were so happy, not moping, not paranoid, not looking over your shoulder all the time. I didn't want to threaten that with just a feeling. I don't know if it's Billy talking to me, or just the memory of his voice, but it's been strong lately. Something is just not right and I cannot put my finger on it."

"How long have you had this feeling?"

Ernie thought about it and answered, "About four months now."

Rainey nodded her head. "I've had it too. I thought it was all the talk of you retiring, Mackie getting older, me being so busy and tired all the time. There's also my track record. Things were going too well. Something was bound to go wrong. Then tonight happened and I thought maybe this was the bad thing, and we made it through it, but —"

"But you still have that feeling in your gut," Ernie finished for her, and then added, "I think your instincts are awake now. Mackie going down woke them up. That voice is telling you to watch your back."

"Funny, but that's exactly what Dad said."

"Then listen to him," Ernie pleaded.

"Always."

#

An hour later, Dr. John Herndon sat across from Rainey and the rest of Mackie's friends and family gathered in the waiting room. John was Rainey's stepfather and a highly respected heart surgeon. Though they were not close for most of Rainey's adult life, she liked him. When the triplets were born, John was instrumental in repairing Rainey's relationship with her mother, and they both became doting grandparents. After the trauma physician came out to tell them Mackie's problems were multiplying due to heart complications, Rainey called Katie to tell her what was happening. It was at her suggestion that Rainey then called John. He came without hesitation. John Herndon loved his stepdaughter and knew Mackie personally, but he came because he was a great doctor and a better man.

Silver-haired and handsome, John patted Rainey's knee and gave them the news. He addressed Thelma first. "Mackie is in stable condition, so you can relax for the time being. That said, he has a long recovery ahead. It was actually opportune that he was shot this evening. The trauma impact caused a hemothorax— bleeding between the chest wall and the lung. The bleeding depressed his breathing and put pressure on his heart. He was stabilized here in the ER by the removal of some of the fluids through needle aspiration and later a tube was placed to remove the rest. The two broken ribs and the soft tissue injuries from the impact, though painful, are not a worry at this time. That's the good news."

Rainey swallowed against the fear rising in her throat.

John took a breath, his tone more serious when he continued. "He experienced a cardiac arrest from an acute coronary thrombosis, probably due to the trauma. In layman's terms, Mackie's heart stopped. The trauma team was able to restart the heart in a reasonable amount of time, but with some difficulty. Further examination uncovered major blockage in four coronary arteries. I'm waiting for his primary physician's files, but I'm sure he has discussed Mackie's high cholesterol and risk for atherosclerosis with him, though it appears he did not heed the warnings. Mackie was well on his way to a heart attack before tonight. Fortunately, he had that episode here. Had it occurred elsewhere, I'm not sure he would have survived. As soon as we feel he is ready, we'll be doing a quadruple bypass. Our friend Mackie is going to have to undergo some serious lifestyle changes, if he wants to live."

"He will survive the surgery, right?" Junior asked.

Rainey admired John and the way he handled his answer, honestly and directly. "There are no guarantees, it's major surgery with risks. Mackie is strong and motivated. I see no reason why he would not do well and recover without complications. We will work for that result and deal with any problems, should they arise. That's the best promise I can give you."

"May I talk to him?" Thelma asked.

"He's a little groggy, but I'll walk you back," John offered, rising to his feet.

"Thank you, John," Rainey said, standing, and then uncharacteristically initiated a hug between the two of them.

He hugged her close and whispered, "He'll be fine, Rainey. I'll take care of him."

She gave him one more squeeze and whispered back, "I know you will," before letting him go.

He smiled and turned to Thelma. "Let's go see how your husband is feeling."

She had taken a few steps with John, before Thelma turned back to Rainey. "You come, too. He'll want to see you."

She waited outside in the hall, while Thelma spoke to Mackie. Theirs was a childless marriage, so it had been just the two of them for over thirty years. They spread their love among nieces and nephews, and of course Rainey and Billy Bell, and Ernie, too. They were all one conglomerated family, but the love was strong. Rainey hugged Thelma when she came out of the room. She reassured her that Mackie would make the changes in his life to keep him around for a long time, at gunpoint if necessary. Rainey knew this day was coming. The playful sparring she did with Mackie about his eating habits and lack of exercise were rooted in true concern for his wellbeing. There would be no more joking.

John walked Thelma back to the waiting area, while Rainey slipped into Mackie's room for her moment with him. A pretty little nurse smiled and excused herself to check on another patient, leaving Rainey and Mackie alone. Upon stepping up to his bedside, Rainey was struck by how fragile and vulnerable Mackie appeared. It was the first time in her life she perceived him as anything other than invincible. Monitors blipped and bleeped, tubes and IVs extended from his body, which was barely contained on the trauma gurney. His eyes were closed, and she hesitated to wake him, but she was haunted by a memory that would not allow her to let him sleep.

Rainey was never able to tell her father good-bye. He was there one day and gone the next, no warning, no chance for her to say, "Hey Dad, thank you for loving me. Thank you for believing in me." Her father knew she loved him, but she never told him how much his fighting for her had meant. She was never able to tell him that he saved her. It was the will to live he instilled in her that got her through the darkest days of her life. Mackie had been there, too. Rainey would not let the moment pass this time.

"Hey, big man," she said softly.

Mackie's eyes fluttered open. A breathy, "Hey," rumbled from his chest.

"Don't try to talk, just listen. You are going to come through this, just like every other near death experience you've faced." She smiled down at him. "I guess you went about as near death as you'd care to, so you and I are going to start running the trails again, out at the lake. Like we used to when I first moved out there with Dad."

Mackie coughed, about to say something, but Rainey stopped him.

"Shh, we will walk them at first, but you're getting healthy again, no arguments—and no more fried food, period."

"Rain—" he started to say.

"Stop trying to talk. Let me say this. I love you. You have always been there for me. Always. I could have given up a few years ago, but you wouldn't let me. I'm going to be here for you now. You are very important to me, Katie, the kids, but mostly me." Rainey smiled and sniffled, unaware that she had started to cry. She laughed to cover the emotion, and said, "Unfortunately, your job watching my back is a long-term contract and I think you owe me a few more years—fifty will do."

A nurse entered the room. Rainey recognized him from the trauma team earlier. He nodded and proceeded to check monitors, tubes, and drips. Rainey felt Mackie's hand against her side and refocused on him.

With some difficulty, he tried to speak again, "Rainey, I saw some—"

His eyes fluttered shut. Rainey looked over at the nurse with concern.

"It's the meds," he answered her unspoken question. "He'll go in and out. He's fine. They should be moving him to the cardiac unit soon. They'll monitor him there until he's ready for the bypass. Your friend is lucky. He was a walking dead man. Dr. Herndon is one of the best in the field. Mr. McKinney here will be back on his feet shortly."

Rainey looked down at Mackie, who was now breathing slowly, in a deep sleep.

"He's your stepfather, right?"

The question startled her. Her head snapped around to face the nurse. "Excuse me?"

"Dr. Herndon. The word at the front desk is he's your stepfather."

That was not common knowledge. Rainey went to great pains to protect her extended family members from the attention she attracted, for both privacy and security reasons.

The nurse kept talking. "We knew there had to be a family member or somebody important involved for Dr. Herndon to personally oversee treatment in the ER. He just doesn't do that. One of his residents maybe, but not Dr. Herndon."

Rainey avoided a direct answer. "Mr. McKinney and Dr. Herndon are acquainted."

The nurse tilted his head, a questioning expression on his face. "You are the one they call Agent Sexy, right?"

Rainey bristled. "What did you just say?"

The nurse threw his hands up in surrender. "Hey look, I'm just warning you. Someone just posted a picture on a blog of you hugging Dr. Herndon in the waiting area. The caption said he was your stepfather and called you Agent Sexy. One of the clerks at the desk was showing everyone. I'm just giving you a heads up."

"I'll give you a heads up," Rainey said. "Don't call me Agent anything."

The waiting room was full of people. Anyone of them could be the person stalking her family. She leaned down to kiss Mackie on the forehead, whispering, "I love you, big man," and then started for the door. Rainey wanted to get a picture of everyone in the waiting room, look at security tapes, whatever it took. This was her first break in the hunt for the Triangle Lesbian Blogger.

The nurse called after her, "Hey, Cookie Kutter is out there now. If you decide to plant that microphone up her ass, please wait until my shift ends in an hour."

Rainey emerged from Mackie's room fully intent on taking out her frustrations on a bleached-blond reporter with boundary issues. Junior was waiting for her, both arms out, like the defensive end he used to be, attempting to contain a running quarterback.

"Rainey, just walk away. No good can come of you talking to that woman again."

Rainey ignored his pleas and kept moving forward, while issuing requests that sounded a lot like orders. "Find security. I want copies of the camera feeds in the waiting area since we've been here, and get the emergency room entrance too."

"We're not law enforcement. They're not going to hand that over to me," Junior said, still trying to slow Rainey's progress toward the waiting room.

Rainey took out her cellphone, noted the time was midnight, and dialed the number anyway.

"Rainey, are you okay? Is Mackie all right?" Molly asked, as soon as she answered.

"I guess you saw the news."

Rainey imagined most people had, as the "Breaking News" casts flooded the airwaves. She could tell by the looks she was receiving from some of the people in the hospital that they had watched the scene unfold in vivid color.

"I'm fine. Mackie is recovering from the gunshot to the vest, but he has to have a quadruple bypass as soon as possible. He was lucky he was in the hospital when his heart stopped."

"I'll keep him in my thoughts, and you," Molly said, with the sincere concern of a friend. Then, in a tone more in line with her role as Rainey's lawyer, she added, "Leslie came in the office and told me turn on Cookie's feed. You know, if you're going to knock her lights out, just do it, but try to refrain from threatening her in public. It makes it harder for me to argue no premeditation, when you do finally lose it."

"Well, that might have been the last public threat, because I'm about to physically remove her from this hospital if I have to. She's posting pictures from the waiting room on that blog now."

"Rainey, until we have proof, as much as I respect your instincts, we cannot accuse her of running that blog."

"I'll have the proof," Rainey argued, "if you will get a subpoena for the security tapes of the lobby and waiting room for the last couple of hours."

"Okay, I'll work on that, but until we have the evidence, don't do anything I can't get you out of."

"I'll take that under advisement, counselor," Rainey said, now able to see Cookie at the end of the hallway.

"Rainey, call Katie. Let her talk you down. I can hear it in your voice. You are about to make a monumental mistake," Molly pleaded.

"I've had enough, Molly. This stops now."

"All right. Just call me when they schedule the bail hearing. But you might want to think twice about making your public downfall on television with strained peas in your hair."

Rainey stopped walking and laughed. "How did you know what it was?"

"Katie called Leslie."

Katie and Molly's girlfriend, Leslie, were thick as thieves. They formed an instant bond upon meeting and spent a lot of time together. Leslie, a psychologist, volunteered at Katie's women's shelter, loved kids, and thought Molly and Rainey were way too serious, all things that endeared her to Rainey's wife.

"Katie didn't mention the peas when I talked to her," Rainey said, momentarily losing her desire to strangle Cookie.

Molly chuckled. "Leslie said Katie didn't have the heart to tell you that your menacing threat to Cookie was somehow diminished by the baby food in your hair, which was prominently framed in the shot."

Molly had accomplished her goal. She had calmed Rainey sufficiently.

"I guess I should go home and take a shower."

Sounding relieved, Molly said, "Yes, I think that would be a good idea. I'll work on getting access to the security data. I know it's not as enticing as punching Cookie in the mouth, but it's the best way. If she's involved, we'll get her, Rainey. Just be patient."

"Thanks, Molly. Always the voice of reason. I'll talk to you tomorrow."

"Good night, Rainey. Get some rest."

Rainey hung up the phone and slipped it back in her pocket. Junior, who had relaxed while Rainey talked on the phone, sprang back into defensive mode.

"It's okay, Junior. I'm not going to talk to her. Someone posted a picture of me with my stepfather on that damn blog, but they are probably gone now anyway. I'm going to find Gunny, see if she retrieved my weapon, and then I'm going to go home and wash the peas out of my hair."

"Is that what that is?" Junior asked, smiling and pleased she was under control.

"That little girl of mine has quite the arm," Rainey said with pride.

"A natural athlete like her momma," Junior said, slipping an arm around Rainey's shoulder and ushering her in the opposite direction from Cookie, toward another exit. "Okay, you go home. I'll stay here with Thelma and Ernie. Gunny left your Glock in the Escalade. She took the Expedition and the other guys back to the office. She said call if you need anything. I'll walk out with you."

"I'll be back after I help Katie with the kids' breakfast. I'm not sure exactly what time that will be, other than shortly after sunrise."

"Still can't get them to sleep later, huh?"

"No, but I'm thinking of putting blackout curtains in their room," Rainey said, and then out of curiosity asked, "Did you hear what went on between Mackie and Detective King, before I got here?"

Junior opened the door and they exited the building into the parking lot, while he answered her question.

"I only heard the last part, before I asked that asshole to leave. Mackie shouted at him, 'You should tell her before she figures it out on her own.' King yelled back that it 'would be a cold day in hell.' That's all I got."

"Hum, I wonder if the 'she' is me," Rainey pondered aloud.

"Mackie said he had to tell you something earlier. Maybe when he's feeling better you should ask him what that was."

"I will," Rainey answered, remembering that Mackie was trying to tell her he saw something.

They reached the Escalade, where Junior opened the back gate and leaned in to unlock the gun safe secreted beneath the floor mat. Rainey saw an evidence box, like the ones used to secure weapons before trials.

"What's in the evidence box?" She asked.

Junior pulled two Glocks from the safe, his and Rainey's. Most of the law enforcement people Rainey knew carried the same model. It was a durable weapon, and very reliable, an important factor when your life depended on it. Junior answered Rainey's question, while he tried to determine which weapon was hers. "King gave your Glock back completely disassembled and in that box. I thought I'd save you the trouble and put it back together."

"What a dick! I'm not sure what I did to piss Rex King off, but he sure has a problem with my existence."

Junior nodded in agreement. "He's like a dog with a bone over that Chambers thing."

Rainey reached for the weapon in his right hand. "This one is mine. See the nick in the back of the grip." She checked her weapon and holstered it. "He never liked me, even before Chambers was killed." She sighed. "He's the least of my worries at the moment."

Without warning, a chill crept up her spine and the fine hairs on her neck sprang to attention. Rainey scanned the parking lot. There were people moving about, getting in and out of cars. Clouds of smoke billowed from two men and a woman, huddled around the lone ashtray in the shadows. A couple of nurses were saying goodbye as one was going on duty, the other ready to call it a night after a long shift. No one looked out of place. Her eyes trailed through the windshields of the cars parked nearby, searching for someone watching her. She saw nothing, but could not shake the feeling that trouble was near.

"What is it, Rainey?"

Those who knew her had come to know that look, that intense concentration on her surroundings.

Rainey put her hand on Junior's arm, still scanning the area for the source of her unease.

"Do me a favor, Junior. Don't leave Mackie alone. You sit outside his room and keep watch. Get some of the guys together. Make a schedule. Mackie is never to be alone. I'll clear it with my stepdad, so there should be no problems."

"What's wrong, Rainey?" Junior asked.

She took one last look around and then met his worried eyes. "I just have a feeling something isn't right, and when it feels wrong, it usually is."

CHAPTER FOUR

"Before we declare a serial killer present, there must be evidence. Fuck Rainey Bell."

CRACK!

Bladen bit down on the ball-gag and moaned. He came back about a half an hour ago. It could have been longer. She wasn't sure. She lost track of time after the beating began.

He had arrived in a fury, ranting about Rainey Bell not recognizing his work. "Bodies, she wants bodies. Crime scenes to profile. Victims to analyze. Why can't she recognize that she can't say it's a serial killer, because I'm so much smarter than she is? She knows I'm out here. She has to. Why won't she admit it?"

"I don't know," Bladen answered, unsure if she was supposed to comment or not.

He backhanded her. "Shut up! I ought to just throw you out on her doorstep. She'd have a body then."

Bladen remembered what Rainey Bell said about defiance and avoiding his temper, but since he was in the process of tying her feet to a hoist, she thought she had nothing to lose. He was going to kill her eventually. Maybe if she defied him, he would lose control and do it now. Bladen would rather die, than live through anymore of his torture demonstrations. Her will to live had turned into longing for a swift death. She did not want her parents to suffer their remaining years not knowing what had happened to her, wondering if she was out there trying to find her way home. She did not want them to discover what actually had happened either, but she knew her father would read the autopsy report. He would scour her murder file into the night, because he would never rest until he found the man who killed his daughter.

The pain and anguish this madman had caused her, and knowing what he was about to put her parents through, raged out of her as she shrieked, "Kill me then, you bastard. Kill me so I can be done with you, you sick freak."

Bladen began to fight him, something she had not done since the Pear was introduced into play. She would take any beating, lashing, rack, and rape he had to throw at her, if he would just never use the Pear again. She could not imagine anything worse. If Bladen was going to die, she wanted to leave him with her last wish, a prophecy she hoped. A low primal growling voice emerged from her throat.

"She's going to find you. You'll screw up somehow. Guys like you always do. Narcissistic, egocentric, little men with little dicks, all of you. You better hope Rainey Bell finds you, because if my dad does, you'll wish you were already dead."

That was when the ball-gag went in her mouth. Her attempts to fight pleased him. Her fear and rage made him laugh and dialed up his sadistic fury. Afterwards, he indulged his fantasies on her as never before. Bladen only thought he had done his worst. Now she prayed even harder for death. She closed her eyes and tried to block out his ranting and the unyielding pain. She had almost reached that place where the agony would be too much and she would black out. Bladen would welcome the darkness and hope she never saw the light again, if only the pain would stop and she could not hear his voice anymore.

"I'll give her a body to examine. She still won't be able to figure it out."

CRACK!

Bladen's last thought before she lost consciousness was, "I hope it's me."

#

Rainey pulled up to the guardhouse at the entrance to her gated community. An armed guard stepped out and approached her window. Most cars could enter without stopping, a simple wave through the windshield and a swipe of a security card would do. Rainey could do that too, but the staff was under orders to stop her and Katie every time they entered, at Rainey's request. The guard waited for Rainey to roll down the window, before speaking.

"Good evening, Ms. Bell," he said, while trolling a flashlight beam through the interior of her car.

This precaution was necessary. Should an assailant in the backseat force either her or Katie to drive into their neighborhood, Rainey wanted this to be the result. An armed guard inspecting her vehicle was a small price to pay for security. Rainey ran all the scenarios, all the ways a determined killer could invade the carefully placed line of defense encircling her family. Some people thought her obsession with security was paranoia. To them, Rainey responded, "I'm not paranoid, just prepared. There is a distinct difference and a higher survival rate for the latter." With the unsettling suspicion that something was amiss, she was happy even this new guard was spot on with his duties.

"Could you pop the trunk, please," he said, politely.

Rainey hit the release and watched the trunk lid open in her mirror. The guard finished with his search, closed the lid, and returned to her window.

"Is there anything else, Ms. Bell?"

Even though he was new, she knew his name. She made it her business to know all their names, and to confirm the guards had undergone the in-depth background checks she was assured each had to pass. Still, Rainey took advantage of Brooks, her close friend in the Communication and Information Technology Unit of the FBI, and her unique abilities to ensure those checks were accurate.

"Yes there is, Cliff. I'm not sure who or what the threat is, but I need you guys on high alert for awhile. I just have a gut feeling."

Cliff smiled. "Well, you got to go with those. Anything specific I should be looking for?"

If Rainey knew what to look for, she would have found it already. She had no information to offer beyond, "You know about the stalker," which is what Rainey called the person providing the pictures to the blog site, "but this feels different somehow."

"Disturbance in the force, have you," Cliff joked, in his best Yoda impression.

Rainey's first thought was this was not something to joke about, but his grin won her over and she smiled back. "Yes, you could say that. I'm going to shoot an email to the main office, but if you could leave a note in the guardhouse, I'd appreciate it."

"Will do," Cliff said, stepping back and hitting a remote, which caused the big iron gates to begin sliding open.

Just before she rolled her window up, Rainey said, "May the force be with you."

She could hear Cliff laughing, as the window closed and she drove into her neighborhood, following the winding drive to the last lot on the left, near the north end of Lake Jordan. Rainey pulled the Charger up to a small metal box at the end of her driveway, rolled her window down, and placed a finger on the biometric pad. At the recognition of her print, a keypad illuminated where she typed in a code, causing the gate separating her home from the rest of the world to open. Only people with encoded prints stored in the security system could enter without Katie or Rainey letting them in. That was a very short list.

Motion detector lights came on above the garage doors. Standard remote openers were not part of Rainey's security, because they could be cloned. Once the security system recognized her car, through an elaborate coordination of signals being sent from the Charger's onboard computer and received by the sensors embedded in the concrete drive, the garage door cranked open. Rainey halted, surprised to see her mother's Cadillac where she usually parked the Charger. Leaving room for her mother to back out, she reluctantly left her four-wheeled baby in the driveway.

Confused as to why the door did not close automatically when she turned off the car, Rainey was apprehensive when she walked into the garage. Her anxiety dissipated when Katie stood up from the steps that led into the house. She must have overridden the computer when she heard Rainey open the door. Katie pushed a button on the wall and, as the door began to lower, she crossed the floor to Rainey, wrapping her arms around the taller woman's waist.

"I'm sorry I couldn't come to the hospital. I'm glad you're home."

"Me too," Rainey said, kissing her wife on the top of her head, hugging her close. "I didn't expect you to be awake. This is a pleasant surprise." She put her hands on Katie's shoulders and grinned into her upturned face. "You aren't expecting me to finish what you started earlier, are you? I don't think I can do that with my mother in the house. Why is she here, anyway?"

"Oh, I don't know," Katie teased, taking Rainey's hand and leading her toward the door that led into the kitchen. "There's something forbidden about having sex under the same roof with a parent. Might spice it up some."

"No extra spice necessary, and you didn't answer my question."

When Katie opened the door, the aroma of freshly cooked biscuits mingled with the unmistakable smell of bacon cooking wafted out.

"*You* are turning down hot sex? You must be tired," Katie said, smiling over her shoulder at Rainey, and then explaining, "Your mother is asleep in the guestroom. My mother is coming over in the morning. They are babysitting for the next few days, while we deal with Mackie."

"Here, right? They're not taking them anywhere, are they?"

Katie stopped and turned to face Rainey. The smile disappeared, replaced by a no-nonsense expression that went with her question. "What's happened, Rainey? Something else besides Mackie being in the hospital has you spooked."

Most of the time, Rainey hid her fears and concerns from Katie. She always told Katie about overt threats, but the little nagging feelings and suspicions, Rainey kept to herself. Her wife already suspected she was paranoid, so fueling that impression with gut feelings and possible threats was not a good idea. Katie demanded that she not be forced to live in fear, albeit behind a wall of security cameras and alarms. This time, Rainey thought

Katie should know. The feeling was too strong and Ernie felt it too. Something was awry. Hyper-vigilance was called for.

"Let's sit down at the table. We need to talk," Rainey suggested.

Katie put her hand in Rainey's chest, preventing her from moving. "You tell me right now. Is one of those crazy people after you again?"

"I honestly don't know what's wrong, but something is. I feel it. Ernie feels it."

Katie tried to explain it away. "You're both worried about Mackie. That's all it is."

"No," Rainey said, "You don't understand. We've been feeling this for months and it got worse after Mackie had the heart attack. I can feel eyes on me. I can feel danger, but I cannot for the life of me figure out what I should be preparing for. I don't want to scare you, honey, but there's trouble coming."

Katie turned and walked into the kitchen.

Rainey called after her, "Where are you going?"

"We're going to need coffee."

"Are you upset?" Rainey asked, hoping the answer was not yes. She could not help but feel guilty for putting Katie through yet another scare.

"No, honey," Katie said, putting a K-cup in the coffee maker. "We both know that this is our life, one threat assessment after another, but I do have a request."

Relieved at Katie's response, Rainey took off her coat and hung it by the door. She opened one of the many gun safes in the house and stowed the Glock. Katie insisted that all weapons be locked away while they were in the home. All the safes had biometric locks, which only Katie, Mackie, Ernie, and Rainey's fingerprints would open.

Her weapon put away and her stomach growling, Rainey started toward the breakfast table, responding to Katie, "And what would that request be?"

"Before we sit down for this heart to heart over bacon and eggs, go take a shower. The peas are really distracting."

#

Bladen floated above her body, watching the scene unfold beneath her. She felt peaceful, warm, free of pain and fear. It was a wonderful feeling, all she had been told it would be. Death had come so easily when she finally gave up the fight. Once he finished pummeling, torturing, and whipping her this last go-round, and while she was still hoisted upside down, he positioned a large tub under her, filling it with cold water. He would lower her head down into the water and keep her under to the point of drowning, before pulling her up, leaving her coughing and struggling to breathe. He would convince her it was the last time, and then plunge her back under. When she finally stopped struggling, she went rather quickly to this place of limbo. It was a relief to leave the torment. The one thing she could not understand was why she was still there. Why was she being made to hover, to watch as he tried to resuscitate her lifeless body?

She could hear him calling her name as he pounded on her chest. "Come on, Bladen, breathe." He began compressions, trying to keep the blood flowing to her brain. "I'm not done with you yet. Come on." He stopped compressions and blew air into her lungs, then resumed pumping on her chest. His words were clipped as he pumped her heart, urging it to start again. "Come on! You've got—some fight—left in—you. That's why—I picked you. I knew—you would—fight. Come—on!"

"Bladen," a man's voice said softly.

Bladen turned her head from side to side, trying to find the source. That's when she saw the bright white light. It was so beautiful, Bladen wanted to rush toward it, but the silhouette of a man appeared between her and the light. As he came toward her, his features became clear. He was tall with a head full of curly, reddish-brown hair and a beard to match. His green eyes were penetrating. Bladen had the sense that she knew him, but could not place his familiar face.

"Are you here to take me to the light?" she asked.

"It's not your time, Bladen. You have to go back."

Bladen looked down at her body, with her murderer still trying to revive it. The thought of going back there sent her into a panic.

"Please, don't make me go back. He's going to kill me anyway. Don't make me suffer more. Just take me now."

"Have faith, Bladen," the man said, as his image began to dissipate like fog clearing under the warmth of the sun. Just before he vanished completely, he said, "Don't give up. They're coming for you."

Bladen screamed at the man who was now only a mist, "It's too late. Don't you see? It's too late. Please, God, don't leave me here."

#

Rainey sat at the desk in her office sending emails, her hair still damp, but clean and pulled back in a loose ponytail to dry. If she left it free, the curls would expand into a frizzy mess. The thought of doing a Halle Berry on her hair had crossed her mind. Mostly, when one of the kids had a handful between fat little fingers, apparently having lost the motor skills to unfold the tightly clinched fist. If Katie said, "No," it was received with coos and appropriate responses. If Rainey told the triplets, "No," it was a mere momentary distraction and whatever activity they were involved in would immediately resume, until she physically removed the phone from a mouth, took away the shredded book, or rescued the cat.

Freddie Krueger, Rainey's bobbed tail black cat, could identify with her on the triplets' penchant for hair pulling. He had adjusted to the move and the babies fairly well. He roamed the large lot, mostly staying in his yard behind the high-security fence, but was known to head down to the lake from time to time. Rainey knew this from the variety of dead things he left in the garage, where his doggie-door entrance was located. Rainey tried to keep him in at night, and often found him curled up on the floor outside the triplets' nursery door. She was not sure if he was protecting them, or plotting his revenge for the handfuls of fur forcefully removed from his coat. Just in case it was the latter, he was not allowed in their room unsupervised. They installed a screened door over the babies' room doorway, covered in plastic-coated hardware cloth strong enough to keep Freddie out and the babies in. That way, the solid wooden door could remain open.

71

Sightlines and hearing were important, with three clever children and an equally cunning feline.

Family life had changed Rainey and Freddie, but they both seemed to be doing well. Rainey never knew she could love something as much as she loved those babies. They seemed to find her amusing and instinctively knew she was the weaker of the two adults. They pulled all their best stunts when she was the one watching them, but they had fun. Katie came home last week to find them all, Rainey included, covered in finger-paint, when an afternoon at home with mom number two turned into a free-for-all of wrestling rainbow-colored children. Rainey had no hope of ever controlling them like their mother. When Katie entered a room, all three of their heads would turn toward her. They seemed to think Katie was some kind of Goddess to be worshipped and obeyed. Katie said it was not her presence to which they were responding, but the appearance of a major food source.

The food source stuck her head in the doorway of the office, yawning loudly. "Okay, everything is ready for the morning. I'm going to sleep for a bit. You should come too. We'll be up soon enough as it is."

Rainey stood and walked to the door. She gave Katie a hug and a kiss, and then said, "I'll come up in a bit. I have one more email to send."

"Okay, don't stay up all night. You need some sleep." Katie yawned again, before saying, "Goodnight, I love you."

"I love you, too."

Katie went off to bed. It was now after two a.m. They had talked for the better part of an hour, after Rainey returned from a quick shower and a change of clothes. Rainey outlined everything she knew, from the writer preparing her character assassination, Mackie's condition, the risky surgery, hearing her father's voice, Ernie's warning, and the feeling she was being watched and not by the stalker. Rainey restated her belief that Cookie Kutter was involved in the blog, and how she hoped to catch her, or someone who worked for her, on the security cameras at the hospital. She told of Danny's forced betrayal and the leaked Grand Jury testimony. Rainey admitted she felt evil lurking, more malignant than a photographer posting pictures or a writer telling tales. Katie listened, promised to be more aware than usual of her interactions outside the home, and then told Rainey what she needed to hear.

"If you think someone is out there plotting your demise, then I believe you. Do what you have to do to keep us safe. I'll do as you ask."

That was hard for a strong-willed, free-spirited woman like Katie. They had survived two serial killers together, but it was a struggle to get Katie to listen in the beginning. Katie Meyers was determined not to let what happened to her affect the way she lived her life. She would not raise children in a house filled with paranoia and fear. Rainey had to explain it really had nothing to do with living a fearless life and was more about surviving to live it. After their last brush with death, Katie tended to follow the security procedures Rainey set out for them without fail. She still thought Rainey was paranoid, but not nearly as much as she did before.

Rainey sat down to write her final email. She already sent one to her stepfather about Mackie's protection detail, and one to the security company office alerting them to a possible threat. She could not describe the threat to either John or the security company. Unsure of what or whom she was up against, she kept her concerns vague. She also sent a message asking Brooks to tweak the software she designed, which searched twenty-four hours a day for any mention of Rainey on the Web. Her former job as a criminal mind-hunter made Rainey a target for twisted individuals out there fixated on the Behavioral Analysis Unit members. It was common to find reams of information about the unit and their work in a serial offender's home. Rainey needed to know if one of them was focused on her.

Now, the last message had to be written. She held off on this one until the end, not wanting to write it, but knowing she had to. She opened the encrypted email program to insure privacy. This message was for Danny McNally's eyes only, and only he would have the key to open it.

"Danny," she began. "I've thought long about how to broach this subject, but I find no way other than directly. Your Grand

Jury testimony in the Chambers case has been leaked. Martin Douglas Cross, the writer, will be publishing quotes from that testimony in his new book about me."

She stopped typing and looked across the desk at a picture of Danny and his Godchildren, Rainey's children. It was taken at the triplets' birthday party, which he flew in to attend. His goofy grin was so wide, his eyes were forced into smiling slits. Katie had framed the photo and placed it on the desk. Danny had Rainey's back since they joined the BAU together, nearly twelve years ago. He had seen her at her most exposed. Had he betrayed her? She could not know for sure without reading all the testimony, which was unlikely to happen. Marty might be able to get his hands on it, but no one was going to give that testimony to Rainey willingly.

With a heavy heart, she typed, "I know I put you in the position to have to testify to what you heard me say to and about Dalton. You tried to warn me the day would come when you would be forced to tell the truth. I admire your integrity. You were correct in your testimony. Under the right circumstances, I would have killed Dalton Chambers. Still, the fact remains, those circumstances did not arise. Chauncey Barber confessed, and is serving life without parole for Dalton's murder. As you told me before, if I were involved, I left a mile-wide trail right back to my door. I believe you said it was the smartest or dumbest thing I had ever done."

Rainey selected her words for the next paragraph carefully. Encrypted or not, the only safe communication was face to face in a listening device free environment, a luxury she did not have at the moment.

"No one would believe I was that reckless. No one, but Detective Rex King, who has a deep desire to see me rot in prison; author Martin Douglas Cross, who, as it turns out, I should have at least wounded enough to scare into never crossing my path a second time; a certain blond journalist named after a kitchen utensil that my wife would like to punch again; and possibly you, my friend. My position is still the same. If Chauncey Barber did murder Dalton Chambers because of some kindness I showed him, then bless his heart. I did not personally

74

order a hit. Call it semantics if you will, but those are the facts. Read up on Henry Plantagenet and the Archbishop of Canterbury. This story has several parallels, but you're not going to find me wailing at the altar wearing a hair shirt."

That was as close as Rainey could come to telling Danny the truth. As she had just discovered, if placed on the stand and under oath, Danny would reveal what she said. She moved on to the second reason for her email.

"There was one more piece of information from Mr. Cross that I think you should be interested in. He brought up Michael Paul Perry, insinuating that people were talking about the incident, and implicating me in his death. Either he's bluffing, or you have a misinformed leak in the unit. I know we did what we did out of respect for the boy's family, but if this blows up, you and the Bureau will be forced to make a statement. I was following orders from way above my pay grade, as were you. I won't remain silent and take the fall by myself. You might want to let the powers that be know that. I suggest you find out if anyone has been looking at that case and with whom that information may have been shared."

Rainey almost forgot to mention Mackie's situation and added it as a final note.

"Mackie was hit in the vest tonight with a .44 at close range. He suffered the usual resulting injuries, but had a heart attack later in the hospital. He'll undergo bypass surgery as soon as he is deemed stable enough. I'll be tied up with him for a few days. We'll chat about all this when he is out of the woods."

She closed with her standard, "Your friend, always, Rainey," attached a new picture of his godchildren, and sent the message.

After shutting down the computer, Rainey stood and walked to the window. Her office was at the rear of the house, with a view of the backyard. The moon was in the waning of its cycle, with only a sliver of light reflecting down to earth. Here, in her little fortress, Rainey felt safe most of the time, but tonight she had let the evil follow her home. She sensed it out there, watching. Rainey closed the blinds and went to the bookshelf she brought from the old house at the lake. It had been her father's and still contained memorabilia from his soldier days. It also held a secret, one where Rainey broke one of Katie's rules. A thick volume of Shakespeare's Complete Works rested on the middle shelf. Only it wasn't a book at all. It was an empty shell concealing a small, snub-nosed, .38 revolver that belonged to her father. Rainey verified it was still there and in working order.

She left the office to check the window and door locks, stopping in the foyer to scan through the camera images on the wall-mounted security panel hidden behind a hinged painting. One more check of the alarm system to see that all the indicator lights glowed green ensured the security net was solidly cast around her family. Satisfied that she had done all she could do, Rainey climbed the stairs to the master suite.

As she reached the first landing, Rainey was drawn to the large arched window that looked out over the backyard. She stopped and stared into the night, out beyond the thick brick security wall with its heavy iron gate. The wall was imposing, but not impassable. Night vision cameras would capture the image of someone scaling the wall or tampering with the gate. Motion detectors would sound the alarm and lights would blare down on anyone stepping a toe into the net laid out over her property. Everyone in the neighborhood knew when someone violated Rainey's safe space. It caused a clamor at one of the neighborhood association meetings, but Katie handled that with ease.

One neighbor expressed fear that if Rainey felt the need for that much security, what kind of element might she attract to the area?

Katie stood up and replied, "You live in a community behind iron gates and armed guards. You call once a week about some suspicious email you've received, wanting Rainey to check it out. Might we also be concerned about the people of whom you are afraid?"

The neighborhood quieted down about Rainey's presence after that. Some neighbors even hired her to help with security plans for their homes and families. She identified a stalker for a frightened woman, helping her take the appropriate legal steps and security measures. More than one neighborly wife or husband had approached her, wanting a wayward spouse caught on camera during an extramarital dalliance. Rainey did not do that type of private investigating. She had enough business without stooping to long nights of surveillance outside hotels and strip clubs.

Beyond the backyard, Rainey could see the thick woods that led to the shore of the lake. Anyone could be in there watching her search the blackness for movement. She was sure that some of the photos of her family had been taken from the higher limbs of one of those trees. The hair began to stand up on Rainey's neck and arms. Danger was in the air. Cliff was right. There was great disturbance in the force.

"Dad," Rainey whispered, "if you can hear me, I need more clues."

"Get some sleep so you can understand the clues," Katie said from the top of the stairs, in a ghostly voice.

Rainey turned quickly to see Katie holding sleeping Timothy against her shoulder.

"He was restless," she said, still patting the baby's back unconsciously. "Come on, we'll take him to bed with us."

Rainey smiled and bounded up the stairs. "Here, I'll take him," she said, holding her arms out to take her son.

Katie handed the baby over to Rainey, and then steered them all toward the third floor master suite. "Honey," she said, patting Rainey on the back now, "we'll be okay. It's like you say, you're not paranoid, just prepared. I know you'll keep us safe."

Rainey looked down at the precious babe in her arms, the smallest of the boys. "I know why my father was so vigilant with me now. The thought of something happening to one our children—I don't know, Katie—I really do think I could commit murder if someone threatened them."

Katie smiled up at Rainey and said matter-of-factly, "You'll have to get in line."

#

Her cellphone ringing startled Rainey out of a dead-tired sleep. She felt like she had just closed her eyes, but the clock on the bedside table said it was five minutes before six a.m. Three hours of sleep was better than none, she supposed. Fearing something had happened to Mackie, she frantically felt for the phone.

"Hello," she said, not even pausing to see who was calling.

"Rainey, this is Sheila. I'm so sorry to call this early, but this could not wait."

Sergeant Detective Sheila Robertson, of the Durham County Criminal Investigation Division, was an old friend and a frequent colleague. Their most recent endeavor together was as members of the missing women's task force. If she was calling this early, it could not be good news.

"Hang on, Shelia. Let me get where I can talk." Rainey rolled out bed and started for the bathroom, hoping Katie could settle Timothy, who woke with the ringing of the phone, back down for a few more minutes rest. Once she was behind the closed bathroom door, Rainey said into the phone, "Okay, what's up?"

"We have a body," Sheila began. "I need you at the scene."

"I don't know if you heard about Mackie, but I have to go back to the hospital in about an hour. Do you think you can do this one without me?"

Rainey looked in the mirror at her tired eyes and wild hair. It was still slightly damp when she removed it from the ponytail before falling asleep. She was now blessed with a bride of Frankenstein hairstyle, which would require another shower and some heavy conditioning to bring under control.

Sheila brought her back to the conversation with, "No, Rainey. You really have to come out here."

"Out where? What is it, Shelia? You sound shaken."

"I am, Rainey, and you will be too. Look out your back window."

#

Rainey stood under bright portable lights provided by the Medical Examiner's office. Still wearing the tee shirt she slept in, she had jammed a baseball cap over her mop of hair, thrown on some jeans, jumped into her boots, and grabbed her coat on the way out of the house. She arrived still warm from recently being cuddled with Katie and Timothy. It did not take long for the cold to seep into her bones upon seeing the body of a young woman deposited in the woods behind her house. It was obvious, from the condition of the body and the ground beneath it, that this was a fresh body dump, no more than a few hours old.

"This guy is a freakin' animal," a uniformed cop said over Rainey's shoulder.

Sheila shooed him away. "Go string some more crime scene tape or something, but do it away from here." The officer moved on, while Sheila mumbled under her breath, "Chatham County rookie."

Rainey's house was in Chatham County, making it not a Durham County problem, but someone notified the multi-county task force. Sheila had been dispatched to see if this was one of the missing women. No ordinary homicide, this was the work of a sadistic sexual killer, an offender type with which Rainey was all too familiar.

"We're going to need to put that hair in some kind of containment device, if I'm going to let you get closer to the body," a diminutive, salt-and-pepper haired, bespectacled woman said, while smiling up at Rainey.

If she had not been wearing gloves and the protective clothing of a medical examiner, Dr. Helen Wood might have been mistaken for a dainty little grandmother. Rainey had worked with Dr. Wood before. Her presence indicated the North Carolina Office of the Chief Medical Examiner had already been notified. From what Rainey could see of the body at a distance, she was very glad the esteemed pathologist was present.

Rainey dug in her coat's many pockets. "I've got a tieback in here somewhere." She stumbled on the note left for her last night. "Oh, here Sheila. You're going to need an evidence bag. I suspect the UNSUB in the rape cases left this in my coat last night. See if anyone has video of Wiley Trainer's vehicle while I was inside the house."

Dr. Wood shook her head. "Trouble finds you, Rainey Bell."

Rainey put the note in Sheila's gloved hand and continued looking for a hairband, answering, "Yes, it seems to."

Discovering one in the breast pocket, she pulled the band around the bush attached to her skull, calming it into a more manageable ponytail, and tucked it under the collar of her coat.

She added latex gloves handed her by Dr. Wood's assistant, pulled a flashlight from her pocket, and signaled the doctor that she was ready to enter her crime scene. Dr. Wood, satisfied that Rainey wasn't going to shed all over the body, took a step forward, beckoning Rainey and Sheila to follow. She pointed at the lividity staining under the victim's skin.

"She was definitely dumped here. And you're going to find this very interesting. She was frozen, probably some time ago. I can't be sure until we get test results, but she still has ice crystals in her core. She must have been frozen in this position."

Rainey examined the body for clues, and there were many. She was naked, head shaved, and posed with her hands still tied behind her back, ankles bound, slumped to the side. The position and mud on her knees indicated he left her kneeling, face pressed into the mud, buttocks raised in the air, exposing the damage done by the remaining oversized phallus protruding from her rectum. Rainey agreed with Dr. Wood, he had frozen her in that pose. As her body thawed, it fell over, ruining his art. Rainey had seen this type of presentation before. He was displaying his work like a sculpture, drawing the eye of the beholder to the horror first.

Signs of brutal torture were evident from her ankles to the ligature still positioned around her neck. There was hardly a place on her body without trauma. Rainey could not see the victim's face, as it was still partially submerged in the mud, but she was sure he did not leave it untouched. She started talking aloud for Sheila's benefit, but softly, so the curious and untrained would not hear details that should remain guarded for the moment.

"This level of bruising and injury does not look like a single beating. These were multiple attacks over time, possibly weeks, or months."

Dr. Wood concurred, "Don't quote me yet, until I can evaluate the tissue samples, but I think you are correct. There is healing evident around some of the lash marks, scarring, and old bruising. Poor girl went through hell for an extended period."

Rainey squatted behind the body, intrigued by a bite mark on the victim's buttock. "I know you haven't done a thorough exam, but have you seen any other bite marks?"

"No, but her breasts are badly bruised and with lividity, it's hard to tell," Dr. Wood replied. "We've already taken pictures of that one. I think we'll be able to get a good dental match, if you find a suspect."

Rainey looked at the bite mark closely. Struck by its familiarity, she pulled out her phone.

Sheila, put her hand on her arm. "Hey, the brass kind of frowns on personal pics at the crime scene. I'll make sure you have a full set of official photos."

"I'm not going to take a picture. I'm going to show you one."

Rainey typed in some info in a search engine and soon pulled up the picture she sought. She turned the phone so Dr. Wood and Sheila could see the screen.

"Ladies, you are looking at Ted Bundy's bite mark. Doesn't the bite mark on this victim look a lot like this?"

Sheila looked surprised. "Are you trying to tell me this body has been frozen since Ted Bundy was loose in the seventies?"

"No, but as you can see, his bite mark is readily available on the Internet. I think this killer made a set of teeth to look like Bundy's."

"Why would he do that?" Shelia asked, a knee jerk question, one Rainey was sure came to everyone's mind when faced with the depravity of others.

Rainey pointed at the ligature around the victim's throat. "See that hangman's noose, that's mimicking Gerard John Schaefer, another dead sadistic murderer. Although he was only convicted of two, he was a suspect in many more. The pose is reminiscent of several offenders, sadly too numerous to name."

Rainey noticed something sticking out of the mud under the head. "Can we roll her yet?" She asked Dr. Wood. "I think he might have placed something under her face."

Rainey was not ignoring the close proximity of the body to her residence. She could see the top floors in the distance, mostly obscured by evergreen branches, but still visible. The American Tobacco Trail ran behind her house. It was a recreational trail that traversed the Triangle. The body was located a few feet into the woods, just off the well-traveled path. He wanted this body found and placed it where it could be seen at daylight. Sheila told her an anonymous call alerted Chatham County deputies, who located the body. Rainey was sure the caller was also the killer. So anxious was he for Rainey to recognize his work, he could not wait for the body to be discovered by a passerby.

He may have stood in this spot, watching Rainey while she paused on the landing peering back at him. This was a message to her. He was screaming, "Can you see me now?" It did not miss her attention that the positioning of the body, had it stayed in the kneeling pose as he planned, pointed the buttocks squarely at her house. "Kiss my ass, Rainey Bell," he was saying. She kept those thoughts to herself, while Dr. Wood and her assistants rolled the body onto an evidence collection sheet, careful to preserve the pose for the time being.

The body was located in a sunken area that sometimes flooded with the spring and summer rains. This close to the lake, the ground remained damp, if not wet, most of the year. Dark, thick mud caked on the victim's face obscured her features. A partial death mask impression remained in the mud where her face had been. Now that the body had been moved, they could see the corner of a piece of paper sticking out of the muck. Dr. Wood's assistant took pictures and then cautiously removed what turned out to be a twenty-dollar bill. She placed it between two clear pieces of plastic, careful not to dislodge or disturb the mud still attached to half of the bill, should it contain prints. Once inside a sealed evidence bag, the assistant gently handed it to Rainey.

Rainey examined it closely with her flashlight. One end of the bill was fairly free of dirt and she could see something typed along the edge.

Sheila stood next to Rainey, looking over her shoulder. "What does that say?" she asked.

Rainey pulled the evidence bag closer, looking at the tiny print. When the words became clear, she read them aloud.

"Agent Sexy, I believe you're looking for this one."

Rainey looked back at the mud-covered face of the victim. The skin of the body was pale, but could have been a light skinned or mixed race young woman.

She asked the medical examiner, "Dr. Wood, what ethnicity would you assign the victim?"

"I thought she was Caucasian, but now that we've rolled her over, I'm leaning toward light skinned African American-Caucasian mix."

Rainey thought she knew the identity of the victim, but she had to be sure. "Look for a small tattoo on her right shoulder."

Dr. Wood leaned down, brushing some dried mud from the victim's skin. "Yes, I see it. There is a dark bruise under it, so it's hard to read, maybe a capital 'H' followed by a lower case 'a' and—"

"It says Halle," Rainey said. "Halle is her daughter's name. The victim is Jacqueline Upshaw. She went missing in September 2012."

"That's the girl whose mother shot Mackie, right?" Sheila asked.

"Yes, and it also explains why she is the victim he chose to give us and why he placed her in my backyard. I dismissed him last night and spoke to the media about the serial rapist instead. He's jealous. This is his coming out party. He's making sure he gets his notoriety, which may be his undoing."

Sheila was still looking at the evidence bag in Rainey's hands. "Why a twenty-dollar bill? What's the significance?"

"The UNSUB wants us to know he has studied, that he's an expert on serial killers. This is a counterfeit bill, I'm sure, and his ode to James Mitchell DeBardeleben, or Mike as he was called. He has also been called America's most sadistic killer, which explains the torture. If our UNSUB is emulating that particular offender and ones like him, then this woman suffered immeasurably and welcomed death when it came."

Dr. Wood squinted up at Rainey. "There will be more bodies, I presume."

"Yes, many. He's kept them hidden so far, but the media attention will lead him to expose more. He did not learn one very important lesson from DeBardeleben."

"What's that?" Sheila asked.

Rainey handed the evidence bag to Sheila. "DeBardeleben never craved the media attention. It's why he was able to get away with so many crimes for so long, and he spread his evil deeds over many states. He died in prison, having never confessed. Our guy seems to think he's smart enough to hunt in one place and not get caught, even flaunt his presence now. Why not? He's escaped detection so far."

"Why draw attention to himself? Does he want us to stop him?"

Those were both questions Rainey had answered repeatedly during her years with the BAU. She would probably answer them again in the future, just as she responded to Sheila now.

"That's a common misconception. Sure, some killers turn themselves in, or self-destruct, but this is an apex predator. Smart and cunning criminals, committing well-rehearsed, well-planned crimes, do not plan to get caught. But what is the point of being the greatest serial killer ever, if no one knows you exist? They get sloppy, caught up in the game with the police and the media.

They can also start to believe in their invincibility. In Dahmer's case, the police stopped him with body parts in garbage bags in his back seat. Two of his victims sought help and were handed back to him by the police. One was actually carried back into his apartment by officers. He got away with his crimes for so long, he began to think he could not be caught. I think we have the perfect storm with this guy. He wants credit and he thinks we can't catch him."

Sheila verified what she was hearing, "And you think this is just the first body he'll give us? This is the beginning of the game?"

"He is desperately seeking media attention." Rainey pointed at the bite mark. "None of the rest of this scene even remotely resembles Ted Bundy's crimes. He put that there because Ted is sexy. Mention Ted Bundy and the media frenzy will begin. If I were you, I'd keep the bite mark particulars on a need to know basis. It will drive this guy nuts that you didn't mention it."

"Okay, by me. Doc, you okay with that?" Shelia said.

"No problem. Are we done, ladies? I'd like to get her out of here, so you can process the rest of the scene."

Rainey took a few steps back from the body. "I'm done. In fact, I'm going to go back to the house and have breakfast with my children, and then go check on my friend in the hospital. Nice to see you again, Dr. Wood."

"You too, Rainey. Come by, if you want to view the autopsy. I should have her on the table this morning, say ten o'clock."

"Thanks, but I have a feeling you'll have plenty of company on this one." Rainey looked up at the first rays of gold breaking out in the sky. "I'm not sure what the rest of this day is going to bring, other than the sun. With triplets, I've learned not to plan on much more than that."

Sheila turned to go with her. "I'll walk you to your gate." When they had taken a few steps, Sheila said softly, "I'm sorry your involvement with the task force may have made you a target and brought this to your home."

"An evil man brought this to my home. There was something I noticed about the missing women, something I never mentioned to the task force."

Sheila stopped, lowered her chin, and said, "You probably ought to divulge that information now, since there is a dead body at your backdoor."

"I thought it was a coincidence, but now—"

"There are no coincidences," Sheila interjected, repeating something Rainey often said to her.

Rainey continued, "I think he's been fixated on me for a long time. BAU team members usually fascinate these guys. I was all over the news in the summer of 2010—July to be exact. That's when the first woman disappeared. We didn't know that at the time, and he's made no effort to contact me, but I think he's been waiting to see if I would notice him."

"Well, he's got your attention, now," Sheila said, just as they arrived at Rainey's back gate.

"That he does," Rainey answered, while lifting the security panel and placing her finger on the biometric lock. When the keypad appeared on the screen, she punched in the code and heard the two heavy-duty dead-bolt locks recede with a clunk.

"That's a fancy system you have there," Sheila said. "Considering your history, I guess you need to be prepared for the worst."

Rainey turned to her with a smile. "That's why I like you, Sheila. You understand the difference between paranoia and preparedness." She opened the gate, before saying, "You're going to need help on this. The BAU should be notified. It's not that I think they can swoop in and save the day, but they have resources and experience unmatched when dealing with this type of sexual sadist."

"We have you. Why do we need Danny's team?"

Sheila worked with the BAU team several times before. That's how she and Rainey met, back when Rainey's life was on a very different course. The path she was on today dictated her response.

"He made this personal, dumping a body in backyard. He wants to play with me. A few years ago, I would have found that tantalizing and jumped right in the game, but"—she looked over her shoulder at her home, where Katie and her kids were warm and safe—"I have more to lose now."

"So, you want off the task force?"

"You're not going to need me. Besides, if I am his focus and I don't show up at the body recoveries or press conferences, it will unsettle him more. In fact, you should get the brass to publicly fire me. He's fixated on me, draw him off, and give him a bigger target. Bring in the FBI with lights flashing and sirens blaring. He'll start tossing bodies out in no time. That's how you'll catch him."

"Well, okay," Sheila replied. "I'm sure you have a lot on your plate with Mackie going down. Thanks for the help. I'll put in an invoice for your crime scene consultation."

Rainey shook Sheila's hand. "This one's on the house."

"You stay safe, Rainey Bell," Sheila said, shaking her hand.

Rainey grinned. "Always."

CHAPTER FIVE

"In breaking news this morning, a body was found near an exclusive neighborhood in Chatham County, on the shores of Jordan Lake. Police have cordoned off the area and are not allowing our cameras in, but as you can see from our helicopter shot, the area is flooded with law enforcement personnel. In an interesting twist, sources report the body was located just feet from former FBI Behavioral Analyst Rainey Bell's backyard. Bell has been involved in several serial murder investigations here in the Triangle, since resigning from the FBI, and resides in the home you see here in this highly secured gated community with Katie Meyers and the triplets they are raising as a couple. More on this developing story as information comes in. Now, on to the weather. How is our day here in the Triangle shaping up, Elizabeth?"

He had been switching from channel to channel, listening to the news coverage of the discovery of his "present" to Rainey Bell, since he came back from its delivery. He talked to the television, as he watched.

"You can see me now, can't you, Agent Sexy?"

After reviving her from the near drowning, he shackled Bladen's limp body to the wall and left her hanging there. He went away for a while. She had no idea how long, having lost consciousness shortly after he turned off the lights, and only waking upon his return. The concept of time passage was blurred, but she knew it was morning. As he flipped through the channels, Bladen recognized the theme music of the news show she usually watched while eating breakfast.

He came back from his absence excited, turned on the television, and spent the time waiting for the news to break with Bladen. He unshackled her from the wall and placed her on a large dog bed in the corner, telling her all about the "present" he picked out especially for "Agent Sexy," while he bound her in an elaborate web of ropes. He toiled at each knot until it was perfect. Bladen had not resisted, but remained pliable and silent through it all. She kept her eyes tightly shut, with the image of the green-eyed man smiling at her, telling her not to give up.

Not giving up was a tall order in her current condition. Weak from her near-death experience and the torture, Bladen's will to fight had left her. Her hands and feet were tied behind her back, bound together. Another splintery hemp rope was doubled and looped over both shoulders, with one end attached to her hands, and the other end running down the front of her body, pulled tightly through her crotch and brought up to her feet. If she moved at all, the rope dug into her flesh, causing excruciating pain from her already traumatized vagina and anus. Giving up seemed like the best option to Bladen.

Bladen heard the click of the television turning off and then his chair scraped the floor, as he pushed it back from the desk. She remained as motionless as possible, feigning unconsciousness, as his footsteps approached.

"I know you're awake. I've been doing this long enough to tell when someone is faking."

He checked the ropes with which he had bound her.

She whispered through her swollen split lips, "Why don't you just kill me?"

"Now, what would be the fun in that?" He said, laughing. "You'll be fine after some rest and then we'll play some more."

"Just let me die," Bladen said, with her last bit of energy.

He slapped her hard, shouting, "If you don't snap out of it, I will. When I get back, if you aren't any fun, then I'll just finish you off and go get another one with some fight. Maybe I'll just go get Agent Sexy herself. That would be better than a sniffling, half-dead bitch like you."

Bladen had noticed how he could rage one second and then be calm and controlled the next. He did it now, speaking to her like a father to a child.

"Your daddy would be so disappointed in you, Bladen. He expects you to fight, to hang on, until he can rescue you. You think about that while I'm gone. Remember what Rainey said, 'Stay focused, stay engaged.' She should be engaged in finding you any time now."

He patted her still stinging cheek. Satisfied she could not escape the ropes, he moved away, but continued to talk.

"I have to go to work. I'll be gone most of the day. There's a tube with a water bottle attached to it, just above your head. I put a protein drink in there for you. There's water in a dog bowl near your feet. You have to get your strength back. It'll take some working around to get to it, but if you're thirsty or hungry enough, the reward will be worth the pain. I hope you'll think of me when that rope cuts into your cunt. I know I'll be thinking of you."

Her weak, "Fuck you," only made him laugh, as he turned off the lights and left, but not before his parting threat.

"Oh, I intend to fuck you in more ways than you ever dreamed, Bladen Asher. You can bet your sweet ass on that."

#

Rainey walked into the kitchen, leaving her muddy boots in the garage. She spotted the kids first, all lined up in their chairs, pinching Cheerios with stubby fingers. From the smears of baby food on their little tee shirts, Rainey could tell Katie had already fed them. They looked up when they heard Rainey enter and smiled at her, which she returned.

"Good morning, little people," she said, grinning broadly.

The triplets broke into spasms of laughter, immediately engulfing Rainey with all the good things, all the wonderful, fantastic, unimaginable joy she had in her life. If she could only have this—no evil men doing evil things—just this peace and contentment, Rainey would put away her weapons and silence the alarms. One glance at the television on the counter brought reality flooding back.

She could hear the helicopters overhead, and now was watching a recorded telephoto image of the walk she just took across her backyard, while the news ticker underneath read, "Body found behind former FBI agent's home . . ." Thankfully, the volume was off. Rainey could only imagine the damage they were doing to the security net she worked so hard to keep in place. Every wannabe serial killer and deranged nut-job within driving distance would be staring at the screen, taking notes.

"Damn," she said, under her breath, but not quietly enough.

Weather let out a whispered, "Nam."

Then all three started mimicking Rainey. "Nam, nam, nam."

"I told you," Katie said. "They hear everything you say, Rainey."

Weather led the trio into a chorus of, "Nee, nee, nee," which Rainey was sure was going to be her moniker for the rest of her life.

Rainey never dreamed of being someone's Nee-nee. She was fine with them calling her Rainey, but Katie said the kids would call her what they wanted and so far, "Nee-Nee-Nee," was it. Katie was on the cusp of the traditional, "Ma-ma," but then again there were a lot of "Da-da-das" being bantered about without a Daddy in sight. Most of the time, the triplets babbled among themselves in some weird alien language, complete with inflection and hand gestures. They fascinated Rainey, who could watch them communicate with each other for hours, totally engrossed in what she thought they might be saying. Weather seemed to be the most vocal, Mack the most interested in what she had to say, and Timothy, usually the peacemaker, seemed to change the subject when things became loud.

"Got me in trouble already," she said, laughing at her children.

Weather let fly with a handful of Cheerios in a salute to the tall, dark adult she found so entertaining.

"Hey, shortstop, knock it off," Rainey said, picking up the projectiles.

More cackles of laughter ensued, and all three loaded their hands for the next volley.

"No," Katie said softly.

Hands came down and filled little mouths with Cheerios.

"You are the Triplet Whisperer, no doubt about it," Rainey said, hugging Katie to her.

"Good morning, everyone," Constance Herndon sang, making her entrance.

Rainey's mother was dressed in an expensive warm-up suit, her hair and make-up perfect, as if she were headed to the Country Club to sip mimosas on the patio with her friends. She pecked each one of the babies on the cheek, leaving lipstick kisses in her wake.

Always the perfect hostess, Katie left Rainey's arms, asking, "May I bring you some coffee, Constance?"

"Please, dear. I don't have to ask how you are, Rainey. I can see it. I presume the helicopters and heavy police presence in the woods behind your residence to be the cause of your displeasure." Constance glanced at the television screen just long enough to read the caption about the body. "And I see my presumption was correct."

"Good morning, mother," Rainey said, taking off her jacket and hanging it by the backdoor. "Thank you for coming over."

"The hat, Rainey," Constance said, just as Rainey was about to pull out a chair. Indicating her hat should be removed out of good manners.

"Trust me," Rainey replied, refusing to remove the hat in a fashion that summed up most of their interactions during Rainey's adolescence, "it will be more impolite to take it off."

"You always did go through conditioner like water. It's your father's genes. Billy had the wildest bush of hair when you were born. He cut it, because you nearly yanked him bald."

"A shearing has crossed my mind," Rainey said. "It appears to be frizzier than ever."

"That comes with age," Constance dropped casually, adding a little jab at the end. "You'll be turning gray soon."

Rainey followed with a snide, "And I'm sure blonde is your natural color still."

Rainey and Constance called a truce after the babies were born, but theirs was still a tenuous relationship. Rainey could not abide her mother's pretentiousness, and Constance never forgave Rainey for not being debutante material. Rainey did get points for marrying one, though. If Rainey had to be a lesbian, at least Katie's pedigree met her mother's approval.

With impeccable timing, the debutante brought over coffee for Rainey and her mother, and in typical Katie fashion, proceeded to tell Rainey how it was going to go from here.

"My mother is on her way over and so is Gunny."

Rainey raised a questioning eyebrow.

Katie continued, "I called her, because I knew you would not let me leave the house without you, and someone who can protect the kids needs to be here or you won't leave either. We'll go to the hospital together, but Thelma says Mackie is scheduled for a lot of tests this morning, so we may not see him."

She kept up her monologue, the triplets jabbering along with her. A true genius at multitasking, Katie managed to drop bite-sized pieces of fruit on the triplets' trays, and serve the adults at the table plates of fruit and toast, all without missing a beat. Rainey was in awe of Katie's abilities. She sipped her coffee and watched her wife manage their lives, happy to have her do it.

"I've cleared my calendar for the remainder of the week. If I'm not with you, then I will be here at home, safe with your children. You just go do what you need to do without us on your mind. Release the hounds! Go get your man, Rainey Bell. Nobody gets away with leaving a body in our backyard."

Rainey set the coffee cup on the table. "I'm not going to be involved. I told Sheila to have them fire me publicly. I'm going to catch up on some college basketball games I've recorded and sit this one out. I'm not interested in being a target."

"It appears that ship has sailed," Constance said, pointing at the television, where Rainey's image was prominently displayed.

The picture was taken at Maybelline's last night. Rainey could see a little of the strained peas in the edge of the close-up, and from the facial expression, she could tell she was talking to Cookie when it was taken. The caption read, "Killer taunts former FBI profiler, Rainey Bell."

Katie commented, "Well, at least they cropped most of the peas out of the shot."

At that moment, lights flashed on in the backyard, strobes lit the still dawning morning, and a loud alarm jolted the babies, who sent fruit cubes and Cheerios skyward, before adding their own frightened cries to the cacophony. Rainey hurried to the security panel by the backdoor to silence the alarm. On the monitor, she could see a photographer running away from the back gate, where he was immediately wrangled by two uniformed police officers and taken away.

"You should show Constance how to reset the alarm. You know that is going to happen all day," Katie said, calming the children with coos and kisses.

Rainey's phone rang from her jacket pocket. She reached for it and saw Sheila's name on the caller ID. Sheila spoke as soon as Rainey said, "Hello."

"I'm so sorry, Rainey. There will be a uniform on your gate all day. It won't happen again."

"Thank you," Rainey said, and calmly added, "You may want to spread the word, in case it isn't common knowledge, I will shoot the first fucker that comes over that fence."

Sheila laughed. "Well, if they don't die from a heart attack first. That alarm nearly made me hurt myself. Good lord, that was loud."

"It's supposed to be a deterrent. If they keep coming through all of that, then I feel pretty good about putting a bullet in them."

"I see your point." Sheila paused, and then asked. "Are you sure you want off the task force?"

Rainey turned, so Katie could see her face, as she explained to everyone listening. "To use his apparent interest in me as an affective investigative tool, I would have to become the face of the investigation, the one out front, taunting and drawing him in. That's not my job anymore. Call the BAU, Sheila."

"All right then," Sheila said, sighing. "Tell Mackie I hope he feels better soon."

"I will. We're headed to the hospital in a bit." Rainey started to end the call, but she said instead, "Don't let the BAU put you in a holding pattern. Tell them there is a DeBardeleben type sadist in the Triangle. That should get them in the air within the hour. Preserve the site for them. They'll want to see it."

"Okay, Rainey. I'll do that. Thanks, and kiss those babies for me."

Rainey smiled at Katie and their children, saying into the receiver, "Every chance I get."

#

Melanie Meyers, Katie's look-alike mother, arrived shortly after the alarm incident. Rainey excused herself to shower and change, but not before stopping to kiss each one of her children and her wife on the cheek. This hands-on, touchy feely, showing emotion and affection in public persona was new to Rainey, but she had grown into it over the past year. Unconditional love changed her, so much in fact, that she honestly did not want to be involved in the serial killer investigation taking place just beyond her back gate.

As she poured a copious amount of conditioner on her hair and waited for it to soak in, she thought about this new Rainey, the one with no ache for her old life in the BAU. The private investigator jobs were interesting and kept her engaged. The consultant gig satisfied her need to use the skills she worked so hard to obtain. She could drop in, read the files, maybe see a few crime scenes, interview a couple of victims or witnesses, give her recommendation, sometimes testify in court, but above all not take it home at night, where she slept cozy and well—no more nightmares. There was a heavy price paid for achieving a highly sought after position in the Behavioral Analysis Unit. Living with that depravity day in and day out took its toll. Rainey considered her bill paid in full.

It was the weather making Rainey's hair go nuts. She tried to dry it, but the wintertime static in the house forced her to spray it down again with leave-in conditioner. Katie walked in, just as Rainey decided it was no use and put her hair back in a ponytail, and swore at the mirror.

"I am cutting this damn mop off, I swear."

"If you want to cut your hair, cut it," Katie said, slipping out of her clothes and heading for the shower.

"I don't know why I've kept it long all these years," Rainey said to her reflection in the mirror.

Katie grinned, then slipped behind the glass door, saying, "You told me your daddy loved your hair. I think that's why you haven't cut it."

Ignoring the truth of Katie's words, Rainey said, "I haven't had short hair since I was a baby. Suppose I look weird. Maybe my head is really small under this mane."

Katie rubbed the steam from the glass and peered out at Rainey. "Your head is normal size. Besides, if you don't like it, you can grow it back."

"Maybe," Rainey said, contemplating what she would look like with short curls. Her image disappeared as the steam from the shower began to fog the mirror. "I'll see you downstairs."

Katie called after her, "Don't fight with your mother."

Rainey chuckled, saying under her breath, "I'm not making any promises."

#

"We got a problem, boss," Gunny said, as soon as Rainey made it back to the kitchen.

She had stopped in the den to check on the kids and the grandmothers. All was well, so she headed for the kitchen for some coffee, where she found Gunny pacing.

"What's up?" Rainey asked, reaching for her cup and heading for the coffee maker.

"Katie took my weapon and put it in that safe there. Now, how am I supposed to be on a protection detail without my weapon?"

Rainey shook her head. "She won't allow a weapon in the house, at least not beyond the doorway."

"Well, that'd be fine if I could get to my gun when I needed it, but I can't open that safe," Gunny argued.

Gunny had a point, but Rainey was not going to program her fingerprints into the security system. Rainey trusted just three people that much. Mackie, Ernie, and Katie were the only people, who could unlock the exterior gates, open the gun safes, and enter the panic room. Located on the third floor in the master suite closet, secreted behind the wall, the space to install a small panic room was one of the selling points of the house.

They made a few other changes before moving in. Normal things, like a new gourmet kitchen for Katie, a laundry room on the second floor, a nursery beside the master suite, and new carpet in the den. Among the not so normal improvements were replacing all the windows with ballistic glass, the elaborate security system, gun safes distributed throughout the house, and the heavy-duty brick and iron fence around the grounds. Rainey's castle was her fortress, and very few people were allowed beyond the mote of security she created around it.

Rainey thought of a solution. "I'll move my mother's car. You pull yours into the garage. Put your weapon in there. It will be two steps from the door and not technically in the house. That way, we're not breaking the rules, just bending them."

Gunny chuckled. "I like the way you think, boss."

Gunny called Rainey boss, because she was so used to saying sir and ma'am in the military. Rainey finally broke her of saying ma'am to her all the time, and just accepted she was going to call her boss instead. Gunny and Rainey trained together once a week, and there was no doubt in her mind that her children would be safe with the former Marine watching over them. Rainey had the bruises to prove, even without a firearm, Gunny Pierce could put a hurtin' on your ass. With her pistol, Gunny was a master marksman. So, what Katie didn't know would not hurt her.

Rainey walked to the safe and retrieved both her Glock and Gunny's. Like Junior, Gunny carried the same weapon. Rainey could tell them apart easily, because Gunny's had a custom slide cover, with "Gunny" engraved on it in gold, a gift from her unit when she left the service. Rainey closed the safe and handed Gunny her Glock, and then remembered she needed her mother's keys.

"Here, hold this," Rainey said, handing her weapon to Gunny. "For God's sake, don't let Katie see them. I'll be right back."

Gunny laughed. "That little blonde has you wrapped. Just sayin'."

"Yeah, well, she's not above throwing us both out the door, so hide the firearms if she beats me back here."

Rainey trotted off toward the den, where her mother informed her that the keys were in her purse in the bedroom. She ran to one of the second floor guestrooms, wrong one first, and then found the purse in the next room, but not the keys. After turning in a circle for a few moments, Rainey spotted the keys on the dresser, and hurried back to the kitchen as fast as she could, but it was not fast enough. Katie had arrived just seconds before and was wagging a finger in the air. She was about to corner Gunny, when she heard Rainey approach.

Katie wheeled on Rainey. "Why is she standing in my kitchen with your pistol?"

Gunny had concealed one of the weapons, but she had not moved quickly enough. There she stood, holding one of the pistols. This was not good, not good at all, a major infraction of Katie's house rules.

In order not to face Katie's wrath, Rainey scooted by her, grabbed her coat, and pushed Gunny toward the door leading to the garage, saying, "We were just leaving. Meet you in the car."

When Rainey closed the door behind them, Gunny handed her the Glock and started up a hearty laugh. "That little woman is your kryptonite, Supergirl. It's fascinating to watch you go all weak in the knees."

Rainey dropped the clip from the pistol, checked that the chamber was clear, and stuck the magazine back in. It crossed her mind that she had not fired the weapon since Rex dismantled it, but the action seemed fine. She holstered it, and pushed a button on the wall.

"Well, I'd rather not be sleeping on the couch, so go hide your gun, while I move my mother's car."

The garage doors began to open. Gunny walked away still laughing.

Rainey called after her, "You don't understand. You date men. Women are a whole other ballgame."

Gunny turned around, backing out of the garage with a grin. "I lived and worked with women for twenty-four years, witnessed all the drama that went with it. That's *why* I date men."

#

Drip—Drip—Drip—
On it droned, second by second.
Drip—Drip—Drip—

This maddening sound was interrupted intermittently by earsplitting death metal, at least that was the way Bladen would describe it. The loud roar of a distorted voice, screaming undecipherable words, literally vibrated her teeth. Yet, she had begun to experience it as white noise, moments of respite from the drip—drip—drip. She still jumped each time it exploded from the speaker behind her, but she had learned to control the anticipation of its return.

"Just let it happen," Bladen told herself.

There was no pattern to the music's timing. It popped on and off at differing intervals, staying on for seconds or minutes, before abruptly ending. At times, she begged it to come on, because the dripping was agonizing. She would focus on something else, a happy memory, a lesson plan, anything to take her mind away, but the drip—drip—drip would pound its way through, dragging her back to the miserable little room, the pain, and the interminable drip. If she were lucky enough to fall asleep, the death metal would blast from the speaker, causing her to jerk awake, and the ropes to bite and rip her raw skin. He was torturing her without being there.

Drip—Drip—Drip—

#

Upon exiting their neighborhood, Rainey and Katie were met by a media frenzy of flashes from photographers' cameras and reporters running toward the car. Rainey gunned the engine, which sent the paparazzi scattering for their vehicles in an effort to follow the quickly disappearing Charger.

Katie commented, as they sped away, "You may not want to be the face of the investigation, but I think they have other plans."

Rainey pulled the Charger into a parking place at the hospital, looking in the rearview mirror. No one followed them, at least closely enough to have seen them pull into the hospital, but

Rainey was taking no chances. She put her pistol in the console, because even a license to carry did not permit a weapon in the hospital. She kissed Katie on the cheek. "Hurry up. Let's get inside before they find us."

They were approaching the hospital doors, when a detective Rainey knew exited the building. "Well, providence has spoken," he said, smiling at her.

"Good morning, Detective Gardner," Rainey said.

Gardner was a former army man and still carried himself with a military bearing, as he continued toward them. "I was just going out to the car to find your phone number. I've got a rape victim in here that refuses to speak to anyone or undergo an examination until she speaks to you."

"Why me?" Rainey asked.

"She attended the symposium where you spoke Monday night."

"Is it the same guy?" Rainey asked, knowing Gardner was working the serial rapist case.

"We don't know," he answered. "She won't talk. Just walked in here this morning and asked to speak to you. She said she knew you'd be here with your friend."

"There's not much of my life people don't know about, after last night and now this morning."

"Yeah, I heard about Mackie and the body dump. Some guy at the office commented that you were on every channel, like it was the Rainey season." Gardner chuckled at the joke, and then seeing that Rainey did not find it amusing, said, "I guess it's not that funny from your perspective."

Rainey answered coldly, "No, it isn't."

Katie entered the conversation. "Oh, Rainey, that woman must be traumatized. You go on and talk to her. I'll go up and see about Mackie."

"Yoo hoo," a familiar voice sang from behind them.

It was Ernie, carrying a box of Krispy Kreme doughnuts. To look at her, no one would know she was up late and probably had as little sleep as Rainey. Ernie never had a hair out of place and was always dressed professionally, in sharp suits and heels. The sweet, little old lady act did not work on Rainey. She knew the heart of a lioness lived beneath that perfectly coiffed gray bun. Mess with one of Ernie's cubs and a person would get the claws, or a bullet, whichever the situation required.

"Hey, Ernie," Katie said, as the older woman approached. "Did you get some sleep?"

"Yes, I went home to the farm about an hour after Rainey left. I came back to town early, because I wanted to stop by here before I went to the office."

Rainey admired Ernie's dedication, but the business could be closed for a few days. "Don't worry about the office. Take the day off. Take two. We can shut down a bit without problems."

Ernie shook her head. "At my age, honey, it pays to keep moving. I'm just going in to check messages. I'll be back here at the hospital this afternoon, so Thelma can go home for a bit."

Detective Gardner cleared his throat to get Rainey's attention. "I know you've got a lot on your plate, but if you could talk to this victim, maybe we can determine what happened and if this is the same guy."

Ernie was not one to ponder alone what she could ask outright. "The same guy that left the body behind your house?"

Katie answered for Rainey. "No, this is the serial rapist. The body came from the serial killer."

"My Lord," Ernie said. "What in the world is wrong with people?"

Rainey noticed a news van pull into the parking lot. "Katie, go on up with Ernie. I'll be there as soon as I can. Let's get out of the public eye." She nodded toward the van closing in on her position.

Katie rolled her eyes. "You know, I thought being married to a politician was bad, but it appears I jumped out of the frying pan and into the fire with you."

Gardner led the way. "We call it the profiler effect," he tossed back over his shoulder. "And with Rainey, it's extreme. The media thinks the FBI is sexy. Add in profiling, serial killers, and a good-looking former analyst, it's a news director's dream."

"You forgot lesbian," Katie added. "They never forget to mention that."

Gardner chuckled. "Yeah, they don't miss that very often. Face it, Rainey Bell, you're a media darling." He looked back at the parking lot. "And it looks like your favorite reporter just pulled in."

Rainey turned to see a van with Cookie Kutter's smiling image painted on the side. She pushed Katie and Ernie through the door and slipped inside. "Whatever happens, Katie, do not punch Cookie on camera again."

Katie smiled over her shoulder at Rainey. "I've learned to use my words."

Katie's wicked grin did not comfort Rainey. "Don't talk to her, please. I'm begging you."

Katie winked. "Don't want me hogging your spotlight?"

"No," Rainey said, "I don't want to be left alone with the triplets, while you get a new sugar-momma down at the jail."

#

Rainey saw Katie and Ernie to the elevators and then followed Gardner back to the examination rooms, somehow able to avoid Cookie. As they walked, Gardner filled her in on what he knew. The woman had yet to give her name, address, or any details, other than she was raped. She had some visual signs of trauma, consistent with the other victims. Her lip was split, her hair was damp, and there was evidence he used tape on her mouth and eyes.

Rainey could not remember being in the emergency room the night of her own abduction. It was several days later when the memories began for her. Still, waking up to the horror of what had happened was the low point and the beginning of her recovery. The disassociation it took to learn to live with what had been done to her began the moment her brain remembered his face hovering above hers. Although she had seen her attacker take his last breath and knew he could never hurt her again, walking into this woman's room made it necessary for Rainey to double check her mental boxes, assuring the lids were tightly secured. She could not let her emotional memories enter into the conversation.

Gardner stopped outside the door. "See if you can get the location for me, so I can get the scene sealed."

Rainey nodded, and stepped into the room. A nurse greeted her with a smile, but was prepared to protect her patient. She positioned herself between her charge and the intruder. "May I help you?"

The young woman in the bed spoke softly. "It's okay. She's the one I want to talk to."

"Rainey Bell," she said, extending her hand to the nurse.

"Dani," the nurse said, shaking Rainey's hand. She turned to the woman in the bed. "I'm going to step outside, so you two can talk, okay?"

The woman only nodded. The nurse left the room. Rainey assumed she was the SANE nurse. It had nothing to do with her mental state. The acronym stood for Sexual Assault Nurse Examiner, an individual specially trained to collect evidence and deal with the trauma associated with sexual assault. She was usually the first advocate a rape survivor encountered. While her job was to collect evidence to be used in the investigation, her priority was the health and mental wellbeing of her patient, a huge step forward in assault victims' treatment from that of past decades. It was the first step to the restoration of a survivor's dignity.

The young woman in the bed looked to be in her mid-twenties, consistent with the other serial rape victims. The rapist seemed to have only an age range and appealing appearance for target selection criteria. This woman was small, but athletic looking. She appeared to have put up a struggle. In addition to the split lip, there was an abrasion on her left cheek, and her eye was swollen, already turning shades of purple. Rainey could still see tape residue in her thick brown hair and the skin was raw near her eyes and mouth, where she had ripped the tape off after the assault. Her wrists were red, where he bound them, leaving markings associated with the use of plastic handcuffs similar to those used by law enforcement. All consistent with the other women Rainey had interviewed in the serial rapist investigation.

"Do you mind if I sit down?" Rainey asked.

"Go ahead," the woman answered in a whisper.

Rainey took the chair by the bed. She knew the woman would talk about the assault when she was ready, so she did not ask her anything about it. Instead, she said, "Can I get you anything? Are you warm enough? It's always so damn cold in these rooms."

"I'm okay. My hair is almost dry now and the shivering stopped. I don't think I've ever been that cold before."

Another consistency. He made the women get into the bathtub after the assault, where he supervised the washing of his DNA from their bodies. He then drained the tub and filled it again, demanding that they stay there while he searched their homes. He would pop back into the bathroom to remind her he was still there, terrorizing the woman into believing he would never leave. Eventually, he would simply slip away. Some of the women stayed in the cold water for hours, nearing hypothermia, in fear that he was waiting just outside the bathroom door.

The woman in the bed almost let herself go back there. Rainey recognized the pained expression on her face and the coping mechanism that triggered her next question.

"Did I bring my purse? My phone is in my purse." She looked around the room, searching for the normalcy that would be a long time coming. The purse and phone were things from her life before the world spiraled out of control.

"I don't know, but I'll ask, if you like."

"I think it's in my car," the woman said, still trying to put distance between her and the memory she had almost allowed to creep in.

Rainey saw an opening. "Hang on. I can find out for you." She stood and walked to the doorway. Sticking her head out, she asked the diligent nurse, "Did she have keys with her?"

"Yes, they're in the personals bag by the bed. I've already bagged her clothes separately."

Rainey walked back into the room and over to bag, removing a set of keys with a keyless entry remote attached. She smiled at the woman, attempting to keep her at ease.

"I'll have Detective Gardner see if your purse is in your car, if that's okay with you?"

"Yes, that's fine."

"You parked in the ER lot, right?" Rainey asked, now that she had consent to search for the purse.

"I think so," the woman answered, a little hesitantly.

"Just a sec, then. I'll be right back." Rainey stepped into the hall and handed the keys to Gardner. "Her car is in the ER lot, she thinks. Push the panic button on the remote and listen for the horn."

Gardner trotted off to find the vehicle. He would have all he needed to identify her, if he could locate the purse. If not, then a quick check of the registered owner's driver's license picture could yield a verification of identity. Even if the vehicle was registered to someone else, it was more information than they had now. She would tell Rainey her name and address eventually, but the scene needed to be sealed right away. This way, Rainey did not have to push the woman and could let the story unfold when she was ready.

Rainey resumed her seat, saying, "He'll be back in a minute. I don't carry a purse, but I know how unsettling it can be not to know where my phone is."

"I saw you Monday night," the woman said. "I sat there trying to imagine what I would do if I was raped. I saw your scar and thought how brave you were to show it. Does it remind you every day? Do you still remember it like it was yesterday?"

The woman wanted to know what all victims do. Will I be able to forget this ever happened?

Rainey leaned forward. "In time, I was able to put it away. The pain lessened, the nightmares faded, and I came to understand that this happened to my body. It does not define me."

A tear rolled down the woman's cheek. "But you still remember, don't you?"

"Not as much as before, and more than I will remember tomorrow. I don't think we can ever forget it completely, but I filled my life with other things. I don't have time to dwell on it. Survivors find their own path. Everyone deals with trauma differently. I can't tell you the right choices for you. I can tell you the worst is over. You survived. Nothing else matters, not what he made you do, not what you had to do to survive. Nothing matters except that the attack is over. When you can embrace that, the healing will begin."

"They want me to tell them what happened. I don't know if I can do that," the woman said, the tears flowing freely now.

This was the part Rainey hated, the coercive element to a rape investigation. She handed the woman a tissue from the box beside her bed and tried to soften her appeal for the woman's cooperation with the police. "What and when you tell it is up to you. You have control now. That is important for a survivor, to be in control of what happens next. You can leave here right now and never speak of it again, but I don't recommend you do that. You came here seeking help, because deep down you know that's what you need. Let the system help you. If you choose to give a statement to the police and seek justice for what happened, then you've taken the first step."

"I'll have to testify in court. They'll try to say that I asked for this, because I forgot to lock the backdoor. It was my fault. 'You knew I was coming. You left the door unlocked for me.' That's what he said."

There it was, Rainey thought, the self-imposed guilt. The seed planted by the rapist that, if not plucked out before it grew, could cripple this woman's recovery.

"You did not leave the door unlocked. He uses the same line at each of his crimes. He needs to believe it himself, that you wanted him. Nothing could be farther from the truth and it is his fantasy, not reality. He's a criminal. They lie."

The woman stared at Rainey for a moment, her brow wrinkled, as she processed this new information. "I knew I locked that door," she finally said.

"You did nothing wrong. No matter what he said, what anyone else says, or what those nagging little voices in your head will say down the road, you have to know you did nothing wrong. The moment he entered your home without permission, your only option was to do whatever it took to survive. That's all you need to know."

"He had a gun, but I fought him anyway. He hit me with it, then I stopped fighting and he didn't hit me anymore. I remembered what you said about the different types of rapist. He kept telling me I was lucky he was a gentleman."

Rainey smiled at the younger woman. "I suggest you tell anyone who calls you lucky to fuck off."

A slight smile crossed the woman's lips, accompanied by a weak laugh. "I will." She sighed, wiping her tears away. "Well, I guess I better tell that detective what happened, so I can leave."

"Would you prefer a female ask you questions?" Rainey asked, aware a strange man in this woman's space might be upsetting.

"No, he's fine. He kind of reminds me of my brother, and somehow that is comforting."

"You're going to need to call your brother or someone and stay with them for a few days. The police are going to seal the crime scene to collect evidence," Rainey said, standing to go. "You shouldn't stay by yourself for a while. It helps to have someone close by, someone you can trust, so you can rest. It's important to get as much normal sleep as possible. Let your body and mind heal."

"Is that how you got through it? That blond woman you live with, did she help you?"

Rainey tilted her head in question.

"I confess," the woman said shyly. "I watch Cookie Kutter's show. I was watching last night. That's how I knew you would be here." She pointed at the gold band on Rainey's left ring finger. "The blonde is your wife, right?"

Rainey smiled. "Yes, Katie is my wife. And to answer your question, we helped each other through it. She is a survivor, too." Rainey reached into the small breast pocket inside her jacket and pulled out a card. "She runs a center for women and children in need of a safe place, should you require one. They also have counseling and legal advocates available, or if you just want someone to talk to, or a safe place to sit quietly and look at the water. Whatever you need, they can help. This card has all the info. Call this number anytime, day or night. Someone will always answer."

Rainey reached for the pen on the bedside table. She wrote her private number on the back, a rare occasion, but she thought this woman might need it, if for no other reason than to know Rainey cared enough to give it to her.

"I won't hold watching Cookie's show against you. This is my private cellphone number. Call me if you need anything, or you just need to talk." Rainey held out the card and winked. "If Cookie gets this number, I'm coming looking for you."

The woman took the card, clasping Rainey's hand as she did. "Thank you for taking the time to talk to me."

Rainey squeezed the woman's hand. "I lived life after my attack like I should have died, like my life wasn't worth as much anymore. I wasted time living like that. Don't let that happen to you. I promise you, every day will get easier. Remember, surviving was the only thing that mattered."

Rainey was at the door when the woman spoke, causing her to turn around. "Alana. My name is Alana Minott. It was a pleasure to meet you, Rainey Bell."

"It was a pleasure to meet you, Alana Minott. Take care."

Rainey stepped into the hallway. Two uniformed officers were with the SANE nurse, who looked puzzled.

"You can go in now. She's ready," Rainey said to her, but the nurse just stared.

"Rainey Bell?"

Rainey turned to the officer, confused. "Yes, I'm Rainey Bell."

The other officer stepped behind Rainey and grabbed one of her wrists. "Put your hands behind your back," he said.

She was too stunned to resist, when Rex King stepped into the hallway from the next room over. "Rainey Blue Bell, alias Caroline Marie Herndon, you are under arrest for the murder of Bernard "Bobo" Jackson."

CHAPTER 6

Rainey was paraded out of the hospital in cuffs, under the glare of Cookie Kutter's camera lights. "Did you kill Bernard Jackson to cover up your involvement in the Dalton Chambers murder?" Cookie shouted.

Rainey glared at her, but remained silent. She was led to her car, where Katie and Ernie were standing with other officers. There was a small crowd of onlookers gathering. Rainey recognized some of the medical personnel from Mackie's trauma room last night. Detective Gardner was there, holding a purse and looking utterly dismayed.

Katie, phone pressed to her ear, was not happy. As soon as Rainey was close enough, she started talking fast. "Rainey, I let them in the car, because they had a warrant and Molly said I had to. She's on her way. I'm trying to keep them from impounding the car."

Rainey tried to sound calm. "It's okay, Katie. Let them do what they have to do." She turned to Ernie. "Take her home. Make sure she's safe and tell Junior he has to watch Mackie's back."

"Ms. Meyers, I'm going to need a statement from you," Rex said.

"Here's your statement—" Katie began, and then paused to listen to her phone. "My attorney says she'll make arrangements for me to come in and give a statement, but at the moment, she is advising very strongly against me telling you what a little weasel you are."

Rainey laughed, which caused Rex to jerk her toward the waiting police cruiser and hand her off to a female officer. "Book her on suspicion of first degree murder, and make damn sure she's read her rights at every turn. This one is by the book. No mistakes."

"Molly will meet you there, Rainey," Katie shouted. "I love you."

Rainey managed a smile. "I love you, too. Go home. Stay with the kids. I'll call you."

She lowered her head and sat down in the back of a police car in cuffs, for the first time since playing the part of a prisoner during academy training. This was real and quite a different experience, she noted.

Rex stuck his head in the open door. "You think that pretty little thing will wait for you while you rot in prison?"

Rainey didn't take the bait. She smiled. "Don't scratch the car, Rex. It's worth more than your pension."

"Your father was an arrogant ass, too," he snarled.

"Did my dad kick your ass or something? I'd be shocked if he did. He rarely lost his temper, and you would've needed a much larger set of balls to challenge him." Rainey made no effort to conceal her contempt. She knew she should stop, but the opportunity was too great. She took one more manhood-questioning jab at Rex. "Oh wait, did he fuck your wife? Now, that sounds like him. He was a real ladies man."

The fact that he flushed scarlet and slammed the car door told Rainey all she needed to know. Old Billy had a fling with someone Rex cared about. She was mulling that over when the female officer climbed into the front seat, chuckling.

She made eye contact with Rainey in the mirror and smiled. "You told that man he had tiny nads and called his wife a 'ho' with a smile on your face. Girl, I don't care if you did kill somebody. That was some funny shit."

"I don't know," Rainey said. "I'm having a hard time imagining my dad with someone who would sleep with Rex King. That's a bit—disconcerting."

She smiled through the window at Katie, who blowing kisses as the cruiser pulled away. She looked up to see the officer watching her in the mirror.

"That's my wife," Rainey said with pride. Ignoring her circumstances, or maybe because of them, she began to tell the officer about her family. "We have triplets, a girl and two boys, Weather, Timothy, and Mack. They just turned a year old. You should see –"

#

"We can't put a former FBI agent in the general population," the guard on Rainey's right said, as she was being led to a holding cell in the Durham County Detention Center.

"King said put her in with last night's trash," the guard on her left said.

Rainey remained quiet. She stopped talking when they reached the jail, where she was humiliated with a strip search and given an orange jumpsuit and slippers to wear. This was all special treatment, arranged just for her by Rex King, whose demise she was plotting with each step toward the jail cell. She should have been downstairs, in her own clothes, awaiting her lawyer. This was a little treat Rex designed to frighten Rainey. She was not afraid. She was livid.

The guards stopped in front of a large cell with seven women already inside.

"Open twenty-six," the guard on the left said into her radio.

The guard on her right opened the cell door when the dead bolts clunked open. "Don't tell them who you are," she whispered to Rainey.

Rainey did not acknowledge the advice. She was afraid if she opened her mouth, she would not be able to stop the flow of obscene suggestions of what Rex King could do with his arrest warrant. The warning was pointless anyway.

One of the prisoners stood and pointed at Rainey. "Look here, y'all. We got us a good girl gone bad, a real live FBI agent coming to join us."

The friendly guard held fast to Rainey's arm. "We can't put her in there. If something happens, we'll be in big ass trouble," she told the other guard.

Rainey pulled loose and walked into the cell. She backed up to the bars for removal of the handcuffs, her jaw set in defiance.

"All right then, girl," the kinder guard said, releasing the cuffs. "Go on in there, but don't turn your back on them and watch that one in the cell to the left. Don't get close to those bars. That one's real mean."

Rainey rubbed her wrist and moved away from the door, as the dead bolts clanged back into place. She headed toward the back left corner of the cell. All the other prisoners were on the right side bunks, apparently staying clear of whoever was in the adjacent cell. Rainey figured she would have a better chance of defending herself against an assailant separated from her by iron bars, than mingling in the other women's lair. She did not search the cell for the occupant, keeping her eyes averted to the floor. No eye contact and do not lose focus, she reminded herself. She found a good defensive position and waited for the jackals to circle the new prey, prey with a badge. It would make no difference to these women that Rainey no longer carried the credentials. Once a cop, always a cop.

A large woman, with the glassy, red-rimmed eyes of an addict coming down, stood and started toward Rainey. "You an FBI agent? I hate cops," she growled.

"Hold on now, Big Momma," one of the smaller women said. "You kill that girl and you ain't never gonna see the light of day again."

Another woman approached—not as big as the first—eyeing Rainey with murderous intent. "Go on, Big Momma, fuck her up," she said. "You'll get props for that over at the women's prison. They'll make you a hero."

Rainey prepared to make her stand, as the women began to form a semi-circle in front of her. She was trained in self-defense, but the chances of her surviving a beat down by six motivated women were slim. Rainey was tough, in good shape, and could hold her own in a fair fight, but she was also a realist. This was going to be painful. She tried to remember some of the new

111

defensive moves Gunny taught her since they started sparring together. As the women inched closer, Rainey was wishing Gunny were there to help her when her would-be attackers suddenly froze, their eyes widening.

Rainey heard movement in the adjacent cell. She had forgotten about the woman behind her, and moved too close to the bars. She jumped, but did not move fast enough. A large arm snaked through the bars and wrapped around Rainey's chest, pulling her back against the bars. She thought this was it, the day she would meet her maker, and was about to say her goodbyes to Katie and the kids, when the woman in the cell behind her spoke.

"Y'all go on, now. This is my friend."

Rainey glanced over her shoulder and broke out in a big grin. "Maybelline, I am so glad to see you," she said to the giant woman, whose meaty arm held her pressed to the bars.

"You stay right here. They won't mess with you." She glared at Rainey's cellmates. "Ain't that right?"

The mob moved back, returning to the right side of the cell. A few mumbled under their breath, but none wanted to take on Maybelline or the network the smalltime criminal mob boss controlled. Those women hoped to be back out on the street one day. That can be a lonely place when the word is out someone is looking for you. Maybelline released her grip on Rainey, allowing her to turn and face her.

"Maybelline," Rainey said, knowing the news she bore was not going to be pleasant. "I know what happened to Jacquie."

Rainey explained her daughter's fate to Maybelline as the other inmates listened. They seemed to understand that the time for aggression had passed. A woman was grieving her daughter and they respected that, remaining quiet. Rainey sat down in the corner next to the bars, where Maybelline sobbed in pain. She stuck her arm through the bars and around the shoulder of the weeping mother, whispering how sorry she was. They stayed quiet like that for almost an hour, when the guards returned.

"Come on, FBI. Your lawyer is here," the not so nice one said.

The other guard smiled at Rainey, while she handcuffed her again. "Yeah, and that lawyer is pissed. Said we better have you back in your street clothes and downstairs, before she has a chance to rain federal agents down on this jail. Scared the pants off the guys downstairs when she whipped out that phone and got some guy from Quantico to start yelling at people."

The other guard was playing nice, too, now that the tide appeared to be turning. "At first they all thought Jodie Foster had walked in, until they realized it was Molly Kincaid, which seemed to excite them even more. They said her name like she was the righteous hand of God himself. Never seen people moving so fast to get a prisoner released."

Rainey laughed. "Yep, that's my lawyer."

#

"You better bring somebody else in here to question me. I'm not talking to that dickhead, King," Rainey said, glaring at the mirrored glass in the interrogation room. "And turn off the damn speaker. I'm talking to my attorney."

Molly sat perfectly still, elbows on the table, chin resting in her hands while Rainey ranted. When Rainey took a breath, she sat back. "Are you done?"

Rainey stopped pacing and sat down at the table next to the impeccably dressed Molly. The navy blue suit she wore set off her big blue eyes. Attorney Kincaid cut an impressive swath through the courtrooms of the south, much like Sherman brought the realities of the Civil War to the plantation doors of the wealthy men who began it. She was extraordinary, but to Rainey she was just Molly, a colleague, who over the past two years had become a dear friend.

"Thank you for allowing me that little tantrum. I had remained calm for about as long as I was able."

"I could see that," Molly said, grinning. "The vein in your neck was vibrating. That jaw clinch is a tell, as well. I'll have to remember that the next time we play poker. I'm in the hole deep."

"Playing poker with me and Leslie is probably not the smartest thing you've ever done. A behavioral analyst and a psychologist, both trained to read body language. Nope, not in your best interest."

"That's okay," Molly said, a mischievous glint in her eye. "I'm an attorney and devious by nature. I will prevail. By the way, teaching Katie to play poker was not your best move, either. I believe she cleaned you out the last time. You, my friend, cannot bluff your wife."

"Can you believe she went all-in with me, holding only a pair of sevens, with face cards on the table?"

"And you had?" Molly asked, like they were two old friends just chatting on the veranda, not an attorney with a client under arrest for murder.

Rainey liked that about Molly. She stayed in control. The only time Rainey had ever seen Molly flustered involved Leslie and a very wet tee shirt.

"Well, I had nothing, but –"

"Give it up, Bell. Katie reads you like a book. You don't even have the secrets you think you do."

Rainey laughed. "Yeah, you're probably right."

The door opened, and in walked Rex King and Wiley Trainer. The jovial mood instantly left. Molly put her hand up in front of Rainey, signaling her to remain quiet. This was Molly's area of expertise, not Rainey's. Hers was on the other side of the table, trying to question a suspect while people like Molly thwarted that effort. She was happy to let Molly do her thing.

Rainey kept telling herself this would all be an amusing story one day. She chose to ignore her knowledge of wrongfully convicted individuals, who served years in prison before being proven not guilty. What kind of evidence could they have anyway? She did not do it.

"Ms. Kincaid, it's a pleasure, as always," Wiley said.

"Nice to see you again, Captain Trainer, and if we could dispense with the pleasantries, would you mind explaining why my client, whom you trusted in a hostage situation last night, is sitting here in handcuffs this morning?"

"Well, Rainey," he said, directing his answer to her. "It seems we have a ballistics match on your Glock 19 with the bullets removed from one Bernard "Bobo" Jackson at an early morning autopsy."

"How could you have—"

Molly cleared her throat and made a face at Rainey. "Really, why am I here?" she asked her wayward client.

Rainey acquiesced and shut her mouth.

"As my client was about to ask, how could you have a match that fast? You just took her weapon into evidence an hour ago."

"Your client," Rex said, smirking at Rainey, "used that weapon to shoot Jared Howard in 2011."

"In self-defense," Molly said, making sure to get that on the interview transcript Rainey was sure was being recorded in the other room.

Rex droned on, as if she never spoke, "Therefore, there was a record of that weapon in the system. The lab is double-checking the results with the Glock removed from your client's car. What, Rainey? You didn't have time to dump the weapon before the cops showed up in your backyard this morning?"

Molly chuckled. Rainey did not see the humor in the situation. The word "FRAMED" screamed out in her brain in bold capital letters. This asshole was going to put her in prison with evidence he fabricated. She was just about to say that when Molly started talking.

"I see the handy work of the same ambitious prosecutor and the detective with a vendetta involved in the last fiasco of assigning blame where there was none. Prove my client's gun was involved in the shooting and then we'll talk. Until you do, I'm assuming you will be releasing her."

Wiley rubbed his chin, thinking a moment before replying. "Well, we do have this record match."

Molly stood up. "And computers have the wrong data uploaded to them every single day. Until you have a match to the weapon that was removed from my client's car this morning, you have no grounds to hold her."

Rex came unglued. "You're not seriously considering letting her go, are you? She'll run. She knows she's caught."

"My client is well respected. In fact, this very police department uses her services frequently. She has a wife, children, and strong ties to the community."

"Those are not her kids and that sham lesbian marriage isn't enough to keep her here. Those ties don't bind like a real marriage," Rex spat, nearly foaming at the mouth.

Before either Molly or Rainey could respond, Wiley turned to Rex. "Now, that'll be enough of that. Do you have any evidence other than the old ballistics match?"

"The security cameras at the hospital show her leaving just before Bobo was killed not two blocks from there," Rex argued.

Molly jumped in. "That's it? That's all you have. How many other cars left the hospital or were in the area when Mr. Jackson was shot? Who else knew he was a paid informant? Have you spoken to the security firm that logs my client's comings and goings from her home? Did she have time to commit this crime?"

Molly would not have asked the questions, if she did not already know the answers. She had spent the time Rainey was in custody, making the case for her client's innocence. She continued to chastise Rex.

"You haven't done your homework detective. You jumped the gun, so to speak." Molly finished with a satisfied smile that spread to Rainey's face.

"All right," Wiley said, standing. "Give me your hands." Rainey held out her wrists, while he unlocked the cuffs. "I've known you since you were a girl, Rainey, so I'm letting you go, but if your weapon matches the bullets taken from the body, then I expect you to come on in for a chat."

Rainey spoke before Molly could stop her. "I didn't kill Bobo Jackson, Wiley, and you know it. If those bullets match, you'll have to testify that Rex here had my weapon last night and he took custody of it again this morning." She glared at the mirror, knowing the prosecutor was behind the glass, watching. "Rex didn't mention that when he came to you for a warrant, did he? He had ample time to manipulate the evidence. Look at it closely before you come after me again."

"Are you accusing me of framing you? The O. J. defense, now that's original," Rex scoffed.

Molly had grown very interested while Rainey was speaking. They had not talked about the weapon being in Rex's hands, because Rainey just learned of its significance a moment ago.

Molly launched into Rex. "You arrested my client for shooting a man with a weapon that you had in your possession not once, but twice in the last twelve hours. Did you allow anyone else access to the weapon? Was it in your sight the entire time? Is there a documented chain of custody? Did you want to make a case for tampering, or are you just that incompetent?"

Rainey couldn't help herself. "She's too nice to call you an idiot, but I'm not. Fuck off, Rex."

#

Rainey exited the holding area, after having her personal items returned, and joined Molly in the hallway. They walked toward the lobby, while Rainey made a mental note to avoid ever being strip searched again at all costs. She spent her FBI career learning to think like the criminals she studied, examining their experiences closely. The strip search was one more thing with which she could now empathize, but would have happily existed without intimate knowledge of the experience.

She saw Katie waiting on the other side of the glass doors to the lobby. Ernie was there too. So much for following Rainey's instructions. Rainey looked down at Molly.

"Would I go to jail if I put one of those shock collars on her, so she couldn't leave the yard when I told her to stay home?"

"Yes, I'd advise against that. I think your best bet is to have a GPS chip implanted, so you can retrieve her when she strays."

Rainey opened the door to the lobby, smiling at Molly. "I've actually looked into that, for her and the kids."

Molly shook her head, saying, "Why does that not surprise me?"

Katie hurried toward them. "Are you okay?"

"Yes, and why are you here? I told you to go home."

Ernie explained, "I told her to do what you said, but she insisted we needed to come bail you out of jail. I tried to tell her that a murder charge would have to wait for a bail hearing and your best bet was to let Molly here get them to let you go, but you know how Katie is."

"Yes, I do," Rainey said, but could not help the smile that crept onto her lips. "How is Mackie?"

117

"He's scheduled for surgery in the morning," Ernie said. "He's fine. Junior told him you had been to see him while he was asleep. A little white lie, so he won't worry about you."

"Good thinking," Rainey said. "You might want to hide the TV remote, too."

"Thelma is on it. She's not letting him watch any of the local or news channels, during the little time he is awake. He's pretty doped up."

"Agent Bell?" A man's voice echoed off the marble walls and floor.

Rainey turned to see him coming toward her. She instinctively positioned her body in front of Katie, and said, "Not anymore, but I used to be. Can I help you?"

"I hope so," he said.

As he grew closer, Rainey could see the anguish in his eyes. She also thought his face pinged a memory, but was not sure from where.

He extended his hand. "Colonel Patrick Asher, retired Army. I attended several of your lectures at Quantico, when I was still with the Criminal Investigation Command out of Fort Bragg."

Rainey vaguely remembered his face. There were so many law enforcement personnel attending classes at Quantico, very few stood out.

"How can I help you, Colonel Asher?"

His eyes welled with tears. "It's my daughter. She's missing."

"Have you contacted the police?" Rainey felt his pain, but at the moment, she had her hands full.

"Yes, but they are waiting for the BAU to get here. She doesn't have that much time if this serial killer has her."

Rainey knew people went missing all the time. Most of them were not victims of foul play. "What makes you think she was abducted?"

Colonel Asher pulled out his phone and tapped the screen while he talked. "She was supposed to call last night after she got home from class, but she didn't. When her mother and I couldn't reach her, I drove up from Fayetteville. I found her vehicle, not in her space, unlocked, keys in the ignition. Her book bag was on the front seat, with her phone and wallet still in it. This was up against the back tire."

He turned the phone around to show Rainey the image of a hypodermic needle cap on the pavement, just under the edge of the tire. It was new and had not been there long. It had to have rolled there while the vehicle was parked. Colonel Asher was right, there did appear to be foul play afoot.

The Colonel had one more piece of the puzzle to add. "I talked to her last night. She was upset that this red truck kept parking in her assigned space, off and on for the past two weeks. That's why she was forced to park at the end of the lot in the guest spaces. She was walking to her car, and saw the truck again. She commented on it, right before we hung up. I think that was him." He tapped the phone screen again and pulled up another picture, this one the image of a vehicle door with a fresh ding in the paint. "Look at this. This is recent. It's red paint, like someone opened a red car door into the driver's side of her Jeep."

"Did you show this to the investigators?" Rainey knew she was looking at possibly the only break in the missing women's case.

"Yes, and I told them that I asked her to write down the tag number of the truck. It didn't feel right. I don't know if she did. She was in a hurry."

"Where is the vehicle now?" Rainey wanted to know. "Maybe she did write it down and it's in the car somewhere."

"I didn't see evidence of her doing that, but I didn't poke around too much. I left everything in her Jeep as I found it and they sent a team out to bring it back to the forensics garage." His frustration mounted. "I can't wait around for paint test results or the BAU to pull someone off the inauguration threat assessments to come down here. At this point, she's nobody's priority but mine."

Rainey had not thought about the inauguration. Danny and the team would be assisting the Secret Service and up to their elbows in the loony bin—the files where all the nuts were watched carefully for threats that might come to fruition. In addition to other legitimate threats, the loonies all had to be located, checked on, and detained if necessary to ensure the safety of those in attendance at the inauguration. Danny would be hard pressed to find someone he could afford to break away from such a monumental task.

"I'm sure the BAU is trying to free someone up as soon as possible and I know the locals are pursuing every lead until they get here," Rainey offered as some reassurance that the Colonel's daughter was somebody's priority.

He was not placated. "You're here now. They told me you were off the case, but you have to help me. That's my daughter. She'll fight as long as she can. I know she will, but she can't hold out too long." A single tear ran down his cheek. "I saw the pictures in the squad room of that woman they found this morning." As hard as he tried to hold it together, he could not. His knees buckled a little. "Oh, God—Bladen. What is he doing to her?"

Rainey reached out to steady him. Her heart broke for the man, but what could she do? "Colonel Asher, I don't know if they told you, but I'm under suspicion of murder. I've just been released from custody. I'm not sure how much help I can be."

Asher pulled himself back together. "Sergeant Robertson said there was only this one rogue detective that even imagined you were involved. She said she had no doubt that you'd be cleared of the charges. She told me how to find you."

It was good to know other people thought Rex was out of control, too.

"She said you backed off the case because of your family. I know I don't have a right to ask you to put them in danger, but I don't know where else to turn."

Katie had heard enough and took charge. "Colonel Asher, Rainey will help you." She turned to Rainey. "I will go home and stay there under lock and key with Gunny. You go help the colonel. Ernie and Junior will take care of Mackie." She put her fingertips on Rainey's arm, her voice soft. "If it were your daughter, you'd tear the world apart looking for her. Help him. You're his only hope right now."

Rainey had no choice when Katie put it that way. She turned to Molly. "Is there any legal reason I can't carry a weapon?" She was going to help, but not unarmed.

Molly shook her head. "No, you are still licensed to carry in the state until otherwise notified."

"Do you have a car, Colonel Asher? Mine was impounded."

"That detective really doesn't like you, does he?" Colonel Asher replied, his relief evident.

Rainey shook her head. "No, he doesn't, so I'm without transportation at the moment."

"You can ride with me," he said. "I should take you to her apartment, so you can profile the vict—Bladen. I know you like to start there."

Rainey looked at Katie. "And you're all right with this?"

Katie smiled. "You go do what you do, catch this guy and find the Colonel's daughter. The kids and I will be safe at home, I promise you."

Rainey crossed the few steps to Katie, hugging her close and whispering in her ear. "I love you. Please stay home, no matter what. I'll call you." She gave Katie a kiss on the forehead, and turned back to Molly. "Keep that jackass, King, off my back for a few days, and get my car out of impound, if you can, before they have a chance to tear it apart."

Molly answered Rainey's request, "Leslie is out of town and my calendar is clear for the rest of the week, so I can focus on keeping you out of prison, but don't give King an excuse to take you into custody. I'm also working on obtaining a copy of the security tapes from the hospital. Since we need them now to prove your timeline, finding the stalker will be a bonus."

Colonel Asher looked confused. "You are suspected in a murder, a body was found in your backyard, and you have a stalker, too?"

Rainey smiled. "Welcome to the Rainey season, Colonel Asher."

#

Bladen's head lay next to the water bowl. Through much painful maneuvering, she had managed to consume some of the protein drink from the tube and inch around to the water, where she lapped at the contents like the dog the bowl was meant for. She still jumped each time the loud music burst into the room,

121

and the dripping continued, but the nourishment had given her strength. She rested now, awaiting his return. Bladen had reached the low point and was now scratching her way back to the surface, where hope remained.

"Fight him, Bladen," she whispered to herself. "Don't give up." She thought of her father. He would be looking for her by now. "Find me, Dad. I'll hang on, but you have to hurry."

The music blared out of the speaker. Bladen slammed her eyes shut against the demonic screams and the pain the flinching created between her legs. Immediately, her mind was flooded with the image of the red king cab truck that had recently begun parking in her assigned space at random times, forcing her to park in the dark guest area near the woods surrounding her apartment complex. She was walking to the isolated parking lot, talking to her parents on the phone, when she saw the truck backed into the adjacent parking space. She remembered being frustrated, because it had been in her assigned space earlier, and commented to her father about it. The memory failed at that point, replaced by the flash of being forced into that truck and then nothing.

Her phone—Bladen needed her dad to find her phone. Yes, there was hope. It warmed her from the inside out. She smiled for the first time since she awoke in this hellhole. Even though she told him he was paranoid, Bladen was always the good girl and did as he instructed, because Colonel Patrick Asher really did know a thing or two about life. She had learned to listen. He knew that boy she loved in high school was a poor choice and he was right. He knew the weather was going to turn bad, keeping her home and preventing her from being injured in the icy crash that nearly killed her best friend. He knew something was not right about that truck and told her so, asking her to write down the tag number and tell the apartment manager, but Bladen had done better than that.

"Look at my phone, Dad. I took a picture of his truck."

#

The colonel spent the drive down from Durham to Rainey's office talking about Bladen. The twenty-two-year-old was his pride and joy. She was an early education major, student teaching this semester and scheduled to graduate in May. No steady boyfriend at the moment, she was too focused on school. Most of her social interactions were among a small group of friends. Bladen had never been a discipline problem and was always a good student. She was an avid runner, a passion left over from her high school cross-country days. She was careful and smart, trained by a father who knew protective security measures, which made her a low risk for becoming a victim. Her abductor had put a great deal of planning into her capture. This told Rainey he liked the game, the hunt, the laying of the snare, as much as the springing of the trap.

Rainey listened carefully, forming a profile of the victim while she gave directions to the little house Bell's Bail called home. A mile and a half from Chapel Hill on East Franklin Street, the location was selected because seven courthouses were seated within a forty-mile radius of the front door. It sat away from the adjacent businesses on a heavily wooded lot. Through the trees, it was barely possible to see the art gallery to the west and the secondhand store on the east. Ernie had a good eye for what Rainey would consider a safe distance from her neighbors, when the move to the new office was planned. Rainey was reluctant to leave her father's home and the office on the lake, but she was able to visit often since Katie's foundation bought the land and housed the women's shelter there. She had also grown to like the centrally located new home of Billy Bell's Bail. Rainey thought Billy would have approved.

After unlocking the door and silencing the alarm, Rainey led Colonel Asher through the living room/dining room area, which served as Ernie's office. On the right, a hall led to bedrooms and the bathroom. Mackie used the front bedroom for his office space, which he graciously shared with Junior. The other bedroom housed records and office machines. The kitchen, in the back of the house and on the left, was on the way to the stairway leading to Rainey's office over the attached garage. She liked the isolation, away from the foot traffic downstairs, and the fact no one could see in her windows. Rainey sometimes had things on the four dry-erase boards lining her walls that should be shielded from prying eyes. Like today, she realized, when she unlocked the door at the top of the stairs.

Two of the dry-erase boards were placed end to end along one of the long walls, and were dedicated to the serial rape cases. Photos of twelve women were taped along a timeline of the attacks, revealing their injuries, with handwritten notes under each. Shorthand notes, but enough was there to depict in graphic detail what the rapist said and did to them. A map hung on the wall near the timeline with red pushpins indicating where each rape took place. These were the notes and visual aids she used to work the case, things she would not hang on her office walls at home, things Rainey never meant a man searching for his missing daughter to see.

Rainey turned to him. "I'm sorry about the evidence photos, Colonel. I'm consulting on a serial rape case too."

His eyes trailed over the pictures. "As bad as I hate to say this, after seeing what that animal did to the woman found behind your house," he pointed at the photos, "I would rather my daughter be on that board than where I fear she is now."

Rainey did not respond, because she would have reinforced his belief. If his daughter was in the hands of the man that held Jacquie, Bladen Asher was suffering a great deal more than those women on Rainey's boards. It did not lessen the damage done the serial rape survivors. There was no comparative scale or degree of rape, as far as Rainey was concerned. She detested those that would diminish a rape survivor's trauma, merely because she did survive, or because they deemed the resistance too ineffectual to have been a sincere effort. Unlike the deeds of the power assertive serial rapist displayed on Rainey's boards, the man who probably held Bladen was a sadistic sexual murderer, whose gratification was gained from instilling terror and inflicting torturous pain on his victim, ultimately leading to death. Bladen would have fared better with the rapist. Her father knew that without Rainey's confirmation.

After a moment more of studying the rape case boards, he spoke. "I've been following this case. I advised Bladen to go to your presentation Monday night."

"That's interesting," Rainey said, walking to the white board to add a date and name to the timeline. She wrote Alana Minott's name and yesterday's date on the board. "This is the latest rape victim. She, too, attended that lecture."

Colonel Patrick Asher was an experienced investigator, but it did not take a genius to see the common denominator here was Rainey. "If he was following Bladen, he might have been at your lecture. Maybe that's why he left the body where he did."

"The serial rapist was getting too much attention. They're both narcissists and competing for the spotlight. The body was the killer's coming out announcement." Rainey walked over to the opposite wall where a large satellite image of the Triangle area hung. It was stuck with nine red pushpins. She placed another pin where Jacquie had been taken, and then asked, "Where did you say Bladen was abducted?"

The colonel pointed out Bladen's address. Rainey pushed a pin in the location and took a step back from it.

"That fits," she said, pointing at the map. "You see this rough circle the pins form. These are the missing women we think were all taken by the same guy."

Rainey picked up a yardstick from the corner and measured the distance between several of the pins. Finding center, she pressed a blue pin in. Taking some yarn from a nearby table, she looped one end around the center pin. Measuring the scaled distance from the center to the outer most abduction location, she wrapped the loose end of the piece of yarn around a marker, and drew a circle on the map.

"He's in here, within this twenty-mile radius, and I'm guessing somewhere near here." She indicated an anomaly, a lone pin near the center point. "This was the first victim, we think. She was a college student, never came home after leaving a babysitting job. They found her car with a flat tire on the side of the road, here. He moved out to the prostitute areas for a while after that, and then found his preferred targets, young independent women."

The colonel knew how to create a geographic profile. If he had the same information as Rainey, she was quite sure he would have come to the same conclusion. He was looking at the list of women and the dates they went missing, written on one of the other dry-erase boards.

"This timeline is all wrong," he noted. "These first abductions were closer together than the last. They usually escalate, not grow further apart."

"We couldn't be certain it was the same guy, but after seeing the body this morning, I'm pretty sure it is. I think he was experimenting, learning which fantasies worked best for him. The body would indicate that he's discovered he likes sadistic torture and that means spending more time with his victims." Rainey saw the pained look cross the colonel's face. "I'm sorry to be so frank with you."

He waved her apology away. "No, no, I appreciate your honesty. It's the only way we'll find her."

Concerns for the father aside, Rainey addressed the investigator he used to be. "Between these first abductions and the ones that began to space out, I think he was constructing his lair. In order to have the time to do what he did to the victim we know about, he had to have an isolated, private space, one not easily discovered by others." She pointed at the map again. "See all this undeveloped land in the center, here. I'll bet money his torture chamber is in there somewhere."

"And that's where we should look for the red truck," the colonel answered.

Rainey smiled at him, heading for the gun safe on the office wall. "I think I have a friend who can help with that. First, let me get my weapon and then we'll go to Bladen's apartment. That will give the forensics team some time before we go look at her vehicle."

Rainey opened the safe and took out the Beretta 92FS she kept there.

"M-9, good weapon," Colonel Asher said.

"My favorite is the Glock 19, but since the police have that at the moment, this will do."

126

He reached under his jacket, coming out with an M-9 of his own. "My favorite weapon is the one in my hand, when faced with a kill or die situation."

"I hear that, Colonel. I most definitely hear that."

\#

In Bladen's apartment, Rainey found the lodgings of a tidy, organized, young woman. She spoke as she walked the space, a habit that worked for her and her old partner, Danny, on many investigations. Her "partner" on this walkthrough happened to be the father of the victim, but she did not temper her remarks for him. She was not telling him things he did not know. He offered insights of his own, the investigator in him trying to contain the emotional father. Years of military training had allowed him to compartmentalize. Rainey admired this ability, because she knew all too well how hard it was to maintain those boxes, where monster hunters kept their most precious possessions, family.

"Your influence is evident, Colonel. Your daughter's quarters are immaculate, closets and cabinets organized, minimal clutter, the home of a military man's daughter."

He opened the refrigerator, which was a cluttered mess of take-out containers. "Her rebellious side peeks through some of the spit and polish, though," he said, grinning. "She also hates to cook."

First grade worksheets were stacked neatly on the kitchen table, graded with smiley faces. Rainey recognized a few from helping Katie pack up her classroom when she resigned from the first grade teaching job she loved to recover from the trauma that changed her life. Rainey hoped Bladen could return those worksheets to her students personally, but every hour that crept by made that less and less likely.

"What do you see, Rainey?" The colonel asked, after she had been quiet for a moment.

"I see a young woman who added a dead bolt to her door, a pole lock on her balcony door, and I found a pistol in her bedside table drawer."

"I gave it to her. She is licensed and trained, but she never carries it."

Rainey smiled. "Then what does she carry? I'm sure with you as a father, there was either pepper spray or possibly a stun gun in play here."

"Pepper spray and a personal alarm on her keychain. I insisted," the colonel replied. "And she had self-defense training."

"When she ran, was it outdoors, alone?" Rainey asked, examining the books on Bladen's desk and finding only school related material.

"No, she ran on the treadmill here at the complex gym, except for when her running club went out on the weekends. She was careful. She was prepared," he said emphatically.

Rainey knew he was questioning what else he could have done to secure his daughter from the monsters that walk among us. He knew they were there. The colonel was a man who spent the better part of thirty years hunting them for the army. He was in the business of protecting his soldiers, both from each other and from those outside the military that would harm them. Colonel Asher had almost certainly investigated his share of sexual predators in the alpha male world of the armed forces. He had prepared his daughter for the worst, and still he was tormented with the thought he had not done enough. Rainey faced these same fears for her own children, as her father had done for her.

"Colonel, my father did all he could to prepare me for the world. I was also a trained FBI agent, much more capable and aware than a twenty-two-year-old college senior, and still I was abducted. There is nothing you or she could have done. When a criminal like this goes after a target, his patience usually wins out over all precautions."

She gave him a moment to let that sink in. "So, let's use what we know about Bladen to tell us about her abductor. He's above average intelligence. I'd say very intelligent. He stalked her, knew her patterns, and took his time learning about her. Planning like that takes patience and cunning. He's organized, has a vehicle to transport his victims, and if that needle cap proves to be part of his MO, he was prepared to handle someone like Bladen who would have fought him. He may have picked her specifically because she would be a challenge, but he'd have to know he could gain control of her. You saw no evidence of a struggle at her car, correct?"

"No, nothing like that. It looked like she just vanished."

Rainey nodded her head. "That's consistent with the other women, with two exceptions. About the time he changed targets from street people to more affluent women, there was evidence of a struggle. One woman's briefcase fell open, scattering paperwork around the parking lot where she was taken. The next woman struggled with him. A piece of her blouse was found under the edge of her car tire, and she was also abducted from a parking lot. After that, there were no signs of disturbance. That's probably when he started using drugs to subdue them."

"Or his con improved," the colonel suggested.

"That's true, he could have learned how to be more efficient at luring them into his trap. It's probably a combination of both," Rainey said, moving toward the door. "I'd like to see the car now. I'll need to make a call first." The colonel was hesitant to leave. Rainey knew he needed a moment to gather strength for the next phase. "I'll just step into the hall, while you lock up."

Rainey pulled the phone from her coat pocket and closed the apartment door behind her. The screen saver on her phone showed a picture of Katie and the triplets, laughing wildly. She remembered taking it, her hand shaking from laughing with them. This was the only shot that was not motion blurred. Strained peas in the hair and all, Rainey loved being a parent. That realization hit her several times a day. It always caught her by surprise. She had been so sure she would fail miserably at raising children. She looked down at the picture of the four loves of her life and was immediately drawn back to the father of a missing child, inside the apartment. She could not let her empathy overwhelm reason, but the reminder did not hurt. Rainey understood more profoundly than ever before that nine daughters were still missing—one found—and all were someone's child.

She pushed the contact number for her favorite detective. "Sheila Robertson, I might have known you would stoop to sending a devastated father to rope me back into this case."

Sheila chuckled. "Well, I'm assuming my manipulation worked. How else can I help? Do you need me to run over Rex with my car?"

"Not a bad idea," Rainey said, laughing. "Really, what I need is for you to meet me in the forensics garage. I have a plan."

"You're not planning on stealing your car out of there, are you?"

"No, but you better get there before I do and make sure my baby is in the same shape I left her. I wouldn't want to cause a scene. You know how I feel about my car."

"Yes, I do, so I'll go down now and make sure it's being lovingly looked after." She paused, then excitement crept into her voice. "Oh, I forgot. The ballistic report came back on your Glock."

"So, am I cleared now? Can I go on with my life without Rex King up my ass?"

"Well, not exactly. The barrel of your gun did fire the bullets that killed Bobo Jackson."

Rainey was shocked into saying rather loudly, "What the fuck?"

"Wait for it," Sheila said, teasing out the information. "The barrel of your weapon fired the bullets, but the firing pin and breech face impressions, along with the ejector mark on the casing found at the scene, were made by a different weapon."

"Rex took my weapon apart last night. He gave it back to me in a box," Rainey said, very sure now that Rex King was setting her up for murder. "He took it into custody himself, this morning. That fucker is framing me, Sheila. It's so obvious it's almost pathetic."

"Fortunately for you, enough people saw the Glock in Rex's possession. The brass told him he needs more evidence to bring you back in. FYI, rumor has it, he's trying to get search warrants for your home and office."

"Damn, Katie will be pissed if they tear up the house or upset the kids."

"Someone may be framing you for murder, and you're worried about what Katie will say. Man, you have mellowed into an old married lady." Sheila paused, her tone more consoling.

"No one would blame you if you went home to take care of your business. We can look for this girl without you."

The colonel came out of the apartment, locking the door behind him. Rainey saw the grimness of his expression.

"I'm in this for the long haul," Rainey said, "or until they lock me up, whichever comes first."

"No way that murder charge ever sticks to you. You're right, and I'm not the only one who thinks so. Someone is manipulating evidence. The question seems to be who that person is, not whether you killed a man."

"Oh, Molly will see to the already mind-fuckingly-tainted murder charges, Sheila. I'll be going into cuffs for trying out the new self-defense move Gunny taught me on Detective King. It's called the hammer-blow."

"Please let me be the arresting officer," Sheila replied, laughing. "I'll be gentle with the cuffs."

"Bring the pink ones," Rainey said. "See you in about twenty minutes."

She hung up and put her phone away. The colonel's grim scowl had changed into a smile.

"What?" She asked, wondering what he found so amusing.

"I can see why you survived your assault. Up against murder charges and you're all piss and vinegar. You're hard to knock down. You remind me of Bladen."

Rainey did not have the heart to tell him the only reason she survived was an inadvertent siren that scared her attacker away. Luck saved her, nothing nobler than that.

She decided to give him some hope instead. "Then she's giving this guy hell. Let's go find your daughter."

CHAPTER SEVEN

Colonel Asher pulled his sedan into a parking space outside the forensics garage enclosure, as directed by the officer on duty. Rainey's phone rang in her pocket, just as she reached for the door handle. She stepped out of the car, pulled out the phone and saw it was Molly calling.

"I need to take this. It's my lawyer," she said to the colonel, as he exited the car.

He moved toward the entrance checkpoint to give her some privacy, pulling out his own phone to make a call.

Rainey slid her finger across the screen to answer. "Guess you've called to warn me my home and office are about to be searched."

"How the hell do you do that?" Molly replied.

Rainey chuckled. "I have mystical powers. Have you warned Katie, yet?"

"Oh, so your mystical powers don't include telling a certain little blonde that her house is about to be raided. I suppose you were waiting for me to soften the blow."

"I think that was wise, don't you? She won't blame you, and if she does, you can still go home. I have to live with her."

"Well, you're safe for the time being," Molly said. "She's mad, but not at you. I'm at your house. Ernie is at the office, now.

"Should I come home?" Rainey asked.

"No, I think it is best if you stay far away. I'll have my hands full keeping your wife out of cuffs. Oh, and your mother is on the phone demanding an explanation from somebody, not sure from whom, but it appears to be a government official."

"With my mother's social circle, that could be anybody. Let her do what she does. Trying to stop her will only make it worse."

Rainey knew Molly could understand the dysfunctional relationship she had with Constance Herndon. Molly and Rainey both had life altering experiences with their respective mothers at age ten. It was probably one of the reasons Rainey liked Molly so much. Molly had her own demons with which to deal.

"Hey, if your mother wants to call in the big dogs, let her," Molly said. "This whole thing stinks of conspiracy to frame you. Did you see the ballistics report?"

Rainey kicked at a rock on the pavement in frustration. "No, but Detective Robertson told me about it. Should I be worried, Molly?"

"Rainey, if you go to prison for this, I'll be sitting right there in the cell with you. Just let me handle it and keep your mouth shut. I'll let them in here, give them your weapons, and send them on their way. Ernie is at the office, and she'll deal with everything there. You just stay calm. It sounds like you are, which kind of surprises me, actually."

"Well, I'm trying to concentrate on finding this missing girl, rather than the demise of one Rex King. And what do you mean 'weapons'? Why are they taking all my weapons? I thought they were looking for another Glock, which I don't own by the way."

"I argued that, along with having Rex King removed from the case. His obvious conflict of interest precludes his participation. He was removed, but they want all the weapons. The argument being, you may be a dangerous criminal. I had to give them that—the dangerous part anyway," Molly said, with a chuckle.

"I'm dangerous to King right now, that's for sure. I think my dad slept with his wife, but this is extreme payback if that's his motive."

133

"Are you sure he's the only person who had access to your weapon?" Molly asked.

"No, I'm not. Gunny, Junior, and the other runners, they had access to it, and I don't know where it was while Rex had it. Gunny and Junior, I trust them with my kids, so I certainly trust them with my weapon. The runners, I'm not really familiar with them, but I can't imagine why they would do something like this. Besides, how did they change the barrel back?"

Molly was on top of things and looking at every angle. "The Glock was in your car at the hospital this morning. I'm sure it's like your house and sends out an alarm to wake the dead if someone tries to break into it, but has anyone had access to your keys? They can clone those electronic keys now, you know."

Rainey thought about it and remembered her coat being moved in Wiley's car. "Yeah, I did leave my keys in my coat last night. Someone moved it, left a note in my pocket about the serial rapist."

"How long does it take to switch barrels on a Glock?"

"If you've done it enough, fifteen to twenty seconds tops."

"Well, there you have it," Molly said, "another plausible scenario. If your key was cloned and they were following you this morning, then it is possible the barrel was switched back while you were inside the hospital and before Detective King seized the weapon. It's also possible someone else in the chain of custody has a problem with you."

"I guess that's why you get the big bucks," Rainey said, truly glad someone was thinking of possible reasons her Glock barrel killed a man, but not the weapon itself. "Speaking of bucks, I'd like to do something for Bobo's family, make sure he gets a decent burial. It appears someone killed him to get at me. I feel bad about that, but under the circumstances, I'm not sure I should contact them."

Molly answered quickly, "No, don't do that, at least not yet. Let's get through this search and see what else they throw at us first. They won't do anything with the body for a few days, anyway. It's an open investigation and less than twenty-four hours old. You'll have time to make arrangements later, when you are completely in the clear."

"And that's going to happen, you're pretty positive?" Rainey asked, allowing a bit of apprehension to slip into her voice.

Molly was reassuringly confident. "You find the Colonel's daughter. I've got this."

"Thanks, Molly. I appreciate you dealing with my problems." Rainey turned to see the colonel had finished his call and was handing his weapon over to the officer in charge of the checkpoint, which prompted her next question. "Hey, what about the weapon I'm carrying? Should I turn it in while I'm here at the forensics garage?"

"How convenient. Sure, make it easy on them," Molly said. "And Rainey, watch your back. If it isn't King, then it could be someone else in that department or even somebody closer to you."

"Yeah, I hear you. I've got to go. Don't let Katie get into to trouble. She's hard to wrangle when she's mad."

Molly laughed. "Oh, I know. I've discovered she really gets angry when someone questions your integrity. Your children may have learned some new words. I'm just glad her mother was here when I told her. She was able to calm her down and convince her not to hide all the weapons in the panic room."

"That's my girl," Rainey said. "Okay, call me if she needs bail money."

#

Sheila waited for Rainey at the checkpoint.

"I came to tell you the search warrant request went through and Rex King is in the garage, two things I was sure would not make you happy."

"On the contrary," Rainey said, "Molly is handling the warrants and I'm told Rex is off my case, so there shouldn't be any problems."

Sheila tilted her head to one side, an expression of confusion on her face. "Are you all right? You seem very calm for someone being framed for murder."

The colonel spoke up. "You can remain composed, when you're trained to ignore distractions."

"A murder charge is a hell of a distraction," Sheila commented.

Rainey removed the Beretta from her holster, dropped the ammunition magazine, and made sure the chamber was clear, before presenting it to Sheila. "I'm calm, because there are more pressing matters. Take this, and turn it into the lab. I'm also not worried, because I've got nothing to hide. Let them search and test all they want. They'll never find proof I killed Bobo, because I didn't. Now, I'd like a look at Bladen's vehicle and the personal items that were inside. Can you arrange that?"

"Already done," Sheila said, nodding at the colonel. "Colonel Asher has some friends in high places. Access to whatever you need is to be given, as long as you stay away from the Jackson murder investigation."

"I have no intention of coming anywhere near that case," Rainey said. "Let's go see what the forensics team found."

"Follow me then," Sheila said, moving to lead the way. "So, when are you letting me in on this plan?"

Rainey stepped up beside her and smiled. "I need a few more pieces of information and then I'll tell you. Until then, as far as anyone knows, you're just keeping an eye on me for the brass. Does that work for you?"

Sheila returned the smile. "Well, since that's what I'm really doing, I have no problem with that at all." Her phone began to ring. She took it out of her jacket pocket with her free hand, the other one still holding Rainey's weapon. "It's Dr. Wood. I told her to call me when the autopsy was complete."

"You didn't go yourself?" Rainey asked.

"No, I'm babysitting you," Sheila pointed out, before she answered the call. "Thank you for calling, Dr. Wood."

Shelia listened for a few minutes, while the colonel and Rainey waited patiently. Before she turned her back to them, the expression on Sheila's face told Rainey the horror they saw on the surface of the body was nothing compared to what a full autopsy had revealed.

Her suspicions were confirmed when Sheila turned back. "Would you mind repeating that to Rainey? She's here with me and I think her insights will be critical in finding out who did this."

Rainey took the phone. "Hello, Dr. Wood."

"Sorry to hear about your troubles, Rainey. Gossip travels fast I'm afraid. My two cents, if you did kill somebody, you would never use a weapon that could be traced back to you."

"Thank you for your vote of confidence," Rainey said, slightly amused that people really thought her capable of cold-blooded murder. At least, Dr. Wood thought her intelligent enough to pull it off. That had to count for something.

"Now, about Jacqueline Upshaw—this young woman suffered immeasurably. Quite frankly, I'm very surprised she lived through what she did. Incredible, just incredible."

"I take it the injuries were severe and many," Rainey said, as a way to move the doctor along.

"Oh yes, too many to list on the phone. I sent the report to Detective Robertson. The cause of death was internal bleeding produced by, if I'm not mistaken and you don't want to know how I know this, but I believe he used a Pear of Anguish, along with another instrument to rip her open internally. He used the phallus to plug her up, keeping the blood inside. Nice and tidy for him, excruciating death for her. There are indications suggesting this young woman was subjected to more than one medieval torture device."

"Really? You recognize the injuries as caused by medieval methods? How can you be so sure?"

"I spent a summer with a team of forensic pathologists uncovering a thirteenth century mass grave from the massacre of Cathars at Beziers, France. It was an education into the handiwork of the Inquisition's torturous methods, and a reminder that often what is done in God's name is indeed an example of the pure evil in man. A lesson not easily forgotten."

"How long did he keep her?"

Dr. Wood cleared her throat, as if to clear away the memory of what she had seen. "Without the test results, I can only give you an educated guess. Based on scarring and healing of injuries, I think this poor woman was tortured for three months, and was killed as recently as four weeks ago."

"Thank you, Dr. Wood. As bad as it sounds, that's good news for the woman he has now."

"Oh, good Lord. He has another one? My prayers are with her."

"She's going to need them," Rainey replied, silently contributing her own prayer for Bladen Asher, as well.

#

"You're probably asking yourself by now, why me?"

Bladen jerked awake from the momentary drift into not knowing. She did not think of it as sleep, but more a respite her mind took from reality. The drift would send her far away from her torment, sometimes to a blank nothingness, other times to a warm memory. Bladen could only achieve these short intervals of relief when the music was not vibrating through her bones. The maddening drip would begin with the abrupt end to the demonic snarling of unrecognizable lyrics, and with it, her anxiety would build. It took all her mental strength to calm herself into the drift. These moments of peace were the only thing keeping Bladen from losing her mind.

Lying in her own stinging excrement, raw from the ropes digging into her skin, her muscles cramping from immobility, Bladen had drifted to the beach. Her mother was beside her on the blanket, head tossed back, a full throaty laugh filling the air, as the waves crashed to the shore nearby. The sound of his voice startled her out of the memory. Bladen had not heard him come in—but had he?

"You're here because I saw you. I wanted you and I took you. It's as simple as that."

Bladen searched the darkness for movement.

"I spent my life living by other people's rules. What I have discovered is that following the rules gets you fucked, while those who don't follow them just take whatever they want and then some."

Bladen listened carefully, realizing his voice came from the speaker.

"Three years ago, they took everything from me. Now, I take what I want." He chuckled. "And I have to tell you, I wish I had started breaking the rules much sooner."

Bladen thought she heard a whimper, but his voice drowned it out.

"So, here you are. You will be here as long as I find you useful. Give up the fight, and you become a tedious problem that I will dispense with in some macabre fashion. Trust me, your death will be as painful as you imagine, because once you give in, the only pleasure I can get from you is watching you die slowly. I will then place you in my collection and move on to the next. Rest assured there is another in line, one I've watched just like I watched you."

This time Bladen was sure she heard a soft crying as he paused. She could hear him moving around on the recording, and then very clearly a woman begging, a weak, ragged whispered plea.

"Please, I want to see my baby again."

Bladen heard the whip strike flesh, followed by the woman's anguished screams. She flinched at the sound, producing her own moan of pain as the ropes dug in between her legs.

"That's right, Jacquie, scream, let me hear it," he said, as he lashed the woman repeatedly. Bladen could hear the excitement building in his voice with each skin-ripping slap of the whip. "Louder, Jacquie, louder." His bizarre laughter combined with the woman's shrieks of pain, filling the little room with the sound of her suffering.

Bladen closed her eyes and prayed for Jacquie's soul, because she had now taken her place. Jacquie had finally given up at some point. At that moment, as she listened to the torturous screams echoing around the room, Bladen vowed to fight. It was not death for which she prayed now, as she had in her lowest moments. No matter the method, she would have welcomed the peace of moving into the light, as she was sure Jacquie had, but now Bladen prayed for the strength to remain alive. She had something to fight for other than herself. The longer she held out, the more likely he would be caught, keeping more women from suffering this chamber of horrors.

She thought of the man that was surely looking for her, saw him clearly in her mind, reminding her, as he had so many times before, "Never give up, Bladen."

Over the sound of the other woman's horrendous screams, Bladen answered him, "Hooah, Colonel!" She narrowed her eyes at the darkness, "Come get some, freak."

#

Rainey did not tell the colonel what Dr. Wood said beyond the fact that the UNSUB kept Jacquie up to three months. He did not ask for any details. She thought he probably did not want to learn those facts in front of other people. They followed Sheila into the forensics garage bays, in time to see an evidence technician flip the visor down on a safety helmet and lean into the trunk of Rainey's car with a lit acetylene torch.

"Whoa!" Rainey shouted. "What are you doing?"

The technician stood up to answer, flipping the visor back up. "There's a lock box welded into the trunk."

"I know. I put it there," Rainey said, striding toward the technician.

Sheila was at her elbow. "This would be considered interference with the Jackson investigation."

"No, I'm helping," Rainey answered. She asked the man with the torch, "If you think there are weapons in that box, did it cross your mind that heating it up with a torch might not be a good idea? May I open it for you? You have plenty of witnesses to verify I only unlocked it."

The technician stepped back from the trunk, turned off the torch, and motioned for Rainey to open the box. She leaned in, punched in the code, and moved away from the trunk. She looked at the technician.

"If you should require any further help, please call my lawyer before you damage this vehicle. I'm rather fond of it. There is no need for you to destroy my car looking for evidence that is not there, but should you do that, be prepared for the lawsuit."

"Now that is definitely interfering," Sheila said, handing Rainey's weapon and clip to the stunned technician. "Log this in. It's hers."

Sheila took Rainey's elbow and moved her to a Jeep parked in the next bay. The colonel was already there, standing silently, staring at his daughter's vehicle.

Another investigative forensic technician approached Sheila, holding a file folder in his hand. "Sergeant Detective Robertson, I was told I would find you here. We rushed those test, as requested."

"Thank you for meeting us down here, Conrad," Sheila said, shaking his free hand.

"No problem. So, here's what we have so far." Conrad opened his folder and went right to the matters at hand. "The needle cap contained midazolam and fentanyl in commonly used proportions for sedation. It induces deep sleep rapidly, and more than likely left the recipient with amnesia for the immediate events just prior to and for sometime after it was administered. Neither are common street drugs, but you can find anything if you know where to look."

"That would explain no struggle at the scene," Sheila commented, before Conrad moved on to the next results.

"The paint sample is Vermillion Red, used mainly by Ford, and a very popular color. This particular formula has been used since 1990 on a number of models."

"She said it was a truck," Colonel Asher interjected.

Conrad nodded. "That would be consistent with the picture we found on the phone inside the vehicle." He opened the folder, revealing a photo of the tailgate and license plate of a red pickup truck. "This was the last picture taken with the phone at 6:15 p.m., yesterday."

The colonel grew excited. "That's right after we hung up with her. She must have taken it before she approached her Jeep."

"The tailgate is from a Ford F series, eleventh generation, produced from 2004 to 2008," Conrad explained. "Can't be more specific than that from what we have here in this shot. These tailgates can fit on several makes and models, so I can't guarantee anything other than the paint color. If we had the taillights in the image, that would help." He pulled another piece of paper from the folder. "The license plate was reported stolen over a month ago from a Vermillion Red, 2005 Ford F150 crew cab. I don't think that was a coincidence. Your criminal is smart."

Rainey asked, "Where was the vehicle when the plate was stolen?"

The technician handed Rainey the piece of paper. "It says in the report the vehicle was parked at one of the shuttle lots at State college. Security cameras caught a dark figure, but that's about it. No way to sharpen that image. Even so, he kept his face shielded with a hat."

"You can get height and weight from the security feed," the colonel suggested.

"They did," Rainey said, reading from the report. "He's five-ten to six-feet tall, heavy build, but hard to tell with the clothing he was wearing, an oversized hoody and baggie sweats." Rainey looked up from the report. "He's smaller, I guarantee it. He dressed that way to throw off the cameras. He's too smart not to have known they were there."

Conrad beamed when he said, "There's something else too. I did some more digging." He pulled another page from the folder. "This is a list of stolen plates from Vermillion Red F150 pickups, model years ranging from 2004 to 2008. They were all taken while the vehicles were parked in remote lots around the Triangle, during the last three years."

Rainey took the paper, reading down the list of six stolen license plates. "These are all special farm issue plates. He took two per year," she noted.

"I noticed that too," the technician answered.

Sheila suggested, "He was keeping the tags current."

"The good news is this scratch on the tailgate." The technician held up the image of the truck, pointing at a long gouge in the paint. "You can visually eliminate prospective trucks fairly quickly. This scratch has been there for a while and is deep, exposing raw metal. If he were going to paint over it, he probably would have done so by now. He hasn't had time to have it professionally repainted since yesterday, and you'll be able to tell if he did it himself, unless he does body work for a living."

"May I have a copy of this picture?" Rainey asked.

"You can have this one." The tech handed Rainey the image from the folder, and then continued, "The bad news is there are thousands of Vermillion Red F150 trucks in the Triangle. It is a very popular truck."

Rainey smiled. "Yes, but we know where to look."

"We do?" Sheila questioned.

"Rainey has a geographic profile that makes us think he's in one particular area," Colonel Asher answered. "It's mostly undeveloped land, south of Chapel Hill, still a lot of ground to cover."

Rainey spoke directly to Sheila. "I understand the BAU is tied up at the moment."

"I talked with Danny. Someone will be here in the morning. That's the best he can do."

A commotion on the other side of the garage drew everyone's attention. Rex King was involved in a heated argument with Wiley Trainer. Since Wiley never lost his temper, this was indeed a moment to pause and watch.

"She's the best chance we have of getting a confession. We've got nothing else on this guy," Wiley said, his voice echoing loudly in the cavernous garage.

Rex roared back, "She killed a man and everyone is treating her like she's above the law. Go on, taint your case. I'll bet this guy's attorney's going to have a field day with this, a murder suspect questioning a rape suspect. You people have lost your minds."

Rainey had never seen Wiley angry, but she was seeing it now. He lit into Rex. "And you are supposed to be nowhere near her case, so back off, or I'll have you shuffling papers until retirement. You're not above suspicion here, Rex. I'd remember that if I were you."

"I'm not supposed to be near the case?" Rex was incredulous. "But she can be in here with evidence. This is a crock of shit."

Rex stormed off. Rainey stared after him, shocked to see Martin Douglas Cross waiting by the door. The writer made eye contact with Rainey, nodded, and then followed the fuming detective out of the garage. Wiley approached while she was still trying to process what she had just seen. He motioned her away from the others. "Rainey, may I have a word with you?"

When they were out of earshot, he said, "Rainey, I know you're working this missing girl on the sly, but I've got a rape suspect upstairs that some of the investigators think might be the serial. I'd like your opinion."

Rainey looked over Wiley's shoulder at the colonel. "Okay, but I'm going to need a favor in return."

"I can't fire Rex, if that's what you want," Wiley said, calm again and smiling.

"It would be nice if you could, but no, I need something else. I'm going to have a list of vehicles pretty soon. We're going to need personnel to run those down. They'll need to work in teams of two, no exceptions."

"How many are we talking about?" Wiley asked, rubbing his chin.

"I don't know yet, but I don't want Sheila running into any paperwork or overtime issues when she asks. I think we can find this guy, Wiley."

"You think his daughter is still alive, don't you?"

Rainey turned so the colonel could not read her lips, just in case he knew how. From her experience with military personnel at Quantico, she knew them to be very resourceful.

"She's alive. She may not want to be, but she is. The man that has her is capable of unfathomable torture, but he kept the last one for months. We catch the right break, we can find her."

"Whatever you need, just ask," Wiley said. "I can't help but think about my own daughter. I can't imagine what this man is going through."

Rainey nodded in agreement. "I hope we never have to find out."

#

Rainey left the colonel with Sheila, telling him he should go through the rest of Bladen's personal items and look through her phone for anything that stuck out to him. She followed Wiley to an interrogation room, where they found Forest Sutton sitting across the table from his arresting officer, Blake Little. When Wiley opened the door, Officer Little was berating his captive.

"Knock off the bullshit, Sutton. Once these women get a look at you in a line up, you're going away for a very long time. Cut a deal. Maybe they'll keep you in isolation. You know what they do to rapist up at Central Prison, don't you?"

Wiley interrupted Little's rant. "Hey, I asked you to sit with him, not question him."

Little stood up immediately. "Sorry, Captain."

"Leave us alone with him," Wiley said, with a bit of reprimand implied in his tone.

"Yes, sir," the officer answered, leaving quickly.

Wiley eased back into his calm, soothing drawl. "Sorry about that, Forest. He's up for a promotion to Sergeant. It tends to make them a little anxious to get that big bust under their belts."

Forest Sutton smiled at Wiley, giving Rainey the impression that a rapport had already developed between the two men. She also noticed the scrapes on Sutton's face and hands, and the little purple mouse forming on his cheek. It appeared there had been a struggle at his arrest. He was nervous, antsy, unable to sit still, constantly pushing his long bangs from his forehead. Rainey's immediate reaction was this is not the serial rapist. His body language was inconsistent with the confident alpha male that had been breaking into women's homes.

When he spoke, Rainey heard the voice of a timid, confused young man. "Man, that guy just won't listen. Please find my girlfriend. She'll tell you I wasn't breaking into her apartment. Well, I was breaking into it, but she wanted me to."

"We're trying to locate her," Wiley said. "She has not returned to the apartment and she isn't at work. Do you have any idea where she could be?"

"No, and now I'm really worried," Forest said.

Rainey believed him. Still, this could all be an act, and if it was, this guy was doing an Oscar winning performance of the anti-suspect in a serial rape case. But one thing was gnawing at her. When they walked in, she caught a whiff of the cologne she smelled on her coat last night. She wasn't sure if it was the leather warming and releasing the smell, or if Forest here had

145

been in Wiley's car. So, she pulled out the chair next to Wiley and sat down.

"Forest, this is Rainey Bell. I've asked her to come talk to you. She may be able to help you clear this up."

"Okay," Forest said, barely looking up from the table.

Rainey smiled to put him at ease. "Forest, I'm not a police officer, but I'm acting as an agent for them, so I need to know that you've been read your rights and understand them."

"Yes, I signed that paper waving my rights. Really, I haven't done anything wrong."

Wiley had filled Rainey in on the arrest details, but she wanted to hear what Forest had to say. She began with easy questions, things he would not lie about, facts easily checked, most of which she already knew from looking at the arrest report, but she needed a baseline of body language when he was being truthful.

"Okay, Forest. Let's start out simple. How old are you? Where do you work?"

"I'm twenty-nine. I've been a paramedic with the fire department for seven years."

Rainey noted that his head came up and his shoulders straightened when he mentioned his job. He made solid eye contact with her for the first time too. He was proud of his profession. It gave him confidence. Her next question was meant to test that confidence and was one of the reasons Forest was sitting in an interrogation room. He did not fit most of the profile Rainey developed for the rapist, but one aspect of Forest's life sent up alarm bells.

"That's right. I read that in the arrest report. It also said you applied to the police academy, and after being rejected, you enrolled in the forensic science program over at State college."

Forest grew defensive. "I was rejected because I was sick during the PT test. I had the flu. I also realized that I really wanted to be in forensics instead of patrol duty, so I went back to school. I graduate in May."

Rainey observed Forest lean forward, look her in the eyes, and defend his pride. He was being truthful. She knew that because Wiley had checked out his background, but it did put

146

him squarely within the parameters of the profile. One other aspect of Forest's demeanor made Rainey suspicious. He was not displaying the typical behavior of an innocent man, no demanding of his rights, no real outbursts of indignation at the charges, more pleading to be let go than professing of innocence. He was guilty of something. She pressed him for details.

"All right then, why don't you tell me why you were arrested breaking into the backdoor of an apartment at quarter to five this morning?"

"I was supposed to," Forest began, and then hesitated. "Man, she's going to kill me."

"Who?" Rainey asked.

"My girlfriend. This was her idea. I wouldn't do something like this if she hadn't, well, she pretty much insisted. She's, uh, she's—Oh man, she's going to kill me."

"Forest," Rainey said, trying to focus him. "Let's attempt to string a whole thought together. Just one at a time would be best."

Forest ducked his head. Here was his guilt, his shame. "My girlfriend wanted me to break in her apartment and role play a domination scene."

"You mean she has a rape fantasy and she wanted you to be the attacker." Rainey stated it plainly, so the words would sink in.

Forest leaned forward, cuffed hands on the table. "I'm not like that. I didn't want to do it. She insisted and she's, she's—"

"She's hot, Forest. I saw her picture in the file. So, explain why she wasn't at home when you planned your break in."

"I have no idea. I thought she said last night." He flopped back against his chair, exasperated, and Rainey caught the cologne scent again. "I've been on duty for three days. I left my phone in my buddy's car, when he gave me a ride home from the firehouse last night, and I haven't been able to track him down. Man, I am so going to catch hell for this."

"What kind of cologne is that you're wearing?"

"I don't wear cologne. My girlfriend has allergies." Forest sniffed of his shirt. "It was that guy that tackled me. He must have bathed in the stuff."

The rapist did not wear cologne either, but every woman Rainey interviewed commented that the attacker had a robust manly odor, not overly unpleasant, but strong, pervasive. It lingered in their homes after he was gone. It occurred to Rainey that the rapist knew this, and masked his scent at other times with cologne. When they caught him, Rainey believed he would prove to have been chastised at some point for his manly odor.

Forest leaned forward again, looking from Rainey to Wiley and back. "Look, I know I was stupid. I can't believe I actually did it anyway. The reason that guy saw me was because I was so nervous I couldn't unlock the door."

Wiley sat up a little taller. "Are you usually faster at picking locks?"

"Yeah, I've been doing it since I was a kid. I'm pretty good at it most of the time. My granddad was a locksmith. He taught me how."

That was another reason Forest was in handcuffs. He was found in possession of a lock picking kit. The rapist was also adept at entering locked doors, prompting speculation that he possessed the same skills of which Forest was now bragging.

A knock at the door stopped the questioning. Officer Little stepped in, a sheepish expression on his face. "We found the girlfriend. She said the break-in was planned for tonight, not last night. She thought Forest was working last night and stayed over at a friend's house. She came home a few minutes ago to get her phone charger before going to work because her battery died."

Forest, feeling vindicated, said, "See, I told you."

Rainey smelled the cologne again, heavy in the air as before. She watched Officer Little walk over to Forest and remove the cuffs. He fit the rapist's height and build, as described by the women he attacked. He also fit Rainey's profile, the alpha male cop involved in the investigation, and she remembered seeing him at Maybelline's. She listened as he spoke to Forest, watching for clues.

"I'm sorry you had to go through this. Under the circumstances, with all the rapes going on, you can understand why we had to take a close look. You were breaking into a woman's apartment in the wee hours."

Forest stood up, rubbing his wrists. "Yeah, well, that's not going to happen again. She can find another boyfriend if that's what she's into. I'm done."

Little chuckled. "She's a firecracker, all right. She's downstairs waiting for you."

Forest looked stricken. "Can you show me the back way out of here?"

Little handed Forest off to another officer in the hallway and then stopped to talk to Wiley and Rainey.

"Sorry to have caused a false alarm. I really thought he was the guy," Little said, watching Forest slink away toward the back exit.

Rainey watched Little. "Hey, what's that cologne you're wearing?"

Little wrinkled his nose. "It's not me. The campus cop that tackled the guy, he's bathed in the stuff. It follows you everywhere."

The observation room door opened and two men joined them in the hallway. With them came the strong smell of the cologne. Rainey knew one of them—a detective working on the rape cases. The other man was younger, maybe late twenties, dressed in black pants and turtleneck, much like the police tactical teams wore. He was also the source of the cologne. Wiley stuck out his hand toward the younger man.

"Thank you for your help on this." Wiley turned to Rainey. "Jason is an officer with the State College police department. As their liaison, he's been working on the serial rape case with us. Jason Brand, this is Rainey Bell. She developed the profile we've been working with."

Jason smiled broadly. "Yes, I know who you are." He extended his hand for her to shake. "It's an honor to meet you."

Outwardly, Jason seemed calm and at ease. When Rainey clasped his hand, she felt him vibrating beneath the surface.

The whole time she was in the room with Forest, Rainey had been wondering why an experienced investigator like Wiley Trainer needed her to tell him they had the wrong guy. She glanced at Wiley and saw the twinkle in his eye. This was the real suspect Rainey had been summoned to evaluate. His interrogation was taking place right here in the hallway and Jason Brand had no idea.

Something was also tickling Rainey's nose. Since she started living with a woman, Rainey had noticed that she could smell men more readily now. She could detect the lingering odor of a man in her home, long after they had gone. It had been one of those things at which Rainey marveled, the way her brain readjusted to what she now found pleasurable, the scent of a woman. What may have tripped her sexual antennae before Katie no longer held appeal. The human brain was an amazing thing, and hers was telling Rainey that a strong male musk was detected and it did not like it. Under all that cologne, Jason was concealing his manly scent.

Rainey decided her plan of action immediately, and set out to crack Jason's outer calm.

"Yes, I think I've seen you before." It was a guess, but a good one. "You were at the lecture I gave Monday night, but didn't Wiley say you were an officer at State College?"

He was about to lie. Rainey looked for the tell tale signs and they were there. It was thought to be nearly impossible to fake a genuine smile. Called a Duchenne smile, it engaged the muscles around the mouth and eyes. A fake smile cannot induce the same effect, especially the wrinkles at the corners of the eyes. Rainey had no doubt that Jason's smile was forced.

"I heard you were speaking. I thought I could learn something from your lecture that could help me in future investigations, and of course this one, too. It was very insightful. I'm glad I went."

His eye contact was very intense. Rainey recognized that, too. People who lie a lot know one of the signs of deception is averting the eyes, which they overcompensate for by holding eye contact too intensely. The concentrated effort to focus on a person unnaturally could cause the liars blinking rate to change as well. Correspondingly, Rainey knew he was searching for her reaction to his explanation, watching to see if she bought it. She called that peeking.

Even the most accomplished liars peeked out from the veil of innocence they desperately tried to hide behind, giving themselves away in the split second she glimpsed the real person behind the facade. Jason's peek was well disguised, but she saw him hiding in the deadness behind those baby blue eyes. Like the blink of a shark's eye, Rainey saw the same cold, nothingness of an apex predator. Jason Brand was a small Tiger Shark swimming where Great Whites had been. He was no match for the sociopaths in Rainey's realm; the monsters in boxes with tightly closed lids in the corners of her mind. Jason Brand was out of his league.

Rainey knew how to pry the mask of innocence away for a peek of her own. *Okay, Jason,* she thought, *how good are you?*

"That's great," she said. "I wish more officers would take the initiative to learn about sexual assault. I'm very happy you could be there."

Ah, there it was, the mark of deception only the best, most sophisticated of liars could control, the urge to gloat over their successful duplicity. Jason smiled, this time a genuine Duchenne smile. He was demonstrating duping delight, a common phenomenon among liars. They cannot help the smile they produce when they think their falsehood has been accepted as truth. Sometimes it was just a slight upward turn in the corners of the mouth, or like Jason's, a full grin, but it was usually there.

Now, to apply the heat, Rainey challenged him to tell his version of the recent arrest of Forest Sutton. "It was very fortunate you were on the scene tonight. It wasn't our UNSUB, but it could have been. Good police work. Do you live there?"

Jason crossed his arms over his chest, positioned himself with his feet facing the exit, and altered his voice to a lower pitch. "To tell you the truth, it was just luck."

These were all red flags, especially the qualifying language, "To tell you the truth . . ." While not all those behaviors signaled deception, in combination they were screaming at Rainey, "BIG OLD LIAR." He confirmed her suspicions even more by the level of detail in his lie, another red flag.

"I'm coming off the overnight shift, switching to afternoons. I'm not used to it yet. Sometimes I just drive around until I can settle down. I was driving by, when I notice this patrol car pulled into the parking lot, kind of at an angle, like he was called there for something and rushed to park his car. So, I pulled over to see if I could help. It took me a while to find him. It also crossed my mind he might shoot me, if he saw me in the shadows. I tried to stay where he would be able to see me clearly, but I couldn't yell out in case he was about to catch the guy. I saw the suspect running and heard Officer Little yell at him to halt. He ran right past me so I tackled him."

Little offered more. "I couldn't tell who I was chasing there for a second. I was responding to a prowler call in the next unit, when I saw the Sutton guy behind another one. I yelled at him, and then this other guy comes from between the buildings. They were both wearing all black. Then Jason tackled Sutton. That's how I knew which one to cuff."

Wiley slapped Jason on the back. "Good work. Too bad it wasn't the right guy, but maybe we'll get him soon. Word of advice, wear some identifying hat or jacket next time. Would have been a shame if you were shot or mistaken for a suspect while trying to help. I'll be sure to put in a good word for you on that State Police application."

Jason relaxed into his duping delight smile. His lies had been accepted. He was clear to continue doing what he was doing without suspicion, or so he thought. They said their good byes, leaving Rainey standing in the hall with Wiley.

As soon as they were alone, Rainey said, "You know that's him, right?"

Wiley grinned at her. "Oh, yeah. Knew it the minute he walked in. Give Officer Little credit, he suspected him too. He put on a good show in there, all to make Mr. Jason Brand very comfortable. We're already pulling records and getting warrants in order. While we've been occupying him here, his supervisor was checking his workstation and patrol unit computers. He ran the license plates of at least three of our victims that we know of so far."

"You're going to find he was stalking someone at that apartment complex."

"The woman you spoke with at the hospital this morning, she lives there too. He ran her plates three months ago. The 911 call came from her neighbor who heard Jason leaving her unit." Wiley said, a real Duchenne smile wrinkling his eyes.

"And you needed me, why?" Rainey asked, smiling back.

"Just wanted verification and to show you that your profile was on the money. Thank you, and now, whatever you need, you just call. I know you will be cleared on this murder charge, but I'd worry if I were you. Somebody is out to get you, Rainey Bell. Watch your back."

"Funny, but that's the message I seem to be getting from everyone these days." Rainey remembered that Wiley knew her father. "Do you have any idea what my father did to Rex King?"

"I believe the word for Rex would be cuckold. He managed to wrangle a pretty woman, but she was not the most faithful gal. That I know is fact. I don't know the details of your father's involvement, but there were rumors about twenty years ago. They started up again after Billy's death. Some people thought Rex had something to do with that."

"Oh, really?" Rainey was intrigued. "We know who killed my father. He was just a kid making his gang bones, wasn't aiming at anyone in particular. But you say Rex was a suspect, that's interesting."

"Only for a bit. Mackie tracked that kid down pretty fast, so the rumors died out, and then you moved back. He's been hell bent on keeping you away from this department since then. I believe he thinks if he harasses you enough you'll refuse to consult with us."

"It takes a mighty small penis to take out your frustrations on the daughter of the dead man that may have screwed your wife," she said. "Are you sure he has one?"

Wiley slapped her on the back gently, laughing. "You sure as hell are Billy Bell's daughter, no question about that."

CHAPTER EIGHT

"Are you okay?" Rainey asked, hoping for a positive reply.

"Yes, I'm just angry that they are doing this to you," Katie replied through the phone.

"They didn't make a mess or anything, did they?"

"No. It was a couple of guys who know you. They seemed rather apologetic through it all. They did run into a bit of trouble with Gunny, when they found the Glock in her car. We're going to discuss that, by the way. She's a little pissed they took it."

"I bet she is. That's her baby," Rainey said, completely dodging the discussion comment. "Have you heard from Thelma or Ernie? How's Mackie?"

"Thelma called. She told him about the missing girl and that you're looking for her, so he understands why you're not there. Don't worry about him, Rainey. He's in the best of hands. Your stepfather is brilliant. Let him take care of him."

"I'm still going to try and get by the hospital to see him. If you talk to him, tell him—"

Rainey felt the stress crack her veneer, the wall she built to keep emotions in check. The Rainey season was in full swing, hammering at her from all directions, threatening to blow the lids off her boxes. Urging her mind to stay focused, she slapped some mental duct tape on the lids and gathered her composure.

Katie understood and said just the right thing. "He knows, Rainey."

Rainey collected herself with a deep breath. "So, all is well there, then."

"Yes, we're all fine. The grandmas are in heaven and I'm catching up on some paperwork for the women's shelter. We break ground on the halfway house next month, and Molly still hasn't decided if the 'Sarah Harris House' is what she wants to call it."

Molly was putting up most of the money for a facility where women recovering from substance abuse could get a fresh start, a roof, employment help, therapy, a new outlook, leaving both the substance and the reasons for its abuse behind. Molly wanted a place that would have benefitted her own mother. "A place like this would have saved Sarah Harris many years of torment. No more women through the cracks, Katie," Molly had said, as she signed the check over to Katie's foundation. She sealed the deal with a promise to round up every woman she knew, which was quite a few, for a fundraising reception for the rest. Rainey was looking forward to the reception. She wanted see all the women Molly had slept with in one room, number one, and, number two, watch Molly watch Leslie see them, too.

"Don't push her, Katie. It's a big decision, honoring her mother that way."

"I'm not. I just have to make sure the reception invitations go out on time. I showed her a mock-up today and almost had her final approval, when the trouble erupted with Gunny in the garage. We *are* going to talk about that."

Forewarned, Rainey ignored Katie's comment again. "Okay, well, I don't know when I'll be home."

"Take your time. It's kind of nice to have a crisis so I can work. Built in babysitting, now why didn't I think of that? Oh wait, I did. A part time nanny, I think it was, but alas, no one could pass the security check."

Rainey's reply was a little defensive. "We're doing fine. We have our mothers several days a week, Ernie helps, Mackie and Thelma, even Junior and his girlfriend babysit sometimes. Those are the people I trust. I stay home as much as I can. If you need more time to work, say so. I'll adjust my schedule to accommodate you." That last part came out a bit too antagonistically, Rainey was thinking, but Katie did not respond in kind.

Her tone changed, softening. "I'm sorry, honey. I know you're stressed. You're right, we're doing fine. Be careful. I love you. We're all safe, and will be waiting here when your job is done."

Rainey hesitated, but considering the agreement they shared, she said, "Katie, someone close to us could be responsible for framing me."

Katie's answer was a quiet, "I know, I'm watching."

"Good girl. I love you, too. Kiss the babies. You call me if you notice anything, the slightest thing out of order. Got it?"

"I got it. Love you. Stay safe."

"Always, Katie, always."

Rainey hung up and headed back to the conference room where Sheila had set them up. It was a familiar space to her, after having been involved in two investigations the BAU conducted out of that very room. Lunch of sandwiches and sweet tea had been brought in, while they began the task of sorting through what they knew and needed to know. A list of vehicles matching the truck's description was being generated. Colonel Asher was doing his best to keep his own boxes tightly closed. He had to excuse himself for a bit, after reading Jacquie's autopsy report. Rainey had warned him not to, but he said he needed to know. He understood that in the investigative process the autopsy report was a vital link to ascertaining the UNSUB's behavior. Rainey had taken the time to step out to call Katie. It appeared the colonel made it back ahead of her.

"Gary Heidnik," he said to her, as she walked back into the room.

Rainey had decided to respect the colonel's wishes and treat him like any other investigator. She responded, "Kidnapper, rapist, torturer, held six women captive in his basement. Same general profile, brilliant narcissist, but his goals were different. Our UNSUB is not interested in breeding with his enslaved harem. Torture was a means to an end for Heidnik. This guy," Rainey pointed at the autopsy report, "is all about the torture."

The colonel prompted Rainey with, "Narcissism and paranoia go hand in hand with these types, right?'

Rainey nodded her head in agreement. "At his core, he is a narcissist. He's created an illusion of supremacy around himself, insulating him from insult or humiliation. He must control everything and anyone close to him. He will demand respect and any questioning of his authority will provoke rage and potential lethal consequences for the person who crossed him."

"And his paranoia is him projecting what he fears and loathes on others," the colonel added. "He detests women, strong women, if I'm reading the victim profiles correctly."

Sheila was in the position of dealing with a rogue analyst and a distraught father, while the rest of the Triangle law enforcement agencies prepared to search for the colonel's daughter. She took notes to present to the task force, as Rainey continued.

"These types of murderers almost always have a dysfunctional relationship with a mother figure. He will also come from a broken or abusive home. If the parents stayed together, then it was probably not a healthy environment. There are exceptions, but something probably went terribly wrong in this UNSUB's childhood."

Colonel Asher contributed to the impromptu profile. "He's smart. I'd say well above average intelligence. Despite that, he will have many failures in school or employment goals. He will blame his lack of success on others. He probably has a job he feels is beneath his intelligence and feels superior to those he works with. He'll present the attitude that he knows more than he lets on, as if he could accomplish wonders if he wanted to."

Rainey continued his thread of thought. "Along with that superior attitude, comes difficulty with authority and boundaries. He will have overstepped his authority at work and reacted badly when put in his place. These men are often drawn to the military, but can't handle the command structure. He may have excelled as a soldier, but his narcissism would have made it difficult for him to remain in the service. His time would have been short, if he made it through boot camp."

"In my experience," Sheila said, "They shy away from conflict with male authority figures, but take out those frustrations on their victims. A man like this gets reprimanded at work, then goes home and beats his wife."

"Yep, that's our guy. You might want to look for domestic abuse charges on these truck owners," Rainey suggested, and then continued the profile. "This type of offender is indifferent to his fellow man, irresponsible and self-centered, the classic psychopath. People who know him well will find him manipulative, deliberate in his actions, full of guile, but outwardly cordial for as long as it suits his objectives. Should he be thwarted, his true personality revealed, his outburst would be over the top with indignation."

The colonel stated the physical particulars. "The victim profiles suggest he is a white male. His age is older than the range we would normally use. Because of his organization, the crimes themselves, I'd say he's in his late thirties or early forties. He'll be articulate, extroverted. He will take great care with his health and appearance."

"So, we're looking for a good-looking man?" Sheila asked.

"Not necessarily," Rainey answered. "His vanity about his looks may be because he isn't handsome. He may spend a great deal of time trying to improve his looks. DeBardeleben was not handsome, but was obsessed with his appearance. They found combs everywhere in his belongings. His wives talked about the amount of time he spent combing and caring for his hair."

"You think he's married?" Sheila asked, still taking notes.

"If he is, she's subservient to him. He's done things to her, forced her to participate in his fantasies. She is his victim as well. The minute she stops being compliant, she will suffer. I'm leaning toward divorced with this one. Something happened three years ago, when he started abducting women. Willing or coerced partners supplied his source of pleasure, the suffering of women, until his tastes turned too violent for them. He sought a more readily available source, one where he did not have to control his most sadistic fantasies."

"A lot of the things we know about this type of sexual murderer will only be revealed to be true after we catch him," Colonel Asher said. "He'll have the trilogy of childhood behaviors, bedwetting, arson, cruelty to animals. He'll have youthful alcohol or drug abuse, but his behavior now will indicate use, not abuse. He'll probably have a juvenile record of stealing, shoplifting, possible voyeurism.

"We can use those things to narrow the search, if we develop a list of suspects," Sheila said, listing the items in her notes.

"If he doesn't have a record, people will remember a troubled childhood, with discipline handled at home, and poorly I might add." Rainey's phone rang and she pulled it from her pocket. Danny McNally's picture grinned at her. "It's Danny. Hold that thought," she said to Sheila.

"I hope you're calling to say you are on your way," Rainey said into the phone.

"As soon as I can clear these files off my desk, I'm on the jet," Danny said. "We're shuffling assignments right now. Detective Robertson emailed the information on the current missing case, the ME's report, and the other missing women's files. You've just become a major priority."

"I guess having her tell you we had a DeBardeleben down here wasn't good enough. You had to see the proof." Rainey's teasing held an edge.

Despite attempts to prevent it, Rainey could not stop the nagging sense of betrayal she felt toward her oldest friend. Now was not the time to let those feelings surface. She stuffed them back down for the sake of a more important issue, the colonel's missing daughter.

Danny ignored her tone. "Not me, the management. The autopsy pictures were all it took to clear us for the trip, and that call from the Army brass probably had a bit of influence. We'll be on this tonight and there before dawn. Do you have anything to add to the information we already have?"

"We're generating a list of possible vehicles to track down. I'm sure you're developing your own geographic profile, and you'll see the area where he is most likely located. If you could have Brooks contact the officers working on the list down here, I think she can narrow the search for them."

"Will do. Anything else?"

Rainey thought it was a good idea to let him in on her plan. "I'm going to put you on speakerphone. I have an idea and Sheila needs to hear it. Colonel Asher, the missing woman's father is also in the room. He's retired Army CID. Treat him like an investigator. That's what he wants."

"Okay," Danny agreed.

Rainey put the phone down on the table and introduced the colonel to Danny. "Colonel Asher, you're speaking with SSA Danny McNally of the BAU."

"I'm familiar with you, sir," the colonel said, leaning toward the phone. "We met during my training at Quantico. I don't expect you to remember me. I was one among many."

"I'm sorry you're in this situation, Colonel. We'll do all we can to locate your daughter. That is the main focus of my team from this moment on."

Rainey heard Sheila's sigh of relief. Some local law enforcement agencies did not want interference from the FBI, but most welcomed the BAU when the cases were overwhelming, as this one portended to be.

"Danny, I want to bounce an idea off you. Would you agree that this UNSUB is focused on me?" Rainey asked.

"I think the body in your backyard would be a good indicator, yes," Danny answered.

"We know from the clues he left on the body that he wants the recognition for being in the same league with, if not exceeding the depravity of DeBardeleben or Schaefer, and I'm sure you caught the flagrant grab for media attention with the Bundy bite mark."

"I'm following you," Danny said.

"I suspect it was you Molly called at Quantico, so you know I'm under suspicion of murder." She did not wait for his confirmation. "They are about to make a big bust on a serial rapist. I think we can work both of these situations to our advantage."

Danny understood immediately. "You want him on page two."

"Exactly," Rainey agreed. "I think the media should be flooded with info on the serial rapist bust. It would also be good to have an official statement precluding me from any involvement with ongoing investigations, until I am cleared as a murder suspect. A very brief statement should be made about the body recovery, maybe even hint at a tie to the rapist. I think that statement should include that the BAU has been contacted, but until more of the missing women's bodies are found and a serial murderer is proven to exist, you have more pressing matters with which to deal."

The father overwhelmed the investigator in Colonel Asher. He objected, "That could push him to kill Bladen."

Rainey put up her hand. "Hear me out, and Danny, feel free to jump in. He may very well lash out at Bladen, but he needs her right now. He needs someone to listen to his ranting and raving, who will agree he's being disrespected, and that once again society has failed to recognize his superiority. He contacted the police and drew my attention because he's devolving. We should help push him over the edge."

Danny concurred. "He will have to show us he's worthy of attention, and I think you're right about his current captive. It is a risk, but I think he'll keep her alive. He'll vent his rage on her, but if she survives that, if she's smart and plays to his narcissism, it could buy her time or an escape opportunity."

Neither Danny nor Rainey told the colonel the other reason he would not kill Bladen. He was not done with her yet. This UNSUB favored long term confinement, a slow and painful breaking of a woman's spirit. He had invested too much time in Bladen's acquisition to dispose of her so quickly. Her worth was tied up in his narcissism. If he devalued her by killing her quickly, or if she proved not to fulfill his fantasy, then he had wasted his time, chosen poorly, and that would reflect badly on his self-image as all-powerful and superior. No, Bladen would suffer much more before her death, Rainey was sure. She was betting the young woman's life on it.

#

Drip—Drip—Drip—

Bladen's counting of the drips halted at the sound of a—what was it, a car door slamming? He was coming. While her body began to tremble and her thoughts to race, part of her mind was working out the clues. She heard the sound. It originated outside of this room. The music had been ear-splittingly loud. Her location, she concluded, was in the middle of nowhere or someone would have heard the music. Bladen cycled through what she knew. She was underground, away from other structures. The sound of the car door slamming, if that was what it was, came from above her. The smell of oil was stronger when he opened the door. Could she be under a detached garage? It would have to be very detached. Unafraid of being discovered, he encouraged her to scream and shriek. But if Bladen could hear a car door slam, then her screams could be heard, opening a possibility of hope. She filed that information away. The slim chance that someone may hear her anguished cries was all Bladen Asher had to hang onto, as the door opened and pure evil walked back in.

He beat her while she was still tied up. Kicked her repeatedly, telling her his dog knew better than to "shit in his house." Once done with the "behavioral modification session," as he referred to it, he cut the ropes loose, making sure to yank them away, ripping more skin in the process. Unencumbered by ropes for the first time in hours, she crawled, stumbled, and finally gained her feet again on the way to the bathroom, where he made her haul the dog bed into the shower. She was told to wash it spotless, but was not allowed to clean herself until the bed met his specifications. Her own waste burned fire between her legs, where the ropes had worn her skin into a bloody rash. Finally, his attention wandered to checking the early afternoon newscasts, leaving her free to clean herself. The bastard made sure to turn the water down to no more than a cold trickle, before he left the room.

Free, a totally different concept to Bladen now. She was not free to turn on the hot water or increase the flow of the cold. He had not specifically forbidden it, but she knew she was not free to do anything on her own. It took a while, but once she was able to clean her raw skin, she sat down over the drain. Pooling the water in the bottom of the shower stall, Bladen let the icy liquid cool her feverish flesh and reduce the swelling. Her ribs ached from his kicks and punches, but he spared her head, forcing her to remain conscious for her lesson. He was always careful to keep her aware of the pain as long as possible.

He only raged occasionally. All through the previous night, he carried out his torture calmly, his voice droning on, as if he were a boring instructor lecturing on the subject of human suffering. Then there was the forced dialogue, where he made her repeat how much she enjoyed what was happening to her, or beg him to stop using specific phrases. He would record her attempts to follow the script, play them back, and make her repeat each line until she said it to match whatever fantasy he was living in his mind.

The worst parts were his "Tell me about the pain" moments. Like a scientist in a laboratory, he would ask, "How much does it hurt, Bladen? Describe it to me."—"Can you compare it to any other pain you've felt?"—"Which was worse, the rack or the picquet?" He wanted honest answers, and "modified" her behavior when he did not believe he was receiving them.

Alone in the shower, able to move her limbs again, Bladen worked the stiffness out of her joints. These rare moments of freedom were the only bright spots she had to look forward to. She massaged her muscles, encouraging the blood to flow again, after hours of restriction. She needed to be ready to take advantage of an opportunity, should one arise. Bladen knew she had to maintain her strength any way she could. She would eat what was given to her, drink when she could, and stay alive, whatever it took.

"Stay focused. Stay engaged," she whispered.

Suddenly, he was standing over her again. She flinched at his unexpected appearance. He held a hamburger and a soft drink cup in his hands. He saw that she was trying to relieve the pain by soaking in the few inches of water she managed to accumulate. Bladen thought he was going to kick her again, or at least make her stand up. But he only smirked under the black mask, crumbled the hamburger, and tossed it into the water pooled between her legs. He poured the soft drink over her head, tossed the cup in the water, and left her alone.

Freedom was indeed an altered concept for Bladen.

\#

Jason Brand's perp-walk was well attended. The traditional parading of a high profile suspect before the media, shortly after his or her arrest, was controversial at best. In this instance, the suspect's head was covered to prevent tainting of the witness identifications, but the press conference that followed left no doubt that the serial rapist was in custody. After an afternoon of working out the details of the statement with the department spokesman, and coordinating with Wiley on Jason's arrest, Rainey was quite sure they were setting the right lure.

The media was informed of an important press conference, and given plenty of video of the perp-walk for the nightly news. The spokesman hammered home the message that the Triangle could rest easier tonight. The rapist who terrorized young women in the area was behind bars. All questions about the body found behind Rainey's house were deflected as "being under investigation," and not "yet" tied to the rapist. Questions concerning Rainey were answered with, "Former agent Bell is not involved in any active investigations at this time. She is a person of interest in a murder inquiry and that is all we are willing to comment on."

Sheila hung around long enough to give Cookie Kutter a statement, with other media outlet microphones tucked close to her chin. She pulled off the casual presentation brilliantly. Rainey watched the performance on a television in the conference room, alone. The story seeded, all Sheila had to do was wait for her cue.

With no way to get more information on Rainey's situation, Cookie concentrated on other rumors. Since she prided herself on having all the best behind the scenes crime-beat gossip, it was, of course, Cookie who shouted the anticipated question. "Sources say the body you found was dumped by a serial killer connected to the missing women, and the FBI has declined to participate in the investigation. Can you comment on that, Sergeant Robertson?"

Sheila almost walked away, paused, and then turned back to Cookie. Excellent sell, Rainey thought.

"Just so the families of these missing women know, we are doing all we can to find out what happened to them. The FBI has been contacted, but until we have more evidence to share with them, there really is nothing they can add to the investigation."

Cookie could have been reading from Rainey's script, if she had written one. "But are you now willing to admit there is a serial killer in the Triangle?"

"No, not at this time," Sheila replied, and then moved away quickly, refusing to comment further.

"Now, we wait." Rainey said to the television screen. "Come on asshole, show yourself."

The door opened behind her. She turned to see Colonel Asher enter. The soldier's stiff upper lip had slipped some, replaced by the worried frown of a desperate father. His eyes were rimmed red. He went off by himself to release the emotion, something Rainey saw countless times working with the BAU. She had done it herself, when a case burned through the layers of protection. At those moments, it was best to discharge the built up tension, rather than attempt to stay in control. A quick release and back to work she would go. She doubted it was that easy for the colonel in this instance.

"I pray you're right," he said. "I hope Bladen can withstand his fury. You just threw down the gauntlet. My daughter may be the collateral damage in this war you've begun."

Rainey addressed the father, not the investigator. "She'll make it, Patrick. You said yourself that she's tenacious when challenged. Bladen is smart and she has the advantage of having you for a father."

His reply was almost a whisper, as he tried to remain composed. "My brain knows this is her only hope. My heart is afraid it won't be enough."

He sat down in a chair at the end of the long conference table, the files of missing women scattered out in front of him. Rainey crossed the room and joined him, this time addressing the investigator, not the father.

"Colonel, you have many more years experience in law enforcement than I do, but I'm not sure how many of these types of offenders you've come across. None, I'd venture to guess. Less than two percent of serial murderers are true sexual sadists, and of that number, only a very few could compare with this

UNSUB's desire to inflict long-term suffering. It's interesting that you used the term 'war,' because that is what we are engaging in, a war of manipulation, domination, and control. This is the goal of most rapist, stalkers, and multiple murderers. Boil these crimes down and those three things are at the heart of them all. They also engage in manipulating law enforcement and the media. We engage them right back, play the game, and try to control the outcome. It is war, Colonel. We must know our enemy and attack his weaknesses. This particular UNSUB wants attention. We deny that and he'll announce himself in a big way. I'm sorry to sound so callous, but it is my belief that a live Bladen serves his needs more effectively. He's going to reveal much more to us than her body—he hasn't had the time to make her presentable. He wants to be the greatest serial killer ever, and he's going to show us the proof."

The colonel listened intently, and then asked, "You surmised all that from looking at one body?"

"No, not one body, many. As much as these guys would like to believe they are special, they pretty much fit into certain categories and behaviors. That's the basis of profiling—if you see a, b, and c behaviors, then the offender will usually follow the same pattern as others before him. That's how we get out in front of them, anticipating their next move. This guy was going to contact the police again. We're just prodding him to make a big statement."

"If that was your daughter with him, would you be doing the same thing?"

Rainey did not hesitate to answer, "Yes, sir. I would be concerned, as you are, but I have to trust what I've learned—" Halfway through the spiel she had delivered countless times before, she stopped. Her parent box flew open and the words tumbled out. "Who am I kidding? Concerned? Colonel, if that were my daughter, or either of my sons, I would be a crazed animal. I admire your ability to remain rational, while suffering the worst of a parent's nightmares. I would hope that I could remain so and entrust my precious child's recovery to the men and women of the BAU. I have faith in their methods. I believe that if it were possible, they would bring my child home. I expect nothing less from them in Bladen's case. They take it personally, sir. No stone will go unturned."

"It appears you take it rather personally yourself," the colonel said, a slight smile in one corner of his mouth.

"Yes, I do."

He leaned forward, placing his forearms on the table, lacing his fingers together. His voice softened, he said, "It's a gift and a curse to see into the hearts of men. We can spend our lives searching every human interaction for deception or ulterior motives. I tried not to bring that home with me, the paranoia."

Rainey nodded in agreement. "I understand completely. It's hard, but like my wife says, at some point you have to try to live among the other humans. We can't raise children in a home filled with fear."

"I never wanted Bladen to be afraid, but I did tell her evil was out there. She did everything right, and he still took her."

"Evil finds a way, Colonel. We walk the streets with evil every day. We unknowingly work with it, live next door to it, invite it into our homes. Unless it is shown to us, even a trained behaviorist can't see evil when it is cleverly cloaked."

"You've seen a lot, haven't you? I've been to war. I've seen horrible things, but you, you've seen the worst of humanity, and now it's right here in your backyard."

"That's another reason I think Bladen will survive his rage over the press conference. He hasn't had the time to do what he did to Jacquie Upshaw. He'll have to raise the bar, if he wants to impress the BAU. He'll show us something that separates him from the other killers he's studied. He wants to be a star, but don't confuse that with wanting to be caught. He'll give us a body or bodies he's already disposed of. It's less risky. If he's as smart as I think he is, he knows we're playing games with him. However, his narcissism won't allow him to ignore the opportunity to prove his existence and his superiority to the police. He can't help the smirk."

The colonel sat back, composure restored. "So, what now?"

"It's going to be a while before they have the list of pickup trucks narrowed down to a manageable number. Brooks, a computer specialist with the BAU, can do most of the eliminations. She's fast, but it takes time to weed out the records that would be of no use to us. I know it's agonizing to wait around, so let's take a drive."

Rainey stood and the colonel followed suit. He asked, "Where are we going?"

"That satellite map image in my office was two years old. I'd like to see that area now."

The colonel followed Rainey to the door. "Do you have access to a helicopter?"

Rainey grinned. "No, but I do know someone with access to a satellite. I just have to contact her from my secured network at home. Come on, you're about to meet the family."

#

Bladen heard his roar begin and knew something had happened. He came into the bathroom ranting. She caught the swearing, but could not understand what he was saying. He was so angry he could not finish a sentence. He yanked her up from the shower drain by her hair. Bladen fought him, but she was wet, and slipped on the slick concrete floor. He dragged her the rest of the way, backhanded her so hard she saw stars, and then lifted her onto the rack. He slammed her wrist and ankles into the shackles. When she fought again, he smashed his elbow into her abdomen, leaving her struggling for air.

Once she was completely strapped in and unable to resist further, he climbed on top of her. Spittle dripped from his bottom lip onto her face, as his angry breath heaved the oxygen from the air. He was literally foaming at the mouth. Bladen looked into his contact-covered pupils, seeing the veins bulging in the whites of his eyes. He wrapped both hands around her throat, squeezing the life out of her, panting like an animal. She felt the blackness creeping in from the edges. This was it. He was going to kill her right then. She stopped fighting and made her peace with it. It was better than many of the other methods he could have employed to end her life in his chamber of horrors. The darkness closed in around her, the light becoming a pinpoint at the end of a long tunnel. Abruptly, the light flooded back, as he released his grasp on her throat, bellowing in frustration.

"Rrrruuuurrrr!"

While Bladen coughed and gasped for air, he hovered over her. Finally putting nouns and verbs in order, he yelled, "Fuck the FBI! You'll fucking make time for me, assholes. You'll see. Fuck you, and fuck Rainey Bell."

He climbed off her, caught up in his rage again, ranting about Rainey Bell. Bladen's only concern at the moment was breathing. That changed when he went for the whip. He began to lash her, but almost as an afterthought, while he imagined what he would do to a real live profiler.

"If I see her where I can get her, that bitch will be stretched out on this rack and fucked six ways to Sunday. Profiling me would be the last thing on her mind. I bet she would fucking fight like hell, but I'd break her. They all break, eventually. Becoming useless lumps, they whimper how they'll do anything, even kill each other if I ask. Maybe I should just go get her. See if she'd kill you to avoid having her asshole ripped open."

Bladen screamed with each slap of leather, but it seemed her captor could no longer hear human suffering. The whip moved up and down her body, as if he were lazily beating a rug out on the clothesline. While excruciating, the sound of the whip biting into her skin and her shrieks of agony appeared to have a calming effect. He lowered his volume, and the rant became the telling of a fantasy

"I should have grabbed that nosey bitch, Katie Meyers when I had the chance. Next time, she won't be so lucky. I'll teach her to meddle in a man's family. That rich bitch needs to mind her own fucking business. Yeah, I'll grab that little blonde whore next. She'll leave the compound sometime. That's better than grabbing the FBI bitch herself." His maniacal laughter filled the air. "Rainey Bell will never forget me."

Bladen Asher would never forget him either.

#

As they made their way out of the courthouse, Rainey and the colonel met Sheila coming back from the press conference. After congratulations on the successful duping of Cookie and the rest of the media, Rainey explained that she was taking the colonel to her house. She used the excuse that Katie prepared dinner for them, because she could not betray her satellite source, especially to someone that may have to testify in court how certain information came to her knowledge.

Sheila pulled Rainey to the side, slipping a flash drive in her hand. "Take this. There are two videos on it. You'll know what to do with it when you see them. I also included the image of the cartridge found at the Jackson murder scene. The shooter cleaned up two of the ejected rounds. This one was found under the body. Jackson rolled on top of it, trying to get away. Whoever shot him delivered the final two shots standing over a wounded man. That's a cold killer, Rainey. Watch your back."

"Thanks, Sheila and, it goes without saying, I didn't get this from you."

Sheila winked. "I knew I liked you for some reason."

"Call me as soon as you hear from him. It won't be long," Rainey said.

Sheila called after her. "You stay safe out there."

Rainey smiled over her shoulder. "Always."

#

Rainey called Katie to tell her they were coming. The rest of the ride over was quiet, as they both ran the clues through their brains. Rainey's directions were the only words breaking the silence, until they pulled up to the guardhouse at her neighborhood.

"Just roll your window down, Colonel," Rainey said.

One of the senior members of the security staff stepped up to the car. "Good evening, sir. How may I help you?"

Rainey leaned over, giving the guard a good look at her face. "Hey, Reese. It's me."

She saw Reese's hand slide closer to his weapon. Rainey and Reese had a long discussion when she moved into the neighborhood. He was very aware of her circumstances and the lengths some very disturbed criminals might go to gain access to her home.

She eased his mind, asking the colonel, "Could you pop the trunk so it can be inspected."

The colonel raised his eyebrows, but pulled the trunk release.

"It's procedure when I enter the neighborhood," Rainey explained.

After closing the trunk, Reese walked to Rainey's side of the car. She pressed the button, lowering her window glass. Reese eyed her suspiciously.

"Considering all that's been happening, Ms. Bell, would you mind telling me my dog's name?"

He wanted the failsafe code. If she said anything other than the arranged name, he would pull his weapon immediately. She made it easy for the guards to remember. Smiling up at Reese, she asked, "How is old Buddy?"

"He's just fine," Reese responded. "Have a good evening, Ms. Bell."

Reese stepped back to the guardhouse and opened the gate. As they drove through, the colonel glanced over at Rainey, but he did not comment on the security measures. At least, not until they pulled into her driveway. She told him to stop, exited the car, and approached the security panel. The colonel rolled his window down, watching her access her home. When the gate began to slide open, Rainey motioned him to go through, but he just sat there. Rainey approached his window.

"Colonel?"

"You've looked into the eyes of the devil, haven't you?"

"Yes, sir, and I intend to see him coming next time."

"These security precautions imply you believe there will be a next time," he said, beginning to roll the car up the driveway slowly.

Rainey walked beside the car, continuing the conversation. "Katie may talk of not living in fear, but the only reason that is possible is because of the net I've thrown around our family. Yes, I believe there will be a next time and a next. As long as these freaks find me fascinating, I'll be a target, as will the people I care about. Some people think I'm paranoid. My history and recent events suggest otherwise."

The colonel smiled up at her. "Haec protegimus," he said, bringing the car to a stop where Rainey indicated he should park.

Rainey laughed. "Yes, sir. 'This we'll defend.' My father was an Army man, too."

Colonel Patrick Asher had done his homework on Rainey. He stepped out of his car and rattled off, "Master Sergeant William Bell, Special Forces, Vietnam, '70 to '75, Purple Heart, Silver Star. A hell of a soldier raised a hell of a daughter."

"Hooah, Colonel."

Rainey remembered the Army affirmative slang, as opposed to the Marines' "Oorah." Her father told her it stood for "Heard, Understood, Acknowledged," or anything but "No." The colonel's smile told her she got it right.

She returned a broad smile and gestured toward the front door. "Welcome to our home."

CHAPTER NINE

Katie met them at the door.

"Welcome, Colonel Asher," she said, and then stood on her tiptoes to kiss Rainey on the cheek. "After you put your weapons away, Rainey, Mack has something to show you."

"Thank you for having me," Colonel Asher said, though it was not really his choice.

He gave Rainey a quizzical look over the weapons comment. Rainey pointed at a brass sign on the foyer table, which read, "All weapons must be checked at the door." He took out his pistol, dropped the clip, and cleared the chamber, before handing it over to Rainey. Katie, who was nearly bouncing with excitement, grabbed Rainey's hand as soon as she closed the gun safe, pulling her toward the den, with the colonel following.

When Rainey reached the top of the two steps down into the den, she could see the grandmothers standing, watching the triplets. Gunny was sitting on the couch and everyone was grinning from ear to ear. Weather, Timothy, and Mack were hanging on to the coffee table, balanced on wobbly legs. Their heads turned simultaneously, as their mothers entered the room.

Katie opened the baby gate and stepped down into the den. "Come on," she said, urging Rainey to hurry. She dropped to her knees at the bottom of the steps and smiled at the triplets.

Rainey followed Katie down to the floor, anticipating what she thought would happen next. She smiled at her children. Mack turned toward her and dropped his grip from the table. Rainey held out her hands, encouraging him. "Come on, Mack. Walk over here."

Mack was the largest of the triplets, thick and strong. He had been flirting with his first steps for a few weeks. His face broke into a wide smile, as he threw his right foot out in front of him, and then he toddled over into her arms, his momentum flinging him into Rainey's chest, while he giggled with delight.

"Well, look at you, big guy," Rainey said, laughing.

Weather let go of the table and tried to follow Mack, but only made it a few steps before toppling over and crawling the rest of the way. Timothy held on the longest, choosing to drop to his diaper-cushioned butt, before following his siblings into Rainey's lap. All the adults were laughing and clapping, while Rainey squeezed her children into a hug that ended with her rolling in the floor with giggling babies crawling over her. If only she could freeze these moments, keep the world out and simply love her family. Awash in baby giggles and "Nee nee nees," Rainey could not imagine life without the family she never thought she would have.

Katie kissed her on the forehead, and stood up. "Play with the kids while I put dinner on the table. Then you can go off to your office to plot and plan."

Rainey watched her walk away, still unable to believe Katie was hers, these children were hers, and this was their home, their lives. She looked up at the colonel and was reminded that the other shoe could always drop. He stood there smiling at her children, but there was sadness in his eyes. He no doubt was remembering his own little girl's first steps.

From her position flat on her back, with a baby on her chest and the other two trying to pile on, Rainey made the introductions. "Colonel Patrick Asher, this is my mother, Constance Herndon."

Constance stepped forward, extending her hand. "It's a pleasure to meet you, Colonel. I am so sorry about your daughter."

Rainey indicated the older version of Katie. "And this is Katie's mother, Melanie Meyers."

Melanie stepped forward to shake the colonel's hand. "Nice to meet you, Colonel. I, too, am sorry to hear about your daughter. You've come to the right woman for help. Rainey saved my Katie. I will always be grateful for that."

Gunny stepped forward. Rainey nodded in her direction. "Colonel, this is retired Marine Gunnery Sergeant Naomi Pierce."

Gunny shook the colonel's hand with a strong grip. "It's a pleasure to meet you, sir," she said. "Just call me Gunny."

"The pleasure is mine, ladies," the colonel said.

Rainey sat up, holding out Weather to the colonel. She did not know anyone that could be sad while holding the little strawberry blonde with green eyes. Rainey's daughter was a charmer and she knew it.

"Here, hold her a sec, while I wrangle these two brutes," she said with a grin.

The colonel looked shocked at first, and then took Weather into his arms. He smiled at her and she smiled back. Weather seemed to be searching his eyes, as she touched his face, and then nuzzled under his chin. Yes, Rainey's girl was a charmer and she melted the sad man's heart.

"Isn't she the sweetest thing," Melanie said.

Constance chuckled. "She's just like Rainey was, very in tune with people. She always seemed to know what people were feeling, even as a baby."

The colonel patted Weather's back, hugging her to him. "What's your name little one?" He asked, as Weather leaned back and tried to stick her fingers in his mouth, studying his face.

Rainey remained in the floor, a giggling baby boy under each arm, and introduced her children. "That's Weather, and this is Mack and Timothy."

The colonel looked over at Rainey. "You have a beautiful family."

"Thank you, Colonel. We got a late start and there were all these bedrooms, so we had them all at once."

The colonel handed Weather back to Rainey. "Spend some time with your children. It passes so quickly. I need to talk to my wife. I'll step into the hall."

"Come with me, Colonel. I'll show you where you can have some privacy," Melanie offered, escorting the colonel out of the room.

Weather wriggled out of Rainey's arms to stand in front of her, using Nee Nee's chest for balance, while babbling a series of sounds. Mack hung off Rainey's right shoulder bobbing up and down, doing a dance to his own drummer, and occasionally jabbering back at his sister. Timothy knelt on her left, completely engrossed in one of Rainey's pants pockets. While her children used her for an activity center, Rainey turned her attention to Gunny.

"I understand you were not happy about your weapon being seized."

"No ma'am, I was not," Gunny responded, with more than a hint of military in her tone. "As I explained to the officers, the warrant was for your weapons, not mine. I also explained that I was on protection detail."

"A legitimate argument," Rainey commented, waiting for the rest.

"Your lawyer told me the warrant read all firearms on the premises, including the garage, so I was not given much choice in the matter. Your wife then subjected me to an interrogation, as to why my weapon was out of the safe. I regret to inform you that you are in deep shit, boss." She quickly added, "Sorry, deep guano."

Rainey smiled at her. "We're going to have to work on your weapon- hiding skills."

"Oorah, boss. And may I add, I can see why you don't like to cross her."

"Hands on her hips, huh?" Rainey asked, able to imagine exactly what Katie looked like when she questioned Gunny, and fully expecting to see it herself again, very soon.

"When she gets going, you can't get a word in there, can you?"

Rainey chuckled. "No, you really can't."

Gunny winced in pain and her hand shot to her temple.

"Are you all right?" Rainey asked.

"Just a headache. If you don't mind, while you're here, I'm going to lie down for a bit."

"Are you sure you're okay? I could call Junior, so you can go home," Rainey suggested.

"No, no, he's with Mackie. I'll be fine. I just need to close my eyes for a minute or two," Gunny said, still rubbing her temple.

"Really, if you need to go home, I can find someone else to stay here."

Gunny hated her disability, and that's what these headaches were. They ended her military career, the only life she had known since the age of eighteen. Rainey saw flashes of brain injury behavior, moodiness, irritability, but Gunny tried to maintain an even keel. She disliked having someone ask her if she needed to rest. Gunny prided herself in showing no weakness. Rainey should have remembered that.

Gunny's reply had an edge to it. "If you don't think I can take care of your family, then maybe you should call someone else." As soon as it was out of her mouth, she apologized. "I'm sorry. I just need a few minutes."

"No problem. Go rest. I'll tell Katie to save you some dinner."

After politely excusing herself, Gunny left the room, leaving Rainey alone with her mother and the triplets. She was trying to extricate her tightly clasped breast from one of Weather's tiny hands without losing skin, when Constance started speaking.

"Are you all right, Rainey? You seem rather calm in midst of the current tempest surrounding you."

Prying Weather's little fingers from her shirt, Rainey said, "I think I may be mellowing with age."

Constance chuckled, and took a seat on the end of the couch near Rainey and the children. "You, mellow? That would be a first. Beware the raging current beneath the smooth surface, I'd say."

Rainey grinned at her mother. "That's your tax dollars at work. They train us well at Quantico. Emotional involvement precludes brain function."

"You know, when you grin like that, you look just like your father. I'm not sure you have a single strand of my DNA."

177

Rainey's smile grew. "Dad always said I reminded him of you when I was mad."

Katie's mother stuck her head around the corner. "Food's on the table."

Rainey handed Weather to her mother, stood, and took a boy into each arm, thinking she had gotten away with that shot across the bow.

Her mother, following closely behind her to the dining room, was not about to let that pass. After all, it was at the knees of Constance and her grandmother, Martha Lee, where Rainey learned the art of retort.

Constance said softly, "Well played, Caroline."

"Touché, Connie," Rainey said, smiling over her shoulder.

"Billy Bell, as I live and breathe," her mother said, sighing.

They both started laughing and headed into family dinner. Like resigning from the FBI, falling in love with Katie, and becoming a parent, sitting down to dinner with Constance and being happy about it was something Rainey never imagined. She smiled, hugging the boys closer. Yes, she was a swirl of raging currents underneath, but for these precious moments, Rainey was determined to float peacefully on the surface with her family.

#

"This is going to be good."

Those were his parting words to Bladen. He left her suspended from the picquet, one wrist attached to a bar above her head, her opposite foot on a blunted stake on the floor. It was blunted, but sharp enough to cause severe pain if she tried to relieve the strain on her wrist. He told her this form of punishment was used on soldiers in medieval Europe. It would not kill her, unless he left her there for days. He knew this because he had done it to one of his first conquests, as he called them. Bladen was being disciplined for kicking him in the ribs when he unbuckled her leg from the rack. She did not care at that point if the kick made him angry. She had decided she was going to take one good shot at this guy before he killed her. She saw her chance and took it. Instead of anger, he was pleased that she still had some fight left in her, after the torture he just administered.

He laughed at her, even though she was sure she hurt him. "I guess you didn't like that last little ass fuck. Maybe another session with the Pear will make it easier for you."

Bladen screamed in rage and tried to kick him again, but this time he jumped out of the way. His fist to her jaw was the quick response. While she was still dazed from the blow, he removed her from the rack, dragging her by her hair to the picquet.

"I see some discipline is in order while I'm out. I'd love to stay and see to your correction personally, but this will have to do until I get back. I don't want to miss the show," he said, as he pulled the rope tight around her wrist.

"You're fucking insane," Bladen shouted.

"No, I'm not. I'm quite sane. I just don't give a fuck."

#

After dinner, Rainey retired to her office with the colonel. The first thing she did was look to see if the .38 was still secreted away. It was.

The colonel chuckled. "They missed one, eh?"

Rainey smiled back at him. "Only you, me, and my deceased father know about this. Let's keep it that way."

"I take it Katie would not approve."

It was Rainey's turn to chuckle. "Oh no, she would hit the ceiling if she knew this was in here. My philosophy is what she doesn't know doesn't hurt."

The colonel shook his head. "Word of advice from an old married man, that philosophy will get you a night or two on the couch."

"I'll remember you said that," Rainey said with a wink.

She crossed to her desk and sat down, where she attempted to make contact with her satellite image source. She received only a standard recorded message stating Brooks was out of the office, which was highly unusual, both in style and content. Rainey sent an encrypted email requesting a new satellite image for the GPS coordinates she supplied, and waited for a reply.

"She might be out of the office," Rainey explained to the colonel, "but she is never far from her email."

179

Curious about the videos on the flash drive Sheila gave her, she plugged it into the computer and clicked on the file labeled "Hospital Security." A video of the emergency room waiting area began to play. Rainey recognized the moment, because she saw herself stand and hug her stepfather. She stopped the video and restarted it, this time watching the other people in the room.

Looking over her shoulder, the colonel pointed at the screen. "There. See that guy. He's watching you."

Rainey restarted the video again. Leaning on the wall near the entrance of the waiting area, a man was focused on her, while pretending to be engrossed in his phone. She actually saw him snap the picture that ended up on the Triangle Lesbian blog minutes later. Regrettably, Rainey could not see his face. The stalker/blogger was concealing his identity with a baseball cap and seemed to know right where the security cameras were. Rainey replayed the video, this time catching a glimpse of Martin Douglas Cross, the writer, standing on the other side of the exterior wall of windows, looking in on the scene. She was pondering that, when the video skipped forward to another short clip attached at the end. Rainey forgot all about the writer.

"Gotcha!" she said with delight, as she watched Cookie Kutter give the stalker money. Rainey still could not see his face, but she clearly saw him hand Cookie a flash drive.

"I assume this is good news," the colonel commented.

"You have no idea how good," Rainey said. "I'm about to send a copy of this to my lawyer and then I'm going to watch Cookie crumble."

Rainey saved a copy of the video to her hard drive and then sent an email to Molly with the video attached. She wrote, "Make an appointment with the judge," in the subject line, and "See attached," in the body of the message. Uncharacteristically, Rainey added a smiley face icon at the end. As an afterthought, she wrote, "I want this guy's name, whatever it takes."

She checked to see if Brooks had responded to her earlier email and then opened the second file on the flash drive. The view from a patrol car's dashboard camera popped on the screen as the video began to play. The patrol unit was parked behind Rex King's unmarked vehicle.

"Well, I'll be damned," Rainey whispered, as she watched Rex hand her Glock to Martin Douglas Cross.

Rex then exited the vehicle, leaving Cross alone with Rainey's weapon. The video went on for several minutes, as Rainey stared in disbelief. Three minutes and thirty-two seconds into the video, Cross exited the car.

"Reasonable doubt," the colonel commented. "Probably ought to send your lawyer a copy of that one too."

Rainey agreed. This time she simply wrote in the subject line, "We need to talk."

She then clicked on the images of the shell casing, noting the markings left by the weapon that fired it. She was zooming in on the image, when her phone rang. Rainey did not look at the caller ID, assuming it was Molly calling.

"That was fast," she said into the phone.

"No kidding," Sheila said. "How did you know?"

"Sorry, I thought you were Molly. What's happened?" Rainey asked.

"I'm on my way back to the office. Just pulled into the parking garage," Sheila said, excitement speeding her words. "They patched a call through to my cell phone. It was him, the killer."

"What makes you so sure? What did he say?" Rainey asked, knowing so many nuts inserted themselves in investigations, even falsely confessing to garner attention.

"First, he asked for me specifically and flat out told the dispatcher he was the man who was holding Bladen Asher. Second, he said, 'Tell Rainey Bell she might need to refer to her notes.' I asked him what notes he was talking about and he said, 'Schaefer, DeBardeleben, Bundy, they are just part of my study.' Only a handful of people know we discussed those killers and I trust every one of them without reservation."

"Did you tell him I'm not on the case?"

Rainey could hear Sheila's heels tapping on the parking garage floor as she answered, "Yes, but he said if we wanted to keep Bladen Asher alive, then we better call you in. We haven't released anything about her abduction, so how would he know her name? He also said he didn't want a bunch of amateurs evaluating his work, since the FBI couldn't be bothered. Boy, you really nailed this guy's reaction to the press conference."

"Was the call recorded?" Rainey asked, already preparing to leave.

The colonel knew something had happened and was anxious for information, but did not interrupt. Rainey held the phone to her ear as she walked out of the office, the colonel following, while Shelia relayed the conversation she had with a killer.

"Yes, we have the recording. Rainey, he was cold, almost pleasant, as if he were inviting me to an art gallery exhibit. He said he was giving us his 'museum of serial murder' and then rattled off GPS coordinates, but the location is in the Indian Ocean, off the coast of Perth, Australia."

"Try the antipodal position," Rainey said. "Send the position and the recording to my phone. We're leaving my house now."

"Antipodal? What's that?" Sheila asked.

"The exact opposite place on the earth's surface. North Carolina's antipodal position is in the Indian Ocean, off the coast of Australia. Once you have the location, send out some covert surveillance teams first. This guy will be out there watching your arrival. Pay close attention to the vehicles that pass more than once. He may even stop to ask what's going on. If you block one lane with emergency vehicles after you arrive, you can slow the cars down and get a good look. By the way, he won't be driving the truck. His car will resemble a law enforcement vehicle, or a muscle car, something manly."

"Okay, I'm about to get into the elevator," Sheila said. "I'll send you the correct coordinates when I get upstairs. Are you going to meet us there?"

"Yes," Rainey said, arriving in the den, where Katie and the others were now gathered. "I just need to tell my family good night and then we're on the road."

"How do you know where to go?" Sheila asked.

"I'll bet it's within a few miles of where they found the first missing woman's car. We'll head that way."

"That's over by your old office, where the women's shelter is, isn't it?"

"Yes, and remember, there are no coincidences," Rainey said, smiling at Katie playing with triplets. "Oh, and thanks for the video. I owe you one."

"And I'm about to collect. See you in a few," Sheila said.

Rainey turned to the colonel. "Let me talk to Katie a second, and then I'll fill you in on the way."

Katie noticed Rainey and came out into the hallway. After the colonel thanked her for the hospitality, he went to wait by the front door. Rainey took Katie across the hall to the formal living room they never used.

"Honey, I have to go. I don't know when I'll be back. Wake Gunny up after I leave. If her headache gets worse, you call Junior. Understand?"

Katie wrapped her arms around Rainey and hugged her tightly. "Don't worry about us. You be safe."

Rainey bent to kiss Katie's lips, before smiling down at her. "I will. Call and check on Mackie for me, and you call if you need me, promise?"

"I promise. Now, go kiss your kids good night." As Rainey passed, Katie popped her on the butt. "And don't think you're getting out of that conversation about Gunny's weapon being in her car."

"Technically, it wasn't in the house," Rainey said, skipping out of Katie's reach.

Katie narrowed her eyes. "Technically, it was a deliberate attempt to circumvent the rules. Program her prints into the system, if you think she'll need to get to her gun. I'd rather you do that than hide things from me."

Rainey stopped moving and turned back to Katie. "Okay, you're right, but I think we need a separate safe for people like Junior and Gunny. They do need to be able to reach their weapons in an emergency. So, call the safe company tomorrow and have one put in. Will that work for you?"

"Yes, and that is how adults handle conflict. Don't sneak around, Rainey. That bothered me more than the gun in her car."

Ooh, that hurt. Rainey hated to disappoint Katie. She tried for redemption. "I'm sorry. It won't happen again." She silently vowed to remove the .38 from her office before she ended up on the couch.

#

"My best arabesque and no one is here to see it," Bladen said, her foot in demi pointe on the wooden stake, her other leg stretched out behind her, trying desperately to balance and relieve the strain on her wrist. "All those years of ballet are paying off, Mom," she said with a little laugh.

At least the dripping was not a problem this time. In his excitement to leave, her tormentor also forgot to turn on the music. To pass the time, Bladen played through childhood memories of tutus and nutcrackers, the annual holiday tradition of ballet and candy canes. She performed in "The Nutcracker" from age six to twelve, before she discovered running was more her passion. When Bladen declared at dinner one night that she was no longer interested in becoming the Sugarplum Fairy, she was sure her mother was secretly glad the days of afterschool dance class chauffeuring and endless recitals were over. Although she had not continued dance, Bladen's heart still quickened when she heard Tchaikovsky at Christmastime.

She closed her eyes and began with the party scene, remembering how the period costumes smelled like dry cleaning and mothballs, and how she relished that smell each year. She recalled the excitement of the first time she was chosen to dance in the opening waltz. A shortage of boys forced her into knickers and a waistcoat, but she did not mind. Bladen was simply glad to have graduated from tiny winged fairy in the sugarplum scene. She relaxed her pose, putting pressure on her wrist, and relieving the stabbing pain in the ball of her foot. While her body hung suspended in the dark room, her mind took to the stage. Beneath a behemoth Christmas tree, "The Nutcracker Suite" began to play, and Bladen waltzed.

CHAPTER TEN

"Three years ago, about a month before the first woman went missing, the company developing this land declared bankruptcy. They cleared some of it, started landscaping, and paved a drive. It's been tied up in court since then, but recently changed hands. Construction is scheduled to begin again next month. The search warrant is on the way, but we have verbal permission from the new owners to enter the property."

Sheila huddled close to a small group of detectives from the task force, while she told what she knew about the property they were about to enter. She was no longer wearing heels, and looked prepared for a hike in the woods. Rainey stood by her as they waited for the chains on the large gate to be cut. Rainey had been right about the location; it was exactly where she said it would be, just off U.S. 501, south of Chapel Hill. The first missing woman's car had been found less than two miles away. The area was heavily forested and about a half a mile from the western shoreline of Jordan Lake. Rainey's old home was a little more than five miles to the south.

"The construction starting up again. That's why he gave us his museum. He knew it would be exposed soon," Rainey told Sheila. "That's his stressor. He needed to manipulate and control its discovery."

Wiley Trainer stood to her left, shining a flashlight on a map in his hand. He drawled out, "Looking at the satellite image, there's quite a lot of forest to cover in there. Where should we start?"

Rainey looked at the map. "Before we let anyone in there, let's drive this lane. I want to look at these areas here." She pointed at several places. "See how these old paths through the woods come in from several directions? He didn't come through this gate, but used these paths. You need to put patrol cars at these access points. I'm guessing we'll find most of his victims pretty close to where these paths enter the property, at least the first ones."

Wiley turned to the assemblage of patrol officers, standing a few feet away. "Y'all wait out here. We're going to take a look and then come back to set up the grid search." He then spoke to the young detective next to him, showing him the map. "Put patrol cars at each of these access points. Nobody in or out."

While Wiley discussed sealing the area off with the detective, Sheila spoke to Rainey. "I'm worried about displacing evidence in the dark. Shouldn't we wait until daylight?"

Rainey nodded in agreement. "I understand what you're saying, but I think he dumped the last body in here months ago. He took Jacquie in September and he kept her body. Unless he grabbed someone we don't know about, any evidence was washed away long ago. Still, we don't want the search team crashing through the site. Make sure the search is slow and deliberate."

Flatbed trucks carrying high-powered outdoor lighting lined the narrow two-lane road running in front of the property, accompanied by large generators. Rainey could hear the police helicopters coming nearer. They were equipped with searchlights that could turn the night sky into day. The state medical examiner had been called in advance of finding the bodies, at Rainey's suggestion. She was sure this was no hoax. The ME's vans were arriving now, lining up behind the flatbeds. All traffic was being diverted through roadblocks surrounding the area. Rainey knew the killer was watching and she imagined he was enjoying the show.

She looked over at the colonel, who stood anxiously waiting by his car. Rainey understood that he needed to be involved, and also knew she could not let him see what was beyond the gate.

She tapped Wiley on the shoulder. "Hey, can you find someone to stay with Colonel Asher? He isn't to come on the property under any circumstances, so you better make sure it's someone that can handle him."

Rainey and Sheila went to the SUV parked in front of the gate and climbed in. While they waited for Wiley to join them, Sheila said, "If there aren't any bodies in here, I'm going to look really foolish."

Rainey stared straight ahead, where the headlights illuminated what was to become a gated community much like her own. "No, the people feeling foolish will be the folks that just bought this land. No one is ever going to forget what was found here."

"You're that positive? How do you know?"

"I listened to the recorded call. Pure narcissism. He planned to reveal his body farm from the beginning. This is his artwork. He needs it to be appreciated, and not by some developer or local hiker stumbling on it by accident." Rainey indicated the massive law enforcement presence with a sweep of her hand. "This spectacle he's created is all part of the grand theatre in his mind."

"So why play into that? Why didn't we just come with a few cars and check it out on the down low?"

Sheila was really trying to understand how Rainey thought and why, after listening to the recorded call, she had recommended storming the location with lights and sirens blaring.

Rainey turned to face Sheila. "While he's watching us, Bladen Asher has a chance of surviving. Keep him busy. That's the only chance she has. The press will be here soon. I'll make sure they see me. You make sure they have ample reason to stay live on the site, or at least continue breaking news. He won't be able to stop watching."

Sheila started nodding her head. "I get it. And while he's watching us, we will be looking for him."

"If I'm right about this guy," Rainey said, "he will think he is so far out in front of us, there is no way we have a clue who he is."

Sheila's eyebrows rose. "We don't, do we? We have a truck description, but that could turn out to be a dead end, just some college kid with a girlfriend in the apartment complex."

Rainey grinned at Sheila. "A coincidence?"

"Yeah, yeah, I know—no coincidences," Sheila said, with a chuckle.

"Brooks should have something on the truck for us soon. The UNSUB doesn't know we have that picture or that we're looking for his truck, and we should keep that advantage. We can't tip him off. His behavior will become very unpredictable, if we do."

Sheila nodded that she understood and informed Rainey, "I called Danny, told him of the search about to take place. He asked that you be on site and I assured him you would be. They were on the tarmac, about to take off."

"Good," Rainey said, "and if you could get the ME to hold off on moving the bodies, that would be even better. Let Danny and the team get a look at the scene first. They should be here in a couple of hours."

"Are you going to stay on site, after they arrive?" Sheila asked.

Rainey looked out the window at the colonel. "I need to help that man find his daughter. The BAU can profile the UNSUB for the task force. I'll get you started, but Danny will be the one leading this investigation."

Sheila sighed. "I sure hope you're right and that girl is still alive, though Lord knows what he's done to her."

Rainey saw Wiley approaching the colonel with a large uniformed officer. "If she's half the young woman her father thinks she is, she's fighting for her life. As long as she is a challenge to him, this UNSUB will keep her alive. The moment she gives up, she's dead."

"Unh, unh, unh," Sheila said, shaking her head from side to side. "I used to think I wanted to know what you know about these sickos. After that body this morning, I am damned glad I don't."

Rainey turned back to Sheila. "I think you are about to get more education in sexual murderers than you could have imagined. When this is over and the nightmares come, you call me anytime, day or night. I've been there."

Sheila had no time to respond, but the anticipated horror showed on her face, as Wiley climbed in behind the steering wheel. A video technician joined him on the front seat, camera already rolling.

As the tech swept the inside of the vehicle with the camera, recording all present, Wiley said, "Shall we, ladies?"

Not waiting for a reply, he put the SUV in gear and moved through the now open gates. The construction company had paved a road through the prospective neighborhood and cleared off a few home sites. A small lake had been created on the left of the entrance. When Rainey crossed through the gates, she closed the mental boxes she would not need or could not afford to have open at a crime scene. She opened the ones that allowed her to think like a killer. By studying their behavior, the FBI analyst had learned how these types of killers thought. Part of Rainey's job had been to suspend her revulsion at their horrible acts and walk in the killer's shoes.

She eyed the lake, as Wiley aimed a searchlight across the surface. "How deep is that water?"

Sheila pulled a printout of the architect's plans for the community from her leather binder. Using her flashlight, she searched for the information. "It's not on this drawing. Should I have someone check it out?"

"If this guy studied Schaefer, then there's a good chance you'll find some of the victims in there."

Sheila got on the phone and called in the dive team. Before hanging up, she said, "Don't touch anything. Just tell me if you find something."

Beyond the lake, a sign indicated the foundation work behind it was to have been a large swimming pool and athletic complex. The helicopters arrived and joined in the search, sweeping their bright lights over the unfinished pool.

"If you were coming out here to look at the land, you'd probably drive around and stop to look at the only construction available," Rainey said. "The UNSUB would know that. It's worth a look, but I doubt he put any bodies there. He needed to be able to come visit them. He didn't want them disturbed until he was ready. Again, control and manipulation of events are important to him."

Wiley crept the vehicle along the paved road. Nightsun searchlights lit up the landscape around the SUV, as the choppers hovered over the area.

Rainey looked over the architect's plans. She had a gut feeling, and leaned up to tap Wiley on the shoulder. "Go on down to the very end of the road and stop. I think that's where we should start."

Wiley sped up and the searchlights followed. When they arrived, everyone exited the vehicle and waited for Rainey to lead the way. She saw where an old one-lane path came out of the woods and started toward it. Once she reached where the path met the pavement, she stopped and looked around. She waved the others over to her.

"Wiley, do you still have that map on you?" Rainey shouted over the rotor blades chopping the air above them. They were far enough away not to disturb the crime scene with the blade wash, but the constant engine noise forced conversation to a higher decibel.

Wiley pulled the folded map from his back pocket and handed it to her. She held it out in the light from the helicopter. "You see this?" Rainey pointed at a dark squiggly line that cut through the forest on her right. "It looks like a trail, but I think it's a stream feeding into Jordan Lake. Let's go back that way. Water draws these guys for some reason. If he knew about the paths, then he knew about the stream."

They started into the woods, the searchlights illuminating the ground around them. Sheila walked beside Rainey. "So, you think he's from around here?"

"Oh yeah," Rainey said. "There's no question about that. He's close, probably drives U.S. 501 to work every day."

The undergrowth was low and the foliage sparse in the dead of winter. The only bright color in the woods came from the evergreens. Copper-colored pine needles and prickly brown

190

pinecones carpeted the forest floor. Broken limbs and old fallen trees littered the ground, but there appeared to be a worn trail toward the stream. They tromped a few more yards before coming on a small clearing and a valley where a dry streambed lay. There were no large trees in the depression, opening up the area to the sky above, where one of the searchlight beams poured through. Rainey grabbed Wiley's arm, before he could take another step forward.

"Stop," she shouted over the constant chop-chop-chop above.

Sheila, Wiley, and the cameraman froze in mid step. Rainey squatted on the ground, looking at the oblong bowl shaped depression.

She pointed up at the helicopter. "Call the search light off for a minute. I need to see what he sees."

Wiley barked orders into his radio and seconds later they were plunged into darkness. After a moment to let her eyes adjust, Rainey began to scour the ground in front of her. There was no moonlight. The sky reflected the illuminated haze of the not too distant metropolitan areas, allowing only the brightest stars to shine through. Rainey clicked on her flashlight and held it close to the ground. She swept it over the bank closest to her and saw no anomalies.

Rainey stood and turned to the others saying, "Wait here," before walking down the slight slope to the dry streambed. She knelt, holding the flashlight parallel to the slope of the other bank. As the beam skipped just above the surface, three distinct piles of leaves, branches, and pine needles appeared, and were too symmetrically spaced to be naturally occurring. Rainey shouted back to the others.

"You can turn the lights back on. I found them, well, three of them anyway. Tell the ME to come on in, so we can take a look."

Rainey flashed her light around the area, while Wiley and Sheila made the appropriate communications. She noticed a small tree standing alone at the crest of the embankment, obviously planted there. It did not look like the other evergreens in the area. The cameraman came down into the streambed with her, recording the scene. He focused where her light was shining and commented on the tree, the first words Rainey had heard him speak.

"That shouldn't be here," he said.

"Why? What kind of tree is that?" Rainey asked.

"It's a Western Hemlock. I'm from Seattle, Washington. That's our state tree."

Sheila worked her way down the slope to stand beside Rainey. "The ME is on the way," she said.

The light from the helicopter popped back on and focused on the spot where they were standing. The three piles of debris were more obvious now that Rainey had located them. She pointed them out to Sheila and Wiley, who had just stepped down into the streambed. "See those three evenly spaced piles of leaves and branches? Shallow graves on a stream bank with a Western Hemlock planted above them. This is either his homage to Gary Ridgway, The Green River Killer, or Ted Bundy, both from the state of Washington. I'll have to see the bodies to determine which."

"How will you know?" Shelia asked.

Rainey said matter-of-factly, "If they were strangled and still have their heads, then it's Ridgway. The UNSUB mentioned 'his study.' If he truly conducted a study on serial killers, then he could not have skipped over old Gary. He was originally convicted of forty-eight murders, had another tacked on in a plea bargain, but confessed to committing more than ninety in his sixteen-year killing spree. If this is his Ridgway staging, then these bodies will be the missing prostitutes. We'll need to check for signs of necrophilia, as well."

Wiley stared at the shallow graves for a moment. "So where do you think the others are?"

"Let me see that map again," Rainey said, holding out her hand.

Wiley handed over the map and leaned in for a better look, as Rainey held it out in the light.

"See how the main road branches off into these planned cul-de-sacs? I'd have your search grids start at the end of each turn around and expand out from there. He took the time to plant a tree here. If you stand back on the other bank, this looks like a museum exhibit. He used the paved road to create pathways to his exhibits. If he's done what I think he has done, then this will be the least horrific of his displays."

Wiley's radio cackled loudly with an excited voice. "Captain Trainer, come in. Captain Trainer, respond."

Wiley put the radio to his mouth and answered, "Trainer, go ahead."

"You've got to come back to the lake, now. Oh man, you need to come right now!"

"I can't come right now. I'm waiting for the ME to get here. Have they started back this way?"

"Well, yes and no, sir. They started that way, but then they saw—Really, you need to come as soon as you can."

"I counted five ME vans out there on the road. You send one of them to my location and I'll be back to the lake in a few minutes."

"Ten-four, Captain. And hey, you better bring that profiler back with you, too. She's never going to believe this."

Rainey smiled when Wiley looked at her and spoke into the radio. "Son, the only person out here that can believe this shit is that profiler. The rest of us, well, we're going to have to suck it up. Now, calm down and get that ME rolling to me."

"Ten-four, Captain."

#

The site was photographed from all angles, before Rainey was allowed to move some of the debris aside. She only had to brush away a pile of dried pine needles to see that she was correct. Uncovering the upper body of a young woman, with the panties he used to strangle her still tied around her neck, Rainey recognized the posing from having viewed the photographs of Gary Ridgway's victims' gravesites.

"These are going to be the working girls he kidnapped," she said, standing and removing the latex gloves she had donned before approaching the body. She spoke directly to the medical examiner's evidence collection team. "Do what you must to uncover the bodies, but please don't move them until the FBI team arrives. They should be here soon."

193

An evidence technician whined, "Man, we'll be standing around out here waiting on the feds for hours."

Rainey smiled at the young man. "There will be plenty for you to do, before your shift ends. In fact, I doubt you will ever forget this night." She looked back over her shoulder at the skull staring up at the stars. "And don't worry about her. She's been waiting three years for us to find her. I'm sure she has the patience to wait for the people that are coming to help solve her murder."

The technician slipped away, red-faced and humbled by Rainey's admonishment, as more crime scene investigators began to arrive. Wiley explained the parameters in which they should work, keeping the scene as pristine as possible until the behavioral analysts could have a look. Rainey walked out of the woods to the SUV with Sheila. The flatbeds were moving lights into the areas she had indicated needed to be searched first. Orders were given to the helicopters to fly around, basically making a show of searching the adjoining woods. She could still hear them clearly, but at least they could talk now without shouting.

"Where did he put the first victim?" Rainey wondered aloud.

Sheila commented, "I was thinking about that too. If the prostitutes were his Gary Ridgway tribute, what was the first one?"

"The first one was an anomaly. I think she crossed his path at the wrong moment in his life and he finally took his fantasies from his mind to reality. Her body will reveal more clues about who he is. I'm not sure we'll find her out here. They usually don't put as much planning into the first body disposal. He would have wanted to get rid of the body quickly. She's probably closer to where he lives, or was. I wouldn't rule out him moving bodies around."

Wiley joined them at the SUV. "Let's go see what all the fuss is about up at the lake and then we'll get the search groups started. They should have all the lights set up by then."

Rainey stared out the window at the commotion erupting on the site, as they drove past flatbeds and ME vans positioning themselves for the body recoveries she had predicted. She had no doubt that her assumptions were correct. As they wound their way toward the lake, Rainey saw what the killer saw, erasing all the noise and illumination, just him on a slow walk through his museum of horrors. If he were caught on the property, he would claim he was just a local out for a walk in the woods, or an off-road enthusiast riding the back trails. The property did not appear to be disturbed in the least, meaning there was hardly any traffic through here at all.

Rainey turned to Sheila. "Check and see if this area is patrolled by a security company, and talk to the local deputies. Find out if they have any records of trespassers, vandals, anything suspicious—and have them look back for calls that may have come in from the public, reporting activity out here. See if those reports came from people willing to give their names."

Wiley made eye contact with Rainey in the rearview mirror. "You think he may have called something in himself?"

"Yes, I do. If you look at the timeline of abductions, there was a time about eighteen months ago, when no women fitting his MO were reported missing. He may have had a moment of clarity. He may have freaked himself out recreating one of these crimes. He may have tried to have the bodies discovered, as a deterrent to future murders. If he did do that and his crimes still went undiscovered, it fed his narcissistic belief that he could not be caught. Big Ed Kemper had the head of one of his victims in the trunk, while he was inside having his juvenile murder record sealed by two psychologists who deemed him a new man. It emboldened him beyond measure."

"Well, it would take a special kind of freak to do the Bundy body dumps," Sheila said.

Everybody knew who Ted Bundy was, knew his crimes, knew his swaggering good looks, but not everyone was willing to know what really turned Theodore Robert Bundy on. Ted liked them dead. He had absolutely no use for a conscious victim. He revisited the bodies, often putting makeup on the corpse and fixing her hair, before violating her again. If this UNSUB went through with replicating the Bundy murders, it put him in a very special class of criminals. Necrophilia practitioners would admit to the most inhumane atrocities, but rarely wanted to discuss the post mortem activities they enjoyed. Even the sickest of the freaks knew sexual violation of the dead was extraordinarily offensive.

When they arrived at the lake, Rainey could see high-powered lights lining the banks and aimed down in the water. The water was clear bluish-green, indicating a sandy bottom. The dive team's Zodiac boat floated in the center of the lake, with two divers in cold-water dry-suits hanging onto the sides. The young detective who had frantically called Wiley on the radio hurried to the SUV before it came to a stop. As soon as Wiley opened his door, the young man started talking.

"Captain Trainer, we have a video you need to see," he said, trying to remain calm, but Rainey could tell it was taking quite an effort on his part.

Rainey and Sheila followed Wiley and the young detective to the back of the dive team's Humvee, where several officers were gathered around a laptop computer, resting on the tailgate.

"Captain," one of the officers said, dipping his head in an unofficial sign of respect for his superior.

An older, silver-haired officer stuck out his hand to shake Wiley's. "Captain, we got a strange one here. In all my years of recovering bodies from the water, I have never seen anything like this."

"Lieutenant Chambless," Wiley began, "this is Rainey Bell. She's a behavioral analyst consulting on the case."

Chambless extended his hand to Rainey. "It's a pleasure to meet you, and I'm glad you're here. Maybe you can tell us what we've found. We have video of what the divers saw. Nothing was touched. They just took the video and came back up."

Rainey shook his hand and said, "Well, let's see what you got."

The sergeant moved the other officers out of the way and turned the laptop so Rainey could see the screen. He hit play, while he narrated what she was seeing.

"When we turned on the lights, we could see a dark spot out in the middle there. The boys went in and started across the bottom. With our underwater lights, we can see pretty well in clear water. You'll see the dark mass starting to form in front of them here."

He stopped talking and just let the video play. Rainey could hear the divers talking to each other through their full-face masks and the sound of the air bubbles moving through the water. The mass began to take the shape of a white Volkswagen. Rainey recognized the 1968 model right away. Ted Bundy drove the same car.

As the diver grew closer, Rainey heard him exclaim, "Holy shit!"

The driver's side door came into focus. The hollow eyes of a skull stared out the window at them, its short dark hair floating in the water. The skeletal hands of the body were tied to the steering wheel.

The other diver said, "Fuck me. What the hell is that?"

The sergeant reached over and muted the volume, as the video continued to play. The camera moved closer, revealing two bodies buckled into the back seat. One of the bodies was bound with ropes around her ankles, knees, thighs, waist, and shoulders. A gag protruded from her mouth, and there was a plastic bag over her head. It seemed the UNSUB had also studied Dennis Rader, the self-proclaimed Bind-Torture-Kill murderer that terrorized Wichita, Kansas. The second body was also bound with hands behind her back, a hangman's noose dangling from her neck.

Rainey began to describe what she was seeing. "The victims are in varying conditions of decay, which indicates he killed them at different times. He's done quite a bit of work to sink a car that floats and pose the bodies this way. The lake is too exposed to spend the kind of time it took to do that. I think he put the bodies in the car and rolled them in the water together."

Chambless said, "He could have floated it out to the middle and then sunk it. Easy enough to do, even for one person."

Rainey explained what the bodies represented. "The body with the bag over the head is indicative of Dennis Rader, BTK. The noose on this one is copying Gerard Schaefer. I'm sure you all recognize Ted Bundy's car. The passenger seat has been removed, just like Bundy's."

The camera moved around the car and then the diver poked it into the passenger side window. On the floor, by the driver's seat, another body was laid out. This one was handcuffed with a crowbar still embedded in her skull.

Rainey pointed at the screen. "That's how Bundy killed his victims."

Sheila asked, "So what about the driver? Whose victim does that represent?"

Rainey did not take her eyes from the screen, but answered, "I think that's supposed to be Ted. I never profiled this UNSUB as killing men, but I guess he needed one for his artwork. That looks like a tie and suit jacket on the body."

"Sweet Mary," the sergeant said under his breath.

Rainey turned to him. "Could you ask them to open the trunk?"

The sergeant picked up his radio and made the request. He turned off the video and started the live feed from the diver's camera. Rainey watched as the divers descended to the front of the Volkswagen, getting a good view of the macabre scene behind the windshield. It took several tries, but when the diver finally pried open the trunk lid, everyone watching jumped back from the screen. A bubble of trapped air exploded from under the lid, causing three skulls to float up a few inches before settling back down in the trunk space.

"How in the hell did she know that would be there?"

She ignored the comment and spoke to Wiley and Sheila. "That's Big Ed Kemper's MO. We have extreme violence and intelligence here, a ruthless combination. I would not be surprised to find our UNSUB has killed more than we are aware of—many more."

The diver shut the trunk lid to keep the evidence intact. When he did, Rainey saw something written on the paint by the latch.

Rainey asked the sergeant, "Can they get a close up of what that says?"

The sergeant spoke into his radio again and the camera moved in closer to the words. Painted in freehanded small black print, Rainey read aloud, "Lady Killer."

"This guy is a real piece of work," Wiley commented in disgust.

Rainey nodded. "This is his lobby display, like the big dinosaur skeleton that welcomes you to the natural history museum." She pointed at the gates. "That's where you enter and then follow the road to his gallery of killers."

Rainey turned a complete circle, observing the fervor of activity in all directions. Up in the sky, news media helicopters danced on the perimeter, held at bay by the police air patrol. Searchlights crisscrossed the landscape. Emergency lights flashed red, white, and blue, bouncing off any reflective surface. The ground troops of the media forces had arrived at the gate. Cameras rolled under bright lights, electronic flashes popped repeatedly. It rivaled any Hollywood red carpet event.

"This is his gala opening, ladies and gentlemen. Welcome to the 'Museum of Serial Murder,' curator as yet unknown."

#

The search parties descended on the woods and within minutes the radio began to crackle with reports of body discoveries. Rainey made the rounds to each site, before the ME and the crime scene investigators began collecting evidence. In order of discovery, she identified the staged areas by the serial killer they depicted. The headless body parts in garbage bags and strewn about one area were probably a tribute to Edmund Kemper, the six-foot-nine giant known as the Co-ed Killer who terrorized Santa Cruz in the early seventies. It could also have been Jeffrey Dahmer, but Rainey doubted this UNSUB was into men or cannibalism. She was also pretty sure the landscaped flowerbed, meant to entice prospective buyers to the home site, would yield more clues.

"Dig up that flowerbed out there by the road," Rainey told one of the investigators. "You'll probably find a head in there, maybe more."

Bundy's scene was a decomposed body wearing makeup and a wig, along with a skeleton missing its head, both covered only with forest debris. Gerard Schaefer liked to do doubles, so his staging involved two women bound together, hangman's nooses attached to their necks, and buried in shallow graves. Dennis Rader's display followed so closely to the binding of his victims, the materials used, and the posing of the two bodies that Rainey thought the UNSUB must have seen the actual crime scene photos which, sadly, were available on the Internet. The last body she viewed was posed much like Jacquie's. There was only one body found in the James Mitchell DeBardeleben display, but that was enough to see the UNSUB had moved on to the convicted killer responsible for largest collection of sexually sadistic evidence ever found.

"He recreated the crimes of six of the most, if not prolific, then scarily proficient human predators since the seventies," Rainey was saying to the colonel.

She had seen enough and come back outside the gate to check on him and put distance between her and the smell of decay permeating the woods. Sheila was in the middle of an impromptu roadside press conference, with the corralled media jockeying for position to frame the property entrance in the shot. Between the gate and the media, Rainey leaned up against a patrol car talking to the colonel, a prominent figure in any camera angle they could take. She was part of the show for the UNSUB, and it was about to get better.

"Did you learn anything that could help us find Bladen?" The colonel asked, just as everyone's attention was drawn to the wailing sirens approaching.

Rainey ignored the clamor the oncoming vehicles created and answered, "Not much. I know he lives close and that he passes this place every day. I know he gradually moved from strangulation to sadistic torture, as he studied each killer, looking for the one that turned him on the most. I think he's figured that out and is now holding his victims in the kind of chamber DeBardeleben fantasized and wrote about. That doesn't help us with his location or identity, but I know more about the man we're dealing with." She paused, as three black SUVs came into view. "I think these guys can help with locating him. The UNSUB wanted the FBI and here they are."

"Quite a dramatic arrival," the colonel commented.

"That's for him. They understand that he's watching and want to keep him interested. That's why I'm standing in full view of those cameras talking to you. The more he focuses on what is happening here, the less time he spends with your daughter. This isn't how the BAU or I usually operate. In most instances, the locals don't even know we have come and gone."

The colonel eyed Rainey for a moment, before asking, "Do you miss that life? You are so very good at it. I'm sure it was difficult for you to walk away."

Rainey watched as the SUVs passed and drove directly through the gates, sirens still in full voice. Her heart had quickened at the sight of the big black vehicles approaching, lights flashing, announcing someone important was coming. She remembered being buckled in beside Danny, adrenaline pumping, brain racing through her mental encyclopedia of depraved behavior, piecing together what she knew, and anticipating what was to come. It was the career of which she dreamed, Special Agent Rainey Bell of the Federal Bureau of Investigation, Behavioral Analyst Unit, the cream of the crop, the best—and worst years of her life.

She smiled at the colonel. "It was both the hardest and the easiest decision I ever made. I would never give up what I have now to return to the bureau."

He smiled for the first time since they arrived on the site. "No, I don't imagine that you would."

Rainey heard doors slamming, and looked to see her former teammates exiting the vehicles. One very familiar body shape emerged from the back of the last SUV. Seeing only her silhouette, Rainey could still identify Melatiah Brooks. A broad smile crept across Rainey's face, as Brooks turned and spotted her.

She began to walk quickly in Rainey's direction, calling out loudly, "Rainey Bell, Brooks has taken flight and landed in your fair city for only one reason."

Danny fell in step with Brooks. "She wouldn't put the travel vouchers through unless I agreed to bring her."

Rainey chuckled. "And what, pray tell, could pry you away from your computers, my friend?"

Brooks swept Rainey into a hug. "I had to come see those babies." She pushed back and looked up at Rainey, who towered over the short, rotund woman. "And of course I had to come rescue you from these idiots. Did they really throw you in general population at the jail?"

"Why, yes they did," Rainey said, looking over at Danny. His appearance always made her smile. No matter how he tried, he never quite looked comfortable with his tall, broad frame stuffed in a suit. His red wavy hair and freckles made him look as Irish as his name and younger than his forty-five years. She gave him a grin and said, "I hear I have you to thank for my shortened stay behind bars."

Danny smiled and accepted the hug Rainey offered, as she stepped out of Brooks's grasp. He patted her on the back and whispered in her ear, "We will talk when this is over. You know in your heart I would never betray you."

Rainey leaned back and stared into the eyes of her oldest friend. She suddenly felt guilty at ever imagining he would do anything to harm her. She smiled and simply said, "I know."

She released Danny, as all the members of the team had now gathered near. Rainey exchanged hugs and greeting with each one, and then turned to make the introductions. Wiley and Sheila, having heard the commotion of the team's arrival, also joined the group.

"Captain Wiley Trainer, Sergeant Sheila Robertson, I think you're familiar with the team."

Wiley and Sheila extended their hands and exchanged handshakes, both having worked with the team in the past.

Rainey indicated the colonel, saying, "And this is Colonel Patrick Asher. His daughter, Bladen, was abducted by the UNSUB yesterday evening. He took classes at Quantico and is retired Army CID. He's asked to be treated like an investigator, as much as possible. Colonel, this is Supervisory Special Agent Danny McNally, with whom you spoke on the phone."

Danny shook the colonel's hand. "We will do everything we can to find your daughter."

"I'm sure you will," Colonel Asher said.

Rainey went through the rest of the team for the colonel's benefit, introducing Roger, the distinguished oldest member of the team; Paula, recently returned from a year away after the birth of her first child; James, the tech guru and surveillance specialist; Curtis, the handsome cherub-faced youngest member of the team; and the irreplaceable computer expert, Brooks.

Greetings complete, Danny cut right to the chase. "So, what did you find in there?"

Rainey's smile faded. She focused her green eyes on Danny's. "You're going to want to call Quantico. The unit chief will want this documented from top to bottom."

Paula spoke up. "How many bodies are we talking about?"

Sheila looked at her notes and answered. "There may be one body off site, his first victim. Rainey doesn't think she's in there. On this property, we found four bodies, one male and three females, in the car in the lake, and three heads in the trunk. Three full bodies at the Ridgway site. One, maybe two, it's hard to tell, at the Kemper site. Two each at the Bundy, BTK, and Schaefer sites, one body is missing its head at the Bundy site, a complete body at the DeBardeleben site, and we are still looking. None of the bodies have been disturbed, awaiting your arrival."

"That's more than what was on the list of missing women you sent us," Danny said. "And what do you mean by sites? Is there more than one area where he dumped bodies?"

Rainey pointed at the gate to the property. "He created a retrospective, a gallery, if you will, of the killers he studied. They'll be teaching this one at Quantico for years to come. The information age has created the perfect storm of serial killer fantasy material and spawned a monster of epic proportions. Welcome to his horror show."

"Okay, let's go take a look," Danny said, starting away. He turned back to Rainey, who had not moved. "Are you coming?"

Rainey shook her head. "No, I've seen enough. It's your investigation now, but I would like to borrow Brooks for a moment."

"You can keep me," Brooks said. "I have no interest in seeing that freak show."

"Don't take her far," Danny said. "We may need her."

203

Brooks shouted after him. "I assure you, horrifying me will be counterproductive."

"Speaking of production—" Rainey said, before Brooks interrupted her.

"I got your email and am sending you the newest satellite image now." She pulled a tablet computer from the oversized bag slung over her shoulder and began rattling off information. She tapped the screen and moved to her next subject seamlessly. "I worked with the task force and narrowed the list of trucks down, but it still has hundreds of possible hits. This UNSUB would drive the most popular pickup truck in North Carolina. We broke the list into geographic areas and officers are locating these vehicles as we speak, starting with the ones closest to this location." She looked up and smiled at Rainey. "And now that list is on your phone."

Rainey felt her phone vibrate in her pocket and heard the "bing" of a message arriving in her inbox. Rainey turned and grinned at the colonel.

"See, I told you they could help," she said, pulling out her phone to take a look at the list.

"I included a link to a map of the addresses where the trucks are registered, so you can get a visual on their locations," Brooks said. "It will update automatically as the trucks are located and eliminated."

Rainey winked at her. "You always know just what I need. Thank you, magic Brooks. Again, you have outdone yourself."

"Whatever you need to catch this piece of shit." Brooks was not one to mince words.

Curtis came jogging back to retrieve Brooks. "Hey, Danny said to come get you. We need you to run a VIN number and trace this vehicle's ownership."

Rainey gave Brooks another hug. "When this is over, you tell Danny you're going to stay and hang out with me and the kids for a few days. The colonel and I are going to take a look at some of these vehicle locations nearby, while the team is tied up here at the site. Keep me informed."

Brooks was walking away when she grinned and said, "I brought an extra bag and told my husband I'd be back when I got back." She waved, adding, "You be careful, Rainey Bell."

"Always, Brooks, always." She turned to the colonel. "Let's take a ride."

The colonel was already in full stride toward his car. "I thought you'd never ask."

Rainey caught up with him. "You know if we find this guy, you can't shoot him until we know where he's holding Bladen."

The colonel kept his gaze forward. "And after?"

Rainey did not hesitate with her answer. "You do what you can live with, Patrick."

His reply made her smile. "Hooah, Rainey Bell."

#

He came in, flipped on the lights, and went straight to his desk in the corner, completely ignoring Bladen. He opened the laptop and began typing, bringing up several windows. Bladen hung there silently, watching as he opened live video feeds from what looked like a massive crime scene. Bladen could make out flashing lights and patrol cars. There were helicopter shots of other helicopters searching a wooded area. A police spokeswoman was holding a press conference in another window, while black SUVs, with dark windows and emergency lights flashing, cruised through the background. She caught a glance of someone that looked like her father, but Bladen was too far away from the screen to be sure.

Her captor threw his head back and filled the room with howls of laughter. When his self-satisfied celebration was over, he turned his attention to Bladen. His sinister smirk peeking from under his mask, he finally spoke to her.

"You would not believe the show going on out there. Lights as bright as day, flatbed trucks full of them, scattered all over the place. They had three helicopters searching at the same time. The dive team is out there and when I left, I passed more medical examiner vans driving in."

He stood up and came toward her, his smirk turning into a grin. He reached out, slowly sliding one of his fingers from her navel up to her neck, where he seized her throat and gripped it tight, cutting off her air. As Bladen struggled, her foot slipped off the stake, leaving her suspended by her wrist, dropping her weight in his stranglehold. So pumped full of adrenaline from his perceived success, he showed no strain from holding her aloft with one hand as he spoke in an even tone.

"Your friend Rainey was there and guess what? The FBI did have time to come see my little outdoor museum, after all. Guess who else was there."

Bladen hit him with her one free arm, tried prying his hand from her neck, kicked at him, but it was all to no avail. He continued to talk as if they were old friends.

"Hmm? No guesses? Well, I'll tell you then. I saw your father. Surprised I know who he is, aren't you? I saw him when he came to pick you up at the hospital, after you hurt your ankle last year."

The room began to go dark again. Bladen stopped struggling, imagining this was either the end or another time when he would take her to the brink of death, just to bring her back. Whatever his plans were, Bladen decided the sooner it was over the better. She fought the panic and let her body go limp. He let go of her neck, lifted her in the air, and unhooked her wrist from the pipe in the ceiling. Bladen never actually passed out, but feigned unconsciousness, having learned that he only tortured her when she was awake enough to scream. He carried her into the bathroom and handcuffed one wrist to the shower wall.

He slapped her a few times, and then grabbed her chin, pulling her face close to his. "I know you can hear me. I need to go home for a while. I better not smell any shit and piss when I come back. And this shower will be spotless, or you will pay the price with the Pear."

Bladen heard him throw something into the shower with her, but she kept her eyes closed and her body limp. She could hear him breathing, as he watched her for signs of awareness. When she gave him none, she fully expected him to inflict pain in order to draw a reaction. Instead, he abruptly left the bathroom, closing the door behind him. Bladen remained motionless, until she heard the main door open and close in the outer room. Her eyes popped open with the sound of the dead bolts being thrown into place.

Bladen looked at the shower floor and saw he had tossed in a wire brush and a bottle of bleach. She then took a look at the handcuffs and realized her captor had just made a monumental mistake.

CHAPTER ELEVEN

Rainey's laptop was in her car, so she was thrilled when she slid into the colonel's vehicle and saw one on the front seat.

"May I use your computer? The map will be easier to read on a wider screen."

The colonel handed the laptop to Rainey, saying, "Sure. I was killing time looking at Google Earth images while you were inside there, familiarizing myself with the area. There are a lot of little crisscrossing roads running through here."

Rainey placed her phone on the seat beside her and opened the laptop, talking as she worked. "I'm going to go through my phone and use my secured network. I'll erase all trace of my having been on your computer, but I feel more comfortable knowing it would take someone like Brooks to hack my system, especially since she helped build it."

"I take it that only looks like an ordinary phone," the colonel said, watching Rainey and waiting for directions to begin their search.

"That would be correct." She tapped a few more keys, and then turned the screen around, showing the colonel the map. "Voila! The newest satellite image with the trucks in the area indicated by these blue dots. If the dot is yellow, someone is looking into that one, and if it's red, it's already been cleared."

The colonel studied the map, and then said, "I see at least twenty blue dots within a five mile radius of here."

"Well, I guess we better get started." Rainey turned the screen back toward her, searching the image for the nearest blue dot. She hovered the cursor over it, causing a box to pop open with the name and address of the truck owner. She clicked on the button labeled "Investigating," which turned the dot yellow. She pointed out the windshield. "Head down this road, turn left at the stop sign."

#

Bladen wedged the head of the wire brush behind the pipe to which she was handcuffed. She pulled with all her strength on the long wooden handle, finally managing to snap the brush, exposing some of the wire bristles so she could remove them. She collected four of the long, thin metal bristles and began to twine them together, creating one stiff wire bundle about the thickness of a large paperclip. Bladen worked the wire into the keyhole of the cuffs and bent it down, making a small right angle in the end. She pulled the wire out, and then with her teeth made a second bend going in the opposite direction.

As she worked, she spoke aloud. "All right, Dad. I'm putting your parlor trick to good use. Who knew teaching me to pick open handcuffs with bobby-pins would come in handy?"

Bladen examined the handcuffs carefully. They were double-locked, which would make picking them more difficult, but not impossible. She inserted the bent end of her wire pick into one side of the keyhole, and pushed down, releasing one of the locks. She then flipped the cuffs, inserting the pick into the other side, and repeated the downward push. She felt the latch release, allowing her to open the cuff around her wrist.

Bladen squealed with joy, as she pulled her wrist free. It was a momentary celebration, because the fear returned, replacing her jubilation. If he came back now and found her free, there would be hell to pay. She huddled in the corner of the shower, listening, trembling, and even contemplated putting the cuff back on her wrist, before her survival instincts returned.

"Get out of this bathroom and find a weapon, Bladen," she chastised herself. She stood and narrowed her eyes at the bathroom door. "If I die, I'm going to make sure I get one good shot at taking you with me, you son-of-a-bitch. Hooah! Come get some."

#

It was nearing nine o'clock when they approached a crossroads with a small gas station on the corner. It was one of those old country quick-stop marts that had somehow survived, selling fuel and snacks to the locals through the years. Rainey and her father had stopped there several times, during the long, lazy Sunday drives they used to take, winding through the back roads talking about life. Billy Bell was not a man who enjoyed sitting still, watching football. He seemed always to be in motion. Rainey not only inherited her father's looks, she acquired his restlessness too. Knowing what she knew now about post traumatic stress disorder, she imagined it was one of the ways he learned to deal with it, before the condition had a name.

"Pull in there, Colonel. I need to use the restroom and grab some coffee."

They had been driving for an hour, checking the tailgates of the trucks they located for the telltale scratch, eliminating three so far. The last address they visited was nothing more than the burned out shell of an old farmhouse beside a dirt path that led into the woods. The owner and the truck were long gone.

"I could use a little coffee myself," the colonel said, pulling his car into one of only two parking spaces in front of the little store.

Rainey knew he was not sleepy or tired. It would be a long time before Patrick Asher crashed. The amphetamine effect of a missing child would disrupt his sleep for nights to come. Even if they found her alive, the fear would wake him in the dark, panicked and out of breath. Should they find her too late, Rainey doubted the colonel would ever have another good night's sleep.

In the bathroom, Rainey splashed water on her face and re-corralled her hair. She stared into the mirror, talking to the UNSUB. "You are so close, I can feel you."

Her cellphone began to ring. She pulled it out of her jacket pocket and saw Katie's face smiling up at her. She opened the

210

door and stepped outside, careful to bring the key she had to return to the clerk, and answered the call.

"I guess you've been watching the news," she said into the phone.

"Yes, I have," Katie replied. "It's been non-stop coverage on Cookie's channel, and the networks keep breaking in with updates. I saw Danny and Brooks. I didn't know she was coming."

"Neither did Danny," Rainey said, laughing. "She's going to stay a few days, after this is over."

"You sound pretty confident that you will find this guy."

"Katie, he's close, so close I can almost smell him."

Katie was quiet for a moment. When she did speak again, some of the lightness had left her voice. "Are you out there looking for this guy without a weapon?"

"The colonel has one. We're not confronting these people. We just pull up, shine a light on the back of the truck, and drive off. They don't even know we're there, most of the time. These are country folks. They don't park their trucks in garages."

"So you and the colonel are driving around looking at trucks, while your former colleagues are investigating, and I quote, 'the largest body recovery in recent North Carolina history.' Oh, and I think my favorite sound bite so far was the young cop, whose entire quote was, 'This guy is a ...' followed by a long series of bleeps, interspersed with words like animal, freak, abomination. I was kind of glad to hear that last one being used appropriately for once."

"I'm glad the show is still going on. He'll be glued to the screen, probably multiple screens, watching every minute of the coverage. He won't see me coming," Rainey said.

"It's obviously pointless to ask you not to do this without backup," Katie said, followed by a deep sigh.

"If we find the truck, we back off and call it in. I know what I'm doing, Katie. You have to trust me."

"Okay, then you have to trust me. Gunny and the grandmothers are going to watch the children for about an hour. They are already in bed anyway. Ernie and Henry are coming to take me to the hospital to see Mackie. I'm taking food for the boys and Thelma. I can't let him go under tomorrow morning, without seeing him. I will be safe and well protected."

"I'm okay with that," Rainey said. "I need to see him too. Maybe I can swing by tonight sometime. Tell him I'm thinking about him."

"I will, honey. I love you. Be safe."

"I love you, Katie, and you be careful, too."

Katie answered with Rainey's signature, "Always," and then she was gone.

Rainey joined the colonel inside the little store, returning the bathroom key to the clerk. The old man eyed her up and down, and then said, "Aren't you Billy Bell's daughter, that FBI girl?"

Rainey smiled at him. "Yes, I'm Billy's daughter, but I'm not in the FBI anymore."

"My name's Wilton. Knew your daddy pretty well. I remember you coming in here with him when you were younger. Sure was sorry to hear he was killed."

"I'm glad he had friends like you," Rainey said. She pulled the tailgate picture from her back pocket. "Wilton, maybe you can help me. I'm looking for this truck."

She handed the picture over the counter. Wilton studied it for a moment, and then handed it back to Rainey. "Well, Miss Virginia had a truck that color, but she passed about three years ago. I see her oldest son driving it sometimes, but I don't think he's supposed to."

"Why is that?" The colonel asked.

"Well now, that's one of those family tragedies, when greed and guile take over after a death. Miss Virginia had a small farm, just down the road a piece. John, her husband, died ten years back. He worked on heavy equipment and cars, when he wasn't in the fields, and left her fair off. She rented out the land to her neighbor to farm. If she'd had no children, she could have lived to a hundred very comfortably, some say. I'm glad she's not around to see what happened to them boys of hers."

Rainey knew they would have to wait for the point of the story, as this was a southern tale. The narrator of such a story felt compelled to add in the details and embellishments, so the listener not only heard, but was completely immersed in the experience. Southerners were of the mind that too few words were more apt to leave the story up for interpretation. They would rather you fully grasp the situation, than form an opinion on just the facts. She dared not interrupt Wilton, and simply offered a nod of understanding.

The colonel was not so patient. "Was there trouble?"

Wilton took a deep breath, storing up for the remainder of his tale. "That oldest boy, Vance, he stayed around here, but the youngest one, Nate, moved to Maryland. Nate visited often, but Vance spent a lot of time with his mother. He also drained her bank accounts. Virginia was always bailing him out of one financial scrape or another after he got kicked out of the army. His divorce practically broke her. She loved that grandson of hers. It nearly killed her when the judge ruled Vance couldn't see him anymore. I think she died of a broken heart, fighting to see him again."

Wilton shook his head from side to side, a well-known storyteller tactic, giving the listener time to absorb the tragedy, before continuing. "When she died, Vance was befuddled to find his mother had been keeping a running tab on the money she'd given him. The land and everything on it, including her truck, went to Nate. She left Vance a few thousand dollars and called it even."

"I take it Vance didn't like that very much," Rainey said, growing more interested in the story by the moment.

"No, not at all. Wasn't long after the will was read that the farmhouse burned to the ground. Folks around here figured Vance done it to spite Nate. I seen 'em fall out right here in the parking lot, fists a flyin'. They've been in court over the estate ever since, accusations going back and forth. That's why I say Vance shouldn't be driving that truck. It's supposed to be put up in the garage with all of his daddy's tools."

"Are you talking about V. A. Wayne's place, back that way about a mile?" Rainey asked, pointing in the direction from which she and the colonel had just come.

"Yeah, Virginia Afton Wayne, that was her. Knew her all my life."

Rainey was very interested now. "We just came from there. I didn't see any garage standing on the property."

Wilton chuckled. "When John built that garage back in the seventies, Virginia made him put it up in the woods, away from the house. She said she couldn't stand to hear him revving engines all day. You have to follow that little sand path into the woods about a hundred yards."

Rainey pulled out some cash to pay for the two coffees the colonel had placed on the counter. Wilton waved his hand at her.

"It's on the house. Your daddy ran down some bad checks for me once. Wouldn't take no payment for it. I reckon I owe him two cups of coffee."

Rainey could barely contain her excitement, but remained calm until they were back in the car. She didn't want to get the colonel's hopes up, but she had a really good feeling about this. He evidently did, too.

"Back to the Wayne address, right?"

Rainey turned to face him. "We locate and identify the truck, then we back off. Understood?"

"What if Bladen is in that garage?"

"If he is there, we have to back off. He'll kill her before he lets us take her. We're going to need help."

The colonel backed the car out of the parking space, saying, "Like you said, I'll do what I can live with."

"Hooah, Colonel."

#

Bladen stayed in the shower stall longer than she needed to. He was gone, but fear kept her behind the closed bathroom door until she was absolutely sure it was not one of his sadistic tricks. While she waited, she broke the remaining part of the brush head completely from the handle, leaving a jagged stake for a weapon. When she had steeled herself against the paralyzing fear, Bladen turned the handle on the bathroom door, pulling it open slowly. The light from the bathroom spilled out into the dark chamber. She was alone.

The first thing Bladen did was turn on the lights and head for his desk. She opened the laptop, powered it up, but was disappointed to find it password protected. She dug around on the desk for any form of communication, and finding none, she turned her attention to other pursuits. Bladen had one mission on the top of her list. She walked over to the shelf where he kept his "tools," and located the Pear. She picked it up and threw it against the far wall as hard as she could. The force of her throw only bent it a little, so she picked it up and threw it again. Her fury grew, as she chased the torturous contraption around the room, repeatedly throwing it against the walls until there was nothing left but pieces of bent metal.

"Try using that again, asshole," she raged.

Next, she went for his whip, seizing it from the wall hook, where he returned it after each torture session. She found a pocketknife in his desk drawer and took great pleasure in cutting the whip into little pieces. Bladen might die tonight, when he returned and found out what she had done, but she knew two things. He would never use that whip to scourge her naked skin again, and his precious Pear of Anguish was no longer a threat.

Once she was finished with the whip destruction, she set out to remove all the leather straps from the rack, yanked the hinged top off the pillory and used it to break the picquet stake from the floor. She cut all the ropes she could find into pieces, and general wreaked havoc on all his meticulously handcrafted torture devices. Bladen worked herself into such a frenzied state, she collapsed against a wall trying to catch her breath. She did not know how long she had been thrashing away at his possessions, but as she looked around the room, Bladen began to laugh for the first time in days.

#

The colonel drove the car slowly up the sandy path. Neither of them spoke. Both were processing the environment, as they slipped beneath the evergreen canopy. The headlights illuminated a structure in the center of a cleared area and surrounded by thick woods. The fine hairs on the back of Rainey's neck stood up and her instincts screamed, "Alert! Alert!"

"Yep, if I was going to build a lair, this is exactly the kind of place I would do it," she said.

"Rainey, are you willing to kill a man with knife?"

She thought that an odd question at the moment, but answered honestly. "I am trained in knife tactics and would stab an assailant if I had to, but I prefer the distance a firearm affords me from my attacker."

He reached under his seat, never taking his eyes from the road, and pulled out a K-Bar, the seven-inch bladed U.S. Army fighting knife of choice. He placed it on the seat beside her. He then reached under his jacket, pulled his M-9 from its holster, placing it next to the knife.

"Pick your weapon," he said. "You're not getting out of this car unarmed."

Rainey reached for the M-9. "Since I'm very sure that you are capable of defending yourself with that knife, I'll stick with something I know I can use." She looked at the colonel's profile, seeing the muscles tightening in his jaw. "We need him alive, Colonel. Try to keep that in mind."

Right now, all Rainey had was circumstantial evidence. She could not call in the troops on a hunch. She could, however, gather more information and she knew just how to get it. She slipped the firearm in her jacket and pulled out her phone, speed-dialed a familiar number, and waited for Brooks to answer.

"Girl, I hope you have some expensive bourbon at your house, 'cause I'm going to need a drink, make that a bottle, after this."

"I do. I'll even put a nipple on it," Rainey answered, and then got right to her point. "I need everything you can find on a Vance Wayne. He is the son of John and Virginia Afton Wayne, both deceased. I can send you the parents' address. The property is tied up in probate court. I know Vance is divorced, has a son, and was denied the right to see his child about three years ago."

"I'm going to totally ignore the humor in his father's name, because the rest of it sounds like the preliminary profile the team just gave the task force. Give me a sec, and I'll get right back to you with all things Vance Wayne. Send me the address. Bye."

A click and Brooks was gone. Rainey sent the address and then said to the colonel, "Just because this guy fits the profile does not mean he is the UNSUB. There are plenty of narcissistic momma's boys out there that never commit a serious crime. We need evidence."

The colonel pulled the car to a stop, the headlights illuminating two garage bay doors and a single door at the far left end of the forty-year-old cement block building. The bay doors had three horizontal windows each, allowing the lights to penetrate the dark interior.

"Something like that," he said, pointing out the windshield.

Rainey peered through the windows of the door on the right at the cab of a red pickup truck, but she thought the colonel was probably more interested in the hangman's noose dangling over the truck bed.

"Yep, that's looking like probable cause," she said.

The colonel shut the engine off and doused the headlights. They sat quietly for a moment, taking in the surroundings. Nothing moved, the building was dark again, but if Vance Wayne were just a few feet into the woods, they would never see him.

"Okay, let's go see what we can tell from outside the building," Rainey suggested.

They exited the car together, closing the doors softly. Rainey pulled the M-9 and her flashlight from her jacket pockets. She took the weapon off safety and gripped it at her side, while trailing the beam from her flashlight on the ground in front of her.

"Someone's been driving in and out of that bay on the left," she said, "and very recently. The dew settled earlier this evening, but these tracks have moisture on either side of them." She pointed the beam of her flashlight at the concrete under the bay door. "Look, his tires left wet sand under the door. He was here within the last two hours."

They approached the garage door concealing the truck. The colonel was tall enough to look down through the glass at the tailgate, but it was so close to the door, he could not see it. Rainey studied the hangman's noose with her flashlight and then trailed the beam through the garage. It was a typical two bay mechanic's garage, with tools hanging on the walls and scattered on workbenches. The larger trappings of the trade—torches, lifts, compressors, and the like—were pushed up against the wall, allowing plenty of space for two cars. The smell of fuel and oil hung in the air.

The sound of a compressor kicking on startled both Rainey and the colonel into defensive positions. It was several seconds before she realized the sound was coming from outside the building, around back. She motioned the colonel to follow her, and then slipped around the corner, sweeping the area with the beam of her flashlight and the barrel of her weapon. Seeing nothing, she continued to the rear of the building, cautiously turning the corner to find the source of the noise. A fairly new heating unit whirred away, pumping air into the garage. The ground behind the building was covered with old fifty-gallon drums and car parts. The shiny new heater looked out of place. Rainey was about to comment to the colonel, when she realized he was not behind her, and at the same time heard wood splinter at the front of the garage.

"Dammit."

She ran toward the sound, catching a glimpse of the colonel entering the now opened door at the far left end of the building.

#

Bladen ran to turn off the lights. She needed the element of surprise. She had not heard his car door slam shut, but something loud just happened above her. After trashing the place, Bladen had searched for weapons she could use to overpower him, or at least inflict some serious damage. She found a hospital scrub shirt folded in the bottom drawer of his desk and put it on, then assembled her arsenal.

Bladen gathered pieces of the rope she cut earlier, tying enough together to create a tool belt of sorts. Carefully crafted leather loops, made from parts of the whip and the rack restraints, held the little pocketknife, a pair of scissors she found, and the stake she made with the wire brush handle, which she had spent some time sharpening to a fine point. She also had the handcuffs tucked into the belt and several lengths of chain at her feet. She modified the bleach bottle, cutting away a portion of the top and one side, which would enable her to throw the blinding liquid at his face upon his entrance.

Prepared to fight to the death, Bladen crouched in the darkness near the door, gripped the bottle of bleach with both hands, and waited.

#

Several things happened all at once. Rainey stepped into the garage, her phone rang, and the colonel shouted. "It's the truck. It's him."

Rainey dug in her pocket for the phone, while she crossed the empty bay, joining the colonel at the back of a Vermillion Red pickup truck with a deep gouge in its tailgate.

She saw Brooks's number on the caller ID and answered, already spewing information, "We found the truck. It's at the address I sent you. There's a burned out house by the road. Tell them to follow the path into the woods about a hundred yards. He's not here now, but he's been here recently."

"Okay, I got all that, but you should know, this guy is a nurse at Memorial Hospital." Brooks paused, which cranked Rainey's already thumping heart into high gear. "Katie, rather the women's shelter, has a protection order against this guy, and so do his ex-wife, his brother, and the owner of the farm next door."

This was a complete surprise to Rainey. It appeared Katie thought there were some things Rainey did not need to know. At the moment, that was the least of Rainey's worries.

"I have to call her. She's at the hospital," Rainey said, frantic to hang up.

"Hang on," Brooks said. "Katie is in protective custody and being escorted home, where she and your children will be under armed guard for the duration of the investigation."

Rainey sighed with relief. "Okay, I'm good with that."

Brooks explained further, "That information you requested set off alarm bells out here. Danny asked that Vance Wayne be located and brought in for questioning. We tied the car in the lake to his father. He had a mechanic's lean put on it back in the eighties—"

Danny's frantic voice interrupted, "Get out of there, Rainey. He's not at the hospital or his home. Units have been called to his ex-wife's address. A child in distress on the 911 call says his dad killed his mom. Seems she called the tip line earlier, saying she thought her ex-husband was involved with the bodies we were finding. No one had a chance to talk to her yet, and she must have said something to him. He's devolving at a rapid pace."

Rainey saw the flash of headlights come through the bay door window and reflect off the back wall of the garage.

"It's too late, Danny. He's already here."

"We're on the way to you. Ten minutes out, tops. Stay on the phone," Danny said, excitement elevating the pitch of his normal baritone.

Rainey watched a black Charger pull up behind the colonel's car and stop, a single occupant behind the wheel. She started describing what she was seeing to Danny.

"He's driving a Charger, typical law enforcement emulation. He's stopped outside, just sitting in the car. When he comes in, I'm going to put the phone in my breast pocket. I might need both hands."

She took another quick look around the garage, while the colonel watched Vance Wayne watch them.

"We're in a mechanic's garage. Bladen is not in sight, but something isn't right. It's cold in here, but there is a new heating unit running full blast out back. The truck is parked over a pit, like you find in oil changing setups." She paused and flashed the light around the oil soaked walls of the pit. "There's nothing in it but old oil."

She focused on the electrical wiring, following the wires across the exposed beams to a box on the wall. She crossed to it quickly, trying to absorb as much information as she could before Vance Wayne made his entrance. Rainey opened the door on the fuse box.

"I'm at the electric service. It's new, like the heater, and heavy duty, enough power for two buildings this size."

The power outlets in the garage were connected to the cables coming from the top of the box. Heavy cables descended from the box down the wall behind a workbench. Rainey started pulling old oily car parts out of the way.

"There are power cables running into the floor, and there is a digital cable run as well." Rainey placed her palm on the floor.

"The floor is warm. There is a room under this building. She's here, Danny. She's under us."

A car door slammed outside. "He's coming," the colonel said softly.

"Okay, Danny. You better get your ass here fast. I'm about to meet our boy face to face."

Just as she pulled the phone away to drop it in her pocket, she heard Danny say, "Try not to kill him, Rainey."

Vance Wayne stopped just outside the door and shouted into the building. "I got a shotgun on you. You might as well come on out. If I come through that door, I'm blowing everything in there to bits."

Still down on the floor, Rainey held up her hand, signaling the colonel to let her speak. "Don't shoot. I'm a fugitive recovery agent in search of a skipper. That's his car out there. We tracked him back here and he took off through the woods. He's the one that kicked the door in."

She turned off her flashlight and leaned back into the shadows under the bench, keeping aim on the dark figure outside the door. The colonel's silhouette was now crouched near the rear bumper of the truck and the steps leading down into the pit.

"Where's your vehicle?" Vance asked.

She knew he was playing along. He knew exactly who she was and why she was there. Rainey was buying time for Danny and her rescuers, who were at this moment barreling toward her location.

"My partner took it. He's circling around to see if the fugitive comes out on the other side of these woods. I stayed here, in case he came back for his car."

When she heard his laughter, she knew the game was up. "That's good, Agent Sexy. Thinking on your feet, but your partner is in the hospital surrounded by the rest of your staff. You're alone in there with Patrick Asher. A rogue ex-federal agent and a distraught father, kicking in doors, breaking laws, anything to find a missing daughter."

Rainey spoke softly into her jacket pocket, hoping Danny could hear her. "He's dropped all pretense. This is the end game. Move your ass."

221

The particular model of M-9 she held was a double-action weapon, requiring hammer cocking for the first round. Rainey slipped her thumb to the hammer and slowly lowered it until the lock clicked home, sounding like thunder in the silence of her hiding place. If she was going to shoot him, she needed a good reason, so she prodded him for one.

"So, what's going to happen? Are you going to stand out there and wait for the cops to get here, or run for your life? DeBardeleben ran, you know. So did Ted, who actually turned out to be very afraid of dying. Schaefer turned himself in after two of his victims escaped. He thought he'd go free after a few years, but I think the guy who stabbed him to death in prison will be out sooner. BTK and Ridgway couldn't wait to confess every detail. Or are you like Kemper? He called in crying, because no one even considered him for his crimes. Which one of your heroes do you choose to go out as?"

Vance took a step closer to the door. "The original Nightstalker was never caught."

"Well, you're not him, Vance. You shopped in one market, so to speak. The original Nightstalker moved around quite a bit. He also liked to make the husbands suffer the degradation of listening to him rape their wives. No, you're no Nightstalker, Vance. You didn't have the guts to enter a home occupied by a man." Rainey laughed, adding, "Hell, you don't even have a nickname. Maybe they'll give you one for your trial. How about 'The Impersonator,' seeing as how you simply copied other people's crimes."

Vance did not grow angry. Instead, he remained calm and controlled, which was not a good sign. "There will be no trial, and they can call me what they want. I'll be long gone before your friends get here, and so will you. You have exactly three minutes to make your peace with God."

Above her head, on the underside of the workbench, a small green indicator light flashed on. Rainey clicked on her flashlight and saw the source of Vance Wayne's confident claim.

She called out to the colonel. "He just started a timer on this bomb above my head. Get out, Colonel."

"Lay down cover fire for me," the colonel said. "Get him away from the door."

Vance apparently heard the colonel's directions and stepped to his left, taking him out of Rainey's line of sight. She fired three shots out the door to make sure Vance could not focus on the colonel, who was running toward her. He slid on his knees, coming to rest beside her under the workbench.

"Rainey, find Bladen. I'll deal with the explosives."

#

Those were gunshots, Bladen was sure. She thought she heard muffled shouts, too. Someone was here, someone other than her captor. The thought crossed her mind that he may have just shot someone, but she had to take the chance that her rescuers were up there. Bladen put the bleach container on the floor, flipped on the lights, and found the thick piece of lumber she had ripped from the top of the pillory.

"I'm down here," she screamed, as she began to pound the door with the large piece of wood. "I'm here! Down here..."

#

Rainey heard muffled thuds that appeared to be coming from under the truck. She fired two more shots at the doorway and sprinted for the steps leading down into the pit. Her shots were answered by a shotgun blast. She felt the sting of shrapnel hit her thigh and heard it pelt her jacket, but she did not stop. She slid under the rear of the truck and scrambled down the steps of the pit.

Flipping on her flashlight, she searched the oil stained walls for an access point. She could hear the faint sounds of a woman's screams and the steady thump-thump of something crashing into the wall in front of her. The stains on a portion of the wall looked newer and intentionally applied. Rainey started knocking on the wall with the butt of her flashlight, listening for a sound difference. That's when she saw the seam in the concrete and heard the hollow return of her tapping. She clawed at the seam to no avail. There had to be a release mechanism somewhere.

She jumped at the sound of the colonel coming down the steps. He joined her in trying to pry the seam open. "There's more than one device. We don't have time to defuse them all," he said. "Get out, Rainey, while you still can."

"We're all going out together," she said. "There has to be a way to open it."

Rainey stopped scratching at the seam and moved the flashlight beam around the pit. Old oil rags were piled in the corner. She kicked them out of the way, revealing a small metal door about the size of a light switch cover with a hasp and lock. Shooting at the lock could disable the mechanism, or ricochet a fragment back at her. Rainey de-cocked the weapon and crashed the butt of it into the lock until it fell open. She flipped open the cover to find a hydraulic control box, with a red and green button.

"Green means go," she said and pushed the appropriate control.

The colonel jumped back as the seam separated, revealing a thick concrete door panel slowly creeping open. Rainey ran back to join him as he pulled on the door, encouraging the hydraulics to work faster. As soon as the opening was large enough for Rainey to pass through, she slipped behind the still moving panel into a small empty room. She found a light switch on the wall and flipped it on.

This was his staging area. A black mask lay on a small table in the corner, with a bottle of contact solution and a contact case. Hospital scrubs and other clothes hung from a hook on the wall. Opposite the panel the colonel was now squeezing through, Rainey saw a heavy metal door and heard the screaming and pounding from the other side.

The colonel began to shout. "Hang on, Bladen. I'm coming." He frantically pawed at the two deadbolts that required a key.

Rainey's mental clock was counting down the seconds they had left before the garage exploded. She realized their time had grown too short for escape. Seeing an identical hydraulic control box on the wall by the now opened concrete panel, she hit the red button. The panel began to close again. She watched the painfully slow process and hoped the bunker she was sealing them into would hold against the blast.

Before the door could close all the way, she shoved the pistol into her jacket pocket, yelling out to anyone that could still hear her on the phone. "Stay back! There's no time left." She hoped they heard her next words. "Remind Katie, I loved her."

The door closed with a final hiss of releasing air. Then everything went black.

CHAPTER TWELVE

The concussion from the explosion sent Rainey crashing to the floor. She was disoriented by the cloud of dust from the crumbling concrete and the ringing in her ears. Blinking, she shook her head, attempting to clear the concussion fog from her brain. A slab of the ceiling had fallen in on them. She was tucked next to the wall in a tent shaped space created by falling debris. All around her, she could hear parts of the garage returning to earth after the force of the blast sent it skyward.

Rainey called out, "Colonel, are you all right?"

The returning moan indicated that he was not.

"Hang on. Help is coming."

Rainey could move, but she was constricted to the small space. Debris would have to be removed to open an escape route from her little concrete tent. Shining out from under the edge of a huge slab of ceiling, she could see the beam of her flashlight illuminating the dust particles dancing in the air. The beam also revealed the butt of the pistol pinned under a ton of concrete. It must have jettisoned from her pocket when she hit the ground. The sound of movement drew her attention. A beam of light began to search the debris.

She was about to call out, when she heard Vance Wayne's voice. "I heard you talking, so I know you're still alive, Agent Sexy."

Rainey clawed at the butt of the pistol. She could hear him coming closer, picking his way through the rubble. A beam of light hit her face, blinding her.

"There you are," he said, squatting down outside Rainey's tomb.

That was the perfect name for it, because Rainey Bell was about to take her last breath. He lowered the flashlight from her eyes, and when they adjusted, Rainey could see the barrel of a shotgun pointed squarely at her face. The beam of his flashlight bounced back from Rainey's little tent-shaped prison, illuminating Vance Wayne's face.

"You!" Rainey said, staring into the eyes of the nurse from Mackie's trauma room, the one that warned her of Cookie's presence.

"We only have a moment. They'll be coming soon, but I couldn't leave without knowing for sure that I had defeated the great Rainey Bell. I knew you would come. I knew your arrogance would lead you right into my trap. I'll be going to get your little Katie Meyers next. So don't worry, she'll be joining you soon."

Rainey closed her eyes. Katie's face came into view, surrounded by laughing babies. She heard the hammer being pulled back on the shotgun. She whispered, "I'm sorry, honey," and prepared to die.

The instant Rainey believed would be her last on earth, a high-pitched screech, she could only describe as a banshee shriek, pierced the air around her. Her eyes flew open in time to catch a flash of blue behind Vance Wayne. His attention diverted to the noise, Rainey grabbed the barrel of the gun, pinned it against the wall, and ducked out of the way of the blast she expected to follow. It did not come. Instead, she felt the shotgun fall away from his hands.

Rainey looked back at Vance. He wore a surprised expression, just before he toppled over with a small crazed woman on his back. A soul-shattering scream from the depths of Bladen Asher's misery reverberated off the walls of Rainey's tight quarters. She watched as the young woman raised both hands in the air and plunged a bloodied wooden stake it into

Vance Wayne's body again. Beyond the point of hearing Rainey call out to her, "Stop, he's dead," Bladen Asher repeatedly plunged the homemade weapon into her tormenter's back, her anguished cries punctuating each strike.

Rainey laid the shotgun down on the floor, careful to release the hammer, and then crawled as far forward as she could. She reached through the opening, where Vance's head had fallen, and grabbed Bladen's wrists on her next downward arc. She gripped the young woman's arms tightly, trying to get her attention.

"Bladen, Bladen, it's okay. He's gone."

Lost in her murderous frenzy, Bladen tried to wrestle her hands loose.

"Bladen, he's dead. He can't hurt you anymore."

Bladen Asher looked like a child reared by wolves. Her hair hung down over her blood-spattered face, partially obscuring eyes wild with rage. The crimson drops falling from her chin added to the animalistic illusion. She stared at Rainey, appearing to grasp at reality, attempting to regain her humanity. Rainey saw that Bladen was dressed only in a scrub top, with scissors and handcuffs dangling from some kind of makeshift rope belt around her waist. The colonel's little soldier had survived on her wits.

"Your father needs help, Bladen."

Bladen blinked, let the bloody stake fall from her hands, and began to weep.

"Where's my dad?"

#

After Rainey and the colonel were extricated from the rubble, the three injured victims were taken to the hospital. Vance Wayne's blood soaked corpse was taken to the morgue.

Danny stood by Rainey's emergency room bed now, a familiar scene for both of them. He was explaining that a Cookie Kutter live broadcast from Vance Wayne's body farm had triggered a cascading set of events.

"Somehow, Cookie found out about the red truck we were looking for and blabbed. Maureen Elliot—she dropped her married name in a further attempt to distance herself from the years she spent as Vance Wayne's battered wife—was watching that broadcast. When she saw the bodies being recovered and heard about the red truck, she knew her ex-husband was the one we were looking for."

"She called it in, right?" Rainey asked, adjusting the sheet over her exposed thigh.

Once again, she was stuck in a hospital gown. Her pants and shirt were taken, because she was pulled out of the rubble through a puddle of Vance Wayne's blood. The leather jacket had been spared because her rescuers made her take it off, before trying to squeeze her out of the would-be tomb. Rainey had a slight concussion, hence the ringing still in her ears, and a white-gauze bandage on her thigh where a piece of shrapnel was removed. It only required a few stitches. The rest of her wounds were covered in brightly colored children's adhesive bandages. She told the nurse the triplets would enjoy them more than the plain tan ones. All in all, Rainey felt pretty good about having survived a building exploding above her.

Danny pointed at Rainey. "You know, it's kind of hard to take you seriously with a Winnie the Pooh bandage over your eye."

Rainey reached up and pulled the bandage off. "Now, finish your story."

"You were a petulant child, weren't you?" Danny said with a chuckle. "Anyway, Maureen did call the hotline. The message had just passed to the appropriate personnel, when the 911 call came in from her seven-year-old child. When Vance placed his one allowed phone call per week to his son this evening, Maureen would not let him speak to the boy. Instead, she told him she had called the police."

"So he went over there and finally killed the object of his rage." Rainey finished Danny's thought, as they so often did for each other.

The partitioning curtain at one side of Rainey's bed was flung back suddenly, revealing Katie clutching a change of clothing for Rainey to her chest. She walked over and gave Rainey a nonchalant peck on the cheek.

"This scene is getting old, don't you think? Me showing up in the emergency room to find you and Danny huddled together after another harrowing escape from the clutches of a madman."

Rainey grinned at Katie. She knew this was an act. If she had not taken one already, Katie would need a moment to process the reality of the situation. At some point, she would show her fear of what could have been, and what might be her future.

"Trouble finds you, Rainey," people commented time and again. No matter how Rainey tried to stay out of trouble's path, it crept in under the doors and through the cracks in the walls. It followed her on the street, peeked in through her windows, posted pictures on the Net, tried to frame her for murder, or make her the murdered victim. Short of a new name and face, Rainey was pretty sure she was doomed to have trouble as a companion the remainder of her days. The life she built with Katie made facing that prospect a lot less daunting.

Rainey slid an arm around her wife's waist. "I thought you were under armed guard at home, but I am very glad to see you."

"You're just happy I brought your clothes," Katie said with a wink, "and the armed guard is in the hall."

They would hold each other close later, say all the appropriate thank you prayers, and always remember each moment was precious, but for now an arm around a waist, a nonchalant peck on the cheek, and a wink said all that needed saying.

The crowd around Rainey continued to grow, as a nurse came in with her release papers, followed by Brooks who announced loudly, "Rainey Bell, you are one hard ass woman to kill. There, I said it. It's what everybody else was thinking."

Rainey signed documents for the nurse, and smiled at Brooks. "I think that's a good thing, don't you?"

"You have an angel on your shoulder, that's for damned sure."

"Hey," Rainey said, playfully wagging a SpongeBob bandaged finger. "You need to clean up your vocabulary or Katie won't let you near the kids."

"She's right," Katie interjected. "Rainey is only allowed short supervised visits."

"Speaking of visits," Danny said, "I'm afraid I have to head back to Quantico tomorrow afternoon. Paula and Curtis will stay to help with evidence collection and a victim statement. There won't be a trial, but a lot of families need answers."

Rainey took the clothes from Katie. "Could you guys give Danny and me a second?"

Once they were alone, Rainey climbed out of the bed, peeled off the hospital gown, and began to dress. There was no need for the pretense of modesty. Danny found her staked out naked with a Y-incision carved into her chest. Diffidence was no longer an element of their relationship. When her head popped out of the black turtleneck she was pulling on, she saw Danny was holding out an envelope to her.

"Here, this is my entire grand jury testimony," he said, careful to lower his voice. "It matters what came before and after that statement."

"I know that, Danny. Keep it. I don't need to see it."

He slipped the envelope back inside his jacket. "I do believe you had nothing to do with Dalton's death and that you don't know who did. I suspect you do not want to know. I also believe, under the right circumstances, anyone can commit murder."

"I expect that you would do so for my kids," she said, pulling on a worn pair of jeans.

"That I would," he said, and there was no further need to discuss it.

Katie brought comfort clothes, her subtle way of signaling it was time for her wayward investigator to come home and stay awhile. Rainey sat down in a chair to put on her shoes. Danny leaned in very close, his hands on the arms of the chair. What he had to say, he wanted no one else to hear.

"The information on the Michael Paul Perry case is not, and I repeat, not coming from inside the bureau. His family is the reason we had to cover up the autoerotic asphyxiation, so I doubt they are leaking anything."

"Someone at the jail, maybe?" Rainey whispered. "I don't care, really. I just don't want to be hung out to dry. I let them make it look like I scared that boy into suicide, when the truth was I turned him on so much, he could not resist the temptation to jack off in his preferred fashion. By the way, proving my point that he had very poor impulse control and should be denied release."

Danny straightened and took a step back, allowing Rainey the space to put on her shoes. "Who's framing you for murder? Any ideas?"

"A few. I'm not really worried. My Glock was in so many hands, no way that charge sticks to me."

"Committing a murder just to discredit you is a bold move. This person feels wronged by you and wants to see you suffer. Be very careful, Rainey. If the attempts to bring you down continue to fail, physically attacking you or someone you love becomes the only option."

"Let's hope I figure it out before that happens," Rainey said, standing, and reaching for the jacket she managed to keep from the evidence collection team.

Danny pulled her into a hug. "I really thought you were gone this time," he said, clutching her to him.

Rainey hugged him tightly. "You're not getting rid of me that easy. I love you, Danny." She pulled back to smile into his face. "Come for a long visit soon. We'll watch basketball, play with the kids, and not mention murderers or crimes. It'll do us both good."

Danny released his hold on her. They walked out side-by-side. "You know, I've got to get me one of those," Danny said.

"One of what?" Rainey asked.

He smiled over at her. "A life, Rainey. I need to get a life. It looks good on you."

Sheila and the armed agent waited with Katie and Brooks by the nurses' station. Rainey did not know the agent, but the suit was a dead giveaway that he was FBI. She could see the strain of the last few days written on Sheila's face. Even a seasoned investigator like Sheila Robertson would need time to process the horror of what she had seen this evening. This was just the beginning. Someone had to sift through all the evidence and then tell the families what happened to their loved ones. She did not envy Sheila that task.

"Good to see there was no serious damage. Thank you again for all the help," Sheila said, as Rainey approached.

"You'll be getting a bill, don't worry about that," Rainey said, chuckling.

Sheila leaned closer, speaking softly. "Stick some extra charges on there for having to deal with Rex. He's coming up behind you."

Rainey turned to see Rex King homing in on her position. Katie saw him, too, and was about to launch into him when they heard and witnessed the strangest thing. A young woman with chestnut brown curls, green eyes, and wearing a Durham Police Academy sweatshirt, stepped out of an examination room on crutches, one ankle bound in an air cast.

"Hey, Dad, thanks for coming. Can you grab my gym bag?" She said to Rex.

"Sure, honey," Rex replied, in a sweet fatherly tone that Rainey was unaware he possessed.

He ducked into the room and emerged with the girl's bag slung over his shoulder. Rex caught up with his daughter in the hall, still not noticing Rainey was there. The dropped jaws of the people near her were an indication everyone was as stunned as she was. Brooks, who had no idea who Rex King was, spilled the beans loudly.

"Damn, that could be your clone, Rainey Bell."

Katie joined in. "How do we know it isn't?"

"I remember when you looked like that," Danny said.

"Well, now that explains a lot," Sheila said under her breath.

Rex turned ashen and came to an abrupt halt when he spotted Rainey. He watched as the two people he was so desperate to keep apart met in a head-on collision with fate.

The young Rainey clone was the first to speak. "Look, Dad, it's Rainey Bell." She didn't seem to notice that her father was no longer following her. She hopped over to Rainey, gushing with excitement. Balancing on one crutch, she extended her hand. "Hi. I'm Wendy King. I think you know my father."

Rex was panicked, and Rainey felt compelled to help him out. She could have been an ass about it, but she chose not to play games using a young woman who was apparently her half-sister

as a pawn. "Yes, Detective King and I are old acquaintances."
She shook the girl's hand. "It's nice to meet you, Wendy. So,
you're in the academy?"

"Yes, sprained my ankle training on the obstacle course
tonight."

"You were running the course this late at night?" Rainey
asked, intrigued by Wendy's commitment.

"If you want to finish at the top, you have to work hard,
especially if you are a woman. But I'm sure you understand how
that is," Wendy answered. "You're one of my role models."

Rainey saw Katie grin out of the corner of her eye. "Thank
you. I consider that high praise from such a dedicated recruit."

Wendy flashed a smile that sent Rainey crashing back
through time to her own twenty-one-year-old image in the mirror.
This girl was born when Rainey was on the cusp of joining the
bureau. She was the un-jaded version of an enthusiastic young
Rainey, both their father's daughters. Rex may have nurtured the
child, but there was no denying Billy Bell's genetic contribution.
Rainey was quite sure that it was easier for her to see the
resemblance in Wendy, than for the younger woman to see her
reflection in Rainey's forty-two-year-old face. Everyone else
certainly saw it.

"I finished my criminal justice degree at State, last semester.
I'm trying to get into Quantico, but the waiting list is long,"
Wendy said. "Thought I should get some training and experience
and try again."

Rex had joined them by now, sheepishly quiet in his greetings
to the group. When he made eye contact with Rainey, she could
see the fear that she would expose his secret. She let him sweat
while she reached in her jacket pocket and pulled out a Bell's
Bail business card. She borrowed a pen from the nurses' station
and wrote two numbers on the back of her card.

"Wendy, this is Supervisory Special Agent Danny McNally."

Danny shook Wendy's hand. "It's a pleasure to meet you."

"It's an honor, sir," Wendy said.

Rainey smiled. Her half-sister had learned to play the game
well. She handed Wendy the card. "I've put SSA McNally's
private number on the back of this card, along with my own. Use

the numbers wisely. You'll know when it is appropriate. Good luck on your quest to join the bureau. I'm sure you'll make a very fine agent."

"Thank you very much," Wendy said, taking the card and grinning at Rainey. "Everyone says I look like you. I take that as a compliment. I hope I can have a career like yours as well."

Rainey mirrored her sister's smile. "I'm sure you will far exceed my accomplishments." She shook Wendy's hand again. "Let me know if I can do anything to help you."

"We should go, Wendy," Rex said. "You need to get that ankle elevated."

"Okay, it was nice to meet you and thanks again," Wendy said, and crutched away.

Rex followed his daughter, walking very close to Rainey. "Thank you," he whispered as he moved past her.

When they were out of earshot, Sheila turned to Rainey. "I see it now. Rex didn't want you around the department because of his daughter, who is obviously related to you in some very big way."

"I'm no geneticist," Brooks said, "but if that girl isn't your daughter—"

She paused long enough to give Rainey the opportunity to say, "No, I did not have a child no one knows about."

"Then your daddy got busy with that girl's momma."

Katie smiled up at Rainey. "You know she's going to come knocking on your door looking for answers, don't you?"

Rainey watched the sister she had not known she had limp away. "Yes, but that needs to be her decision, not mine."

#

Sheila, Danny, and Brooks left the hospital to rejoin the investigation, leaving the armed guard with Rainey and Katie. Rainey did not think it was necessary to keep him around, until Katie explained he would have to give them a ride home. She sent Katie and the agent up to Mackie's room, promising to join them in a few minutes. She had a couple of people she needed to see first.

The colonel and Bladen were placed in a double room, so neither would have to be without the other. The falling concrete ceiling had broken Colonel Asher's leg, but he would be fine. He was sleeping when Rainey stuck her head in the room, but Bladen stared back at her. She walked over to stand by her bed.

"How are you feeling?" she asked.

"I'm not sure," Bladen answered honestly.

"It'll feel like that for awhile. Just be patient with yourself," Rainey offered, remembering the fog in her brain after her attack.

"My dad said he would not have found me without you."

"He wouldn't let me give up on you. He said you would make it." Rainey reached out and squeezed Bladen's hand. "I owe you my life. Had you not come along when you did, I'm sure he would have pulled the trigger. Thank you. You are an incredibly brave young woman. I can see why your father is so proud of you."

A tear trailed down Bladen's cheek. "After the explosion, I woke up and saw the smoke and fire. When I came up out of the rubble, I could hear him talking. I don't remember much after that."

"Don't try. Just know that you are my hero," Rainey said, patting Bladen's hand. "You never gave up."

Bladen tried to smile. "I couldn't give up. I knew you were coming. An angel told me." She peered into Rainey's eyes. "He looked like you, my angel. I'll never forget those green eyes."

Billy Bell had been busy of late. Rainey did not mind sharing her guardian angel with Bladen, and silently thanked him for looking out for the colonel's daughter. She dug in her pocket for another card. Finding a pen on Bladen's bedside table, she wrote her number on the back.

She handed the card to Bladen. "You're going to need someone to talk to. My private cell number is on the back. You call me anytime, day or night."

Bladen's tears came faster now. "Thank you."

"Tell your father to call me when he's feeling better. And Bladen, please remember the most important thing. You did what you had to do to survive. Nothing else matters."

Rainey crossed to the colonel's bed and patted his sleeping hand. "Hooah, Colonel," she whispered, and then left the Asher family to their healing. She had family of her own just a few floors up.

#

Junior was talking with the agent outside of Mackie's room. He rushed to Rainey and hugged her, lifting her from the floor in his excitement.

"I am so glad to see you in one piece," he said.

"Put me down. You're going to break my ribs, Junior," Rainey said, but she was laughing.

Rainey was glad to be alive, but she had not forgotten that someone tampered with her weapon. She looked up at the man she considered a little brother and shooed away any doubts.

"Junior, when Mackie is on his way to recovery, you and I need to sit down and look at these runners we've hired. One of them may be involved in setting me up. I don't know that for sure, but something isn't right, and I'm going through everything in my life to find out what it is."

"We did deep background on all of them. Nothing came up," Junior said.

Rainey nodded. "I know you did your job. What I'm looking for, I think, and this is just a hunch, but I believe there is a connection to Martin Douglas Cross."

"That writer," Ernie said, coming out of Mackie's room in time to hear the last part of Rainey's conversation. "He's tried every way he can to get around me to get to you. It wouldn't surprise me if he found someone willing to sell information."

"We need to know who that is," Rainey said.

Junior agreed. "I'll start looking for financial connections and dig around a bit." He hesitated before asking, "Do you want me to look at Gunny too?"

Rainey trusted Gunny enough to leave her with the children, but she didn't want Junior to overlook anyone or anything. "Yes, look at everyone," she said, and then smiled mischievously. "Look at Ernie, too. You never know what she might be capable of."

Mackie's deep bass voice rumbled into the hallway, preventing any retort from Ernie. "Get in here, Rainey Bell."

Rainey dodged Ernie's attempt to swat her butt. "You're slowing down, old woman," she said over her shoulder as she escaped into Mackie's room.

"So, this is where you've been hiding," she said, crossing the room to his bed. She paused to give Thelma a hug, before delivering a peck to Mackie's cheek. "You look better than you did last night. I guess being able to breathe has a lot to do with that."

Mackie chuckled, which caused him to wince in pain, but he smiled through it. "I hear you survived a building exploding over your head. Cookie Kutter called you 'unbreakable.' I think that's the nicest thing she's ever said about you."

"She won't be talking about me much longer. I have proof she's paying the guy who's taking pictures for the blog site. I'm fairly sure we'll be closing the chapter on the stalker/blogger soon." She frowned. "Wait. I thought they weren't telling you what I was up to."

Katie supplied the answer. "We told him you were alive and well first, before we let him watch the helicopter surveillance footage of the fireball you survived."

"Really, they have footage?" Rainey said a little too eagerly.

"Yes, Rainey, they do. Imagine what it was like watching it live," Katie said, a little edge creeping into her voice. She pointed up at the television. "They just keep showing it, so we thought it best to tell him."

The volume was muted on an aerial shot of law enforcement vehicles screeching to a halt in front of the burned out house seconds before the garage exploded, sending a massive fireball into the night sky.

"Today I am thankful for building codes and criminals compulsive enough to add a few more inches of concrete," Rainey said, still watching the television as the shot changed to the burning shell of the garage. "Look, it only collapsed in the middle of the open areas."

"I'm thankful for all of you," Mackie said, drawing everyone's attention away from the television. "I love you all, but

I think Rainey wants to talk to me, and then I need to get some rest. Nurse Ratchet is getting antsy." He motioned toward Thelma with his head.

Everyone filed out of the room, after wishing Mackie well during the scheduled morning surgery. Thelma said she would use the time to grab a fresh cup of coffee from the canteen.

It was already Thursday, nearing one a.m., just over twenty-seven hours since Mackie's ordeal began. He reached for and enveloped Rainey's hand in his huge paw.

"Katie said you met Billy's other child downstairs. So, I guess you know why Rex King hates you."

"Why didn't he tell me, Mackie?"

"He didn't know. I would not have known, if I hadn't seen her at the academy Tuesday morning. Remember, Wiley asked me to come in for a Q&A with the trainees on proper bondsman behavior?"

Rainey nodded that she did. "So, Dad never knew about her? You're sure?"

"Billy and I had no secrets. Besides, Rex didn't know for sure until you moved back here. Once he got a good look at you, he knew. That's what we argued about. I told him he should tell his daughter before she figured it out on her own."

"It won't be long now," Rainey said. "She'll put it all together—the mannerisms and tastes she could never explain, how differently she looks from her cousins. She'll want to know what happened. She'll want it to be a love story. It wasn't, was it?"

"No, more like a bar story. Horny people, booze, and a one-night stand—the perfect concoction for a surprise pregnancy. I suppose Rex's wife decided to keep it to herself."

Rainey had to ask. "Might there be more of these bar stories I should know about?"

"Like I said, Rainey, I didn't know about this one, and I'm sure Billy didn't either."

Mackie took a deep breath. She could see he was growing tired, so Rainey tried to end the conversation. "You need to rest now. We'll have plenty of time to discuss Billy Bell's mating habits while you heal."

"Trust Junior, Rainey. He can handle the load," Mackie said.

It sounded like the kind of thing Rainey did not want to hear. "I'll trust him until you can come back to work, how's that?"

Mackie squeezed her hand, his big voice rumbling low. "You are not alone, Rainey. You will never be alone. No matter what happens, you remember that."

"Nothing's going to go wrong, Mackie. You have the best heart surgeon in town, and he says a positive attitude is paramount to speedy recovery, so stop talking like that."

"I just need to know you'll be okay if something does go wrong."

Rainey knew what he meant. There was a time in her life when another loss may have sent her over the edge. "I'm good, Mackie. I'm in a good place. You rest now. I'll see you tomorrow afternoon, as soon as they'll let me in." She kissed him on the forehead. "I love you Miles Cecil McKinney."

"I love you, too, Rainey Blue Bell."

"I'm sure Thelma would *love* for us all to go home and let them rest," Ernie said from the doorway.

Rainey turned to her. "Ah, my galvanized friend, you don't know how lucky you are not to have a heart."

Katie popped into the doorway. "Sorry Ernie, she's been watching the Wizard of Oz a lot. The flying monkeys mesmerize her and Weather. They aren't afraid in the least. That's somehow frightening in itself, isn't it?"

"Good night, big man," Rainey said, and then joined Ernie and Katie at the door. "What's there to be afraid of? Everybody knows flying monkeys aren't real." She turned back to look at Mackie. "Vance Wayne could have killed him, pushed just a little too much medication during his resuscitation, and no one would have been the wiser. Vance saved countless lives in his profession. We may never know how many he killed in his obsession. That's what frightens me. Real monsters don't have wings and tails. They are not that easy to spot."

#

As soon as the agent dropped them off at home, Rainey bounded up the stairs to the nursery. She did not stop to say hello to Gunny or the grandmothers, who waited up to see her. Rainey wanted to see her kids. She had to smell them, touch their hair, and kiss their cheeks. She wanted to pick them up, wake them, see them smile and know that she was home. Instead, she only patted their diapered bottoms. She stood by the cribs, listening to her children's soft and steady breathing. Katie slipped in behind her, sliding her hands around Rainey's waist, laying her head softly against her back.

No words. Rainey had no words to describe how she was feeling, because she never felt these emotions before. Losing her life had been a real prospect for many years. She was prepared for that. Losing a child, Rainey would never get used to that thought. She held her emotions at bay while they searched for Bladen. The time to release the stress had finally come for Rainey. She sighed loudly, and with the exhale came the first tear, slowly trailing down her cheek. The last body count from Vance Wayne's macabre museum, the garage, and his residence was twenty-one. Each stolen life was someone's child.

She crossed to the daybed beneath the window and sat down, pulling Katie with her. She leaned back against the overstuffed pillows, holding her wife, watching their children sleep. Mental box lids closed, horrible memories were tucked away, forced back into the recesses of her mind. The knowledge Rainey possessed, the human depravity she witnessed, new bodies tortured beyond recognition, the residual fears from staring down the barrel of a shotgun and almost being blown to bits, it all had to go somewhere. The life she lived within these walls had no room for the trappings of such evil things.

After a few minutes of silence passed, Katie whispered. "Come on, honey. Let's go to bed. We will all be here when you wake up."

Rainey barely heard her. Surrounded by family, safe and sound in her fortress home, she was already drifting peacefully into dreamland, where SpongeBob danced with Winnie the Pooh down a yellow brick road toward an always-happy ending.

CHAPTER THIRTEEN

"I really don't think this is a good idea," Molly said for probably the tenth time since Rainey got behind the steering wheel of the Charger.

Rainey and Katie had let the grandmothers and Gunny sleep in and were feeding the herd when the Rainey's cellphone rang. Molly had arranged a meeting with Cookie and the judge in the stalker/blogger case. She also informed Rainey that she was no longer a suspect in the Bobo Jackson murder, and the police were actively seeking the person that attempted to frame her. They could pick up Rainey's car after the meeting with the judge, and her weapons would be returned as soon as they could be processed out. Things were looking up.

Cookie had been arrogant and obstinate in the judge's chambers. That is, until the judge explained that her order to cease the publication of the private and intrusive pictures of Rainey's family extended to Cookie and anyone else aiding and abetting the stalker. Molly had done her homework. She showed the judge how the same pictures found on the Triangle Lesbian Blog were being used during Cookie's broadcasts and ended her presentation with the video of Cookie paying the stalker for the flash drive.

Rainey had remained quiet while Molly handled the show. She was seething with indignation, but resisted the temptation to tell Cookie the microphone up her ass was not a threat, but a promise. Molly was more eloquent and finished her statement to the judge with information Rainey gave her on the way to the courthouse.

"Ms. Kutter's interference in a police investigation nearly led to my client's death last night, and did lead to the death of a mother in front of her child. While we think there is ample evidence to show Ms. Kutter's actions continually present a threat to my client and her family, we are not pursuing monetary damages at this time. We simply want the harassment to stop and the identity of the man seen in the video taking payment from Ms. Kutter."

"You can't be serious," Cookie said. "You want to penalize me for having good police sources and disseminating information to the public. Go ahead, sue me."

Molly was ready for Cookie. "Ms. Kutter, I've spoken with the legal team at your broadcast company. They are not willing to go to court on this issue. In fact, after I showed them the video of you paying Ms. Bell's stalker, they offered to cancel your show in order to avoid that possibility."

Cookie actually laughed. "Let's go to court, Ms. Kincaid. I'm sure the jury will be made up of people who appreciate my candor in reporting the facts and really don't care how I get them."

Molly grinned, showing her dimple. This was Molly's tell. If that dimple showed up, Molly was holding a winning hand. "Oh, did I forget to mention I also showed them the video of your drunken tirade in which you swear to use any means necessary to—and I quote—'Fuck with Rainey Bell until the day she dies.' You really should leave your ex-girlfriends smiling, Cookie. A scorned woman can be very dangerous."

Molly had withheld that information from Rainey, probably to prevent her from doing something stupid, like punching Cookie in the face. Rainey could not prevent the chuckle from escaping, when she saw Cookie's mouth hanging open and Molly's deepening grin. Cookie was more than happy to inform them of the stalker's name after that.

The judge also warned Cookie to remove all images of Rainey and her family from her webpage and video archives, which Cookie agreed to do. On the way out of the judge's chambers, Cookie tried to smooth things over.

"I think you should know this guy is not stalking you, Rainey. He's been stalking Katie since before the Y-Man case. He sends me way more pictures of her and the kids than he does of you. He's obsessed with her."

Rainey walked away without commenting. Her mind already racing with the information. As soon as Cookie said his name, Rainey remembered him.

Since Molly had told her chauffer that Rainey was going to give her a ride home, she was now an unhappy passenger on Rainey's quest.

Rainey retrieved the stalker's address from the computer in her car, while listening to her attorney rattle off all the reasons she should not go there. Molly made her last attempt to stop her in the stalker's driveway.

"Not a good idea at all, Rainey, and you're making me a party to it. When I left the house this morning, I didn't think it would be the last day of my law career."

"Stay in the car. I'll testify that you tried to stop me," Rainey said, opening her door.

"Suppose this guy has a gun. Katie will never forgive me for letting you go in there unarmed."

Rainey stuck out her hand. "Then give me yours."

"I don't have mine," Molly said. "We were in the courthouse, remember? They frown on concealed weapons in the judge's chambers."

"Okay, well, if you hear shots, call the police. Otherwise, stay put. This won't take long." Rainey exited the car and started for the front door. She turned when Molly opened the passenger door. "I told you to stay in the car."

"I can't hear the gunshots if I stay in there," Molly said, just as the front door opened on the house.

The man who stepped out looked like a clean-cut frat-boy. He froze when he saw Rainey.

She smiled at him. "Mike—Mike Hopkins. Bet you never thought you'd see me at your front door."

Rainey met Mike Hopkins during the investigation into the Dalton Chambers copycat murders. He was taking pictures of Rainey and Katie in the bar, the night Katie slugged Cookie in the parking lot of Feme Sole. Rainey caught him with a phone full of images he was sending to Cookie, and had let him go because he was too timid to be the killer they sought. She left him with a warning to cease taking pictures of her. The warning had evidently not been stern enough. Rainey was at his house now to make sure her next admonition would be the last she needed to deliver.

Mike panicked. He ran back in the house, slamming the door behind him. Rainey was on the move, too. She jumped the two steps onto the porch and kicked the door open, before he had a chance to slide the deadbolt into place.

Just before she stepped inside, Rainey heard Molly say from the driveway, "Well, shit!"

The quiet house was dark and smelled of decay and mothballs. The hair rose on her neck, as a familiar aroma tickled her nose. Air fresheners lined the hall floor and the steps leading upstairs. Maybe Molly was right. It probably was not a good idea to go any further. Something was bad wrong in Mike's house.

She heard movement at the end of the hall, just as she was about to step back out on the porch and tell Molly to call 911. It was too late for that. Mike Hopkins appeared, holding a long barreled .45-caliber revolver in a trembling hand, trying to aim it at Rainey's chest.

"Now, Mike," she said, evaluating her would-be assailant. "That is entirely too much gun for you. The chances of you holding on to it when you fire are very slim, even slimmer than your shaky aim actually hitting me."

"Get out of my house," he said. "You have no right to be here."

"Let's talk about rights, Mike. I have a right to live my life without fear. That's impossible to do with you posting pictures of my wife and family on the Internet, pictures taken of my private residence, illegally."

"I never entered your residence," Mike offered in his defense.

"No, but your camera lens did, and that is not allowed, Mike. I've come to give you fair warning. I'll make your life miserable, if you continue to harass my family. What will your mother think, Mike? I remember you were concerned about her finding out what you were doing. Where is she? Maybe I should talk to her."

"She's in bed upstairs. She's sick. Don't bother her," Mike said, becoming very anxious.

The gun shook violently, forcing him to grip it with both hands. At this point, Rainey was more worried about a wayward bullet striking Molly in the driveway than Mike actually hitting her with one.

"Why don't you put the gun down, Mike? Let's just talk about this. I understand that you are infatuated with Katie. She is captivating, I'll give you that."

"You don't deserve her," Mike said, his agitation growing.

Rainey smiled. "You're right about that, Mike. She deserves better than me, better than having to worry all the time about the sick freaks that come out of the dark to terrorize us. You know, that really upsets her. She doesn't like living in fear."

Mike did not like her inference. "Are you calling me a freak?" he shouted.

"No, Mike," Rainey said, trying to calm him down.

As Mike began to wave the gun around haphazardly, Rainey shifted her stance to give him less of a target. The hallway was dark, making the pictures on the walls hard to see. When she moved, her new angle revealed the family photos on Mike's wall were of Rainey's family. Most of the candid shots were of Katie and the kids. None of them were of Rainey. If Mike viewed her as the obstacle to his relationship with Katie, he could become very unstable quickly. Rainey changed tactics.

"I know you really care about Katie. That's why I came to talk to you. I thought I could make you understand that what you are doing upsets her. I knew you would stop, if only you realized how distressing those pictures are to her."

"I just want people to see how beautiful she really is," Mike explained.

"Would you like to talk to her, Mike? I can call her on the phone. Maybe if you talk to her, you'll see how upset you're making her."

Mike lowered the gun slightly. The opportunity to talk to his obsession was too great to ignore. He stuttered out, "Y-y-you would let me talk to her?"

"Sure. I'm positive that this is all just a misunderstanding. Let's clear this up, so we don't have to involve the police and upset your mother. I'm going to reach in my pocket. I don't have a weapon, so don't worry."

He scowled and blinked rapidly as he watched her take out the phone. She could tell he was still not convinced she was being truthful. She wasn't, but he wanted to talk to Katie badly enough to ignore his instincts. An erotomaniac, like Mike Hopkins, deluded himself into believing the object of his obsession simply needed to understand the depth of his devotion, then she would have no choice but to fall madly in love with him, her stalker. Mike was actually licking his lips at the prospects of speaking to Katie.

Rainey did not dial Katie's number. She dialed Danny's instead. Mike kept his eyes on her, still shaking the gun in her direction, but took a few steps closer. Rainey waited for Danny to answer and started speaking immediately.

"Katie, I have someone here who wants to talk to you. His name is Mike Hopkins."

Danny questioned her. "Are you in trouble, Rainey?"

"Yes, Mike Hopkins. I know you don't know him, but he's a real fan of yours. He's the one that took all those pictures of you. I'm at his house."

"Okay, Rainey, keep talking. Mike Hopkins. Can you give me more on the address?"

"I know I have to be at the hospital soon. How did you know I'm out in Wake Forest?" She paused as though Katie were answering, and then added, "Oh, you're following the GPS on my phone. Smart girl. I won't be late. I'll leave as soon as you talk to Mike. I told him you didn't like the pictures he was posting, but he needs to hear you say it."

Rainey could hear Danny giving information to Brooks. She needed to stall a bit longer.

"No, Katie, he won't listen to me. He's really upset, and I thought if he talked to you, we could work this out so the police don't have to be involved. He's worried about his sick mother. He doesn't want them coming here to disturb her."

Danny came back on the line. "Is the mother there?"

"I can understand not wanting to upset his mother. He says she's bedridden."

"Do you think she's really there?" he asked.

"No, I think we're long past that. I think you're the only one that can make Mike understand how you feel."

"Norman Bates, is it?"

"Oh yes, exactly," Rainey answered.

"Okay, there is a patrol unit a block away. It's rolling to you. Hang on," Danny said.

Mike took a few more steps in Rainey's direction. It was time for her to make her move.

"Okay, I'm going to hand the phone to him now," Rainey said. She held the phone out to Mike, talking loudly enough for Danny to hear. "Give me the gun, Mike, and I'll let you talk to her."

Mike Hopkins loved Katie Meyers beyond reason. Had he thought it through, he would have known that Rainey would not let him near her wife. She certainly would not hand him a phone to talk to her. His delusion made it impossible to resist her offer. He stuck the gun out for her to take and snatched the phone from her hand. Rainey took the revolver, opened the cylinder, and dumped the bullets onto the floor.

Mike did not seem to care. "He-hel-hello, K-K-Katie."

The weapon secured, Rainey set it down on the hall table and grabbed for Mike's wrist. She twisted his arm behind his back and swept his legs out from under him, while he continued to talk to his imaginary Katie. His obsession prevented him from recognizing that he had been duped.

"K-Katie, I've wanted to talk to you forever," he said, just before Rainey landed a knee in his back and forced his face into the floor.

"Rainey, what are you doing?" Molly said from the doorway.

"Get my cuffs out of the console, Molly."

"I am not participating in a kidnapping, Rainey," Molly argued.

"The cops are on the way. I just want to secure him. He had a gun on me," she said, chuckling at the look of horror on Molly's face.

The phone had fallen on the floor by Mike's head. He was not struggling to get free, but fighting to pick up the phone, as he yelled repeatedly. "I love you, Katie Meyers. I love you."

Rainey leaned over him. "Mike—Mike, hey, hey, relax."

His face was red and he was slobbering like an animal, as he professed his love for Katie through spit-laden words of devotion.

Rainey popped his face against the floor, not too hard, but enough to get his attention. He craned his neck, peering up at her out of the corner of one eye.

"There you are," Rainey said, smiling at him. "Just relax, Mike. The sad truth about Katie Meyers is she would be telling me not to hurt you—that I should understand you are in need of mental health care. Katie's sweet like that."

Rainey heard Molly explaining to the patrol officer that her client was in the process of making a citizen's arrest that had somehow spilled into the man's home.

Rainey put her lips close to Mike's ear. "But I'm not sweet, Mike. In fact, I'd like to end this all here, snap your neck and be done with you. Here's your warning, M-M-Mike. Don't come near my family again. Find a new obsession or the next time I see you will be the last breath you take. Don't fuck with me, Mike. I'll kill you."

She slammed his face into the floor again, this time a little more forcefully, just as the officer entered the hallway. Rainey looked up at the breathless female officer, who did not look a day over eighteen. She smiled, knowing this young woman would not soon forget this day.

"You should call your supervisor," Rainey said, her knee still in Mike Hopkins's back. "I think you'll find a body upstairs. It's his mother. I think she's been dead for quite some time."

The officer went pale.

"Hey," Rainey said, softly. "Take a breath and cuff this guy."

Rainey helped handcuff Mike's hands behind his back and then stood to face the young officer. She looked at her nametag.

"Officer Hammond, study this case. Interview this man. Careers are made on understanding how these guys think."

Hammond studied Rainey's face for a moment. "You're Rainey Bell, aren't you?"

"Yes, and I'm giving out free career advice today. If you can close off your emotions, walk up those stairs and evaluate the crime scene, then welcome to the launch of your career. What you have here is a real life 'Psycho,' not a movie. If you're going to go pale when faced with the evil that men do, find another career before the nightmares find you."

"Yes, ma'am," Hammond said, warier now after the reprimand.

Rainey felt a little remorse for stating the facts so plainly. She buoyed the young woman with her next comment.

"Call it in, officer, and read this asshole his rights. Don't let the big dogs come in and take your arrest away. Get your paperwork started and stand your ground."

Hammond smiled broadly. "Yes, ma'am!"

Rainey left Hammond to her tasks. She felt no need to verify her suspicions. There was definitely a body in that house. No amount of air freshener and mothballs could mask the scent of human decay.

Molly, who had remained on the porch, peeked in the doorway as Rainey was coming out. "He didn't have a bloody nose a minute ago," she observed.

Rainey smirked. "He slipped."

She sat down on the porch steps, waiting to give her statement so they could go.

Molly joined her. "Before or after he was in cuffs? I'm only asking while it's fresh in your memory, in case he sues you for breaking his nose. And what exactly are you having him arrested for? The blog is a civil matter. I have to serve papers on him, before he is in violation of the judge's order."

"Don't worry, Molly. Where he's going, they don't allow access to the Internet."

"Why? Any good defense attorney could argue he had a right to pull a gun on you. You did kick the door in," Molly argued.

"Yeah, are you volunteering for the job?" Rainey teased her. "Before you do, you might want to find out if his mother's rotting corpse was a result of natural causes."

Molly blinked, and then shook her head. "It's never normal around you, is it?"

Rainey grinned. "Nope. Not by a long shot."

#

"It never ceases to amaze me what you stumble into," Gunny said, taking another bite of her sandwich.

Katie was feeding Rainey and Gunny lunch, while the grandmothers played with the triplets in the den. "Stick around. Norman Bates types are the least entertaining of the freaks that find her fascinating," she said as she refilled Rainey's glass of tea.

Rainey swallowed a bite of sandwich. "Need I remind you, this particular freak was obsessed with you? Speaking of that, why didn't you tell me about the protection order on Vance Wayne?"

"His ex-wife brought her son to the shelter last summer until she could move again. Even divorced, he terrorized her. He tried to enter the property and was removed. Molly filed the order on behalf of the shelter, among many others. If I told you about every protection order we file, you'd spend all your time investigating them. The security team is doing its job. You put the measures in place. They did what you told them to do when a threat was made."

Gunny chuckled into her plate.

"What's so funny, Marine?" Rainey asked playfully.

"You might as well give up, boss. She has an answer for everything."

Katie was just about to reply, when the alarm erupted in the backyard. Rainey darted to the security monitor, where her eyes narrowed on a figure rattling the back gate and yelling into the camera. She shut off the alarm and started for the backdoor.

Katie called after her. "Wait, you don't have a gun."

"I do," Gunny said, springing from her chair, heading for the garage door.

"You have another gun in your car?" Katie demanded.

Rainey kept moving. The last thing she heard before leaving the house was Gunny saying, "I don't think right now is a good time to argue about it."

Rainey did not need a firearm. She sprinted across the long lawn to the back gate and yanked it open, launching into the man. "Martin Douglas Cross, I'm about to make you piss your pants again, and I don't even have a weapon this time."

Martin backed up with both hands up in front of him in surrender. "Hey, hey, look, I just need to talk to you. It's really important."

"Come here," she said, grabbing him by the shoulder and throwing him into her backyard. "I want to make sure this is legal when I kick your ass."

He stumbled through the gate, pleading his case. "Wait! Wait! You need to hear this. Really, I don't want to cause any trouble. You need to know someone close to you is feeding me information."

"Rex King is feeding you information. He's hardly close to me. And that bullshit you took out of context in Danny's testimony? Just go ahead and print that." She took a step closer to him, which made him flinch. "I also have reason to believe you had something to do with trying to frame me for murder," she growled through clenched teeth. "I saw you with my weapon."

She had not worked out in a week. Punching a bag kept her inner rage at bay. The frustration of the past few days was rushing to the surface and Rainey really wanted to hit something. Martin's face looked like an excellent target.

"No, no, that's wrong," he cried, swaying back and forth like a drunk in a fight.

Gunny thundered up behind Rainey. "I got him, boss. I can drop him where he stands."

"Wait, wait, listen to me." Marty was growing more and more afraid for his life. Desperate, he started spouting information. "I don't know who is framing you, but it has something to do with Michael Paul Perry. That's where I got my information, an anonymous source that knows all about his adoption into that powerful DC family, and accuses you of causing his suicide. This person contacted me about your gun being used in a crime, before the police even knew about the murder. I told the police that."

"You had access to my weapon, Marty. I have the video of Rex giving it to you. How do I know you aren't the one setting me up with your partner, the dick detective?"

"Rex just doesn't like you. He let me look at your weapon, he got me the testimony transcripts, but honestly, I don't think he's the one framing you. How would he know about the Perry kid? It's someone much closer to you than Rex King."

Rainey goaded him. She wanted a good reason to kick his ass. "Why so generous, Marty? I thought you wanted to see me get what's coming to me. How's that going to help sell your book?"

"You don't deserve to go to prison for something you did not do. Besides, the truth about you is more interesting than myths and innuendo."

Rainey dropped her aggressive tone. "Okay, I'm listening. How do you know it's someone close to me?"

Martin relaxed just a little, but kept his eyes on Gunny and the weapon she had aimed at his chest. "My informant knows too much about you, your comings and goings, the cases you're working, the pictures that hang on the walls in your office."

"That's all doable with the right surveillance equipment," Rainey countered. She was still unwilling to believe she let someone inside her security net who would do her harm.

"The guard's dog's name is Buddy, if he asks. You cannot enter your home without defeating four levels of security. There are no weapons allowed past the foyer or garage door. The panic room is in the master suite closet, behind a hidden panel, accessible only by biometric lock."

Rainey dropped her hands to her sides. "Enough." She took a step toward Martin and he ducked, anticipating a blow. "I'm not going to hit you. Give me your business card."

Astonished at the request, Martin asked, "What?"

Rainey held out her hand. "Give me your card. I have things to do today, but I will sit down and talk with you. I will call you as soon as things settle down around here."

Martin dug around in his coat pocket, producing a card emblazoned with, "Cross Examinations: The real story."

"Catchy, Martin," Rainey said, slipping it in her pocket. "Now, out you go. I don't advise trying this approach again. They're giving me my firearms back today."

She escorted the still trembling writer out the back gate.

"Thank you for not kicking my ass," Martin said.

Rainey smiled and looked down at his crotch. "Sorry about the pants, Martin. I'll call you."

She closed the gate and turned to Gunny. "You know she's going to rake us both over the coals for the firearm violation, a second offense, I might add."

"No, I don't think so. She shouted at me to go get it and go after you. I think she's glad I broke the rules, and I may have actually won a point in my argument."

Rainey laughed, patting Gunny on the back. "Oorah, Gunny."

"Oorah," came the reply.

On the outside, Rainey was calm, almost serene, laughing and joking with Gunny on the way back to the house. On the inside, her mind was racing through the list of construction workers, architects, employees, friends, and acquaintances, even family members who had access to her home. Her cellphone rang, as she chuckled at the argument Gunny was preparing in favor of allowing weapons in locked vehicles in the garage. She pulled it out of her pocket, seeing Junior's number on the screen. As hard as she tried not to allow it, doubt crept into mind. That's what Martin had just set in motion, Rainey's inability to trust anyone, even a man she considered a little brother.

"Hang on, Gunny. I need to take this. It might be about Mackie." Rainey stopped walking and answered the phone. "Hey, Junior. Is Mackie all right?"

Junior proudly announced, "He came through with flying colors. That's what Dr. Herndon said. He should make a complete recovery, and be healthier than he was two days ago. He's in recovery now. We should be able to see him in a few hours."

"Great. Katie and I were planning on coming after we get the kids down for their afternoon nap."

"Okay, I'll tell Thelma and Ernie. They haven't left the waiting room all day."

"Gunny is going to stay here at the house. We'll drive separate cars, so I can stay for the night if I need to. Thelma would probably like to go home for a bit. I'm sure you could use a break, too. You haven't left him either, have you?"

"Why does Gunny need to stay at your house? I thought you caught the stalker guy. Who are you afraid of?" Junior asked.

"Someone tried to frame me for murder. Until I figure out who that is, I'm not standing down. It may take days or years, but I'm going to figure out who this is."

"I hear that," Junior said. "I contacted Brooks." He paused to chuckle. "She likes me."

"You're pretty, Junior. Just her type," Rainey said, laughing with him.

"I asked her to run deeper background check on everybody associated with the bail business. Brooks can dig a little deeper than the rest of us, as you know. She said she was coming over to your house to stay a few days and would work on it for me."

"And what did she wrangle out of you in return?" Rainey teased.

"She said I had to come serve her drinks at your house with my shirt off, just so she could look at me. I don't think she was serious."

Rainey cackled into the phone. "Oh, Junior. She was so serious. You better work on those abs." The phone vibrated in her hand. She tipped it down to see Brooks's number on call-waiting. "Speak of the devil, she's calling me now. I'll see you soon."

"My girlfriend would kill me. Tell her that."

"A deal's a deal," Rainey said into the receiver, and then hung up with Junior to answer the other call. "Hello, Brooks. Are you calling with your ETA?"

"Rainey, Danny is on his way to you. Be calm," Brooks said, with uncharacteristic seriousness.

"I thought he had to go back to Quantico," Rainey said, worried but not sure what she should be worried about.

"He was about to leave for the airport when I showed him what I found. He told me to call you and ran away with his head pressed to his phone." She paused. "Where are the children, Rainey?"

"Why, what's wrong?" Rainey said, beginning to sprint for the backdoor.

"It's Gunny. She was raped at age eighteen, her first year in the service. She's Michael Paul Perry's birthmother."

Rainey stopped running. Gunny, who had been running beside her, skidded to a halt, too. Her eyes darted around the yard and to the house, looking for the enemy. When she made eye contact with Rainey, it only took a split second for the recognition to hit her. They locked eyes long enough for Rainey to see the transformation. Like the nictitating membrane retracting on a shark's eye, Gunny blinked the psychopath into view.

At that moment, Katie opened the backdoor. It distracted Gunny, but not Rainey. She threw her cellphone down and leapt for Gunny's weapon, yelling, "Panic room, now Katie!"

Rainey heard the door slam, but could not look up to confirm Katie was gone. She knew she was. One thing Katie recognized was Rainey's "get to safety" voice, never hesitating to do what that voice said. Rainey got her confirmation, when seconds later the panic alarm exploded from the house. The guards would ignore it for the fifteen seconds allowed for resetting, after false alarms and appearances by the likes of Martin Douglas Cross. Katie was following procedure. By now, she would be rushing everyone into the panic room, where they would be safe. She would call the proper authorities from the emergency phone and wait for help. Rainey on the other hand had a major problem, surviving until that help arrived.

Gunny Pierce was fully capable of killing with her bare hands, so it made no difference that Rainey had managed to knock the pistol from her grasp. She grabbed two fists full of Rainey's hair, and began banging her knee repeatedly into Rainey's face.

She was not so much speaking as snarling. "You killed my son, bitch. You told him he would never get out of prison and he hung himself because of it."

Rainey took a second to recover from the first couple of blows, thankful for the training Gunny put her through. They had worked on fighting while dazed by a punch. She had Rainey run in circles with her forehead on a bat, then kicked the bat away, and ordered her to flail away at the heavy bag.

"Just swing. Keep moving. You're bound to land something and a moving target is harder to hit," Gunny would shout at her.

Rainey took that advice and began to pummel any part of Gunny she could reach, gaining the upper hand by the sheer force of running her into the patio furniture. Rainey's advantage was size and strength, and she used it to launch them both on top of the wooden table, snapping the umbrella pole, causing the open canopy to close on the wrestling women beneath it. Rainey's range of motion became limited immediately. When she drew back to land a punch on Gunny's face, her shirt snagged long enough to lose control of her opponent.

Gunny kneed Rainey in the ribs with sufficient force to knock the breath out of her. She stumbled back, tangling in the canopy further. Gunny sat up and kicked out with both feet, sending the umbrella incased Rainey tumbling backward. She landed hard on the blue slate patio, a piece of the splintered umbrella framing piercing her arm. Rainey fought to catch her breath, and ripped her arm free of the wooden spike. She'd rather bleed to death than lie there and get pummeled.

Gunny was no longer talking. She growled like an animal, leapt off the table and landed on Rainey. The women exchanged blows, but Rainey was taking the brunt of the fight. Gunny grabbed a handful of hair on either side of Rainey's head and tried smashing her skull against the slate. Her head hit the umbrella frame instead—a painful blow, but far less damaging than having her brains bashed out on the patio deck. Rainey could hear sirens now. She only needed to hold on for a few minutes more. While Gunny gripped her hair, she left Rainey's hands free. She had one shot to knock this crazed, but highly trained combatant off her chest, before the umbrella frame gave way, and her brains were turned to mush.

Gunny taught Rainey how to deliver a strike to an opponent's open jaw that was almost guaranteed to knock them out. Rainey clasped both hands together, fingers interlaced. She pulled her elbows close to her chest, rocked to one side, and then flung her weight back in the other direction. All of Rainey's strength went into the swing of her double fist, up through Gunny's outstretched arms, connecting the hammer blow to her open jaw with a snap of bone.

The effect was instantaneous. Gunny fell on top of Rainey, who scrambled out from beneath her as fast as she could. She stood over Gunny's unconscious body for a moment, making sure she was out cold. Rainey looked down at the blood spreading on her shirt. It was not too bad. She had worse. Locating Gunny's pistol became her priority. Rainey was not going to bleed to death from her wounds, but if Gunny woke up and found her pistol, things could get bad very quickly.

Rainey thought she saw the weapon fly over by Katie's prized rose bush, the only survivor of last summer's blight. The sirens were in front of the house now. Katie would be controlling the gate from inside the panic room, letting them in. Then she would have to disarm the alarm for them to enter the house. The alarm continued to wail, so finding the wayward firearm was still Rainey's biggest concern. She was digging around under the rose bush, thinking she really needed to weed-eat some of the taller grass, when she heard a shell being racked into the chamber of a nine-millimeter Glock, an all too familiar sound.

"Convenient that you're already down on your knees," Gunny snarled, her words a little warbled by her swelling jaw. "Turn around, stay on your knees, hands on your head."

Rainey turned slowly, searching hate-filled eyes for the woman she had once thought of as a friend, but not finding her there.

"I didn't kill your son, Gunny. You're going to kill me anyway, but you should know the truth. He was a very sick boy, much like the man that raped you. It's true that I recommended he be moved from the juvenile facility straight to prison to serve the remainder of his sentence. He died committing autoerotic asphyxiation, masturbating while he cut off his airflow. The powerful family that adopted him would rather people think he killed himself, than let the truth be known. That's what happened, Gunny."

"Still toeing the bureau line, are you? Staring down the barrel of a gun and you still lie for those people. Who were you to decide Michael wasn't rehabilitated? You took his hope away. Do you know what they did to him in that cesspool they called juvenile facility."

"How would you know, Gunny? I know all the people who visited him in there. You were not one of them."

"Michael contacted me after he turned eighteen. I got one letter, before he was taken from me. That's all I have. He reached out to me for help. They were torturing him in there."

"Did he tell you about the eleven-year-old boy he raped at the facility, so violently he had to be hospitalized?"

That was the wrong tactic to use. Rainey discovered that very quickly. Gunny took a step forward, raised the pistol in the air, and brought the butt of it down on Rainey's cheek. The blow sent blood running from a jagged gash and stars danced into Rainey's vision. The alarm began to sound funny, taking on a wah-wah echo. The black tunnel of unconsciousness wavered around her.

Gunny grabbed her by the hair again, preventing her from toppling over. She let out a wicked laugh, the self-satisfied cackle of a psychopath. It was the epitome of duping delight, the ultimate "I've got you now." It was the sound of pure evil, often requiring the tossing back of the head for emphasis. In Gunny's case, the head toss was unnecessary. The Glock was there to make her point.

She lowered her crazed eyes again on Rainey. "Oh no, you don't. You're not passing out. You're going to see this coming."

She jerked hard on Rainey's hair, pulling her up, lifting her knees from the ground. She pointed the barrel of the gun at Rainey's face. Rainey squeezed her eyes shut, just as the alarm was silenced. She fully expected the next sound to be a gun blast that she would never hear.

"Hey!"

Startled, Rainey opened her eyes. She and Gunny both turned to see Constance Herndon pull the trigger of a snub-nosed .38. It was the last thing Marine Gunnery Sergeant Naomi Pierce, retired, saw before she hit the ground.

Constance was at her side in seconds, prying Gunny's hand from her hair, while Rainey wrenched the firearm from Gunny's other hand. Constance shoved Gunny over into the rose bushes with her foot, and then took the weapon from Rainey. She put both pistols on the ground, as the police poured into the yard.

"That woman was attempting to shoot my daughter. I shot her. We need an ambulance," Constance announced to the police and then sat beside Rainey, cradling her against her chest. "Are you all right, Rainey?" she asked calmly.

"I'm okay," Rainey said, still dizzy and stunned by what just happened. "How did you know about the revolver?"

Constance smiled at her daughter. "My father gave that book-safe and gun to Billy before we ran away to get married. He said Billy should use it on my mother if she came after us. Thankfully, he did not."

"Things might have been different if he had," Rainey said, a little sad at the moment that her family had been torn apart before it really got started.

This moment of nostalgia was probably the result of the blow to her head on top of the concussion she already had from the explosion, or it could have been the pained look on her mother's face. Rainey saw it for a second, the fleeting thought of what if Romeo and Juliet had not ended so badly. Constance covered it by examining the cut on Rainey's cheek. Rainey grabbed her mother's hand and asked the question she never got an answer to as a young girl.

"Why did you leave him, Mom? Why didn't you just tell your mother to go to hell?"

Constance answered truthfully for the first time. "My mother was willing to part with her daughter, but not her grandchild. She would have taken you from me. I gave up my life as Billy's wife to keep you."

"But after I knew the truth—"

Constance cut her off. "After you knew the truth, it was too late for Billy and me, but not for a father and daughter destined to be together."

The two women stared into each other's eyes for a moment of the deepest understanding that ever passed between them, while police and security company employees milled about the broken patio furniture, commenting on the "hell of a fight" that went down there. Paramedics went to work on Gunny first, as she appeared to be the most in need of care, seeing as how she was barely breathing. Rainey only wanted her to live for her mother's sake. So she would not have to live with taking a life, even for a noble cause.

Constance pulled a handkerchief from her pocket—monogrammed, of course—and applied it to her daughter's cheek wound.

"Ouch, not so hard," Rainey whined, ignoring what had just passed between them. She blamed her mother for leaving her father since she was a child. The guilt for doing so was too much to bear at the moment, so Rainey tucked it away. "I didn't know you could shoot."

"There are a lot of things you don't know about me, Rainey Blue Bell. I wasn't so different from you once. I gave you that name for heaven's sake. I haven't always been a stick in the mud."

"I guess you haven't," Rainey said, taking a good look at her mother and really seeing her for the first time. "Why didn't you go in the panic room?"

Constance supported Rainey as she struggled to her feet, steadying her while she gained her balance. "Because you are my daughter and you needed help."

Rainey smiled at her mother and knew what she said was true. "I think I may have some of your DNA after all."

Constance winked. "Who do you think taught your father how to shoot?"

#

Several hours later inside the criminal psychology critical care unit, Rainey called in a favor. Her arm bandaged, head examined, face stitched up, and finally released from the emergency room again, Rainey asked Katie to wait in the hall with Danny, while she paid one last visit.

261

Machines beeped and whirred in the background. The patient was strapped down with locked restraints. Gunny was awake and staring as she approached. The bullet Constance fired entered her cheek, hit her jaw, and glanced off her skull. Rainey had already shattered one side, her mother got the other, but Gunny was alive. Her jaw wired shut, she was unable to speak, but she had nothing to say that Rainey wanted to hear. On the other hand, Rainey had something to say to her.

"I'm sorry about your son and how he manipulated you. If you were well enough to understand his mental disease, I would explain it to you. There is such a thing as a bad seed and your son was one, incapable of remorse or empathy. Now, whether it came from his genetic makeup—in light of recent events, it seems both natural parents had some issues—or a combination of things, Michael Paul Perry saved a good many lives by accidently ending his own."

Gunny fought the restraints, but Rainey just smiled at her.

"It's a shame really. We could have been good friends. I liked you. Unfortunately, the brain injury you suffered created the perfect storm for paranoid delusion and the emergence of a severe personality disorder. You are a wounded soldier, and I hope you get the help you need. Get well, Gunny. Don't come near us again. Get us off your mind, because you don't want to be on mine."

Rainey leaned down very close to Gunny's face and whispered, "You were with my children. There is no love lost here. I won't hesitate and I don't miss. That's what goes wrong with these diabolical plans. I'm for taking the shot and ending the damn thing when you have the chance."

She stood up straight and smiled down at the stranger that had once been a friend. "Oorah, Gunny. I wish you well—very far away from me."

CHAPTER FOURTEEN

"I really do think you should see a plastic surgeon about that scar."

"Katie says it makes me look mysterious," Rainey said to her mother. "Besides, it keeps people from concentrating on my hair."

"Well, at least you took off the Dora the Explorer Band-Aid."

"Yeah, you do look a little different from the last time I saw you, make that a lot different," Alana Minott said. "What happened to all that hair?"

"I donated it to people who make wigs for sick children, before mine removed it a strand at a time. Besides, once you've had your hair used as a weapon against you, chopping it off is an easy decision," Rainey said.

She had not seen Alana in the four weeks since the morning they spoke in the hospital, but had spent hours with her on the phone. The calls came often at first, but not so much now. Rainey spoke openly about how it felt to fight for her life again. The stress, balancing emotions that were out of sync, the mental trauma that comes with the physical injuries, Rainey talked about it all with the young woman. She shared her experiences in hopes that it would make it easier for Alana to understand her own healing process. With Katie's help, Rainey learned the healing power of helping others. Katie truly believed it took a village, and Rainey had certainly witnessed the power of women uplifting each other.

"Perfectly tussled pixie curls. Using unruly to your advantage. Very smart," Constance said. "You look just like you did as a toddler."

"I'm not sure that's a compliment, Mother." Rainey reached to sweep the hair off her neck that wasn't there. "I can still feel it, like an amputee feels the absent limb."

"It's really cute, Rainey. You'll get used to it," Alana said in support of Rainey's shearing.

Alana was Rainey's fellow wallflower among a sea of women in Molly's elegant home. The fundraising reception for Sarah Harris's Second Chance House was in full swing. Alana had spoken earlier on behalf of women who benefitted from the women's shelter services for rape survivors. Now, Katie had abandoned Rainey for a turn through her old social circle. Constance drifted over, appearing out of the whirling mass of women, and only women, ranging in ages from teens in braces to geriatrics with walkers.

The well-heeled elite roamed the rooms dripping diamonds and dropping fat checks in silver bowls carried by very handsome androgynous bois and pretty girls. Whether assuaging their guilt for never having needed a second chance or just repaying the karma for the kind hand held out along the way, the money flowed freely.

"I see there are quite a few couples among tonight's guests," Constance noted. "I take it this is what it feels like at one of our functions, when everyone is coupled up and you're left to the speculation of the other lonely party goers."

"Be careful, Mother, if you hang with the lesbians too long, the country club crowd may grow suspicious."

Constance saved Rainey's life. This had somehow left her with the assumption that she and Rainey would now have those long chats and mystical connection common among mother-daughter relationships. Rainey thought it necessary, in order to keep her sanity and respect for her mother, that she rebuild the walls Constance was hell-bent on eliminating from their bond. After so many years of mutual disdain, she really did not want that kind of dependent relationship with Constance. Rainey loved her mother, appreciated that life had forced her to be what she was, but a healthy distance needed to be maintained. Katie walked up with a champagne flute for each of them and Rainey seized the opportunity.

"Katie, isn't that Martha Ann Smith over there with your mother? Mom, I know you two go way back. You should go talk to her."

Constance nodded, but didn't take the bait. She, instead, stayed to chat. "I see that Molly tapped every deep pocket in the Triangle. Martha Ann brings old money to the table. Where she drops a donation, fifty will follow. That lawyer of yours is shrewd, Rainey, very shrewd."

"Pockets aren't the only things Molly tapped in this room," Katie quipped. "But you have to hand it to her, she always left them smiling. Oh, except that tall blond one over there. That's Anne. It took her a bit to get happy again."

Constance followed Katie's surreptitiously pointed pinky and gasped. "Good lord, that's Anne Broadmoor. You don't mean Anne Broadmoor is—that she and Molly Kincaid were—"

"Yes, Mother. Molly bedded half the women in this room. We're watching them pay for the privilege of an up-close and personal look at the woman who finally landed the elusive Ms. Kincaid. I'm watching Leslie watch Molly watch Leslie see them all. It's quite intriguing on a psychological level and entertaining from a purely voyeuristic perspective. You're spoiling the view."

Constance was an old hat at party politics. Rainey should have known she would catch on rather quickly. "Oh, I see, this is the unveiling of the off-limits sign. Your friend Leslie seems to be handling the revelation that Ms. Kincaid's prowess was not a myth fairly well."

Katie tipped her champagne glass in Leslie's direction. "Do you see that shiny object on Leslie's chest? It is a diamond and platinum miniature of Molly's house key, delivered with roses and a card that said: 'You have the only key,' exactly thirty minutes before the party started."

Constance placed her hand over her heart. "How absolutely romantic. This Ms. Kincaid is quite chivalrous isn't she? No wonder half the room is swooning."

"Yes, but the other half of the room is swooning over Agent Sexy's new hairdo," Katie said, elbowing Rainey in the side to make her laugh, and to indicate she should be nicer to her mother.

"There she is," Alana said at Rainey's elbow. "She came. I'm proud of her."

Alana had made great strides in her recovery and was volunteering to work with other women. One of the first women the shelter paired her with had become a close friend. Rainey craned to see the expected guest and almost did not recognize her. She looked very different from their last meeting. Rainey, with Alana at her side, crossed the floor to greet the young woman. When she saw them approaching, Bladen Asher broke out in a huge smile.

Rainey hugged Bladen. "You look great. How's the colonel?"

Bladen laughed, something she had learned how to do again. "He's fine. He's outside. He's never going to let me out of his sight again. I keep telling my parents they can go home now."

Rainey chuckled. "Give them time. They'll come around."

Bladen waved at Katie, who had been left behind with Constance. "Katie has been so kind to me. The shelter is a Godsend, and I can't thank you enough for answering my late night phone calls, both of you." Bladen included Alana with a nod. "I'm going to be okay, I think. It will take time. One step in front of the other, right?"

"Yes, and this was a big step," Rainey said. "You're safe here. Have some fun, meet some people. You're doing great, Bladen."

Katie had slipped from Constance's clutches and made her way over to Rainey. She hugged Bladen. "You look stunning. I'm so glad you could be here."

Alana saw some other young women she knew. "Bladen, come with me. I'd like to introduce you to some of the other volunteers." She turned to Katie. "Bladen is thinking of becoming one of the volunteer teachers at the shelter school."

"That would be fantastic," Katie said. "We would love to have you. Go enjoy yourselves, now."

Bladen hugged Rainey again. "I really can't thank you enough."

Rainey hugged her back. "No. Thank you. I wouldn't be standing here without you."

Katie got the next hug and didn't wait for a thank you from Bladen. "I owe you, young lady. You saved my girl for me."

Bladen accepted the hug with a chuckle. "You're welcome," she said, as Alana swept her into the party.

"Is she going to be okay, Rainey?" Katie asked.

"I think so. Medically, she's done with restorative surgery. She should make a complete physical recovery. Mentally, only time will tell."

Katie sipped her champagne casually, but her question wasn't casual. "And how are you doing? Have you forgiven yourself for not seeing what no one else saw either?"

"I let that woman into our home, Katie. I should be upset about that."

"Brooks and Danny both said there was no way you could have accessed that file as a private citizen. Brooks only found it because she was looking into Michael Perry's adoption for Danny. You couldn't have known, Rainey. No one did."

"That's the thing about these people. They could be standing right beside you and you would never know it, until they show you their hand."

"Well, hopefully the Rainey season is over and we can rest for a while," Katie said, slipping under Rainey's arm.

Katie was forever an optimist, but Rainey had no such illusions. Someone was probably out there right now, trying to figure out a way to get to her. The danger in Rainey's life, like the real rainy season, would cycle through again. Rainey smiled down at Katie, unable to spoil her good mood with the truth.

"I think we're good for a bit. It'll take the wackos sometime to recognize me with no hair."

Katie grinned and grabbed a handful of Rainey's ass. "I think that haircut is sexy and if you play your cards right, you might get lucky."

"I'm calling that bluff," Rainey said, with a chuckle. "It's already past your bedtime, Cinderella. I'll be lucky to get you up the stairs before you fall asleep."

"Well, the babysitter is spending the night, so just let me have a nap and wake me up," Katie said, grinning.

Rainey started moving them toward Molly. "Let's just say our goodnights. Everyone knows we have triplets. They won't think it's rude that we need sleep. No one would ever guess we're slipping off to have sex."

"So, are you ever going to tell the soon-to-be deputy you hired to babysit that she is your sister?"

Rainey laughed. "I think she knows. She said she was glad that Constance wasn't her mother."

"I'm glad you warned Constance not to say anything. She surely would have let the cat out of the bag by now."

"It's not my mother that I'm worried about," Rainey said. "It's Weather that's going to give it away. She keeps calling Wendy, Nee-Nee."

"You know you're going to have to tell her."

Rainey knew that. She also knew why she had to tell Wendy King who she really was. The conversation would go something like this. "Because we share DNA, your life is in danger. Welcome to Rainey's world."

#

"May I see your license?" The patrolman asked.

"Yes, officer. Here you go."

"May I ask why you're pulled off the road here?" The officer moved the beam of his big flashlight over the passenger area of the box van.

"I ran out of gas. My gauge isn't working. My roommate is bringing some out to me right now."

The rain started coming down heavier. The officer, not seeing any reason to be suspicious, handed the driver's license back through the window.

"You stay inside until your friend comes. It's dangerous to stand out by the road. I'll check back by here in a bit, make sure you got along all right. Stay safe."

"Thank you. I will."

The man watched the officer walk back to his patrol car and drive away, before he opened the laptop again to resume watching the evening's choice of entertainment. A person wearing a lapel camera carried a tray of hors d'oeuvres through a party of only women.

"Now, where were we Agent Sexy?"

About the Author...

Lambda Literary Award Finalist, R. E. Bradshaw, a native of North Carolina and a proud Tar Heel, now makes her home in Oklahoma with her wife of 25 years. She is the proud mother of Jon, a very fine young man raised by lesbians. (Authors note: "Bite me, Family Research Council.") Holding a Master of Performing Arts degree, Bradshaw worked in professional theatre and taught University and High School classes, leaving both professions to write full-time in 2010. She continues to be one of the best selling lesbian fiction authors on Amazon.com.

Made in the USA
San Bernardino, CA
03 May 2013